International Praise for Miss Read

"That rare combination of humo

Review

"Endearing and enduring . . . If you have never met Miss Read and her gentle friends . . . this is a fine time to get acquainted."
—*St. Louis Post-Dispatch*

"The more turbulent the real world, the more charming we may find the stability of Miss Read's tiny fictional world."—*Los Angeles Times*

"Humor guides her pen but charity steadies it . . . Delightful."
—*Times Literary Supplement* (London)

"Miss Read has three great gifts—an unerring intuition about human frailty, a healthy irony, and, surprisingly, an almost beery sense of humor. As a result, her villages, the rush of the sun and snow through venerable elms, and the children themselves all miraculously manage to blend into a charming and lasting whole."—*The New Yorker*

"What you will find in the novels of Miss Read is an aura of warm happiness."—*Columbus Dispatch*

"Pure gold."—*Omaha World-Herald*

"Miss Read's loving evocation of life in the [English] village of Fairacre tells us that it is possible to go home again . . . Fairacre is an excellent place to visit."—*Publishers Weekly*

"A world of innocent integrity in almost perfect prose consisting of wit, humor, and wisdom in equal measure."—*Cleveland Plain Dealer*

"Her humor is delightful and her quiet style with its simple and innocent content gives proof of the fact that there is still a large audience for the decent book about normal people."—*Chattanooga Times*

"Miss Read is a master . . . So relax, put your feet up, sip your tea, and enjoy the slow pace of village life and the memorable inhabitants of Fairacre."—*South Florida Sun-Sentinel*

Books by Miss Read

THE FAIRACRE BOOKS AND THEIR COMPANION VOLUMES

VILLAGE SCHOOL
VILLAGE DIARY
STORM IN THE VILLAGE
MISS CLARE REMEMBERS and EMILY DAVIS
OVER THE GATE
THE FAIRACRE FESTIVAL
TYLER'S ROW
FARTHER AFIELD
VILLAGE AFFAIRS
VILLAGE CENTENARY
SUMMER AT FAIRACRE
MRS. PRINGLE OF FAIRACRE
CHANGES AT FAIRACRE
FAREWELL TO FAIRACRE
A PEACEFUL RETIREMENT
CHRISTMAS AT FAIRACRE (*Village Christmas, The Christmas Mouse,* and *No Holly for Miss Quinn*)
THE CAXLEY CHRONICLES (*The Market Square* and *The Howards of Caxley*)

THE THRUSH GREEN BOOKS

THRUSH GREEN
WINTER IN THRUSH GREEN
NEWS FROM THRUSH GREEN
BATTLES AT THRUSH GREEN
RETURN TO THRUSH GREEN
GOSSIP FROM THRUSH GREEN
AFFAIRS AT THRUSH GREEN
AT HOME IN THRUSH GREEN
THE SCHOOL AT THRUSH GREEN
THE WORLD OF THRUSH GREEN
FRIENDS AT THRUSH GREEN
CELEBRATIONS AT THRUSH GREEN

OTHER WORKS

FRESH FROM THE COUNTRY
COUNTRY BUNCH
MISS READ'S COUNTRY COOKING
TIGGY
THE WHITE ROBIN
A FORTUNATE GRANDCHILD
TIME REMEMBERED

MISS CLARE REMEMBERS

and

EMILY DAVIS

Miss Read

Illustrated by J. S. Goodall

HOUGHTON MIFFLIN COMPANY

Boston • New York

First Houghton Mifflin paperback edition 2007

www.houghtonmifflinbooks.com

Library of Congress Cataloging-in-Publication Data
Read, Miss.
Miss Clare remembers ; and, Emily Davis / Miss Read ;
illustrations by J. S. Goodall.—1st Houghton Mifflin paperback ed.
p. cm.
ISBN-13: 978-0-618-88434-6
ISBN-10: 0-618-88434-3
1. Country life—England—Fiction. 2. Villages—England—
Fiction. I. Goodall, J. S., ill. II. Read, Miss Emily Davis.
III. Title. IV. Title: Emily Davis.
PR6069.A42M57 2007
823'.914—dc22 2007030762

Printed in the United States of America

EB-L 10 9 8 7 6 5 4 3 2 1

MISS CLARE REMEMBERS

To My Father
with love

•

EMILY DAVIS

To Beryl and Philip
with love

CONTENTS

Miss Clare Remembers

•

Emily Davis

MISS CLARE REMEMBERS

He who, in the vale of obscurity, can brave adversity, can behave with tranquility and indifference, is truly great.

OLIVER GOLDSMITH
The Disabled Soldier

PART ONE *Caxley*

CHAPTER I

A FINGER of sunlight, wavering across the white counterpane, woke Miss Clare from a light sleep.

The old lady lay for a while, without moving, watching it tremble like water across the bed and down the uneven bulging wall of her cottage bedroom.

She knew the time without troubling to turn her head to consult the china clock which ticked busily on her bedside table. Her own easy waking, and the strength and direction of the sunbeam, told her that it was a little before six o'clock on this June morning.

And there was no need to get up, thought Miss Clare, with a little shock of pleasure. Each morning, since her retirement from schoolteaching, this tremor of elation had stirred her waking moments. To be freed from the tyranny of the clock, after so many years of discipline, was wholly delightful. Almost every day of her working life Dolly Clare had resolutely thrust the bedclothes from her as the clock struck six. The habit of years dies hard, and still she woke at the same time, and rose very soon after, but with the blessed relief of knowing that, at long last, her time was her own.

She lay now, frail as a bird and very still, beneath the light covers, listening to the early morning sounds. Above her a starling chattered on the chimney pot. To thwart just such nest-builders she had prudently had wire netting stretched across the mouths of the chimneys, and now she could hear the starling's claws and beak plucking the wire and making metallic music. Far away a cow lowed, and farther still a train hooted imperiously as it rushed towards London. Miss Clare could have slipped back easily into slumber again.

But suddenly there came the roaring of a motor-bike kicked into life. The clock vibrated in sympathy, and Miss Clare sat upright.

'That's Jim off to work,' she said aloud. 'Time I was up.'

The motor-bike thundered by, shaking the old lady into wakefulness.

'And this is the day that Emily comes! Plenty to do today!'

She put back the bed clothes and thrust her bony legs towards a patch of warm sunlight on the rug. Miss Clare's day had begun.

It was strange, thought Miss Clare, half an hour later, moving methodically about her small kitchen, how little Emily Davis knew of the important part she had played in her own life. For almost seventy years now she and Emily had been friends. For several years they had taught side by side as pupil teachers, and when their ways had parted, weekly letters, lengthy and beautifully penned, had sustained their affection. No matter how long their partings, on meeting they fell together as sweetly as two halves of an apple. Now, in old age, the warm friendship had an added quality, for the knowledge that it must end before long quickened their love for each other.

They had first met under the steep slated roof of Beech Green school, when Emily Davis was seven years old and Dolly Clare a forlorn newcomer of six. Standing now in the kitchen, her brown breakfast egg poised in a spoon above the saucepan of bubbling water, Miss Clare looked back across the years and saw the scene as sharply as if it had all happened that morning.

* * *

It was the same kitchen that she and her mother had left to make their way to the nearby school. It was a wet Monday morning in March and the Clare family had moved into their new home on the Friday before. Two hours earlier Francis Clare, Dolly's father, who was a thatcher by trade, had set off to work, pushing before him a little handcart containing his tools. Upstairs lay Dolly's sister Ada, two years her senior, and smitten this morning with a timely cold and a violent cough which meant that school was out of the question for her. Envying her from the bottom of her heart, Dolly set out for the unknown, clutching her mother's hand.

'Don't you stir till I'm back, Ada,' called Mary Clare, her face tilted up to the bedroom window. 'I shan't be ten minutes.'

She hurried off so briskly that Dolly was forced to run to keep up with her. Her mother's hand was hot and comforting through the cotton glove. The child had need of comfort. New black boots pinched her toes and rubbed her heels. Her long tartan frock, decently covered with a white pinafore, bundled itself between her legs as she ran along. Her straight yellow hair had been strained to the top of her head and tied there so tightly with a black ribbon by her over-anxious mother that she could feel the skin over her temples drawn upwards in sympathy.

But her physical pain was as nothing to the ache in her heart. Fear of the ordeal before her, the entry alone into a strange and possibly hostile world was bad enough, but even this was less than the misery which had gripped her since the move from their old home at Caxley. This was the third day of grief for young Dolly Clare, the third day of mourning for her lifelong companion, her other half. Emily, her rag doll, had disappeared during the chaos of moving day, and for her young mistress the world was in ruins.

The road to the school was muddy and rutted deeply where the cart wheels made their way. This morning rain lay in long bright bands on each side of the rough flints in the centre of the lane. Other children were making their way to school, shabby satchels or plaited rush bags containing their dinner bumping on their backs. They looked curiously at breathless Dolly, scuttling at the heels of her mother, and nudged each other and whispered as they passed. Dolly was glad when they clanked over the door scraper and entered the high schoolroom.

Mr Finch, the headmaster, was a solemn figure in black with a silver watch-chain drawn across his waistcoat just on a level with Dolly's throbbing temples. The room was very quiet, and a number of children were already in their desks sitting very prim and upright, but with their eyes fixed unwinkingly upon their new schoolfellow. Dolly was too overcome to return their gaze, and looked at her new boots already splashed with chalky water from the lane.

'Yes, sir, she's already been to school at Caxley,' her mother was saying. 'She can read and reckon, and is a good hand with a needle.'

'Date of birth?' asked Mr Finch sombrely.

'Tenth of October, sir, eighteen eighty-eight.'

'And her full name?'

'Dorothy Annie Clare, but she's called Dolly, sir.'

'I will tell my wife. She will start with her.'

'I've another girl to come. Ada, sir, she's eight, but in bed poorly this morning.'

'Very well,' said Mr Finch with a note of dismissal in his voice. Taking the hint, Dolly's mother gave her daughter's cheek a swift peck and disappeared homewards, leaving her younger child as lonely as she was ever to be.

She stood on the bare boards of the schoolroom trembling from her tight black boots to the top knot on her head, fighting against tears and longing for the comfort of Emily's hard stuffed body in her arm. But Emily had gone, even as her mother had gone, and though in an eternity of time, when the great wall clock struck twelve, she would see her mother again, yet Emily had gone for ever.

The figures in the desks wavered and swelled as the hot tears pricked her eyes.

'You can sit by Emily for now,' said a woman's voice above her head. She found herself being led to the further end of the long room. Emily, Emily! The word beat in her head like a bewildered bird trying to get out of a closed room. In her present dream-like condition it seemed possible that she might be advancing to meet her long-lost familiar again, although the dull ache at her heart counselled otherwise.

She found herself in front of a double desk. At one side sat a grave dark child, with black hair smoothed from a centre parting to fall into two long plaits. Her eyes were grey and clear like water and her smile disclosed a gap where her two front milk teeth had gone.

'This is Emily,' said Mrs Finch.

It wasn't, of course, to Dolly Clare; but the smile was engaging and the grey eyes reassuring. Ana, amazingly, the stranger was called Emily!

Tremulously, through her tears, Dolly smiled back, and the friendship began.

Buttering a finger of toast on her breakfast plate, Miss Clare mused on that far-distant meeting with the second Emily in her life amid the misery which had engulfed her in the schoolroom. That such 'old, unhappy, far-off things' should have the power to prick her into acute feeling so many years after, made the old lady marvel. Yet, she told herself ruefully, she had difficulty in remembering the name and aspect of a friend's house she had visited only three days earlier! Memory played queer tricks as one grew old.

Emily's face at seventy was far more difficult for her to recall than that seven-year-old's which flashed so vividly upon her inward eye. As for the earlier Emily, who had shared the first six years of her life, why, Miss Clare could see her more clearly still. She could see the brown painted curls, the wide painted eyes and the dented nose which had suffered much banging on floors and chairs. She could smell the stout calico of which she was made, and see the quilted bodice and green-striped long-legged drawers painted upon it; and she could feel even now the delicious scrunch of the hard-packed wood shavings with which she had been stuffed. The sharply indented waist could be spanned by little Dolly's two joined hands, and the legs and arms were prickly at the ends where the calico had worn thin. There was something infinitely reassuring about the smell and weight of Emily as she leant drunkenly against her. No possible harm could befall anyone, thought young Dolly, if Emily were there.

For Emily was the good spirit of the home and, young Dolly felt sure, her blessing embraced Father, Mother, Ada and every living thing in the little house at Caxley where it had all begun so long ago.

CHAPTER 2

IN 1888, the year of Dolly Clare's birth, Caxley was a compact, thriving market town. Its broad main thoroughfare was lined with lime trees and behind these stood shops and private houses built mainly of good rosy brick and weathered tiles.

Here and there, a Georgian front was decorated with grizzled grey bricks known locally as 'vuzz-fired' or 'gorse-fired'. There were several handsome doorways, some hooded, some with elegant fanlights above the well-kept paintwork, and the general impression was one of solid prosperity. Travellers from London, journeying westwards, had paused at Caxley to change horses, or to eat or to sleep, for countless generations and had gone on their way refreshed. There was warmth and beauty in the rose-red aspect of the town and a bustling hospitality among its prosperous tradespeople which won the affection of many a stranger.

The broad High Street narrowed to a stone-built bridge at its western end and crossed a river which wound its placid way to join the Thames. Beyond that, on rising ground to the north, a few cottages constituted the outskirts of the market town, and among these was the four-roomed house belonging to Francis Clare and his young wife.

What the hurrying stranger did not see as he took the highway beyond the handsome bridge was the poorer part of Caxley. The river made its way round the southern part of the town in a series of wide loops. Here was an area of marshland dotted with a few ancient cottages. As the town grew during the nineteenth century, several mean streets were built also on this marshy wasteland by speculators. They were slums within ten years of their building, liable to flooding in the spring and damp from the rising mists for the rest of the year. 'That marsh lot', as the townspeople called them, were scorned, pitied or feared by their more prosperous neighbours, and children from respectable homes were warned against venturing into those narrow streets after dark.

Here lived the humblest of Caxley's citizens. From these dank dwellings, very early each morning, issued the old crones who cleaned steps or scrubbed out shops, the labourers on nearby farms, and those employed in digging a new way for a branch line of the local railway. More often than not there were children left behind in the homes to get what poor breakfast they could before setting out to school. The Education Act of 1870 meant compulsory schooling, and the pennies to pay for it were hard to come by in many a marsh home, and handed over grudgingly on a Monday morning.

But though poverty and hunger, aches and pains were common in these mean streets, conditions were not as stark as in the industrial towns further north and west. Very few children went barefoot and very few older people were callously neglected. Caxley was small enough to know its people, and a rough and ready charity did much to mitigate real need. Though little was organised officially for the relief of the poor in the town, yet shop-keepers, the local gentry and the more prosperous citizens were generous to those in their employ or who were brought to their notice as being in want. This casual and spasmodic generosity had something to commend it in a small community, for the feckless and improvident had small chance of waxing fat at others' expense, while those truly in need were given help. It would take some years before the conscience of the town as a whole was roused by the sight of 'the marsh lot' and their dwellings, but meanwhile they were accepted as 'the poor man at the gate', and an inevitable part of the social structure of any town at that time.

The marsh people themselves frequently said how lucky they were. The parents of some of them had taken part in the bitter riots earlier in the century. The marsh dwellers knew all too well true tales of the starving farm labourers who had marched to demand a wage of half a crown a day, in the winter of 1830. The fate of these unfortunates at their trial, when sentence of death was recorded against many and others were transported as convicts to Australia, was fresh in their memory. Consequently, although their own conditions were deplorable, they considered themselves more fortunate than their predecessors, sharing, to a small extent, the growing prosperity of the latter part of Queen Victoria's long reign.

Perhaps those who felt the pinch most at this time were the small tradesmen, the clerks and the shop assistants, too proud to seek charity, and keeping up an air of respectability with precious little to maintain it. There was a great company of such people in Caxley at that time, dressed in neat, dark attire, much-darned and much-pressed, whose pale faces spoke of long hours and poor nourishment, and whose main anxiety was not so much the serious difficulty of living on their small wages as concealing their difficulties from those about them.

Francis Clare and his wife were of this company. To be sure,

Francis's round face was not pale, for his outdoor occupation gave him a weatherbeaten aspect, but Mary's wore a pinched and sallow look. It was she who bore the major part of their poverty, making each penny do the work of two, and depriving herself so that Francis and the two little girls should benefit.

She had been in good service before her marriage, employed as a general maid in a farmhouse some miles west of Caxley. The farmer and his wife were hard-working and kindly. Despite the low conditions of agriculture at that time, and the recent disastrous harvest of 1870, yet there was wholesome food for all the household produced there. Outside, the logs were stacked in hundreds, sawn up by the farm hands when the weather was too cruel for fieldwork. Coal was cheap and was bought by the truck load. The farm carts trundled to Caxley station once a year bearing sacks of corn, and brought back enough coal for the winter instead.

At Michaelmas the pigs were killed, salted and jointed and hung in clean muslin from the beams in the kitchen. Strong beer was brewed, in an enormous copper, from home-grown barley, and provided a nourishing drink for the men. There was milk in abundance, and butter was made once a week, Mary herself turning the churn more often than not. All the bread, the massive pies and puddings, were made from home-ground wheaten flour. Vegetables and fruit were picked fresh each day from the garden, and the farmhouse kitchen seemed always to be filled with the fragrance and the clatter of cooking.

Only when night came and the oil lamp glowed on the kitchen table, a round pearl of light in its milk-white globe, did the bustle die down. Then the single men, who lived on the premises, and the farmer and his wife, with Mary, quiet as a mouse in the corner, would settle round the fire or at the table, and read or talk or take out the mending basket, until the yawning and nodding began. Then the young men would say

their good-nights before stamping across the cobbled yard to their bothy above the stables, and Mary would climb up the creaking stairs, candle in hand, to her windy little room under the roof. Finally, the farmer and his wife would rake through the fire, put up the massive fire guard, shoot the heavy bolts on the doors and make their way to bed. By ten o'clock on a winter's night the farmhouse would be wrapped in silent darkness, and the only sounds to be heard would be the snort and stamp of a horse beneath the bothy, or the croak of a startled pheasant from the spinney.

All too soon, it seemed to young Mary, the morning would come, and she would hear the carters taking their horses across the yard, the rumble of heavy wheels and the rhythmic squeak from the pump handle in the yard as the farm hands set about their work. Soon, she too would have to clamber from her truckle bed to rekindle the great kitchen fire, the first of many jobs.

The days were long and busy. Mary learnt how to keep a house clean, to cook and to sew. The farmer and his wife were childless and treated Mary with affection. She was a docile girl, willing to learn and fond of her employers. Life at the farm was hard but happy, and no doubt she would have been content to stay there for many years had Francis Clare not crossed her path.

He was twenty years of age when first she saw him. He came in the early autumn, with his father, to thatch the six great ricks of wheat and barley which stood majestically in a nearby field. His hair glinted as brightly as the straw among which he stood and his blue eyes appraised Mary as she carried an earthenware jug of beer to the thatchers. The two men were at work there for a week, and Francis made no secret of his interest in Mary.

Later that autumn he came again, this time alone, to repair the thatch on one of the barns. He appeared so often at the kitchen door, and Mary seemed to have so many occasions to cross the yard to the barn during his stay, that she was sorely teased. The farmer and his wife liked young Francis. He and his father were known for miles around as respectable and honest workers. There was no reason in the world why Mary should not welcome the young man's advances. There would always be work for a thatcher, they told each other, and they could not keep a good girl like Mary, now almost twenty and as pretty as ever she would be, on a lonely farm for ever.

By Christmas it was generally understood that Francis and Mary were 'keeping company'. Now Mary's needlework was for her trousseau and her bottom drawer. The farmer's wife, when sorting out her linen or her crockery would say:

'Here, my dear, put that aside with your things. 'Tis a bit shabby, maybe, but it'll prove useful, I don't doubt.' Later, Mary was to count these casual gifts amongst her dearest possessions.

On Michaelmas Day in the following year Mary was married to Francis and the young couple went to live in the little house on the outskirts of Caxley. They paid a rent of two shillings a week to the baker in Caxley who owned the property. Francis had ten pounds in savings, and Mary had five new golden sovereigns, a wedding present from the farmer and his wife. There was plenty of work to be had. Francis owned a fine set of thatching tools and had abundant strength and skill to use them. Queen Victoria had reigned for almost fifty years, England was beginning to enjoy prosperity, and Francis and Mary, young and in love, prepared to be as happy as larks as the year 1885 drew to its close.

* * *

Mary Clare's first home was one of a pair of cottages close to the road which ran northwards from Caxley. Francis's own home lay less than a mile away, and his parents were frequent visitors.

A narrow strip of garden lay between the road and the front door, and the little brick path was edged with large white stones. This tiny patch Mary claimed for her own and busily planted pinks and columbines and a great clump of old-fashioned purple iris to flower the next year. A moss-rose already flourished by the gate, and still bore a late bloom or two when Mary arrived at the house as a bride.

The front door led directly into the main living-room of the house, and behind this was a small scullery. A box staircase led from the living-room to the main bedroom at the front of the house, and a narrow slip room, above the scullery, which was really nothing more than an extension of the minute landing, constituted the second bedroom.

It was a small house, but enough for the young couple, and they arranged their few pieces of furniture to the best advantage and were well content. Mary's taste was good. Her own home, a farm labourer's cottage, had been humble but beautifully clean and neat, and at the farmhouse she was accustomed to seeing solid pieces of well-made furniture, and well-designed utensils of copper and wood in daily use.

She spread the scrubbed deal table with a red serge cloth in the afternoons, when the midday meal was done, and enjoyed the sight of a white geranium in a pot set squarely upon it. Round the edge ran fringed bobbles which were to delight her little daughters in the years to come. On the mantelpiece stood bright tins containing sugar, currants, tea and salt. The rag rug before the hearth was of her own making, and the fender and fire-irons of steel were polished first thing every morning with a small square of emery paper, until they shone as brightly as silver.

Their only regret was the smallness of the garden. Only a few yards of light soil stretched beyond the back doors of the two cottages.

'Not enough to keep us in potatoes,' said Francis, 'let alone a bit of green stuff.'

He planted onions, carrots and a row of cottagers' kale, and set down some old flagstones near the back door for Mary's wood and iron mangle to stand upon. This done, there was no room for anything else in the garden.

To have to buy vegetables seemed shocking to the young couple, and certainly an unnecessary expense. As the first few months went by Mary was appalled to find how much it cost to run even such a modest establishment as their own.

Not only vegetables, but meat, eggs, flour and fruit, which had been so abundant at the farm, and which she had hitherto taken for granted, now had to be bought at the shops in Caxley High Street or at the market. Despite her care, Mary found that she frequently had to ask Francis for more housekeeping money, and she began to dread the look of anxiety that crossed his face when she told him that she had no money left in her shabby purse.

For the truth of the matter was that Francis was even more discomfited by the cost of married life than his wife. Although there was always thatching to be done, yet it tended to be seasonal work. After harvest, when the ricks needed to be thatched, the money came in well; but in the winter time when bad weather made work impossible, a thatcher might go for weeks with no earnings.

Francis was beginning to find, too, that the customers who had employed both his father and himself now tended to ask his father alone to do their work. It had been agreed between them, at the time of Francis's marriage, that they would set up separately, and it was only natural that the older man should be asked first to undertake those jobs which he had done for many years. There was no doubt, too, that Francis was not as skilful or as quick as his father. He began to find that he had a serious rival here, and though they were outwardly as devoted as ever, yet Francis could not help feeling that his own trade was decreasing steadily while his father's prospered.

He took to going further afield for work, and set out very early to any job he had been lucky enough to get. Clad in thick clothes, wearing heavy hob-nailed boots and leather leggings, he trudged off, before daybreak during the first winter, along the muddy lanes to the north and west of Caxley. He had built himself a little handcart in which he pushed the tools of his trade, his shears, roofing knife, eaves knife, twine, and the bundles of short hazel strips, called sprays in those parts, which were bent in two and used as staples to hold down the thatch.

There were many hazel thickets on the chalky slopes around Caxley, and Francis had permission to cut from several of them. Mary used to enjoy these outings to collect the hazel sticks, and never came back without a few flowers or berries from the woods to decorate the window sill. Later she used to help Francis to slice the sticks and to sharpen each end so that the straw would be pierced easily.

Despite the pinch of poverty, the two were happy, although neither of them enjoyed living so near to a town, and Mary missed the boisterous friendliness of the farmhouse. Although she did not admit it to her husband, she found life in the cottage lonely. Her immediate neighbours were an aged couple, both deaf and quarrelsome, who had rebuffed her innocent country-bred advances when she first arrived. She was too timid to do more, and knew no one of her own age in Caxley.

Consequently, she was obliged to fall back upon her own resources during the long days when Francis was away from home. She scoured and scrubbed, cooked and sewed in the little house, and worried constantly about making ends meet. She was determined not to lower her standards and become like 'that marsh lot' who lived within a mile of her own doorstep. She had lost her way among those dank streets one day when she was exploring the town, and had been distressed and frightened by the dirt and violence she saw there. In the first few months of married life Mary adopted an attitude of proud respectability which was to remain for the rest of her life.

In the summer of 1886 their first child was born. The baby arrived during one of the hottest spells in August, a small, compact child, fair like her father, and as neat and beautiful as a doll. Francis and Mary were delighted. She was christened Ada Mary and throve from the first.

'But it's to be a boy next time,' said Francis, bouncing his little daughter on his knee. 'Must have another thatcher in the family, or who's to carry on when I'm past it?'

'I'll see what I can do,' promised Mary.

But it was not to be. When Ada was rising two, a fat toddler already tugging the fringed bobbles from the red tablecloth, a second daughter arrived.

It was an April day. This second birth was more complicated than the first, and Mary had paced the little bedroom all day, watching the showers sweeping across the window and drenching the primroses in the tiny front garden.

It was early evening when the baby was born. The showers suddenly stopped, and the sinking sun lit up the room with golden brilliance.

'Open the window,' whispered the mother to the old woman who acted as midwife.

The cool breeze carried with it the fragrance of wet earth and spring flowers. On the glistening rose-bush a thrush sang his heart out, welcoming the sun after the storm,

' 'Tis a good omen,' pronounced the old crone, returning to the bedside. ' That'll be a lucky baby, just you wait and see.'

'But it's a girl!' cried Mary, tears of weakness springing to her eyes at the thought of Francis's disappointment when the news should reach him.

'That don't matter,' replied the old woman sturdily. 'That child be blessed, I tell you, boy or girl. And the day will come when you'll remember what I told you.'

Mary need not have worried. Francis welcomed this second little girl as warmly as the first. Although she had not the beauty, nor the lusty strength of Ada, she was equally fair, and very much quieter in temperament.

One Sunday afternoon in May, when all the lilac was in flower and Mary's clump of irises hung out their purple flags, the Clare family, dressed in their best clothes, carried the baby to the parish church. She wore the same long christening robe which Ada had worn, a garment of fine white lawn, made by Mary, covered with innumerable tucks and edged with hand-made crochet work.

Mary felt a glow of pride as she handed this elegant bundle to the vicar at the font.

'I name this child Dorothy Annie,' intoned the vicar sonorously, and dipped his finger in the water.

CHAPTER 3

MEMORIES of her first home crowded back to Miss Clare as she cleared her breakfast table in the kitchen at Beech Green. To be sure, she thought, the things that one would have expected to see most clearly escaped her. The faces of her mother and father, the aspect of the home outside and the simple geography of its interior, the view of the lane seen through the wooden palings of the gate, and even the appearance of her sister Ada at that time, evaded her memory.

And yet there were other things, objects of no particular merit or beauty, whose feel and smell – and taste, too, in some cases – she recalled with a thrilling clarity after all these years. The white stone nearest the wooden front gate, the first of the row leading to the door, was particularly beloved by little Dolly. It rose to a substantial knob, large enough for a small foot to balance on, and so afforded her a better view of the world outside the front garden. At the foot of the knob was a hole, about two inches across, which held rainwater to the depth of a child's finger. It glittered in the whiteness like a grey eye in a pale face, and gave the stone its individuality. Sometimes the child propped a flower in this natural vase, a daisy or a violet, and once she had dropped in one of the scurrying wood lice which lived beneath the shelter of the stone. The pathetic attempts of the creature to climb out, and her own remorse when it died in the hollow of her palm, were never forgotten.

There was, too, a certain knot in the wood of the back door whose satin smoothness Miss Clare could still feel on her finger tip. Below it a drop of resin had exuded, sticky and aromatic. These two fascinating lumps, one cold and hard, the other warm and soft, within an inch of each other, were a source of wonder and joy to the child. Nearby was the handle of her mother's heavy mangle, white as a bone with drenchings of soap and water, and split here and there so deeply that a child could insert tiny leaves and twigs and make believe that she was posting letters.

Other memories were as fresh. Miss Clare recalled the slippery coldness of the steel fire-irons beneath her small hand, the delicious stuffy secrecy of hiding beneath the table, and the sight of the red bobbles quivering at the edge of the tablecloth. She could still feel the mingled love and terror which shook her when her father held her high above his head near to the oil-lamp that swung from the ceiling, and the roughness of his coat and the prickliness of his cheek.

But clearer than any of these early memories was that of Emily the doll. Heavy, ungainly, battered, but ineffably dear, the look, smell, feel and taste of her rag doll flashed back across the years to Miss Clare. Her home and her family might be hidden by the mists of time, but the image of Emily shone still, as splendid as a star.

* * *

With the arrival of her second child Mary Clare found her life busier than ever. Throughout the summer of 1888 she struggled against an overpowering weariness. As was the custom at that time, the young mother had fed her first baby for over a year, and prepared to do the same with the second. But poor diet and the constant nagging worry of making ends meet had taken their toll. Little Dolly's progress was slower than her lusty sister's had been, and Mary faced the unpleasant fact that she would have to stop feeding the child herself and undertake the expense of buying milk for its consumption. It was a bitter blow.

With the coming of autumn Mary's spirits sank still further. Now came the added expense of coal, oil and candles, winter boots for Francis and warmer clothes for the children. She spoke despairingly to her husband, and he did his best to cheer her. His was a resilient nature, the open air blew away his cares, and he had no idea of the intensity of his wife's misery cooped up in the little house with her babies and with nothing to deflect her mind from the cares around her.

'You let me do the worrying, gal,' he told her with rough affection. 'I guaranteed to look after you when we was wed, and I'll do it, never you fear!'

He gazed round the lamp-lit room, at the firelight glinting on the polished fender and the black pot which bubbled on the hob sending out wafts of boiling bacon. Upstairs his daughters lay asleep, bonny and beautiful. He could see no reason why Mary fretted so.

'We may be a bit short – but that's only natural. We're in no debt, and now the harvest's in there's work aplenty for me. We'll be able to put something by this winter, for sure, then one day we'll be able to get somewhere further out in the country to live. Be better for you up on the downs, I reckon. 'Tis lowering to the spirits, living near the marsh here.'

Mary did her best to be comforted. She had not the energy to point out the drawbacks of the little house, nor did she want to appear dissatisfied with the home that Francis had provided. Compared with 'the marsh lot' they were superbly housed, but the autumn gales had lifted several slates from the roof and had driven rain into the bedroom through the gaps. The window frames had shrunk with age and fitted poorly, and many a keen draught whistled through the rooms. There was no damp course, and the walls of the scullery glistened with moisture. The strip of matting which Mary spread on the flag-stoned floor there was dank and smelt musty.

Francis was a handy man and cheerfully undertook household repairs. It was as well that he did, for the baker landlord in Caxley took no interest in his property at all. He knew, though his tenants did not, that the pair of cottages was to be demolished within a year or two to make way for an extension of the railway line already being prepared from Caxley to the northern part of the county. He did not intend to spend another penny on his houses, and told Francis so flatly when the young man timidly approached him.

'What d'you expect for two shilluns a week?' growled the baker. 'A palace? And how far d'you reckon two shilluns is going to go when it comes to putting a new set of slates on the roof? You wants to come down to earth, me boy. If that ain't grand enough for you, you knows the answer.'

After this encounter, Francis was even more determined to move house as soon as he could find somewhere that he could afford. Meanwhile he and Mary stuffed the cracks with folded paper, and Francis borrowed a ladder and did a little rough thatching here and there among the slates of the rickety roof, to keep the worst of the weather out.

Mary stuffed long strips of sacking with more straw, and put these sausages along the foot of the outside doors which let in the fiercest draughts. They were makeshift measures, but they helped to make the little house more habitable, and gave the young couple a comfortable glow of self-reliance, despite their poverty.

'Where there's a will there's a way!' quoted Mary, ramming a draught-stopper hard against the lintel.

'We'll find somewhere by the spring,' promised Francis, glad to see a momentary return of her spirits.

But his brave hopes were doomed to be dashed. The winter of 1888 still lay ahead, and worse troubles than poverty were to visit the Clares' home during those bitter months.

One November morning, soon after his encounter with the landlord, Francis Clare was at work for another landlord, more zealous than his own.

His employer on this occasion was a man called Jesse Miller, who farmed several hundred acres of land lying between Beech Green and Springbourne. He was reckoned to be a hard man of business but a good master to his men. He had more conscience than many of his fellow farmers at that time, and saw to it that his men were housed well. To be hired by Jesse Miller at the Michaelmas hiring fair in Caxley meant hard work but above average living conditions, as the local workers knew well.

Francis was busy thatching a long row of four cottages, and expected to finish the work by the end of that particular week. The day in question was clear and sparkling, and from his lofty perch Francis had a fine view of the distant downs, a soft blue hump against the bluer sky. A clump of elm trees at the edge of Hundred Acre Field had turned a vivid yellow, and reminded Francis of the sprigs of cauliflower, stained with turmeric, that were to be found in his wife's home-made piccalilli.

The sun was overhead, and his stomach told him that it was

dinner time long before the clock on Beech Green church struck twelve. He descended the ladder and fetched his satchel from the handcart.

Seated on a bank, at the rear of the cottages, he enjoyed the warm sunshine on his face. He undid the knot of the red and white spotted handkerchief that held his meal and took out a generous cube of fat boiled bacon, the heel of a cottage loaf, and a small raw onion.

He ate slowly, paring the food into small pieces with his old worn clasp-knife. A tame bantam sidled closer as the meal progressed, looking with a sharp speculative eye at the feast. Now and again Francis tossed her a crumb which she pecked up swiftly, and afterwards she would emit little hoarse cooing noises, half purr and half croak, in the hope of further largesse.

He heard the click of a gate at the front of the cottages and guessed that one of the men was coming in for his midday meal. The appetising smell of rabbit stew from the end cottage had tickled his nostrils most of the morning. Only one other cottage was occupied that day, by an old lady whose son was working on a distant quarter of the farm. Two younger women from the other two cottages had gone together by the carrier's cart to Caxley market.

Although Francis Clare knew pretty well all that was going on in the houses upon which he was engaged, he made it a rule to be as unobtrusive as possible. His father had taught him the wisdom of such conduct many years before.

'People don't want you prying into their affairs,' the old man had said. 'You be enough nuisance anyway, sitting atop their roof days on end. And there's another side to it. Say you gets chatting one day, come the next the women'll come chatting to you when you wants to get on – or, worse still, asking you to chop 'em a bit of firing or mend the clothes line. You keep yourself to yourself, my boy, and get on with your own job.'

It had been good advice, thought Francis, putting the last piece of bread in his mouth, and leaning back for a brief rest. He closed his eyes against the dazzle of the sun. The food made him content and drowsy, and for two pins, he told himself, he could doze off. But the days were short, there were still a few yards of roof to thatch, and he must get back to the job. He stood up briskly, brushing the crumbs from his thick corduroy trousers, observed the while by the attentive bantam.

He was halfway up the ladder, emerging from the shadow of the cottage into the bright sunlight on the roof, when the accident happened. His heavy boot slipped on a rung, he lunged sideways to catch at the roof, missed his hold, and crashed to the ground, with one leg trapped in the ladder which fell across him.

The noise brought the labourer and his wife running from their back door, and the old crone, who lived next door, hobbling after them. They found Francis, with his eyes closed, blood oozing from a gash at the temple, and his left leg bent at an unusual angle, and still threaded through the ladder.

''E be dead!' said the old woman flatly. She took off her apron calmly and began to spread it over the unconscious face of Francis.

With some exasperation her neighbour twitched it off.

'Give 'im time,' begged John Arnold roughly. ''E's winded, that's all. Cut back and get a drop of water, gal,' he commanded his wife.

Francis Clare came round to feel the sting of cold water upon his forehead, the blue sky above him, and an over-powering smell of rabbit stew blowing upon his face from the anxious countenances that bent over him.

'Take it easy, mate,' said John Arnold kindly. 'You bin and done a bit of damage to your leg. We'll lift you inside.'

'You looked dead to me,' quavered the old lady. She sounded

disappointed. 'Cut down like grass, you was. White as a shroud. I said to John 'ere: "'E's dead!" Didn't I then, John? I thought you was, you see,' she explained, her silver head nodding and shaking like a poplar leaf.

The journey from the hard earth to the rickety sofa in John Arnold's living-room seemed the longest one of Francis's life. He lay there with sweat running down his ashen face, listening to the three making plans for him.

'I'll run up to Mr Miller. He'll know what's best, and meantime you get on up to Doctor's and see if he be home to his dinner,' said John, taking command. 'And you, granny, bide here with the poor chap and see he don't move. Come 'e do, he'll have them bone ends ground together or set all ways. That wants setting straight again in a splint, but us'll do more harm than good to meddle.'

He turned to Francis and patted his shoulder encouragingly.

'Don't fear now. We'll be back afore you knows where you are.'

'But you haven't had your dinner!' protested Francis weakly, looking at the plates which steamed upon the table.

'That don't matter,' said John heartily, and disappeared through the door, followed by his wife who tugged on her coat as she ran.

Francis heard their hurrying footsteps fade away and thought how good people were to each other. John must be hungry, his wife had spent all the morning preparing that savoury dish, yet not a flicker of reproach had crossed their faces at this interruption. Their only concern was for his comfort.

The old lady had turned a chair sideways to the table and sat with one elbow on the scrubbed top, gazing at him with dark beady eyes.

Francis smiled weakly at her, but his head throbbed so violently and he felt so giddy that he was unable to talk to her.

He closed his eyes and listened to the whisper of the fire in the kitchen range and the rhythmic wheezing of the old woman's breathing. Within two minutes he had fallen asleep.

The doctor could not be found. He was still out on his rounds, rattling along the country lanes in his gig, and not likely to be back until well after dark, his wife said.

Francis was carried back to his home in one of Jesse Miller's carts. A bed of straw and sacks lessened the jolting, but the deeply rutted road caused many a sickening lurch and Francis could have wept with relief when the cart stopped at his gate and John Arnold went in to break the news to Mary.

For almost three months Francis was unable to go to work, growing more anxious and dispirited as December made way for January and the weather grew more bitter. It was now Mary's turn to comfort, and this she did as well as she could.

Lack of money was their immediate problem, for with the bread winner useless nothing came into the house. Francis's father came forward at once and insisted on doing his son's outstanding work as well as his own, handing over the money to Francis and waving his thanks aside. Francis and Mary never forgot their debt to his parents, and the two couples were more closely knit by this misfortune than ever before.

The kindly farmer and his wife, from whose house Mary had been married, heard of her plight and sent a bundle of mending for Mary to do weekly, and paid her for it very generously. The carrier's cart brought the mending, and a big basket of vegetables, eggs and butter as well, and such kindnesses warmed their sad hearts during that cold winter.

Sometimes, in his blackest moods of inaction, Francis would brood on the unjust state of affairs which cast a man still further into despair when he needed help most. He was grateful to his father, to his friends and neighbours, but he did not want charity. Somehow or other he ought to be able to ensure that a certain amount of money came into his home to keep his wife and babies while he was off work. People talked about it, he knew. It was to be a long time before such theories were put into practice, and meanwhile Francis and his wife had to endure hard times.

In later years Dolly Clare was to hear her parents talk of that black winter, the first of her life, as the time when they had been driven to the verge of despair.

But time passed, the spring came, and Francis limped about again, burning to get back to work. Mary's spirits rose, Ada played once more in the little garden, and the baby lay there too in its wicker bassinet, gazing at this bright new world and finding it good.

CHAPTER 4

THE baby's first birthday was celebrated by a family picnic in the woods which bordered an expanse of common land north of Caxley.

After the bitter winter, spring was doubly welcome. It was unusually warm. Primroses and anemones starred the leafy mould underfoot, and early bluebells, still knotted in bud, were already to be seen. Mary and Francis breathed in the woodland scents hungrily as they rested on a mossy bank with their backs against the rough comfort of a beech tree.

The battered baby carriage was drawn up nearby, its occupant deep in sleep. But Ada, rosy and sturdy, scrambled joyfully over tree roots, plucking the heads from flowers and gathering twigs, feathers, acorn cups, pebbles and any other fascinating object which caught her excited eye.

'Wouldn't it be lovely,' said Mary dreamily, observing the child's happiness, 'to have a little house of our own in this wood. Or better still, just on the edge of it, on the common.'

Francis smiled at her fancies.

'We'd soon be hustled off, I knows,' he told her. 'No better'n gipsies, we'd be thought. But you take heart, my dear, one of these fine days you shall have a little house away from Caxley and the throng.'

With the sun above him, the warm air lifting his bright hair, and his family closely about him, Francis felt his strength renewed. He had been back at work for some weeks, and although his injured leg was still weak he found that he could get through a day's work steadily. Although money was scarce, to be busy again raised the young man's spirits. In a month's time, he told himself, his leg would be as good as new. In fact, it was never to be quite as strong as its fellow, and Francis walked with a slight limp for the rest of his life.

Mary stirred from her day-dreaming and began to unpack the food from the basket. Ada, breathless with her exertions, came up to this interesting object, and flung herself down beside her mother.

'I wonder where we'll all be this time next year,' said Mary, holding a loaf to her chest and looking across its crusty top to the distant common. 'D'you reckon we'll have that little house by the time our Dolly's two years old?'

'That we will!' promised her husband stoutly. 'Just you wait and see!'

But Mary was to wait for another five years before hope of a country cottage came her way, and little Dolly was to celebrate several birthdays at Caxley before making her home in the Beech Green cottage which would shelter her for the rest of her long life.

* * *

It was in Caxley, therefore, that Dolly Clare spent the first formative years of her life. The lane outside the cottage gate was dusty in summer and clogged with mud in the winter. The child watched the carts and waggons, the carriages of the gentry and the tradesmen's vans, rumble and rattle on their way, raising dust or churning mud, as they travelled to and from the town. The diversity of the horses fascinated her. Ada loved best the shiny high-stepping carriage horses that trotted proudly past, and would call excitedly to her little sister when she saw them approaching:

'Come quick, Doll! Quick, you'll miss 'em!'

But Dolly's favourites were the slow-moving patient great cart horses whose shaggy hooves stirred vast clouds of dust as they plodded towards the market town with the farm waggons thundering behind them. There was a humility and a nobility about these powerful monsters which tore at the young child's heart in a way which she could not express, but which was to remain with her always.

The two little girls reacted differently to many things. To go shopping in the High Street or in the market square was a delight to the volatile Ada. To the quieter Dolly it was sheer misery.

'Ada! Dolly!' The urgent summons from the house in their mother's voice would be the prelude to this ordeal.

First they had to endure a brisk rubbing of hands and faces with a soapy flannel wrung out in cold water. Then came swift and painful combing of hair with a steel comb which seemed to find out every sensitive spot on little Dolly's scalp. Both children had curly hair. Ada's sprang crisply from her head, but Dolly's was softer and fell in loose curls, later to form ringlets. Ada endured the hair-tugging stoically, chattering the while about what she would see and what she wanted her mother to buy.

'Hold still, child!' Mary would command. 'And hush your tongue! Us'll be lucky to get a good dinner from the shops, let alone sweeties and dollies and picture books!'

Dolly's eyes filled with tears of pain during the combing, despite Mary's endeavour to handle her gently. She knew it was no pleasure for the younger child to go shopping, but there was no one to mind her and the two must perforce accompany their mother everywhere.

At last they set out. Sometimes Dolly was pushed in the rickety perambulator, but its days were numbered, and more often than not she would struggle along beside her mother's long heavy skirt, clutching it with one desperate hand, or holding on to the stout shopping basket which her mother held.

Never for a moment did she let go. The thought of being parted from her mother was too terrifying to be borne.

Ada, on the other side, leapt and gambolled as gaily as a young goat, greeting friends, pointing out anything which caught her eye – a lady's pink parasol, a gleaming carriage door with a crest on it, or a pig squealing in a cart, covered with a stout net, and resenting every minute of its journey to the market.

Caxley High Street was always busy. It was a thriving town which served a large area, and the shops always had far too many hurrying people in them for little Dolly's liking. Customers pressed up to the counters to be served, assistants scurried back and forth filling baskets, weighing out sugar, fetching lumps of yellow butter on wooden pats, and slapping them feverishly into shape on the marble slab behind the counter.

Important customers usually waited in their carriages outside the shop while their menservants bustled to and fro carrying parcels, and the proprietor of the business himself fetched and carried too, leaving his premises to pay his respects at the carriage side. Sometimes a horseman, not wishing to dismount, would shout his order to someone in the shop. Out would race the shop boy at top speed, the parcel would be stuffed into a jacket pocket, coins would jingle, and the horse would clop-clop off down the street again.

The bustle was the breath of life to Ada. She scrambled up on the high round-seated chair by each counter, bouncing with such zest that her lofty ill-balanced perch frequently tipped over. From here she watched, with eyes as bright and round as a squirrel's. She loved to see the butter patted, and its final adornment with a swan or a crown from the heavy wooden butter-stamp. She delighted in the scooping of currants from deep drawers with a shiny shovel, and the see-sawing of the gold-bright scales and weights.

But Dolly, crouched between the counter and her mother's

skirt, was in no mood to relish these joys. Bewildered by the noise, hustled to one side if she ventured forth, and half-suffocated by the people who pressed and towered around her, she longed for the time when her mother replaced her purse in the deep petticoat pocket beneath her voluminous skirts and they could make their way out into the street again.

Of all the shops, Dolly dreaded most the butcher's. The headless carcases, split down the middle to disclose heaven knew what nameless horrors in their sinister depths, were frightening enough. The poor dangling hares, with blood dripping from their noses to the sawdust on the floor, were infinitely worse. To see them flung on to the butcher's block and to watch his red hands wrenching the skins, with a sickening tearing sound, from their bodies was even more terrifying to the child, and the final awful tugging to release the head had once caused her to be sick upon the sawdust, thus bringing upon herself the wrath of her mother and the butcher combined.

But the most appalling experience, which happened all too frequently, was the purchase of half a pig's head. This useful piece of meat was very cheap and very nutritious, and Mary Clare often bought it for her family. Dolly watched, with fascinated horror, the whole head placed upon the butcher's block. The eyes, small and blue in death, seemed to look at her. There was something pitiful and lovable about its round rubbery nose and the cock of its great waxen ears. When the butcher, chatting cheerfully the while, raised his cleaver, Dolly squeezed her eyes shut and gritted her milk teeth, remaining so until the ominous thudding had stopped. She had never been able to keep her eyes closed long enough for the butcher to weigh, trim and wrap the meat, and so endured each time the ghastly sight of that cloven head, brains, tongue and grinning teeth exposed by the butcher's onslaught.

Mary, delighting in her purchase and making plans for several meals from it, never knew the repugnance which little Dolly felt. The child could not go near the basket which held this horror, shrouded in newspaper, and was careful to walk on the other side of her mother on the return journey. For Dolly, this was only the beginning of her misery. The pig's head would float, she knew well, in a basin of brine for hours to come, on the floor of the scullery, and every movement would set it swivelling slowly, while one blue eye cast a cold malevolent beam from its watery resting-place.

'Don't pick at your vittles,' Mary would say two days later, when she placed a plate of boiled pig's brain before her younger daughter. 'Look at Ada gobbling up hers! You be a good girl, now, and clean up your plate.'

'That's right, my little love,' Francis would say jovially. 'Thousands of poor children 'ud give their eye teeth for a plateful of brains like that. Why, I wager there's plenty down the marsh would like 'em!'

For all unhappy little Dolly cared, as she pushed the revolting things about, the marsh children could have them. Memories of the butcher's shop, the strain of living with half a pig's head in the house, and meeting the reproachful gaze of that one fearsome eye, completely robbed Dolly of any appetite. Her parents' concern was an added burden, yet how could she explain her revulsion?

And so the pigs' heads continued to appear and to cast their shadow over young Dolly's existence. It was small wonder that shopping in Caxley High Street presented so little attraction for the child in her early years.

Although Dolly's heart sank when her mother slammed the gate and turned left towards the town, it rose with equal speed if she turned to the right, for that way lay the fields, woods and gorsy common land which were becoming so dear to her. That way led to her grandparents' home. Most visiting was done on a Sunday, when Francis was free.

During his enforced idleness, and as soon as he could hobble as far, it had become a habit for the young family to spend Sundays with the old people.

'At least they'll get a good feed,' old Mrs Clare had told her husband. 'That baby don't appear too strong, for my liking; and it takes Francis out of himself to leave that chair of his now and again.'

'Don't overdo it,' advised her husband. 'They don't like to feel they're having charity, that pair, and good luck to 'em. Besides, they won't want Sundays booked here for the rest of their lives. Invite 'em as much as you like while things are bad – but you ease up a bit when our Francis is back at work.'

By the time the little girls were four and six, the Sunday visits were occasional treats. One particular Sunday remained vividly in Miss Clare's memory.

It was a day of high summer. The family set off clad in their Sunday best. Francis wore the dark suit which he had bought for his wedding, and Mary's lilac print was drawn back into a bustle showing a darker mauve skirt below. Three rows of purple velvet ribbon edged the skirt, and on her head was a neat straw hat with velvet pansies to match the underskirt. Both frock and hat had been a present from her generous employers at the time of her wedding, and were kept carefully shrouded in a piece of sheeting on working days. Dolly thought her mother looked wonderful as they set off, and told her so.

'Has Queen Victoria got a hat like that?' she wanted to know.

'Dozens of 'em,' laughed her mother, flattered nevertheless by the child's admiration.

'Not as pretty,' maintained Dolly stoutly. Her own clothes

did not give her as much pleasure. Her two petticoats, lace-edged drawers and white muslin frock had been so stiffly starched that it had been necessary to tear them apart before arms and legs could be inserted. Now the prickly edges dug into her tender flesh, and she knew from experience that the lace on her drawers would print strange and uncomfortable patterns on her thighs from the pressure against grandma's horsehair sofa. Tucked under one arm she held Emily, wrapped in a piece of one of her own old shawls. She was the least well-dressed of the party, but not in her mistress's eyes. She was heavy, too, and Dolly was obliged to hitch her up every few yards.

But these minor discomforts were soon forgotten in the joys of the walk. They crossed a stile and made their way across a meadow high with summer grass. Some of the bobbing grasses stood as high as Dolly herself and she saw, for the first time, the tiny mauve seeds quivering at the grass tips. Ox-eyed daisies and red sorrel lit this sweet-smelling jungle that stretched as far as the small child could see. Above her arched a sky of breath-taking blue where two larks vied with each other in their outpourings.

In the distance the six bells of Caxley parish church chased each other's tails madly. A warm breeze, scented with the perfume from a field of beans in flower, lifted Dolly's hair, and she became aware, young as she was, of her own happiness in these surroundings. Sunlight, flowers, Mother, Father, Ada, and dear Emily were with her. Here was security, warmth, love and life. Nothing ever completely dimmed that shining memory.

At grandma's house there were different joys. There was an aura of comfort and well-being here which the child sensed at once. The furniture was old and solid, unlike the poorer machine-made products in her own home. The old couple had inherited well-made pieces from their families, and the patina of a century's polishing gleamed upon the woodwork. These sturdy chairs and chests had been made and used long before the commons were enclosed and their self-supporting owners became poor men. The difference in the two homes was eloquent testimony to the revolution which had split a nation into classes. Although the young Clares might consider themselves fortunate when they compared their way of life with that of 'the marsh lot', yet the fact remained that they were as poor. Francis's parents were the last inheritors of an older England where a man might live, modestly but freely, off his own bit of ground.

After the greetings and the Sunday dinner were over, the grown-ups settled back to rest and talk and the two children were told to sit up to the table to play.

'I'll take off your sashes, so they don't get crushed,' said their mother, undoing Ada's blue and Dolly's pink ones. It was good to expand, free of their bindings. The sashes were eight inches wide and four or five feet long. Made of stout ribbed silk, they were considerably restricting when tied tightly round a well-filled stomach. Dolly watched with relief as her mother rolled them up, smoothing them on the table to take away the wrinkles.

Ada was given a picture book, but Dolly had her favourite object to play with – a square tin with pictures of Queen Victoria on each side. It had been bought at the time of the sovereign's golden jubilee, the year before Dolly's birth, and had held tea then. Now it was grandma's button box, and Dolly was allowed to spill out the contents across the table and count them, or form them into patterns, or match them, or simply gloat over their diversity of beauty.

There were big ones and tiny ones. Buttons from coats and caps, from pillowcases and pinafores, from bonnets and boots, cascaded across the table. There were buttons made of horn, bone, cut steel, jet, mother o'pearl, linen and leather. Dolly's fingertips, as well as her excited eyes, experienced the gamut of sensations roused by handling the variety of sizes, textures, colours and shapes which were held in the bright button box.

As she bent over her treasures, scraps of conversation floated to her from the grown-ups.

'Found a house yet, my boy?'

'Not that I can afford, Dad.'

'You won't find anything much cheaper than your own, I'd say. Take my advice and stay on a bit till you've built up the work again.'

'Things aren't too good. Straw's scarce.'

'Ah, there's not the wheat grown. Old George Jackson, shepherd to Jesse Miller, was in here this week. He's got more sheep than ever before. He gets twelve shilluns a week, he tells me, and two pounds Michaelmas money. He's not doing so bad.'

'And gets it regular, too,' said young Francis, with a hint of bitterness in his voice.

The women talked of clothes and bed-linen, meals and children. They seemed, to Dolly, to talk of nothing else, unless it were of illness and death, and then it was in low tones meant to keep such things from attentive young ears.

At last the time came when the buttons must be swept from the table back into the jingling tin. Dolly followed the two women into the kitchen and watched the preparations for tea.

Bread and butter at grandma's was quite different from that at home, for here the bread was cut very thin and buttered very thickly. Home-made plum jam could be spread upon the second slice, too – the first must be eaten plain – whereas at home one either had bread with butter on it or bread with jam, never both. Fingers of sponge cake followed the bread and

butter, the top sparkling with a generous sprinkling of sugar.

The children had milk to drink from mugs with a pattern of ivy leaves round the rim, but the grown-ups had tea poured from a huge brown tea-pot which wore a snug buttoned jacket to keep the tea hot.

Grandma's tea was kept in a shiny wooden tea-caddy with a brass lion's head for a handle on the lid. When this was lifted, Dolly saw first two bowls filled with sugar, each settled securely in a hole. At each side of the caddy lay a long polished lid with a small black knob. When these were lifted they disclosed the tea, China on one side, and Indian on the other. This tea-caddy was an unfailing joy to Dolly, and when later it came into her possession she treasured it as much for its intrinsic beauty as for its associations.

After tea the little girls' sashes were re-tied, their hair combed and their hands and faces washed upstairs in grandma's bedroom. The thick eaves of the thatch jutted out beyond the windows and made the room seem dark, despite the golden evening.

Then came the moment which was to stamp this particular Sunday as a day of perfection as clearly as the morning walk through the meadow had done.

The old lady opened a drawer in the chest by the bed and took out a piece of red flannel.

'For Emily,' she said, giving it to Dolly.

The child unfolded the material slowly and with some bewilderment. It proved to be a cloak with a hood, exactly the right size for the doll.

Dolly was speechless with joy. She could do nothing but throw her arms round her grandmother's knees and press her flushed face against the black silk of the old lady's Sunday frock.

'Well, what do you say?' said Mary with increasing asperity. But Dolly could say nothing. With trembling hands she unbound the shawl from Emily' heavy body and dressed her in her new finery. She looked even lovelier than her mother had looked that morning, and far more splendid than Queen Victoria on the side of the button box.

'I made it out of my old petticoat,' said grandma, as they descended the steep stairs. 'There wasn't enough for the children, and I thought Dolly'd like dressing-up her Emily.'

Farewells were said and kisses given. Still no words came from Dolly, overwhelmed with good fortune, but the ardour of her kisses was gratitude enough for the old lady.

Dolly carried the resplendent Emily all the way home, and Francis carried them both for the last part of the journey. Windows and roofs were turned to gold by the sinking sun. The drop of water in the white stone by the gate gleamed like a jewel. From the height of her father's comfortable shoulder Dolly looked down upon the rose-bush, its flowers as blood-red as Emily's new cloak.

The scent brought memories of the bean-flowers' fragrance and the smell of crushed grass in the summer meadow. The ox-eyed daisies, the red sorrel, the rose-bush, and the pansies nodding on her mother's bonnet, seemed to whirl together in a dazzling summer dance.

Dizzy with happiness, dazed with golden light, at last Dolly found her tongue.

'Lovely,' she sighed, and fell instantly asleep.

CHAPTER 5

SOON after that golden day, Dolly started school. Ada had been attending the church school at the northerly end of Caxley for over a year, so that the younger child had heard about teachers and classes, sums and slates, and marching to music.

It sounded attractive, and though she dreaded leaving her mother, yet the thought of Ada's company was supporting. She was, too, beginning to look for more than the little house and garden could provide in interest. Her mother was usually too busy to answer questions or to tell her stories. Her father was much more of a playmate, but he was seldom there. With Ada away at school young Dolly was restless, and when, at last, she was told that she would be accompanying Ada, the child's spirits rose.

She was dressed with particular care that first morning. Over her navy blue serge frock she wore a clean holland pinafore. With a thrill of pride she watched her mother pin a handkerchief to the pinafore, on the right side of her chest, conveniently placed for use in 'Handkerchief Drill Time' which, as Ada had explained frequently, came just before morning prayers and appeared to rank as rather more important. It made Dolly feel important, one of a fraternity, and she wore this emblem of enfranchisement with deep satisfaction.

Her mother sat her on the table to lace her little black boots and tie the strings of her bonnet. The red bobbles on the tablecloth joggled as she wriggled in excitement. Ada, already dressed, jumped up and down the path between the open front door and the gate, looking out for Esther, an older girl, who took her to and from school. This morning she wanted to tell Esther that her sister was coming, and her mother too, and that Esther need not wait for them.

Esther was a tall thin child, with a long pale face and prominent teeth. She looked perpetually frightened, as no doubt she was. Her father was a heavy drinker and violent in his cups. He was a ploughman, but at this time when so much arable land was being turned over to pasture, he had been put to sheep-minding, hedging and ditching, mucking out stables and cowsheds, and other jobs which he considered beneath him. Had he realised it, he was fortunate to have been kept in work at all by his hard-pressed employer. With the influx of cheap grain from the United States and Canada, prices for English wheat had dropped so disastrously in the last few years that he, and many like him, had turned to grazing in the hope of recovery. That, too, was to prove a forlorn hope within a few years, as frozen meat from Australia and New Zealand, and dairy products from Denmark and Holland poured into the country. It was small wonder that men who had spent their lives on the land now uprooted themselves and took their strength and their diminishing hopes to the towns. Others, like Esther's father, too stupid to understand the significance of the catastrophe, either suffered in bewildered silence, watching their families sink and starve, or sought comfort in drink or the militant succour offered them by the evangelical churches.

Transition is always hazardous and distressing. The working people of rural England at that time were largely untaught and trusted the gentry's guidance. They witnessed the crumbling of a way of life, unchanged for centuries, and distress, resentment and fear harried the older generation. The younger people saw opportunities in towns or, better still, overseas, and thousands of them left the villages never to return. Little Dolly, kicking her legs on the table as they waited for Esther, was to be a mature woman before English farming found its strength again, and by that time machines would have come to take the place of the men who had left the fields for ever.

'We don't want you, Esther,' shouted Ada exuberantly from the gate, as the lanky child came into sight. Mary lifted Dolly hastily to the floor and hurried outside, much vexed.

'Ada! You rude little girl!' scolded her mother. 'You come in, my dear,' she added kindly to timid Esther, 'and take no notice of Ada.'

She picked up three small parcels, wrapped in white paper, and gave one to each child. Dolly and Ada knew that they contained a slice of bread spread with real lard from grandma's, and sprinkled with brown sugar.

'There's a stay-bit for you,' she said, 'to eat at playtime. Mind you don't lose it, and no eating it before then, or the teacher will give you the cane.'

Esther put hers carefully in the pocket of her shabby coat, but Ada thrust her own and Dolly's into a canvas satchel which had once been Francis's dinner bag, and now carried such provender, as well as books or a pencil, to school.

'Stay by the gate while I gets my bonnet,' said Mary, lifting her coat from a peg on the door and thrusting her arms into it. Her everyday bonnet was kept on a shelf just inside the cupboard under the stairs. She tied it on briskly. The only mirror downstairs was a broken triangle propped in the scullery window for Francis's shaving operations, and Mary did not bother to waste time in consulting this. She shifted a saucepan to the gentler heat at the side of the hob, locked the front door, took Dolly's hand, and hurried schoolward.

Ada and Esther went before them, the younger child skipping

cheerfully, swinging the satchel and quite unconcerned by her recent scolding. She was beginning to be bored by Esther's attentions. Strong and lusty, Ada could have done without Esther's support after the first week at school. Her boisterous good spirits disarmed any possible bullies, and her tough little fists would have attacked anyone foolish enough to molest her.

Esther adored her. To look after Ada made the pathetic child feel wanted and useful. Mary's bright smile and her occasional present of an apple or rough sandwich as 'a stay-bit' warmed Esther's heart. In the Clares' modest home Esther saw all that she wanted most. Mary knew this, and knew too that her young children were as safe in Esther's devoted care as they would be in her own.

Dolly's spirits were high too, as she struggled to keep up with the others. She could hear the school bell ringing in the distance, and looked forward to the delights of sitting in a desk and having a multitude of children for company. If Ada said school was fun, then it must be. For nearly five years Ada had told Dolly what to expect. So far she had never been wrong. Trustingly, she trotted behind Ada's prancing heels.

The bell had stopped ringing by the time they turned the corner and came in sight of the asphalt playground in front of the school. Children were forming lines, and two or three teachers stood in front of them. One had a whistle and blew it fiercely.

'Straighten up, Standard Four,' she shouted. 'Take distance, there. Take distance!'

The children lifted their arms to shoulder level and moved back to make a space. Dolly watched in amazement.

Her mother kissed her swiftly and put her hand in Ada's.

'You stay with Ada, my love, till your teacher fetches you. They knows all about you, 'cos I filled in the form the other day.'

Dolly's eyes began to fill with tears, and her mother dabbed them hastily with the corner of her scarf. Her voice grew urgent.

'There, there now! Don't 'ee cry. The others'll think you're a baby. I must be getting back to cook your dinner, my lovey, and Ada and Esther'll bring you home very soon.'

Wisely, she hurried away, doing her best to smile cheerfully at her woebegone little daughter, who looked smaller than ever against the bigger children ranked in the playground.

'Hurry up, you three!' called the teacher with the whistle, and Mary saw the three children scurry into place. With considerable relief she noticed that Dolly, though pale, was now dry-eyed. She turned towards home realising, with a shock, that she was alone for the first time for years, and that she would find her house empty.

Twenty minutes later Dolly sat in a long desk close beside Ada. There were four children on the narrow plank seat which they shared, and Dolly was perched precariously at the end, her boots swinging in mid-air.

Before each child was a fascinating square carved into the long desk top. Although Dolly did not know it then, she was soon to learn that each one measured a foot by a foot, and that the little squares inside were each a square inch. Under her lashes she looked to see if her companions were as interested in their property as she was, but they were old campaigners of several terms' standing, contemporaries of Ada's, and were sitting bolt upright with their arms folded tidily across their backs.

Dolly put out an exploratory finger and traced the lines lovingly.

'Don't fidget, dear,' said Miss Turner, briskly. 'Hands behind backs.'

Dolly attempted to put her hands away as neatly as her sister, but found the position extremely uncomfortable. However, Miss Turner seemed satisfied with the effort, and returned to her scrutiny of a large book on the desk before her, leaving Dolly free to gaze about her.

The schoolroom was long and contained three classes. All the children faced the same way, and all sat in desks holding four.

At Dolly's end of the room Miss Turner faced her two rows of infants. In the middle of the room sat the teacher who had wielded the whistle. Her name was Miss Broomhead, Dolly learnt later, and not unnaturally she possessed a multitude of nicknames, none of them flattering. The children in her class were aged from seven to ten or eleven, and their desks were a size larger than the infants', and had four inkwells spaced at regular intervals, whereas the infants' had none.

At the far end of the room the headmaster, Mr Bond, held sway. He was small and neat, with white hair, very blue eyes, and a sharp tongue. He was a stickler for punctuality, tidiness, cleanliness and obedience. Good work took its place after these four virtues. Very often, as he well knew, it followed automatically, for orderly habits make an orderly mind just as surely as an orderly mind expresses itself in a tidy manner. For the eager, clever child, however, whose mind outstripped his pen, Mr Bond's standards could be heart-breaking. He might do a dozen sums of horrid intricacy and get them all correct, but if one small blot or crossing out marred his page then Mr Bond's red pencil slashed across the whole, and he must perforce copy it all out again under threat of a caning. With the amazing patience and endurance of childhood, these conditions were accepted, and Mr Bond was not considered unreasonable in his demands. In fact, he was respected for his high standards, and in an age which was geared to great efforts for a small return, Mr Bond's methods, harsh as they might seem to later schoolmasters, suited his pupils and prepared them for sterner employers in the future.

Two great fireplaces stood at each end of the long wall facing the children. One stood conveniently near Mr Bond's desk, the other by Miss Turner's. Miss Broomhead, unluckily placed in the middle, had to be content with any ambience cast by a large photograph of Queen Victoria which held pride of place in the exact centre of the wall behind her. The Queen was in her widow's weeds, a small crown upon her head, and a veil flowing from it to her shoulders. One plump hand rested on an occasional table, and her gaze was fixed upon some unseen object which appeared to provide her with no satisfaction. Above the heavy frame were lodged two small Union Jacks thick with chalk dust from the blackboards and soot from the fires.

Directly beneath the Queen stood a glass case containing a stuffed fox against a background of papery ferns and tufts of wiry heather. His white teeth looked very sharp and his glass eyes very bright. Dolly wondered, in her innocence, if she would ever be allowed to play with him. At the infants' end, a smaller glass case held a stuffed red squirrel holding a hazel nut in its tiny claws; and at Mr Bond's end a sinister collection of common amphibians, including frogs and newts, at all stages of development, disported themselves among dead reeds and moulting bulrushes arranged around an improbable-looking painted pond.

Six brass oil lamps, with white shades which reminded Dolly of her father's summer thatching hat, hung from the lofty roof and swung very slowly when the door slammed. Three tall narrow windows, set very high in the wall at each end of the room, provided most of the daylight, but two smaller ones, behind the children, added their share, and a constant villainous draught for good measure. Children in the back desks, just below these windows, philosophically endured stiff necks and ear-ache, or used their wits to gain a move to a desk nearer the front.

Almost a hundred children were taught in this one room, and, as Dolly soon discovered, it was amazing how quietly the work was done. Heavy boots on bare boards made far more noise than the voices of teachers and pupils, and when, in the long sleepy afternoons, the bigger children were writing or reading silently to themselves, the atmosphere grew so soporific that many an infant, essaying a wobbly pot hook, let fall both slate pencil and slate, and fell asleep with its head pillowed on the carved square of the desk lid. When this happened, wise Miss Turner let sleeping babes lie, rousing them only when the clock said a quarter to four. Then, with bewildered eyes and one flushed cheek grotesquely marked with inch squares, they would return reluctantly to this world, submit dazedly to buttoning and tying, and so stumble away with big sisters to the haven of home.

School proved much more complex for Dolly than Ada had led her to believe. The parting from her mother affected the younger child severely, although she showed little, and departed docilely each morning holding Esther's hand. She had always been much more dependent on her mother than Ada, and once the older child had gone to school the bond between Mary and Dolly had been stronger than ever.

One incident about this time the child remembered all her life. She came upon her mother sitting by the window one day, holding a needle to the light. She frowned with intense concentration, trying to jab the cotton through the eye. Dolly spoke to her, but so intent was she upon the task in hand, that her mother made no sign, but simply bent closer to the window, her eyes glittering and fixed in awful absorption.

To Dolly the remembrance of her mother's complete mental withdrawal on that occasion was terrifying. Far easier to bear were her brief physical absences to the garden or to the rooms upstairs. But to be so close to one's mother, to put one's hand on her skirt, to speak to her and then to find she was not there, and that one was of no more significance than the wallpaper beside her, was an experience fraught with terror. It was also indicative, she realised later, of the deep need she had of her mother's affection.

But once she had made the daily parting and was on her way to school, Dolly, facing the inevitable, put her mother from her thoughts. Her new companions were overwhelming. Everything about them intrigued the little girl who had known only a few people until now.

In the first place there were so many of them, and they were so diverse. Her path did not cross those of the bigger children very often, but there was surprise and variety enough in the thirty or so boys and girls whose class she shared.

Much to her relief she was allowed to sit by Ada, but she had been moved to an inside position on the bench. and on her right hand side sat Maud and Edith. Edith at the end of the bench was a nondescript five-year-old, the child of a shopkeeper in the High Street. She was the sort of child who fades into the background of a class, having nothing outstanding to make her memorable. Her hair was mousy, her eyes hazel, her dress was drab but tidy. Quiet to the point of apathy, producing neat undistinguished work, dully obedient, Edith existed at the end of the bench.

But Maud was quite a different matter. To little Dolly, pressed so closely to her, Maud was as strange and foreign as a Chinaman. The first thing one noticed about her was her aroma. A sourish, slightly cheesy smell emanated from her, and this became overpowering when the four jumped to their feet, tipping up the long bench behind them, before marching out to play. This movement seemed to release a bouquet of scents from Maud's disturbed clothing, and added to the basic sourness there would be whiffs of stale frying, paraffin and vinegar. Later in life Dolly Clare recognised these mingled smells as the poignant scent of poverty.

Maud was very thin. She wore a tartan frock meant for someone much bigger and stouter. Her long pale neck, shadowy with grime, protruded like a stem from a flower pot, and the shock of red hair atop might have been mistaken for a shaggy bronze chrysanthemum. Her eyes were pale blue and protuberant, her wide mouth perpetually open, and she fidgeted and wriggled without ceasing, thus drawing upon herself a rattle of fire from Miss Turner's tongue.

'Sit still over there!' she would command, turning the frosty glare of her glasses upon Dolly's desk. Poor Dolly would flush pink with shame, but the guilty Maud would be unabashed, and giggle behind a dirty hand.

Maud's mottled mauve legs were bare, which slightly shocked Dolly in those days of muffled limbs. Her bony feet were thrust into a pair of broken boys' shoes, so ill-fitting that they frequently fell off, exposing Maud's claw-like toes. She was constantly hungry, and never owned a handkerchief. Light-witted (and light-fingered, too, it proved later), Maud was the pathetic product of one aspect of England's industrial prosperity. Her home was in the marsh.

Dolly grew very fond of her. Maud was loud in her praise of Dolly's clothes and her soft curls which she delighted in stroking. Her own rough thatch grew more tangled daily as she scratched her head remorselessly. Dolly accepted the scratching, the smell and the giggling of her neighbour without rancour, but wished she would not fidget so much and draw attention to the bench as a whole. Years later, when Dolly herself was a teacher, she wondered that Maud, and many others like her, had not fidgeted more, plagued as they were with the torments of the poor. Unwashed and tangled hair harboured head-lice, bodies packed four to a bed bred fleas, inadequate diet nourished thread-worms – but not their hosts. One stand-pipe of cold water, in a yard, to serve twelve houses, did not encourage cleanliness. Large families meant exhausted mothers, leading to neglect or despair. When you came to think of it, the grown-up Miss Clare mused, it was a tribute to Maud's resilience that she lived at all.

There was a number of children from the marsh in Dolly's class, and young as she was, she soon noticed that they incurred Miss Turner's wrath more frequently than the rest of the class. To Dolly's tender heart this seemed monstrously unfair, but in the nature of things this was understandable. Their work was as dirty and careless as their dress. They lacked concentration and energy. It is difficult to attend to abstract things when one is pinched with hunger in the middle and aflame with head-lice at one end and chilblains at the other. Miss Turner was not unsympathetic, but she had a job to do, and had to do it, moreover, under the eye of a vigilant headmaster.

Consequently, she berated the slow, whipped on the lazy with the lash of her tongue, and encouraged the zealous with hearty praise. She was a good teacher, brisk and cheerful, with a rough and ready way of dealing with the offenders, who seemed, to Dolly, almost always from 'the marsh lot'.

One incident, and its sequel, brought home to the little girl the shattering unpredictability of this new world of school. A squeal of pain from the boys' side of the class made them all look up from the pot hooks and hangers they were writing with their squeaky slate pencils. Miss Turner hurried forward to investigate.

'Miss,' whimpered one five-year-old, holding up a quivering forefinger, 'Fred Borden's been and bit me.'

Sure enough, the tell-tale teeth marks were still red upon the shaking finger, and Fred Borden was pink and sullen.

'Couldn't help it,' said the culprit unconvincingly. Miss Turner swept into action.

'By my desk,' she ordered, following the child to the front of the class.

'Put your slates down,' said Miss Turner, obviously enjoying the chance of a practical lesson in behaviour. 'Here's a little boy who likes to bite other people. Should boys bite?'

'No, miss,' came the self-righteous sing-song.

'Only dogs bite,' affirmed Miss Turner severely, turning to the shrinking malefactor. 'And as you seem to have turned into a dog this morning, I shall have to treat you like one.'

Dolly was appalled. Poor Fred! Did this mean he would be beaten? Dolly shook at the mere idea. He looked so sad, and no bigger than herself, that her gentle heart throbbed with pain for him.

Miss Turner bustled to a cupboard and returned with a length of tape. She tied one end loosely round the child's neck, and there was a titter of laughter which grew to a great shout as she motioned to the child to crouch on all fours as she tied the other end to the leg of the desk.

'There, now,' said Miss Turner, red with bending and the success of her lesson. 'You must stay tied up until dinner time. We can't have dangerous animals that bite running loose in the classroom, can we, children?'

'No, miss,' chanted the class smugly.

'Back to work, then,' commanded Miss Turner, resuming her patrolling up and down the aisles. Dolly took up her slate pencil with a shaking hand.

That anyone – especially someone grown-up – could tie up

another person like an animal horrified the child. To be sure, Fred Borden, who had feared a trip to the other end of the room where the cane lay on Mr Bond's desk, seemed quite cheerful as he sat on the floor by the desk. But Dolly, putting herself in his place, would have been prostrate with shame. To have sat there, publicly humiliated, enduring the gaze of thirty heartless school-fellows, would have broken Dolly. In fact, Fred Borden was enjoying the limelight, felt no hardship in missing a writing lesson, and considerable relief at getting off so lightly.

At twelve o'clock he was released, and the children trooped home to dinner. It so happened that Fred Borden and another boy were dawdling along the road as Esther, Ada and Dolly came up to them. The boys turned and spread their arms out to bar the way. They both grinned cheerfully. They felt no malice – this was just a reflex action when they saw three little girls trying to get by.

Esther stopped nervously, too frightened to protest, and near to tears. She lived considerably further than her charges, and time was short. She dreaded being late back to school.

Dolly, still shocked by the morning's experience, felt that she must tell poor Fred of her sympathy, but could not think how to begin.

At that moment, Ada went into action.

'Bow-wow! Who's a dog? Who bites? Who's a dog?' chanted Ada mockingly.

Fury at her sister's cruelty shook the words from Dolly's tongue. She stepped forward and put one small hand on Fred's filthy jersey. Her earnest face was very close to his.

'I was *sorry*,' she babbled incoherently. 'I was *sorry* she tied you up. She shouldn't have done that. I was *sorry*!'

To her amazement, Fred's grin vanished, and a menacing scowl took its place.

'Shut up, soppy!' he growled fiercely, and with venom he thrust the little girl away so forcefully that she fell backwards into Esther. Fist still raised, Fred followed her.

'What d'you want to hurt her for?' shrilled Esther, finding her voice.

'Because I 'ates 'er!' shouted Fred passionately. 'Because I 'ates all of you! You stuck-up lot!'

And with the hot tears springing to his eyes, he turned and fled down the narrow alley that led to the marsh.

CHAPTER 6

ONE windy March day in 1894 Francis Clare came home from work in a state of high excitement. He blew into the little living-room on a gust of wind that lifted the curtains and caused the fire to belch smoke.

'Well, Mary,' he cried, dropping his dinner satchel triumphantly on the table, 'I've got a house.'

'Francis! No! You mean it?'

'Sure as I'm here.'

'Where?'

'Beech Green.'

'But you've never been to Beech Green today?' queried Mary, still bewildered. The two little girls, playing with Emily on the rag hearthrug, gazed up at him as open-mouthed as their mother.

'No, no. I've been at Springbourne all day, like I said, thatching Jesse Miller's cow shed. He come up while I was working and says: "You the young fellow as near killed 'isself a year or two back and had a ride home in my cart?"

'I told him I was. He's getting forgetful-like now he's old – kept calling me by my father's name, but it appears one of his chaps told him we was looking for a cottage, and he's got an empty one we can have.

' "'Tisn't a palace," he said, "two up and two down, but a pump inside and good cupboards. Take a look at it, and tell me what you think. Two shillings a week rent old Bob used to pay me before he left me to go to work in Caxley. That suits me if it suits you." And he threw the key up to me, and off he goes.'

'Well!' said Mary, flabbergasted. 'And what's it like?'

'Nice little place. Next door to Hundred Acre Field. Good bit of garden and handy for the school. I reckon you'll like it. We'll go over Sunday and you shall see it. Ma'll have the girls, I don't doubt, and we can walk it easy in just over an hour.'

It was the most amazing news, and the family could hardly eat for excitement. By the next Sunday, when Mary had seen it and pronounced it perfect, all that remained to be done was to give a week's notice to their landlord and accept Jesse Miller's offer of a cart to carry the furniture from the Caxley home to the new one.

They were to move on Lady Day, which gave them about a fortnight in which to attend to the multitude of domestic details involved in moving house. For the last few days the Caxley home was almost unrecognisable. Curtains had been taken down, cupboards cleared, boxes stood, roped and massive, in the most awkward places, and chaos reigned.

But for all the bustle and confusion, Mary and Francis smiled. At last, they were leaving Caxley. At last, they were on their way to the open country where their hearts had always been.

Hearing their mother sing, as she washed china and stored it in a box stuffed with their father's thatching straw, the two little girls exchanged secret smiles. Beech Green might be unknown to them, but obviously there was no need for apprehension. Beech Green, it seemed, was the Promised Land.

The day of the move dawned still and cloudless. The Clare family was up betimes and the front door was propped open so that the coming of the farm cart could be instantly seen.

Breakfast was a picnic meal that day, of bread and cold bacon cut into neat cubes placed on a meat dish on the bare table, for such refinements as cooking pots, plates and tablecloths were all packed up.

It had been arranged that Mary and the children should travel on the cart with the furniture, while Francis stayed behind to lock up and return the key to the landlord.

'Jim's going to give us a hand putting our traps in at Beech Green,' said Francis, naming the carter who was to transport them, 'and I should be with you soon after you gets there. We'll be straight afore dark, my love, curtains up and all, you'll see.'

Outside, the early sunshine lit the tiny garden and shone through the open door upon the bare wall of the living-room. Perched on the budding rose bush, a speckled thrush sang his heart out, as if in farewell. It was strange, thought Mary suddenly, that she felt no pangs at parting from this her first home. Here the two babies had been born, and she and Francis had known happiness and misfortune. She had come across that uneven threshold as a bride, and was to leave as a wife and mother, but despite its associations, the house meant little to her. She would be glad to leave it.

There was a distant rumbling, which grew as they listened. Then came the sound of heavy hooves, and Jim's voice.

'Whoa there, old gal. Whoa, Bella!'

'He's come!' squeaked the two little girls, flying to the gate. The adventure had begun.

For the next hour or two Francis and Mary went back and forth from the house to the farm cart, helped by Jim who was almost as strong as the massive mare between the shafts. The children tore up and down in a state of wild excitement, getting in everyone's way, until Francis could stand it no longer.

'You two keep out o' this,' he said firmly. 'Play out the back or upstairs where we've done. We'll all be wore out before we starts.'

Ada skipped out through the back door, but Dolly made her way up the echoing shaky stairs to her empty bedroom. It was queer to see its bareness. There were dusky lines along the walls where the bed, the chest of drawers, and the cane-bottomed chair had stood. A blue bead glinted in a crack between two floor boards, and Dolly squatted down to prize it out.

Near her, where the skirting board joined the floor, was a small jagged hole where a mouse lived. Her mother had set a trap many times, but no mouse was ever caught. Dolly sometimes wondered if this were in answer to her fervent, but silent, prayers on these occasions. Each night, kneeling on the hard floor with her face muffled in the side of the white counterpane, she had chanted:

God bless Mummy,
God bless Daddy,
Aunties and Uncles,
And all kind friends,
And make me a GOOD girl,
For Jesus Christ's sake
Amen.

On the nights when the trap was set, she added fiercely and silently:

'And PLEASE DON'T let the mouse get caught,' before leaping into bed beside Ada, and drawing up the clothes.

Now, she thought, the mouse could have the whole house to live in, and would never see a trap again.

She wandered to the window and looked out into the back garden. Ada was trying to stand on her hands, supporting her legs against the fence. It was strange to think she would never do that again here. Dolly turned to look at the room again. It seemed to be waiting, it was so quiet and eerie. She felt as if she were intruding, as if the place she stood in were no longer hers.

Soon she heard her parents calling.

'Come on, Ada and Dolly! It's all ready now. Let's get you dressed.'

Within half an hour they were off.

Nearly seventy years later, the details of that amazing journey still remained clear in Miss Clare's memory. There had been an iron step, she remembered, to climb on in order to get into the cart. It was shiny with a hundred boot-scrapings, and had a crescent-shaped hole in it through which one had a terrifying glimpse of the road below.

Jim, Mary and the two children squeezed together on the plank seat that ran across the cart. Dolly felt most unsafe, for her feet would not reach the floor. Emily was tucked by her, but Jim said she had better be put in the back.

'Ain't no room for us to breathe, let alone your dolly,' said Jim cheerfully. 'Give 'er 'ere.'

He clambered down again and Dolly reluctantly handed Emily, in her red cape, into his huge knobbly hand. He went to the rear of the cart and propped Emily up in a chair.

'There she be,' called Jim. 'Now 'er's got a clear view of the road.'

Satisfied, Dolly settled down to present delights. The horse's massive brown haunches, moving just below her, fascinated the child. Leather squeaked, brass jingled, wooden wheels rumbled, and the whole cart seemed alive with movement and noises.

A gentle climb, from the river valley where Caxley lay, occupied the first mile or so of the journey. The sun was high now, and from her lofty seat Dolly could see over the hedges into the meadows. They steamed gently in the growing heat, for they were wet from overnight rain.

About half a mile before it entered the village of Beech Green the road plunged down a short steep hill between high banks topped with massive beech trees. It was the first time that the child had seen great roots writhing out of the soil like underground branches. It seemed to make this new world even more strange and foreign.

'Nearly there,' said her mother, putting a steadying arm round Dolly, so that she did not slide forward on to Belle's great back. 'You'll see your new home soon.'

They emerged from the tunnel of trees and began to rumble through the scattered village. Ada noticed the school standing back from the road. A few children, playing in the dinner hour, watched their progress, and one child waved. Ada waved back energetically, but Dolly was too timid.

Their own house lay half a mile or so further, on the outskirts of Beech Green. Three miles further still lay the village of Fairacre where so much of little Dolly's life was to be spent.

Dolly's spirits rose with every turn of the wheel that took her further from Caxley. The light breeze stirred her hair, hanging now, almost to her shoulders, in blessed holiday freedom. The inevitable had happened at the Caxley school. The propinquity of Maud's auburn tangles had soon led to Dolly's head scratching, her mother's shocked discoveries, and the tight tying-back of poor Dolly's locks on school days. The feeling of wind in her hair enhanced the delights of the day as the child kept a look-out for the new cottage.

At last a bend in the road revealed it – a snug, thatched, tight little beauty of a house, set behind a thick hedge just quickening to green. The cart slurred to a stop, the noises ceased, and the full quiet harmony of the wide countryside became apparent.

Jim lifted the two children down. He and Mary began to busy themselves with the load, helped by the vociferous Ada. Dolly, as if in a trance, pushed open the small gate and wandered past the cottage to the end of the garden. She had never realised that the world was so big.

Before her, beyond the garden hedge, sloped the gentle flanks of the downs with Hundred Acre Field at the base, and their tops, hazy in the distance, fading into the blue of the sky. Birds sang in the hedges, in the trees, and far above her in the blue and white sky. The happiness which had warmed Dolly in the flower-lit meadow on her way to her grandmother's returned to her with renewed strength.

She felt as a minnow, long held captive in a jam jar, must feel on being released into a brook; or as a bird set free from a cage into the limitless air. This was her element. These criss-cross currents of scent-laden air, spangled with bird-song, splashed with sunshine, flowed around her, lifting her spirits and quickening her senses.

Dolly Clare had come home.

Now, a lifetime later, white-haired Miss Clare stood in the same garden, gazing at the same view and drawing from it the same comfort and strength which it had always given. Her hands were full of roses. Some would stand in the small sitting room, but the choicest would be put beside Emily Davis's bed in the spare bedroom.

The thought of Emily reminded Miss Clare again of the lost doll. It was dusk, she recalled, before the first Emily had been missed. Distressed though she was, little Dolly had been less upset than her parents feared, for the enchantment of the day still possessed her.

'I'll see Jim tomorrow,' promised Francis. 'He'll have her safe, never fear.'

But Emily was not with Jim. She had fallen from the back of the cart and lay face downward at the side of the lane between Caxley and Beech Green. A ten-year-old boy, who had spent the morning rattling two stones in a tin to scare the birds from his master's crop, found her as he went home to dinner. He turned her over with the broken toe-cap of his boot, and snorted with scorn.

'Some kid's old dolly!' he shouted to the wind, and booted it, in a magnificent arc, over the hedge.

It was a week before she was found, and Dolly had shed many tears of mourning. A man, cutting back the hedge, had discovered the sodden doll and taken it to the local shop, where Francis later collected it.

'There, my dear,' he said to Dolly, 'now you can be happy again.'

Dolly took the long-lost doll into her arms, but never completely into her heart again.

Emily looked so different. She had the pale remote air of one who has been ill for a long time. One eye had gone, and though Mary sewed two white linen shirt buttons in place of her former eyes, this only added to the strangeness of the doll in her young mistress's eyes. She cared for her as zealously as she had always done, putting her to bed, tying on the red cloak before taking her into the garden, and propping a cushion behind her back when she sat at table. But the glory was gone.

It may have been that the new living Emily had taken her place. Certainly she had become very dear to young Dolly.

'And still is,' said old Miss Clare, stirring herself from her reminiscences.

The clock struck twelve inside the house, and from the distant village school Miss Clare heard the shouts of children released from bondage.

'I've done nothing but day-dream,' Miss Clare told herself, returning from the noonday blaze to the shade of the kitchen. 'Emily will be here before I'm ready for her. But then that's one of the pleasures of growing old,' she comforted herself.

Singing softly, roses in hand, she mounted the stairs to the waiting room.

PART TWO *Beech Green*

CHAPTER 7

LIFE at Beech Green was an exhilarating affair, after the confines of Caxley, and made all the richer by the friendship with Emily Davis.

She was a mischievous, high-spirited child, the middle one of seven children. All nine of the Davises lived, as snug and gay as a nestful of wrens, in a tiny cottage at the end of a row of four.

Dolly found her way there before she had lived a week at her new home. There was a happy-go-lucky atmosphere about the Davises' house which enchanted the little girl who had been more primly brought up. She tumbled in and out of their home, revelling in the games, the nonsense and the carefree coming and going of the seven children and their numerous friends.

Emily's father was a gardener at the manor house at Beech Green. He was a giant of a man, with a face as brown and wrinkled as a walnut. Two bright blue eyes blazed from his weatherbeaten countenance, and his laugh shook the cottage.

'My husband's a very larky man,' Mrs Davis would say proudly. 'Likes his joke, and that.'

She was barely five feet high, with a figure so neat and child-like that it seemed impossible that she could be the mother of such a large and boisterous brood. Her energy was boundless. She scrubbed and polished the little house, cooked massive meals, washed mountains of linen, and then knitted and sewed, or tended her flower garden, as a relaxation. Throughout it all she laughed and sang, finding time to play with her children, cuffing them good-naturedly when they needed correction, and seeming, at the end of the day, to be as fresh as when she rose at five-thirty.

Dolly loved Mrs Davis dearly. Her warm and casual friendliness made her feel part of the family, and her self-assurance grew.

In the corner of the cottage living-room sat old Mr Davis, Emily's grandfather. He had been a carter, but now, unable to work regularly, he made a few pence by mending pots and pans for the neighbours. His right hand was encased in a black kid glove, which fascinated young Dolly.

One day, soon after her arrival at Beech Green, the old man caught the child's eyes fixed upon his hand. A soldering iron was heating in the open fire, and between his knees old Mr Davis held an upturned kettle.

'You be wondering why I keeps me glove on, I'll wager,' he grunted.

Dolly smiled shyly.

'Well, I ain't agoing to take it off to show you, me little maid, or you'd 'ave a fright. I ain't got much of me fingers left, if the truth be told.'

He bent forward, breathless with the effort, and removed the red-hot iron from the fire. Dolly, with a thrill of horror, saw how he held it gripped in the palm of his hand. He dipped the iron in a little tin on the fender, and a hot pungent smoke rose from the sizzling liquid.

'I was out in that ol' snowstorm for two days,' said the old man. 'Afore you was born or thought of, that was. In 1881 – getting on for fourteen year ago. I'd taken a load of hay over to Springbourne that day, and it was snowing pretty lively as I went. But how the Hanover I got back as fur as I did that afternoon, I never could tell. Just this side of the downs I 'ad to give in. I cut the horses loose and said: "Git on 'ome, you two, while you can." I felt fair lonely watching them slipping and sliding down the hill, up to their bellies in snow, leaving me on me own.'

'You should have sat on one,' said Dolly gravely.

'Easier said than done,' grunted Mr Davis, applying his soldering iron to the kettle. There was silence while he surveyed his handiwork for a minute or two, and then he resumed.

'The snow was that thick, and swirling around so, them two horses vanished pretty quick. I could 'ear 'em snorting with fright and shaking their heads. They 'adn't seen nothing like it, you see. Nor me, for that matter.

'There I was, and I couldn't make up me mind to stop in the cart or try and plod on home and risk it.'

'What did you do?' asked Dolly.

'Risked it,' said the old man laconically. 'Risked it, and fell in a dam' ditch I never knew was there, and 'ad to stop there two days. I ain't seen nothing like that blizzard before or since. If it 'adn't a been for the two horses getting back I reckon I'd a been there still. They never got home till next day, and it took four chaps searching in turn to find me, it was that cruel.'

'Did you shout?' asked Dolly.

'I was past shouting after the first 'alf-hour,' answered Mr Davis, holding the kettle to the light and squinting inside it. 'By the time they dug me out I was as stiff as this 'ere iron. Stayed in bed a week, I did, and 'ad to 'ave three fingers and two toes plucked orf. The frost-bite, you see.'

Dolly nodded, appalled.

'I shan't forget 1881 in a 'urry,' said the old man, and thrust the soldering iron back into the red heart of the coals with a deft thrust of his maimed hand.

* * *

The Davises were not the only new friends. Francis and Mary Clare blossomed in their country surroundings, and the neighbourliness which they had missed so sorely in Caxley now seemed doubly dear.

The family had for so long been thrust in upon itself. The next door neighbours at Caxley, cross and aged, had been ever present in Mary's thoughts, and Dolly and Ada were often scolded for making a noise that might penetrate the thin dividing wall. Fear of strangers, and particularly of 'the marsh lot', kept country-bred Mary from making many friends in Caxley. Francis's illness and their pinching poverty were other factors in 'keeping themselves to themselves'.

Back in the country again, fellows of a small community, Mary and Francis felt their tension relax. A move is always an excitement in a village, and by the end of the first long day the family had met more than a dozen neighbours, some prompted by kindness, some by curiosity, who had called to welcome them.

Within a few weeks Francis had the cottage garden dug and planted, and found he had already promised to exhibit something in the local autumn flower show which was to be held at Fairacre. Mary, to her surprise, found that she had been persuaded to join the Glee Club, run on Friday nights by the redoubtable Mr Finch in his schoolroom.

'Us makes our own fun,' Mrs Davis said to Mary. "Tis all very fine for the gentry to go to Caxley in their carriages for a ball at the Corn Exchange, but us ordinary folk, as goes on Shanks's pony, gets our fun in the village.'

And Mary, with her two little girls safely at school all day, and a husband back at work, was only too ready to join in the simple homely fun of which she had been starved for so long.

Dolly and Ada took to the village school like ducks to water. They had been well drilled at Caxley and found that the work here was well within their grasp. Their classmates were somewhat impressed by the two new girls who had experienced the superior instruction of a town school, and Dolly and Ada felt pleasantly distinguished.

The smaller numbers made school life much less frightening for timid Dolly, and gave Ada greater scope for her powers of leadership. In no time she was the acknowledged queen of the playground, and had all the younger children vying for her favours, and the thrill of 'playing with Ada'. Mr Finch, who hid a genuine fondness for children beneath his pompous veneer, was glad to have such a bright pupil among his scholars, and Mrs Finch, who had some difficulty with discipline, was relieved to find that Dolly was as sedate as she was hard-working.

But the greatest joy for Dolly in this happy new life was the discovery of the infinite beauties in the natural world about her. That first glimpse of Beech Green and the realisation that she had found her real home, was repeated daily in a hundred different ways. The walk to school took about a quarter of an hour, and revealed dozens of enchanting things.

In that first spring, Dolly discovered that a bed of white violets grew on the left-hand bank just before the farm gate. They were well hidden by fine dry grass, but their heady scent betrayed them, and the child exulted in the pure whiteness, enhanced by the spot of yellow stamens lurking in its depths, of each small flower. Almost opposite grew a rarer type of violet, almost pink in colour, which was much sought after by the little girls of Beech Green. Dolly soon grew wise enough to keep the news of its flowering to herself.

Nearer the school, the lane was shaded by elm trees which grew upon steep banks. Here Dolly found a pink and fleshy plant, which Mr Finch told her was toothwort. It was unattractive, and reminded Dolly of the pink pendulous sows in the farmyard as they lumbered about among their squealing young. But it had its fascination for the town-bred child, and she felt proud to see it put on the window-sill at school, neatly labelled by Mr Finch's own pen.

There were terrifying things too to encounter on the walk to school. Behind the farm gate, just beyond the violet bed, a dozen grey and white geese honked and hissed, stretching sinuous waving necks, and menacing the child with their icy blue eyes and cruel orange bills. Dolly shouted as bravely as the other children when the geese were safely barred, but sometimes the gate was open, and the geese paraded triumphantly up and down the lane. Then Dolly would scramble up the steep bank, over the roots of the elm trees and the toothwort, and try to gain the safety of the cornfield beyond, while the geese stretched their great wings and ran, hideously fast, creating a clamour that could be heard a mile away.

The geese were frightening enough, but even more disconcerting was Mabel, who lived in a cottage half way to school. She was a grotesque, misshapen figure, almost as broad as she was tall, the victim of some glandular disease which was incurable at that time. Mentally she was aged about six, although she had been born thirty years earlier, and she played with a magnificent doll all day long. In the winter Mabel was invisible to Beech Green, for she was closely, and lovingly, confined in the stuffy little house by her doting parents. But during the warm weather the pathetic stumpy figure sat in a basket chair placed on the front path. From there she watched the neighbours go by as she nursed the expensive doll.

'Them poor Bells,' the villagers said, with genuine sympathy, "as got enough to drive them silly theirselves with that Mabel. Got to be watched every minute of the day! But don't 'er mother keep 'er beautiful?'

Cleanliness was a much-prized virtue in Beech Green, and Mabel was held up as a shining example of Mrs Bell's industry. The poor idiot was always clothed in good quality dresses, covered with a snowy starched and goffered pinafore. Her coarse scanty hair, as bristly as that which grew upon the pigs' backs in the farmyard nearby, was tied back with a beautiful satin ribbon. Her podgy yellow face, from which two dark eyes glinted from slanting slits, was shiny with soap, and her fat little legs were always encased in the finest black stockings, with never so much as a pinpoint of a hole in sight.

To Dolly's terror, Mabel took an instant liking to her, and would waddle to the gate, holding up the doll and uttering thick guttural cries of pleasure. Dolly's first impulse was to run away, but her mother had spoken to her firmly.

'You can thank your stars you weren't born like Mabel, and just you be extra kind to that poor child – for child she is, for all her thirty years. No flinching now, if she comes up to you, and you let her touch you too, if she's a mind to! She's as gentle as a lamb, and the Bells have enough to put up with without people giving their only one the cold shoulder!'

And so Dolly steeled herself to smile upon the squat unlovely figure behind the cottage gate, and sometimes put a violet or two into that thick clumsy hand, and admired the doll with sincerity. She never saw Mabel outside the house or the garden, and never understood one word that fell from those thick lips; but when, in three or four years' time, the child mercifully died, she missed her sorely, and could only guess at the loss suffered by Mr Bell, and still more by Mrs Bell, whose clothes line had fluttered daily with the brave array of Mabel's finery.

Looking back later, to those early days at Beech Green, Miss Clare was amazed to think how many subnormal and eccentric people there were among that small number in those late Victorian days. There were many reasons. Inbreeding was a common cause, for lack of transport meant that the boys and girls of the village tended to marry each other, and the few families there became intricately related. Lack of skilled medical attention, particularly during childbirth, accounted for some deformities of mind and body, and the dread of mental hospitals – sadly justified in many cases – kept others from seeking help with their problems. Certainly, when Dolly first went to live at Beech Green, there were half a dozen souls in the neighbourhood who were as much in need of attention as poor Mabel.

There was the boy who had epileptic fits, who sat in the desk next to Ada, and was looked upon with more affection than distress by his classmates, as the means of enlivening Mr Finch's boring lessons. There was old Mrs Marble, who gibbered and shook her fist at the children from the broken window of her filthy cottage near the school, and who would certainly have been ducked in the horsepond had she had the misfortune to have been born a century earlier. There was a very nasty man who delighted in walking about the woods and lanes with his trousers over his arm, frightening the women and little girls out of their wits, but excused by the men as 'only happening when the moon was at the full, poor fellow.'

Then there were the three White children, abysmally slow at lessons, but with tempers of such uncontrollable violence that the whole school went in terror of them. How much of this vicious frenzy was due to mental disorder, and how much to their parents' treatment of it, was debatable. It was the custom of Mr and Mrs White to lock their refractory offspring in a cupboard under the stairs where, in the smelly darkness among the old shoes and coats that hung there, they were allowed to scream, sob, fight, pummel the door, and exhaust their hysteria before being let out again, some hours later, white and wild-eyed and ready to fall into their nightmare-haunted beds.

Even the great ones of the village had their sufferings. The lady of the manor, Mrs Evans, whose visits to the school meant much curtseying and bobbing, had one frail chick among her six sturdy ones, and Miss Lilian was never seen without a maid or her governess in attendance ready to direct her charge's wan looks towards anything of cheer.

As young Dolly soon discovered, Beech Green had its darker side, the reverse of the bright flower-decked face which charmed the newcomers. But it all added to the excitement of daily living. It gave the solemn little girl a chance to observe human frailties and quirks of behaviour, and gave her too an insight into the courage and good humour with which her fellows faced personal tragedy.

These early lessons were to stand her in good stead, for before long she too would be involved in a family disaster whose repercussions were to echo down many years of her adult life.

In welcoming all that life in Beech Green offered her, in both happiness and horror, the child unwittingly prepared herself for the testing time which lay ahead.

CHAPTER 8

THE first intimation of the event which was to colour so many years of Dolly Clare's later life was her mother's visit to the doctor in May 1896.

Mary Clare suspected that she was pregnant again, and she viewed the situation with mixed feelings.

'Just got my two off to school,' she confided resignedly to Mrs Davis one morning, 'and then another turns up. All that washing again, and bad nights, and mixing up feeding bottles! Somehow I don't take to the idea like I did, but Francis is that pleased I haven't the heart to tell him it's not all honey for me.'

'You waits till you has seven,' commented Mrs Davis cheerfully. 'Time enough to gloom then, I can tell you. Why, your two girls can give you a hand, and if it's a boy you'll be looked after proper in your old age!'

Somewhat comforted, Mary Clare made her way, one Tuesday morning, to the converted stable in the manor grounds where Dr Fisher held his weekly surgery.

'There's plenty to be thankful for,' she told herself, as she trudged up the broad drive between the flowering chestnut trees. 'Francis is as pleased as Punch, and he's in work again. And this place is far better to have a baby in than that Caxley hovel. It can lie in the garden, and I'll get the washing dry lovely with the winds we get here. And Mrs Davis is quite right about Dolly and Ada. They're big enough to help now they're eleven and nine.'

Her usual good spirits asserted themselves, and by the time the doctor had confirmed her suspicions she was facing the future with more hope. It is always heartening to be an object of interest, and Mary looked forward to many a cosy chat with her new neighbours, as she returned to her cottage.

Francis was jubilant when she told him that evening.

'It'll be a boy this time,' he assured her. 'You'll see, my love. A real fine son to carry on the thatching trade. The girls will be glad to hear the news.'

'They'll not learn it from me for a few months yet,' replied Mary tartly. 'Time enough for them to know when I takes to my bed.'

'If you don't want them to hear it from all the old gossips in the village,' warned her husband, 'you'd best tell 'em yourself before long.'

'Well, we'll see,' said Mary, more gently, recognising the wisdom of her husband's remark.

The baby was due in November, and the little girls were told one mellow September evening as they went to bed. Mary found it an embarrassing occasion and had steeled herself to it all day. She had rehearsed her short speech a dozen times, and delivered it with a beating heart and a pink face.

'I got something nice to tell you two, my dears. A wonderful secret. God's sending you a little brother next November,' she said, with rare piety.

At last it was out, and she waited, breathless, for the reaction.

Dolly sat up in bed, open-mouthed but silent. Ada bounced unconcernedly on to one side and said nonchalantly:

'Oh, I know! Jimmy Davis told me you was in kitten last June.'

Mary's pink face grew crimson with fury.

'The rude little boy!' she exclaimed, outraged. 'I'll see his mother hears of this, and gives him a good box side the ear, too! And I don't know as you don't deserve one, too, for listening to such rudeness!'

Seething with righteous indignation, Mary left her daughters unkissed, and slammed the door upon them. Relating it later to Francis she found her annoyance giving way to amusement as he gave way to his mirth.

'Looks to me quite simple,' laughed Francis. 'You wrapped it up too pretty, and Jimmy Davis put it real ugly, but one way or another, now they know. You go up and say good night to 'em and see how pleased they'll be.'

By the time darkness fell, peace was made, and the thought of a fifth member of the Clare family brought much joy to the four already awaiting him.

Amazingly, it was a boy. Mary's labour was grievously protracted, and the local midwife had been obliged to send for the doctor after hours of effort. Dolly and Ada had spent the night with the Davis household. Somehow two extra children fitted into the nutshell of a house with no difficulty, and they were thrilled to have a mattress on the floor of the girls' bedroom.

At dinner time next day they were told that a brother had arrived and they could go and see him.

'But mind you're quiet,' warned Mrs Davis. 'Your ma had a bad time with him and wants a good sleep.'

They rushed homeward, and the midwife led them on tiptoe to their parents' bedroom.

Pale, and appallingly tired, Mary smiled faintly at them from the pillows. Beside her lay a white bundle, containing what looked like a coconut from the Michaelmas fair. On closer inspection, Dolly could see the dark crumpled countenance of her brother, topped by a crop of black thatch. His eyes were glued together into thin slits, as though nothing in the world should prize him from the sleep that enfolded him.

Dolly was seriously disappointed. She had imagined someone looking like Mabel's beautiful doll, very small but exquisite. But she sensed that this was no time to express her dissatisfaction, and smiled as bravely as she could at her mother before taking Ada's hand and making her way to the door. Before she put her hand on the knob she noticed that her mother had fallen asleep again, with the same desperate concentration as the baby beside her.

That evening the two little girls returned to sleep at their own home. As soon as Francis came in he kissed them heartily, looking younger and more handsome than he had for many a year.

'Ain't he a lovely boy then?' he said to them proudly. 'Ain't you two lucky ones, having a brother after all?'

He led the way upstairs, and Francis bent over Mary and the baby. Mary looked less deathly pale, and smiled at the family, but the baby still slept, snuffling slightly in his shawl.

'You're all over bits,' Mary admonished her husband, as pieces of chaff fluttered down upon the bed from his working clothes. He laughed, and plucked a long golden straw that had lodged in the leather strap around his trouser leg.

'There you are, son,' he said, threading the bright strand through his child's small fingers. 'Get the feel of straw in your hand, and you'll grow up to be the best thatcher in England.'

It was that small incident that gave young Dolly a glimpse of her father's exultant pride, not only in his son, but in his work, and the new hope he now had of an assured future.

The baby thrived and was whole-heartedly adored by the family and the neighbours. His most fervent admirer was Emily Davis. One might have thought that the child had seen enough of babies, but little Frank Clare seemed dearer to Emily than her own young brothers, and she pushed his wicker pram as frequently as his sisters did.

By the time he was sitting up and taking notice of the world around him, the summer of 1897 had come and Beech Green was busy with preparations for the Diamond Jubilee of the aged Queen Victoria.

The local lord of the manor, Mr Evans, had invited everyone to games and a mammoth tea party, and excitement ran high as the great day in June approached. Many people remembered the celebrations ten years before when the sun had blazed upon a nation rejoicing in a reign of fifty years. This time, they said, it would be better still.

In the great world beyond Beech Green there was perhaps not quite the same fervour for the military pomp and processions as there had been at the Golden Jubilee. Many thinking men felt a growing distaste for imperialism, and distrusted 'jingoism', which they suspected inflamed a love of conquest for its own sake. This did not lessen the devotion to the Queen, who by now was an object of veneration to all her subjects. The majority of her countrymen had never known another monarch on the throne, and as the day of the Diamond Jubilee grew nearer, many tales were told of memorable events in her incredibly long reign.

Dolly's grandfather, on one of his visits to see the new baby, brought the remote figure of the great Queen very clearly to the child's mind.

'I was down at Portsmouth once, staying with my brother. August, it was, in the year 1875, and the royal yacht *Alberta* come over from Osborne one day. The Queen herself was aboard, and there was a shocking thing happened. Somehow or other a little yacht got across the *Alberta's* path and was run down. It sank in no time, and three poor souls was drownded. They told us the Queen was beside herself with distress, pacing up and down in the *Alberta* with the tears falling. Poor lady, she had a wonderful kind heart, and that were a sore and terrible grief to her.'

He presented the little girls with a Union Jack made by their grandmother so that they could hang it from the porch on Jubilee Day. On this occasion he had not brought his wife, for he had pedalled over on his old penny-farthing cycle, an archaic vehicle to which he was much attached. Dolly and Ada

watched him remount after tea, and waved the flag vigorously after his retreating figure.

The day itself dawned clear and shining. 'Real Queen's weather again,' people cried to each other as they bustled about. Household chores were done quickly that day to leave time for the preparations for the afternoon fun. In the grounds at the manor long trestle tables were spread with new lengths of unbleached calico for tablecloths, and on these were dozens of dishes of buns and lardy cakes, sandwiches and pies. Maids fluttered back and forth from the house bearing great trays of cups and saucers, tea urns, jugs, spoons and all the paraphernalia of rural junketings.

Dolly and Ada were beside themselves with excitement. All the schools had a holiday, and it was a thrill to wear one's best white frock with one's best black stockings and nailed boots. Their pink and blue sashes were freshly pressed, and Mary had tied hair ribbons to match upon her daughters' curls.

Dolly felt very sorry for one family who sat opposite her at the long tea table. They had recently lost their mother, and all the four children, even the youngest who could scarcely toddle, were clad in deepest black. From the crêpe bows which decorated their black hats to the toecaps of their heavy boots the gloom was unrelieved. Even their hands were encased in black cotton gloves which they did not remove even when eating. Under the brilliant blue sky, among the laughter and sunshine, they perched like four little black crows in a row, silent, and suffering the heat in stolid endurance.

After a colossal tea, one of the daughters of the house sang patriotic songs, accompanied by her sister, at the piano which had been wheeled out upon the grass from the drawing-room. Applause was polite but not very enthusiastic, and everyone, including the Misses Evans, was relieved when the real festivities began with the sports.

The Clare family did well, for Francis won the men's wheelbarrow race with the eldest Davis boy in the barrow whilst he did the pushing, and later still, Ada tore splendidly across the field in the girls' hundred yards, sash flying, nailed boots pounding, to win by a short head from the butcher's daughter. Dolly came second in the obstacle race, but was beaten by Emily Davis whose wiry skinniness negotiated ladder rungs and wriggled under tarpaulins with amazing dexterity.

Francis received half a crown, but Ada was delighted to have six yards of the unbleached calico which had recently covered the tea tables. It made stout pillow cases for the family which lasted for many years, and was considered by all to be a practical and most welcome prize.

At the end of the long golden day the little family made its way home. Young Frank slept in his wicker perambulator, and across the bottom was lodged the roll of calico. The lane was warm and scented with honeysuckle from the sun-baked hedges, and the smell of hay, lying ready to be turned when the labourers returned to the fields next day after the holiday, mingled with the other summer scents.

Tired Dolly, clinging to the pram for support, thought she would never forget such a wonderful day. 'Nothing ever happens in Beech Green,' she had heard people say. No one could say that now, was Dolly's last thought, as her dizzy head burrowed into the pillow beside Ada's. It was the most splendid thing that had ever happened in her young life.

Although Dolly, at nine years of age, was unconscious of the importance of the Jubilee and its times upon her outlook, yet looking back, as an old woman, she began to realise how deeply events and national movements had influenced even such a quiet life as her own. The Queen's celebrations had brought unaccustomed vivacity and loquacity to the country folk around her. Dolly, unusually excited by the stir, learnt more then about England's place in the world, her great men, her victories abroad and the reforms needed at home, than she had ever done before.

From Mr Finch she learnt of the vast areas of the world ruled over by their own Queen. From him she learnt of the Empire, following his pointer as it leapt from one red splash to another across the map of the world hung over the easel. She was told of the courage and military persistence of those who had subjugated the natives of those parts, and the benevolence of the great Queen whose laws now ruled them. She was not told of the feelings of those subjugated, but supposed that they were as happy to be in the Empire family as she was herself. Certainly the most splendid photographs of African chiefs, Indian princes, and the nobility of many far-flung territories taking part in the Diamond Jubilee celebrations, were cut from the newspapers and pinned up on the schoolroom wall where they were much admired by Queen Victoria's young subjects.

From the newspapers too, Dolly and Emily, both becoming avid readers, soon recognised the modern hero. He was a man of action, willing to tear up his roots and leave his country to explore unknown lands, to seek his fortune – in gold, maybe, in diamonds perhaps – to fight bravely, to dominate and to carry the British way of life to the unenlightened. He was a hero likely to be acceptable to boys as well as girls, for he was a colourful figure of wealth and power to those living amidst the pinching poverty of rural England at that time. The lot of the agricultural labourer grew worse weekly. The trek to find work in the towns continued. More and more white-collar workers struggled along in increasingly drab surroundings. It was small wonder that they craved colour and sensation to add excitement to their lives. The accounts of England's conquests overseas and the blaze of publicity which illuminated her leaders fired many a young man to join the army or to emigrate to those colonies whose exotic representatives marched in the Queen's processions.

The nineties needed sensation. The Diamond Jubilee was an occasion for national rejoicing, not only in the Queen, but in the nation's image as personified by her, proud, beloved, and a world-ruler. It was an image of Britain's greatness which was to remain with Dolly and her contemporaries. It gave them a deep sense of pride which would be needed to sustain them through many a change and the tragedy of two world wars. It gave them too a stability and a faith in ultimate victory which a later generation was to marvel at, deride, but secretly envy.

Later, Miss Clare was to see the follies and mistakes that had accompanied Britain's imperial policy during the nineties, but on that June night, after a shining day of rustic rejoicing, everything seemed wonderful to the little girl, with God in his heaven, the Queen on the throne, and the glory of an Empire everywhere around.

CHAPTER 9

THE friendship between Emily and Dolly deepened with time. They shared a passion for flowers, reading and little children, and were lucky enough to find plenty of each to keep them happy.

The woods on the hill to Springbourne, a neighbouring

village on the other side of the downs, were their hunting ground for flowers almost all the year round. They found wild snowdrops, violets, anemones, primroses and nodding catkins while the year was yet young. Later, bluebells and curling bracken fronds delighted them. Foxgloves and campion followed, and then, in the autumn, they had the joy of collecting hazel nuts and blackberries, as busily as the red squirrels that darted airily across the frail twigs high above their heads. Even in winter the wood offered treasures for those who cared to seek, and the two little girls would return carrying orange toadstools or lichen-covered branches in their cold hands.

Both children were fortunate too in having parents enlightened enough to give them a small patch of garden for their own cultivation. Most cottage gardens at this time were given over exclusively to the growing of vegetables for the family, and there was real need for this. Consequently, very few children had anywhere to play on their own territory, and fewer still were able to count a yard or two as their very own. Dolly and Ada shared a patch, and Emily had a much smaller one in her own garden. Here the children planted any seeds they could beg, and slips of plants given them by indulgent grown-up gardeners. The result was gay and unusual. Radishes and marigolds rioted together, a cabbage sheltered a clump of yellow pansies, and double daisies tossed their fringes beside mustard and cress.

They were lucky too with reading matter. Mr Finch, for all his pomposity and strictness, was a good teacher, and fostered any talent and interest that he saw. Books from the school library shelf could be borrowed, if brown paper covers were made for them and they were returned within a week. Often he lent a book from his own house, and this was greatly treasured. In this way Emily and Dolly were able to read more recent fiction than the Marryats, Mrs Ewings, and Kingsleys on the school shelf. Rider Haggard, Conan Doyle and Kipling were some of the new authors that the little girls met for the first time, and though there was much that escaped their understanding, the excitement of the stories swept them along in a fever of anticipation and made them long for the chance to see the strange foreign places there portrayed. Young though they were, they too had caught the fever for adventure which quickened their elders at this time, and they mourned the fact that they were female, and so never likely to have the opportunities of Allan Quatermain. Dolly's greatest moment came when Mr Finch presented her with a copy of *Three Men in a Boat*, which remained a favourite of hers for many years, though at its first reading she skipped all the moralising bits and the descriptions.

There were plenty of children, in their own families and their neighbours', to satisfy their interests, and mothers were glad to trust their toddlers to two girls who were so unusually sensible. Their sorties to the woods were usually in the company of Frank and another toddler or two straggling happily along behind them, or stuffed in an old pushchair and rattling over the uneven path.

'Fresh air's free,' the mothers used to tell them; 'you get as much of it as you can.' And out the children would be bundled, while cottage floors were swept and scrubbed, and the steel fenders and fire irons were polished with emery paper, and everything 'put to rights', as they said, in the few snatched minutes of freedom from their offspring. Consequently, there were always plenty of young children ready to join in games, or to be petted and admired by the older girls.

Looking back, Miss Clare saw how valuable all this unconscious training had been to her work as a teacher. The love of flowers and reading she passed on to many a country child, and her own response to young children, protective and warm-hearted, never failed her.

Friendship with Emily meant less dependence on Ada, and now that the two sisters were growing older, the differences in temperament became even more marked. Ada grew more handsome as the years passed, and her boundless vivacity made her attractive to the boys at Beech Green school as well as the girls. Fearless and athletic, she could climb a tree or vault a fence, despite her hampering skirts, as bravely as the boys, and Ada Clare was known as 'a good sport'.

Francis Clare adored all his children, but his bonny Ada became increasingly dear to him. Mary looked in some doubt upon her firstborn. There were times when she was headstrong and disobedient, and Mary foresaw a difficult time ahead when young men would enter Ada's life.

Sometimes Dolly was frightened by Ada's bold disobedience of her mother; at other times she was grateful for some small rebellion which proved successful and benefited them both. The weekly dosing was a case in point.

As was the custom at that time in almost all households, the Clare children were given a mild purgative, usually on Saturday evening. Francis had been brought up to expect a teaspoonful of a home-made concoction with nauseating regularity. His mother chopped prunes, raisins, figs and dates, plentifully sprinkled them with powdered senna pods and a little medicinal paraffin oil and mixed it together to form a glutinous and efficient purge. It had the advantage of being reasonably palatable and wholesome, but Mary considered 'Grandma's jollop', as the children called it, very old-fashioned, and substituted castor-oil, which she disguised in hot lemonade.

It was Ada who called Dolly's attention to the suspicious oily rings floating on the top.

'Don't you drink it,' she warned the younger child, in her mother's absence. Mary was at first persuasive, then unsuccessfully authoritative, and finally plain cross, as the two little girls flatly refused to drink the brew.

Francis only laughed when she told him.

'Give 'em Grandma's jollop then,' he suggested. 'They like that, so they say.'

But Mary tried another stratagem. On the following Saturday a plate of dates was offered to the children.

'This one hasn't got a stone in it,' said Dolly with surprise.

Her mother, busy ostensibly with darning, said briskly:

'Maybe it's got some grey powder inside instead.'

'That's right. It has,' agreed Dolly.

'You get some dates like that,' said Mary complacently. 'Some has stones and some has grey powder.'

They ate them unprotesting, thrilled to have such a treat as dates; but Ada discovered the trick before the next Saturday. Other children had grey powder administered in this form, she heard from her schoolfellows.

Fruit laxative tablets, called optimistically by Mary 'nice pink sweets', were tried next. Dolly and Ada held them in their mouths, pretended to swallow them, and then removed them when their mother was out of the room.

'Put 'em under the table ledge, quick!' whispered Ada, and there for several weeks a collection of sucked tablets grew, on a narrow ledge under the table top, well hidden by the red tablecloth.

At last came the day of open rebellion. Ada refused to take any form of medicine again.

'You'll be ill,' warned her mother. 'It's only taking these pills regular that's kept you and Dolly so fit and well. Your mother knows best now.'

'That she don't,' said Ada defiantly, tossing her bright hair.

'If you looks under the table ledge you'll see what we've done with 'em all this time. And we ain't come to no harm!'

The pink tablets were discovered, the two little girls sent to bed in disgrace, and Francis told all when he returned.

He hugged his vexed wife and restored her spirits.

'Well, she've told the truth. Their insides works all right without a lot of oiling, it seems. Let 'em off, my dear, and save a mint of money, and temper too.'

Thus Ada's battle, and Dolly's too, was won. These things happened when Frank was too young to be included in the ritual, but as soon as he was old enough he was told by his sisters just how fortunate he was to have escaped such horrors, and how thankful he should be to those who had smoothed the path before him.

If Mary had a favourite among her three children (and she stoutly maintained that she had not), then it was little Frank. He was darker in colouring than the two girls, who took after Francis. The dark bright hazel eyes that shone so lovingly upon his mother were the same colour as her own, and his hair grew as crisply. More open in his affection than her daughters, Frank charmed Mary by his frequent hugs and kisses, and many a smack was left unadministered because the knowing young rogue disarmed his mother with his blandishments.

'Make the most of him while he's yours,' observed Francis, watching the toddler on his mother's lap. 'He'll break plenty of hearts, I reckon, before he goes off to settle down and leave you.'

'You won't leave your mum, will you, my love?' said Mary, dancing him up and down.

Although she had learnt of the advent of the baby with mixed feelings, the joy which she felt in this boy lay largely in the feeling of future security which he brought, although Mary herself was unconscious of this. The girls would marry, Francis might die first: a son was an insurance against want and loneliness, a joy to her now and a comfort for her old age.

When, in the autumn of 1899, the Boer War broke out, she looked upon her three-year-old and gave thanks that he was so young. Several young men from Beech Green had joined the army to escape from hard times and to seek adventure. Some were now in South Africa and Mary knew the anxiety which gnawed at the hearts of their mothers. She prayed that her Frank would never have to endure the dangers of war, nor she the heartbreak of those who wait for news.

Christmas that year was a sad one, overshadowed by the reverses of the army in South Africa. At the manor, the Evans family were dressed in heavy mourning for the eldest son, who had been shot from his horse whilst attempting to relieve Ladysmith with General Buller's forces. The village was stunned. This seemed to bring the war very near, and people concerned themselves with the direction of the hostilities with real anxiety. Should General Buller have suggested to White that he surrendered Ladysmith? It seemed a terrible thing for an Englishman to think of giving in. But then look at the loss of lives? Look at poor Algy Evans and the Willett boy from Fairacre and the Brown twins from Caxley! So the tongues wagged, and wagged still faster when they heard that Buller had been replaced by Lord Roberts who had lost his only son in the same battle that took their own Algy Evans.

Queen Victoria was reported as saying at this time: 'Please understand that there is no one depressed in *this* house. We are not interested in the possibilities of defeat: they do not exist.' These brave words were heartening, but did not completely quell the fears that shook her less heroic subjects' hearts.

When Dolly visited the Davis' cottage one day, just after Christmas in 1899, she found it clamorous with dismay.

Albert, the eldest son, had just announced that his New Year resolution was to join the army. Some of the family took his part, but his mother hotly attacked him. Dolly watched amazed the change in this smiling little Jenny-wren of a woman to a blazing fury.

'It's always what *you* wants,' she flared at the white, silent boy. 'Thinks yourself a hero, all dressed up in this new-fangled khaki to catch the girls' eyes! What about us? How's the family going to manage with your wages cut off?'

The boy began to explain haltingly, but was overborne. Dolly's heart bled for him as his mother's wrath gradually evaporated into self-pity.

'And what about a mother's feelings? Here I've brought you up from a baby, sat up nights when you was ailing, give you all you wanted, and what do I get in return? You fair break my heart, you do. You can't love me if you treats me like this.' She pulled a handkerchief from her sleeve and mopped the hot tears that coursed down her face. It was the old man of the house who opposed her most bravely. As he shook his black-gloved fist at her, his roars overcame the furious sobbing.

'You let 'un go. He's old enough to know what 'e wants, and you should be proud he's got the guts to want to fight. Don't I know his feelings? I went through the Crimean War – aye, and saw plenty of blood too, my own included, and would've died there but for Miss Nightingale, God bless 'er – and glad to, when we was fighting for the right thing. You women don't know half a man's mind. You try and keep 'im 'ere, tied down to your niminypiminy little ways and 'e'll 'ate you, and 'isself too, for the rest of his days.'

The boy cast a grateful look at the old man, and he continued more softly:

'There, gal, don't take on so. He'll be back before you knows where you are; and you can bet a fortune he won't go no

further than Salisbury Plain for many a long day. Let 'im 'ave 'is fling.'

Arguments flew for the rest of that week, but Albert was not to be deflected, and on the first day of 1900 he went to the recruiting officer in Caxley.

Emily and Dolly thought he was a hero, and defended his action enthusiastically. Here, in real life, was a happening as exciting as those they so often read about. Their interest in the war became redoubled, and they pestered old Mr Davis to tell them about his earlier war-time memories, but all his accounts, they discovered, soon turned to eulogising Miss Nightingale, whose personality had completely ensnared him.

'She's the most beautiful woman alive,' he told them, 'and the bravest. She never cared how rough or foul-mouthed we was to begin with – she soon altered all that. We fair worshipped her out there, and I see her once not long ago when I went to stay with a brother of mine at Claydon. There's a big house there that the Verneys own, and Miss Nightingale stays there sometimes with her sister. She was sitting with her in the garden and I stood behind a tree and looked at her, and looked at her. I thought to myself: "If ever a lady deserves a rest it's that one".'

His old eyes grew so ardent when he spoke of Miss Nightingale and her band of nurses that Dolly seriously considered the possibility of taking up nursing as a profession as she watched him. What could be more rewarding than to see love and gratitude flashing from the eyes of a soldier? A young one preferably, of course. Perhaps Albert Davis? Though, on second thoughts she did not want him hurt at all. And how becoming a nurse's uniform was! Dolly saw herself tripping lightly up and down a long ward, a veil floating behind her, the idol of her adoring patients. She was enchanted by the idea.

Enchantment ended a few hours later when little Frank was sick that evening and she was sent to clear up his cot. Sousing revolting bed linen in a tub of icy water, she realised, with devastating clarity, that nursing was not for her.

CHAPTER 10

DURING the first year of the new century, the object of prime importance at Beech Green school was a large-scale map showing the area in which the Boer War was being waged.

Each morning, before prayers, the boys would gather round

it, moving the little flags to show the day-to-day progress of the troops. Great was the rejoicing when besieged Ladysmith was finally relieved on February 28th, and greater still when, after 217 days of siege, Mafeking too was relieved in May.

Mr Finch was so infected with the national fever on this occasion that he let the children have a bonfire in the playground, and watched their wild dancing around it with an indulgent eye.

The most envied boy in the school was one who wore a tie of the new khaki colour decorated with dozens of tiny Union Jacks. The war, it seemed, was as good as won, as the summer wore on, and when, in the autumn of 1900, Lord Roberts and Buller came home to England, Beech Green felt sure that peace was not far distant.

'Your boy won't never get to South Africa,' they consoled Mrs Davis. 'Just a case of Kitchener clearing up the mess, and it'll all be over by harvest, you'll see.'

At the end of the summer term another excitement occurred. It was announced that Mr Finch was leaving and would take up a new appointment in a large school in the county town. This meant promotion, and his neighbours were quick to congratulate him.

The children were secretly glad to see him go. He wasn't a bad old stick, said some, but it would be good fun to have someone new who wasn't so strict. As one wag put it, in Dolly's hearing:

'Talk about the relief of Mafeking! I reckons it'll be the relief of Beech Green School when old Finch goes!'

The new headmaster came in the autumn. He was young and unmarried, but possessed a fiercely possessive mother who ruled the school house and her son as well.

Ada and the older girls were his slaves from the start. His fair wavy hair, worn a shade too long by country standards, and his pale face made him an object of interest and reverence. His clothes were much less formal than Mr Finch's had been, and he favoured big floppy ties in delicate pastel colours.

'Proper wishy-washy young feller', was what the men of Beech Green called the newcomer behind his back. But the women were inclined to take his part.

'He's just up-to-date, that's all. Very good thing too, to have someone who can teach the children without waving the cane at 'em all day,' they maintained.

His name was Evan Waterman, and he proved to be an ardent churchgoer, much given to genuflection and crossings during the services at Beech Green, which occasioned deep suspicions in the hearts of his Low Church neighbours. The vicar was delighted to have such a devout young man in charge of the school, and his visits there became more frequent and lengthy than ever.

'Lives in the parson's pocket,' grumbled old Davis one day, in Dolly's hearing. 'Don't trust that new chap no further'n I can see 'im! Too good to live, 'e be, mark my words!'

Mr Waterman had not been in school for a week before he told the children that he hoped he need never use the cane again, and to give emphasis to his words he threw it dramatically on to the top of a high cupboard where it lodged among a group of dusty wooden cubes, cones, spheres, and other geometrical shapes which had been undisturbed for years.

The rousing cheer which greeted this display might have warned a wiser man of perils to come, but Evan Waterman simply flushed with pleasure and told himself that he had won a place in his pupils' grateful hearts. Had he known it, it was not gratitude that enflamed those savage breasts, but the thought of a rollicking future where impudence and laziness would go unpunished. The boys winked merrily at each other, quivering with secret mirth. The girls gazed at their new headmaster with rapt devotion. In any case, they had seldom felt the cane, and had nothing to lose.

He told the children that he hoped they would look upon him as a friend, and would tell him of anything that perplexed or frightened them.

'I am here to help you,' he said earnestly, leaning forward in his desk with his pale blue tie flapping dangerously near the inkwell. The red faces of the older boys, choking with suppressed laughter at such antics, he attributed to natural bashfulness. He was determined to put into practice the new ideas in education, and to throw out the repressive methods which he saw had been those used by Mr Finch. To see the children curtseying and bowing to their elders shocked Mr Waterman seriously. The military precision with which the classes stood, turned and marched from the schoolroom to the playground appalled him. In the future, he told himself – and his astonished pupils – all would be freedom and light, and work would be done for the joy of doing it, not because he said so.

He might have known, poor fellow, that such drastic changes take time, and are bound to be accompanied with much trial and tribulation. Certainly the younger children benefited from this easier régime, and the fear that Mr Finch had aroused in them was never inspired by Evan Waterman's presence in their classroom.

The new infants' teacher, who had taken the place of Mrs Finch, was a robust young woman who cycled from Caxley daily on her new safety bicycle. She was a rosy-cheeked young Amazon, called Jenny North, and the village was quite sure that she would soon conquer Evan Waterman's heart and install herself as mistress of the school house in place of the dragon who lived there at present. This topic kept the village gossips engrossed for quite a fortnight, but – alas for their hopes! – the young woman was 'going steady' with a respectable draper in Caxley, and had eyes for no one else. She looked upon her headmaster's methods with a tolerant eye, but did not hesitate to administer a sharp slap upon her young sinners' legs, when her classroom door was safely closed. She and her charges understood each other well enough, and Beech Green parents soon realised that their young ones were getting on steadily under their new teacher.

About the older children they were less happy as the weeks went by. Gales of laughter and a few shouts could be heard from the schoolroom, where only Mr Finch's stentorian tones had been heard before. Rude rhymes were written on stable walls beginning:

Old Milk-and-Waterman
Lost the cane . . .

and the little girls came home, bright-eyed, with tales of kind Mr Waterman patting their hands and telling them they were growing up to be very pretty.

Francis Clare was present one day when Ada burst in from school and threw her books so carelessly on the table that they slid across the surface and crashed to the floor.

'Look out, my girl,' remonstrated Francis. 'That's your school books, you know.'

'Don't matter,' responded Ada carelessly, tossing back her bright hair. 'Mr Waterman says we can do some arithmetic or learn poetry, whichever we like. And he told me not to sit up too late over it, or I'd spoil my pretty eyes.'

She smirked as she repeated the words, and Francis looked at her steadily. Now, at fourteen, in her last term at school, she certainly was pretty, but it wasn't Mr Waterman's place to tell her so, thought Francis with rising anger.

'You don't want to listen to such foolishness,' said Francis.

'And your headmaster should know better than to encourage vanity. Pick your books up, and then go and help your mother.'

When the girls were safely in bed Francis spoke openly to Mary.

'I don't like that chap and I never shall. He's no business to lead them girls on so, and I shall have a word with the vicar about the way he's going on. The best thing we can do, my dear, is to get our Ada settled in a good job and let her leave as soon as it's fixed. No need to wait till Christmas. She's fourteen now and big enough to find a place.'

Mary Clare agreed.

'Mrs Evans was asking for her,' she said. 'It'd be nice to have her handy, and she'd be happy at the manor, I'm sure. I'll have a word with the child.'

'You do that, Mary,' said Francis, 'and I'll give that young feller a straight word or two. There's plenty of talk about him in the village – the work at school is going downhill fast, they say, and the boys just play the goat and get away with it. If you ask me,' continued Francis sturdily, 'a bit of straightforward soldiering wouldn't hurt that young Waterman.'

The next day Mary broached the subject of going into service with Mrs Evans at the manor. To her surprise, Ada was vehemently against it.

'I'm not being maid to no one,' said the girl violently. 'Why should I be at everyone's beck and call! I knows what it'd be! All the greasy cooking pots would be left for me to wash. All the back corridors and stone floors would be mine to scrub. I'd do the vegetables, and clean the mud out of the sinks, and squash the black beetles, and do the flues! Well, I'm not going to, then. I'm going to work in a shop – that's what I want to do!

'But you'd still be at everyone's beck and call,' pointed out Mary. 'And there's only one shop in Beech Green, and that don't want anyone to help.'

'It's Caxley I'm thinking of,' said Ada. 'I don't want to be buried alive in Beech Green all my life. I want to see things going on. There's plenty of shops in Caxley that'd take me on.'

'Well, we'll think about it,' said Mary, taken aback at the assurance of her firstborn. 'I'll talk to your dad tonight and we'll see if we can hear of something.'

Meanwhile, Francis had called at the vicarage and had a few words with the vicar about his new headmaster. To tell the truth, the good vicar himself was beginning to have some misgivings about the new appointment, and agreed to speak to Waterman that week.

'I'm taking my two girls away as soon as I can arrange it,' said Francis as he said his farewells on the vicarage doorstep. 'And you'll find that other folk in Beech Green will be doing the same, sir, unless things alter.'

And the vicar, watching the thatcher's broad back vanish between the Wellingtonias that lined the vicarage drive, sighed heavily. He recognised righteous wrath when he saw it.

To Dolly, now twelve years old, that autumn seemed a time of upheaval and change. She was amazed to hear from her father that he was making plans to transfer her to Fairacre School next term. For her part, she quite liked Mr Waterman, though not with the ardour that the older girls felt for him. Already gaining the cool wisdom that was to be her mainstay in life, the younger child recognised the headmaster's folly as well as his good intentions, but felt sorry that his overtures were so rudely flouted by the boys. She enjoyed his lessons, appreciated his love of poetry and nature, and was beginning to wonder if she too might be a teacher one day.

She knew little of Fairacre except that the school was much the same size as Beech Green's and that it stood near the church. The headmaster had been there for a year or two, had a grown-up family, a jolly, bustling wife who took the needlework lessons, and shared her husband's passion for the local hunt. They always walked a pair of hounds, which frequently burst joyfully into the schoolroom, and on the days when the hunt met near Fairacre, the schoolchildren were allowed to follow on foot. It all sounded happy enough, but it was strange, and Dolly did not like changes.

From her father's manner, though, she realised that the affair was settled, and she made no demur. Ada was found a modest post in the draper's shop in Caxley owned by Jenny North's young man and his father. This stroke of good fortune was brought about by Jenny herself, who recognised a quick bright assistant when she saw one, and knew that Ada's pretty face would attract more business.

It was arranged that the girl should live with Francis's parents and walk daily to the shop in the High Street, not far from the school which she and Dolly had first attended. Sunday was the only day of the week when she could get home, and the grandparents promised to bring her in their old trap or send her with an obliging neighbour.

'But what I really want,' said Ada, eyes shining, 'is a new safety bicycle like Miss North's. Then I could go from here each day, couldn't I, mum?'

'Ah well,' said Mary indulgently, 'you save your wages and see how it goes. I reckon you're a lucky girl to have everything fall out so nice for you.'

The house seemed very quiet without Ada's boisterous presence, and little Frank was promoted to her empty bed in Dolly's room. Dolly was glad of his company, although he was usually fast asleep when she crept up at night, a pink and white cherub with tousled dark curls.

He woke early, and Dolly first discovered her ability to weave stories to amuse the little boy. He liked best one about a naughty child called Tom whose adventures continued in serial form for weeks on end. Years later, Dolly Clare revived Tom's adventures for the amusement of many schoolchildren.

Frank, at nearly four years of age, was increasingly dear to Dolly. She took him with her wherever she could, and was already looking forward to taking him to school at Beech Green after Christmas, when the ultimatum had been given about the move to Fairacre. Now someone else would have to be found to take Frank to school, for Fairacre was too far away for his short legs, and in any case, the teaching which he would get with Jenny North perfectly satisfied Francis and Mary. Time enough to think of Fairacre for young Frank, they told each other, when he was big enough to go into the headmaster's class.

'And if I knows anything about it,' said Francis, 'there'll be a different headmaster sitting in that chair by that time!'

Both parents thought a great deal about their son's future, and Francis was delighted to find that, young as the child was, he already showed an interest in the straw, the knives and hazel spars which one day, Francis hoped, would be the tools of his honourable trade.

They were all glad of the child's gay prattle during that period of autumn gloom, for, besides Ada's absence, other circumstances cast a shadow. The war, which had seemed all but won in September, now took a turn for the worse, and fighting flared up again, on a scattered front, and with renewed bitterness.

As Christmas approached, anxiety grew. On December 22nd it was announced that thirty thousand more mounted men would be sent overseas. Among them, this time, was young Albert Davis, and there was much sadness in the little home. It looked as if the Christmas of 1900 was to be as gloomy as the year before.

The sight of her friend Emily, her face mottled with crying and her eyes puffy and red, brought home suddenly to young Dolly the widespread wretchedness of war, in contrast to the excitement and glory which had so enthralled her a year earlier. She pondered on this new revelation of war's grim side one morning in the Christmas holidays, as she stood by the kitchen copper, watching the clothes boiling gently, the suds sighing up and down like someone breathing. Death was a fearful thing and an ugly one. She remembered the horror of the corpses in the butcher's shop at Caxley, and shuddered. Only that morning she had come across a squashed wren on the road outside their gate – a small round pile of flattened feathers with its tail neatly erect upon it. She had watched that wren, for many weeks, running up and down and in and out of the thorn hedge, and rejoiced in its perky two inches of feathered vitality. And now it lay, stilled for ever, a pathetic scrap, as neat and tidy in death as in life.

To think that men could set out to reduce each other to that dreadful condition made the child feel cold with revulsion, as she prodded the steaming linen with the copper stick. It was bad enough to have Christmas overshadowed, to have to endure the loss of Ada's company, to face the ordeal of changing schools, and to see the Davises – and particularly dear Emily – suffer so, without this final overpowering horror of death to torment her.

Later, she wondered if those black thoughts had been something in the nature of a premonition. For, before a month had passed, death was to come very close to Dolly Clare, setting a grim mark upon that little household which even time itself could never completely remove.

CHAPTER 11

ONE morning in January 1901 Dolly awoke first. It was still dark and she could hear her father and mother moving about downstairs getting ready for the day. Usually, young Frank woke when they stirred and insinuated himself into Dolly's bed hoping for more stories.

But this morning he lay heavily asleep, drawing deep snoring breaths that at first amused his sleepy sister.

'Wake up, Frank,' she called at length. 'You're snoring like an old piggy!'

There was no reply.

Dolly began to whistle a tune that he called their 'waking up' song, a modified version of the army reveille, but there was no response from the sleeping child.

She climbed out of bed and padded across the cold ancient boards to peer at her brother. He seemed much as usual, as far as she could tell in the dim light, but when she put her hand on his forehead to push back his hair she found it hot and wet with sweat. Frightened, she ran downstairs to the lamp-lit room where the smells of breakfast rose from the stove.

'Frank's bad,' she told her parents, and followed them up the narrow staircase, shaking with cold and fear.

The candles were lit, and Mary and Frank leant over the bed. The child woke and smiled at them, and Dolly's heart was comforted.

'He don't look too bad to me,' said Francis. 'Keep him in bed today, my love. He's just got a bit of a chesty cold.'

'He will keep taking his scarf off,' said Mary anxiously. 'And it was that bitter yesterday when he was out in the garden.'

She looked at her son closely.

'D'you reckon we should get the doctor?' she asked hesitantly. Doctors cost money, and were not called unnecessarily to the Clare household. Besides, she did not want Francis to think her unduly pernickety, but Frank had never ailed anything before, and this seemed a severe type of fever.

'You let him lie there today,' repeated Francis. 'I'll get home in good time, and if he don't seem to have picked up, we'll send for doctor then.'

He kissed his womenfolk, bade them cheer up, and set off for work.

Frank slept most of the day, making the same alarming noise which had woken Dolly. Mary Clare's fears were calmed by Mrs Davis, who assured her that her own children had often suffered such symptoms, and a day in bed usually cured them.

'Believe me, my dear,' she told the anxious mother, 'that little 'un's all right. You knows what children are – up one minute, down the next. It's because he's the only boy you're worrying so. You see, tomorrow he'll be fairly.'

But when Francis came home that night he thought otherwise. Dolly had spent most of the day by the bedside, shaken by doubts, and only half-believing the comfort given by Mrs Davis. When she saw her father's face, her terror grew even greater.

'You cut along and get the doctor, Doll,' he said. And Dolly fled through the darkening village for help.

Bronchitis was diagnosed, and the child was moved downstairs to a makeshift bed on the sofa, drawn close to the stove where a kettle steamed for two agonising nights and days.

Mary never left his side for the whole of that time. She sat white-faced and very silent, ministering to the unconscious child's needs, and watching his every movement with awful concentration. When she spoke to Dolly, it was with such tenderness that the child could scarcely bear it.

Dolly was thankful that it was the school holidays and that

she could be there to help in the house and prepare the simple meals that, in fact, none of them had the heart to eat. Throughout the time that she worked, she prayed so vehemently that her head ached with effort. She tried to will God to make Frank better. Surely, she told herself, He wouldn't let him die! Not a little boy like that, who'd done nothing wrong! If men at war were killed, it was understandable, for they knew what they were doing, and God, she supposed, took some of them simply because men did die in wars. But there was no reason why Frank should be so sacrificed. Her distracted thoughts followed each other round and round in a demented circle, and all the time the prayers went up, and she saw them, in imagination, as an invisible vapour rising through the kitchen ceiling, and then the thatch, and finally the lowering grey winter clouds, spiralling their way heavenwards to that omnipotent Being in whose hands the life of little Frank was held.

On the third night, while Dolly slept above, the child slipped away, one hand in each of his parents'. He had never regained consciousness, but there was nothing to show that death was so close. He gave a little hiccup, and the harsh breathing which had dominated the house, quietly stopped. The silence had an icy quality about it, and for a stunned moment the stricken parents were powerless to move.

Then, across the motionless body of their son, their eyes met. Francis took Mary in his arms, and their bitter grief began.

The day of the funeral was iron-cold. A light sprinkling of snow whitened the churchyard, throwing the gaping black hole, awaiting the small coffin, into sharp relief.

In Dolly Clare's memory that day was etched for ever in stark black and white. The sad little family stood watching the coffin being lowered into the icy earth. A bunch of snowdrops trembled upon the lid, as frail and pure as the child within.

Clad in heavy mourning, Dolly remembered that other family she had pitied, so long ago it seemed, on the sunlit afternoon of the Diamond Jubilee. The bare black elm trees were outlined against a sky heavy with snow to come. Black spiked railings round a tomb nearby were tipped with snow, and from the church porch a row of footprints blackened the snow where the mourners' feet had passed. No colour, no warmth, no sunshine, no movement, comforted the spirit at that poignant parting, and Dolly remembered, with sharp intensity, the feeling of loss which had shaken her when she had kissed her brother's forehead, as cold and hard as marble, a few hours before. In the utter negation of death lay its chief terror.

In the weeks that followed, Mary Clare remained calm and unusually gentle with her family. After the first few hours of grief, she showed little sign of her loss. The neighbours shook their heads over her.

'She ought to cry, that she ought!' they told each other. 'That poor lamb's been buried over a week and she ain't shed a tear. 'Tis unnatural! She'll suffer for it, you'll see!'

There was certainly something uncanny, as well as heroic, about Mary's composure, but Francis was glad of it. His own tears were too near the surface for him to have endured his wife's emotion bravely.

It was perhaps as well for Dolly that her departure to Fairacre followed hard on the heels of this tragedy. Great was her joy when Emily told her that she too was starting at Fairacre School, and they could begin the new adventure together.

They set off through shallow snow on the first day of the term, Dolly clad in her mourning black and Emily, in gay contrast, in a bright scarlet coat which had once been her sister's.

They carried bacon sandwiches for their midday meal, and an apple apiece from Mrs Davis's store. The clatter of their strong nailed boots was muffled by the snow as they tramped along, and their breath steamed as they discussed what lay ahead.

'I knows about half of them anyway,' said Emily, seeking comfort. 'There's the Willets and the Pratts. I've played with them sometimes, and they said Mr Wardle's all right if you don't give him no cheek.'

'But what about Mrs Wardle?' asked Dolly.

'Rips up the sewing a bit,' said Emily laconically, jumping sideways into a fresh patch of snow which invited a few footprints.

'But I reckon they'll both be better than old Milk-and-Waterman.'

And Emily was right. On that first morning, as they sat together among their new school fellows, Dolly took stock of Fairacre School and began to feel the warmth of her surroundings thaw the bleakness which had numbed her for the past few weeks.

A massive fire roared behind the fireguard, and though it could not hope to warm completely a room so lofty and so full of cross draughts, yet it was a cheering sight on a cold January day. Mr Wardle, warming his trouser legs before it, proved to be a hearty boisterous man who welcomed the newcomers, and bade his schoolchildren do the same.

He was that rare thing, Dolly discovered later, a happy man. Blessed with boundless energy, superb physique, a lively wife and four children now out in the world, Mr Wardle enjoyed his little domain and liked to see those in it equally happy. His recipe was simple, and he told it to the children over and over again:

'Work hard. Do your best, and a bit more, and you'll get on.'

Sometimes he put his recipe into a different form and read them a homily about the sin of Sloth, which he considered the most vicious one among the seven.

'If you start getting lazy,' he would say, bouncing energetically up and down, 'you'll get liverish. And if you get liverish, you'll get sorry for yourself. And that's when the rot starts. Use your brain and your body to the utmost, and the Devil will know that he's beaten.'

He certainly set them all a fine example. His teaching was thorough, exact and lively. His spare time was taken up with gardening, walking his hounds for miles around the countryside, training the church choir, and adding to a magnificent collection of moths and butterflies. His authority was unquestioned, unlike that of poor Mr Waterman at Beech Green, and Dolly soon found herself responding to the vitality of this man who could kindle a spark in even the stolidest of his country scholars.

The children, perhaps because of Mr Wardle's example, seemed friendlier than those at Beech Green, and Emily and Dolly, who had secretly feared a little teasing and bullying, found no antagonism. Nor were any remarks passed about Dolly's black clothes, much to her relief. Although she did not know it until many years later, Mr Wardle had already warned his children about Dolly's loss and given them to understand that extra kindness would be expected of them, and good manners most certainly enforced, if his vigilant eye saw any shortcomings.

He was a man whose good heart and good head worked well together. Quick to recognise a child's vulnerability, he never descended to sarcasm and ridicule to gain his ends. Severe he could be, and when he was driven to caning them the cane fell heavily, but it rarely needed to be used. Work, exercise, fresh air and laughter kept his charges engrossed and healthy; and from Mr Wardle Dolly Clare learnt much of the ways of a good teacher.

About a week after their arrival, on January 22nd, 1901, Dolly and Emily sat with the rest of the big girls at one end of the main room, with needlework in their hands and Mrs Wardle's eye upon them.

It was called 'Fancywork' on the timetable, and each child had a square of fine canvas and skeins of red, blue, yellow and green wool on the desk in front of her. They were busy making samplers, using the various stitches which Mrs Wardle taught them. 'Fancywork' was a pleasant change from 'Plain Sewing' which involved hemming unbleached calico pillow slips with the strong possibility of seeing Mrs Wardle rip them undone at the end of the lesson.

The room was quiet. The boys at the other end were drawing a spray of laurel pinned against a white paper on the blackboard, and only the whisper of their pencils as they shaded the leaves and carefully left 'high-lights', broke the sleepy silence.

It was then that the muffled bell of St Patrick's next door began to ring, and Mr Wardle, looking perplexed, hurried out to investigate. When he returned a minute later, his rosy face was grave.

'I have very sad news,' he told his surprised listeners. 'Queen Victoria is dead.'

There was a shocked silence, broken only by the distant bell and the gasp from Mrs Wardle, as her hand flew to her heart.

'All stand!' commanded Mr Wardle. 'And we will say a short prayer for the Queen we have lost, and the King we have now to rule us.'

Afterwards, it seemed to the children, the grown-ups made too much of this event, but they were wrong. Their lives were short, and to them the Queen had always been a very old lady near to death. To their parents and grandparents, who had known and revered her for all their lives, this passing of a great Queen was the end of the world they had always known. National mourning was sincere, and tinged with the bewilderment of children who have lost the head of a family, long loved and irreplaceable.

Dolly never forgot Emily's words to her as they crept quietly from the playground that day to make their way homeward.

'Won't Frank be pleased,' said Emily, 'to have the Queen with him!'

It was exactly what Dolly herself had thought when Mr Wardle had broken the news, and the comfort of hearing it put into words was wonderfully heartening. Certainly the shock of this second death was considerably lessened by Emily's innocent philosophy, and the thought of Frank's gain mitigated their own sense of loss.

It was not the first time that Emily had been of comfort to Dolly by her ability to come to terms with the unknown. In the years to come, her child-like simplicity and faith brought refreshment to them both.

Sixty or so years later, Miss Clare, half asleep in the shade of her plum tree, recalled that historic day, and its dark solemnity lit by Emily's touching confidence.

There certainly could be no greater contrast in the weather, thought Miss Clare, watching the heat waves shimmer across the sun-baked downs. In the border, the flaunting oriental poppies opened their petals so wide in the strong sunlight that they fell backwards to display the mop of black stamens at the centre. At the foot of the plant, Miss Clare's tortoise had pushed himself among the foliage, to escape from the June heat which even he could not endure.

She could hear the faraway voices of children at play, and guessed it must be about half past two, when Beech Green school had its afternoon break. Soon Emily would be with her again, as comforting and as hopeful as she had been on that bitter bleak day so long ago.

Miss Clare stretched her old stiff limbs in great contentment, revelling in the hot sunshine and the joy of Emily's coming. Looking back, she saw now that an age had closed on the day that Mr Wardle had called them to prayer, and she who since then had seen many reigns, could imagine the impact which Victoria's passing had made upon her parents' generation.

But for Dolly the twelve-year-old child, that day had been chiefly a turning-point in her own happiness. She could see now, sixty years later, that several things had contributed to the sudden lightening of her misery. Mr Wardle's infectious vitality, new surroundings, work praised and encouraged, had all helped together to raise the child's spirits from the depths into which her brother's death had cast them. The natural buoyancy of youth and time's healing powers added their measure of restoration, but it was Emily's homely words which had really set her free at last. It was as though the Queen had taken Dolly's burden upon herself by entering into that unknown world where Frank already waited, and, fanciful though the idea seemed a lifetime later, yet it still seemed touching in the strength and hope it had given to a sad little girl who had needed comfort sorely.

'Ah! It's good to grow old,' said Miss Clare, contemplating that pitiful young figure across the years, 'and to know that nothing can ever hurt you very much again. There's a lot to be said for being seventy!'

And turning her face gratefully to the sun, she continued to wait, lapped in warmth and contentment, for the coming of Emily.

PART THREE *Fairacre*

CHAPTER 12

FROM the first, Dolly Clare liked Fairacre. It was a compact and pretty village, grouped charmingly about its church, unlike Beech Green, which straggled along the road to Caxley. Some of the cottage roofs had been thatched by her own father, since they had come to live nearby, and still shone golden in the sunshine. More ancient roofs had weathered to a silvery grey, while others, more venerable still, sagged thinly across their supports and sprouted with green patches of moss and grass.

Not all the cottages were thatched. More than half were tiled with small tiles of a warm rosy brown which combined with the weathered brick to give a colourful appearance to the village. A few large houses, built in the reigns of Queen Anne and the early Georges, glowed with the same warm colour among their trees, and little Dolly Clare grew to love the vicarage, which could be seen plainly from the playground of Fairacre school, admiring its graceful fanlight over the front door, and the two great cedar trees which stood guard before it.

Fairacre, in those Edwardian days, was rich in fine trees, planted to give shelter, no doubt, from the roaring winds which swept the whaleback of the downs above it. Limes and horse-chestnuts shaded gardens, and clumps of magnificent elms sheltered the cattle and horses in the farm meadows. Close by the school, protecting both it and the school house, towered more elm trees, in which a thriving rookery clattered and cawed, and several of the neighbouring farms had leafy avenues leading to their houses. There was much more ivy about at that time. The dark glossy leaves muffled many a garden wall and outhouse, and added a richness to the general scene. When, in later life, Miss Clare looked at old photographs of the Fairacre she had known as a child, she realised how denuded of trees the village had become within her lifetime.

She and Emily loved it from the start. Their spirits rose as they turned the bend and approached the church and school. It was almost three miles to walk each morning, but the two little girls were quick to find lifts with obliging carters and tradesmen, and rarely had to walk both ways in the day. Dolly, who had been so frightened by the size of Bella on the day of the move from Caxley, now treated these great-hearted horses with affection and complete trust as she scrambled up from shaft or wheel hub to her high perch beside some good-natured driver who had taken pity on the two young travellers.

In all weathers, riding or walking, they traversed the familiar road. They looked out for the first wild flowers of spring, the pink wild roses that starred the summer hedges, and the bright beads of autumn berries. They watched the birds building nests, and could tell to a day when the eggs would hatch. They knew where a badger lived, and where a white owl would appear as they plodded home on a murky winter afternoon. Those three miles grew as familiar and as well-loved as the faces of their mothers. There was always something new, something beautiful, something strange, to find daily, and the two children learnt as much from their close scrutiny of banks and hedges as they did in the busy classroom at Fairacre school.

As Dolly and Emily neared the end of their schooldays, in the early part of Edward VII's reign, they found that one or the other was frequently called upon to walk from Mr Wardle's room to the infants' room next door in order 'to give a hand', as Mr Wardle always put it, to the teacher in charge.

They were now called monitors, and with one or two other children of fourteen, undertook a number of daily jobs in the running of the school. Numbers thinned after the age of twelve, for those who could pass an examination in general proficiency were allowed to leave, and farmers were eager to employ these young boys now that labour was difficult to obtain. This meant that those over twelve who were left behind were often lucky enough to get closer attention from their headmaster. Mr Wardle looked upon Dolly and Emily as promising pupil teachers of the future, and gave them every opportunity of learning the rudiments of the job under his roof.

Both girls enjoyed their time with the babies. Miss Taylor, a wisp of a woman with two protruding front teeth which were the only outstanding feature of an undistinguished appearance, was glad to delegate some of her duties.

'You take the little boys, dear,' she would say to Dolly, 'and you can manage the girls, Emily, while I hear the big ones read.'

And so, to a background of young voices chanting round the teacher's desk, Emily and Dolly would squat on low chairs by their charges and show them how to write capital letters on their slates, holding small hot hands within their own while wet slate pencils traced uncertainly the mysteries being explained.

Sometimes, when Miss Taylor wanted peace in which to mark sums or tidy cupboards, Dolly would perch on the high chair before the class and tell them one of the stories about naughty Tom which had once delighted little Frank. It warmed her heart to see the joy with which the children listened, and the company and affection of these babies did much to soften the blow of Frank's death.

It was no surprise to the girls when one afternoon Mr Wardle asked them to stay behind to talk about training as pupil teachers. It was a golden June afternoon with the weather-cock on St Patrick's ablaze in the sunshine against a clear blue sky. Their schoolfellows' cries died rapidly in the distance, for hay-making was in progress and the children were racing to join their fathers and big brothers in the meadows.

Emily and Dolly stood demurely in front of Mr Wardle's great desk, eyeing the massive brass ink stand and the array of pens.

'Well, would you like it?' asked Mr Wardle after he had outlined the training involved.

'I think I should,' said Emily hesitantly. Her grey eyes were clouded with concentration. A wisp of dark hair cleaved to her damp forehead. Volatile and exuberant by nature, Emily was pondering earnestly on her ability to stick to a course for four years and then to the profession to which it led. She liked children, she liked the idea of teaching them, but would she tire of it? She raised perplexed eyes to Mr Wardle's lively blue ones.

'You'll like it more every year,' promised Mr Wardle, seeing the child's doubts. 'You'll make a very good teacher in time.'

He turned to Dolly questioningly.

'I will,' said the child steadily. She might have been taking her vows, thought the schoolmaster, both touched and amused by the calm assurance with which she declared herself. It was strange that on this occasion the more timid of the two should be so confident. With a flash of insight, he recognised in that moment, that he was in the presence of someone who would become a much greater person than he would ever be, and he felt unaccountably humble.

'You're a born teacher,' he said quietly, and turned the key in his desk drawer to bring the interview to a close.

Together the three emerged into the dazzling sunlight.

'Tell your fathers that I have spoken to you about this,' said Mr Wardle, 'and ask them to come and see me. Meanwhile, think it over well. You don't want to spend your whole life regretting a decision. Take plenty of time to make up your minds.'

He watched their figures dwindle into the distance. The heat waves shimmered across the lane, blurring the outlines of their pale print frocks and wide straw hats. One of them, he thought, half-closing his eyes against the brightness, has given her mind to it already – and her heart and soul too. He only hoped that she would find as much happiness as he had himself.

Strangely moved and elated, he crossed the shade of his garden and entered the school house.

In the following September the two girls returned to Fairacre with the status of pupil-teacher. This meant that they helped Mr Wardle and Miss Taylor, and under their guidance prepared and gave lessons occasionally, generally making themselves useful. Twice a week they went into Caxley for evening classes, and occasionally they attended an extra class, or a demonstration lesson by a qualified teacher, on a Saturday morning.

Both girls were excited by their promotion. They enjoyed the trips to Caxley, and knew that they were luckier than most village children in continuing their education after the age of fourteen. To be sure, the work expected of them was fairly simple – Arithmetic, English, Geography, History and Nature Study – only a little more advanced than Mr Wardle's final lessons with his top class, but it was stimulating to see different pupils and to be taught by a variety of men and women.

Francis and Mary were pleased with Dolly's choice of career. Their shy one, it seemed, was blossoming. Mary helped

Dolly to lengthen her skirts and to dress her soft hair in a top knot in a manner suitable to her new dignity. Emily's dark braids were now worn wound about her head, and the two girls spent much of their time adjusting each other's hair pins. The conversation on the way to Fairacre these days dealt with fashions rather more than education.

They both longed for 'low shoes' instead of the stout laced boots which they were still obliged to wear. The Misses Evans, also in their teens, were lucky enough to wear shoes with straps every day of their lives, and on high days and holidays, so Dolly heard, they had real silk stockings to wear with them. They surveyed their own cotton-clad legs, terminating in the loathsome boots, with acute disfavour.

On the evenings that they went to evening classes they eyed the young women of Caxley, who appeared to their unsophisticated eyes as positive fashion plates. Sometimes a carriage would rattle past, bearing a beautiful lady, on her way home from a tea party, wearing one of the delicious large Edwardian hats smothered in tea roses and with clouds of veiling tied beneath the chin. Dolly and Emily gazed with wonder. Would they ever be able to have a hat as adorable as that?

Getting to Caxley was a problem. Mr Wardle took them in on Tuesday evenings when he went to play chess with an old friend, and brought them home again. He owned a small governess cart, and it was a tight squeeze to get even such slim people as Dolly and Emily into it with sturdy Mr Wardle taking up more than half the room. On Thursday evenings they relied on the corn merchant's waggon which had been delivering goods in the Beech Green area all day, but this arrangement had its drawbacks, for the driver was a slow, ambling fellow, and the girls were in a ferment of anxiety until they were dropped at the Institute in Caxley High Street.

They returned home in style on Thursdays, for one of the women teachers, the daughter of a prosperous grocer in the town, had the use of her father's carriage and spanked along the lane to Beech Green when the lessons were over.

It was Ada who was responsible for solving this problem of transport in an indirect way. Growing prettier every year, with bright bold eyes and burnished hair, Ada had many admirers. The young men of Caxley were frequent customers at the general draper's where she worked, calling in to finger ties or to try on one of the dashing new straw boaters, while their eyes wandered over the pretty assistant. It was no wonder that old Mr and Mrs Clare grew anxious about this wayward grandchild. Despite their protestations, Ada came home later and later in the evening, and they felt powerless to control her. They spoke plainly to Francis about it one Sunday when they spent the day at Beech Green.

The girls had been sent out with a message while the problem was talked over. Francis was greatly perturbed.

'She'll have to live here,' he said firmly. 'Ada's our child, and we must see to her. 'Tisn't right that you should be bothered with her feckless ways at your time of life.'

'We'll see if Mrs Evans can have her there to work,' promised Mary. 'There's no way for her to get to Caxley every day, and maybe she's better in the village.'

The old man looked dubious.

'She won't take to it kindly, that I do know,' he said. 'And, to be fair, the girl's doing well at the shop, and they want to keep her.'

'Well, she can't get there,' said Francis, 'so that's that.'

'Your father and I,' said old Mrs Clare, 'have been thinking about that. You tell them, my dear,' she nodded to her husband.

'If you're agreeable,' said Mr Clare, 'I'd like to buy both girls one of these new safety bicycles apiece. They may as well have their little something now, when they need it, as wait for me to go to my grave and then get a pound or two. What'd you say, lad?'

'I'd say,' said Francis, with feeling, 'that they're two real lucky girls, and Mary and me'd be proper thankful to you.'

Mary was looking a little apprehensive.

''Tis real kind of you,' she said earnestly, 'but – but d'you think they'd be safe? I mean, Caxley's a busy place. They might get knocked down, or run into something if they couldn't manage the machines—'

Francis broke in upon his wife's misgivings.

'I'll see they learn to manage 'em before they goes to Caxley,' he assured her. 'You tell 'em the good news when they comes in, dad, and watch their eyes sparkle! You'll get plenty of kisses for this!'

'I don't want kisses or thanks,' said the old man, although he looked pleased at the thought, 'but they're good girls, and I'm glad to do it for them.'

And so it came about that once again Ada and Dolly shared a bedroom and set off each morning on their marvellous bicycles, one to Caxley and the other to Fairacre; and on Tuesdays and Thursdays Dolly rode proudly into Caxley to the evening classes, independent of lifts and free to come and go whenever she liked.

Only Emily was sad, and that sadness did not last long, for Mrs Evans remembered an ancient bicycle propped in an outhouse and lent it to the girl for as long as she needed it. Pedalling along together, the wind playing havoc with their insecure coiffures and their long skirts, the two friends felt that life could hold no greater joy.

Francis Clare was delighted to have both his daughters at home again. His gay Ada had always been his secret favourite, and he was glad of her boisterous presence for Mary's sake.

Since the death of Frank, Mary had become much quieter. She rarely spoke of the child, and shrank from any mention of him by Francis. It was only to be expected, Francis told himself at first. The wound was still fresh and any attention to it gave pain. But as the years passed it seemed unnatural to Francis to remain so silent about the tragedy which had smitten them both so cruelly.

Every week Mary made her way to the grave and put fresh flowers upon the pathetically small green mound. She went alone, and this hurt Francis. She chose her time, when Francis was at work, and when he remonstrated gently with her, the tightening of her lips and stricken look in her eyes were enough to silence him. If only he could thaw her, he told himself, if only she would speak of her grief, then it could make things so much easier for both of them. As it was, he dared not hurt her more, and could only hope that the passing of time would bring them both comfort.

Ada's good spirits lightened the little cottage and Francis rejoiced in her vivacity. What if the boys did look at her in Caxley? Who could blame them? Ada had her head screwed on the right way, thought Francis, and knew how to behave herself. It was only right that she should attract young men at her age, and with her pretty ways. To tell the truth, he was half in love with her himself, seeing again the beauty that had been Mary's in years gone by.

So he comforted his wife when she wondered if they should be stricter with their lively first-born,

'There's safety in numbers, my love,' he said. 'Ada won't do anything silly. She may be a bit flighty. What girl at seventeen isn't? But she'll make some young man a good wife, you'll see.'

He spoke fondly, thinking of the years immediately ahead when Ada would still be a daughter in his house, with the possibility of marriage far ahead in the future. He did not see the flicker of doubt that passed across his wife's face.

CHAPTER 13

WHILE Ada enjoyed the bustle of life in Caxley High Street, and felt her spirits lift as she skimmed on her bicycle towards the town, Dolly found quiet satisfaction in the remote tiny world of Fairacre.

The school's setting was sheltered and peaceful. In those days rough turf surrounded the building, with a stone-flagged path leading to the road, and another to the school house. In summer this little green was white with daisies, and the bigger girls showed the younger ones how to make daisy chains with a pin, or a sharp thumb nail. Later, plantains sent up their tough stalks and knobbly heads, and the children used to pluck these and play 'knocking heads off' with skill and energy.

The writhing roots of the clump of elm trees provided more amusement for the babies, who contrived houses and shops in the spaces, and a steep bank which sloped into a field below the trees provided numerous slides in wet or dry weather.

On the grass, under the shade of the trees, stood a bucket of water. This was replenished daily by Mr Wardle, from his own well, and was the only drinking water for the school.

'Tastes a bit funny in the afternoon,' Dolly Clare heard one child say to another.

'Ah! But mornin's it's lovely!' replied the other fervently, obviously grateful for small mercies.

It was Dolly's duty to watch the children during the dinner hour. In the summer, they sprawled on the grass with their hunks of bread with a bit of cheese or bacon to help it down. Sometimes a few radishes or lettuce leaves were added to the meal, when they were in season, and in the autumn plenty of fine apples, plums and nuts were carried to school in the children's dinner bags. Washed down with a swig from the tin mug standing by the 'old bucket', it all tasted good to country children.

In the winter the desks were dragged forward nearer the blazing fire, and the children ate their meal with one eye on a large kettle which lodged on a trivet. Dolly and Emily made cocoa for them all, ladling a spoonful into the cups brought from home and adding a wobbly stream of boiling water from the heavy kettle. There was no charge for this, for years before, in the bitter winter of 1881, the managers had decided to provide this beverage from their own purses, and the kindly custom continued. A jug of milk was sent over daily from the farm near the church, and brown sugar was kept in a great black and gold tin which had come from China years before, to find an alien home at Fairacre. For many of the children the cocoa was the most nourishing part of their meal, for times were still hard for the agricultural labourer, and bread formed the major part of the contents of the school satchels, Dolly noticed.

School began at nine, and ended at four, so that for most of the year Dolly and Emily cycled home in the light. Only at the end of the Christmas term and the early part of the Spring one, when the oil lamps were lit from a long taper and shed meagre pools of light upon the children's heads below, were Dolly and Emily obliged to fix lamps to their bicycles and pedal through the dark lane behind the two wavering beams.

Dolly found the work absorbing. By nature she was methodical, cool-headed and patient. The children responded to her quiet ways with trust and affection. But it was for Emily that they showed most enthusiasm. Her quick wits, her humour, and her ready laugh made the children too excitable for Mr Wardle and Miss Taylor's liking. When Emily took a class into the playground to play 'Cat and Mouse' or 'Poor Jenny Sits A-Weeping', the shrieks would penetrate the stout schoolroom walls, and Mr Wardle, intercepting sly grins among his pupils, would stalk forth to call for stricter discipline outside.

'Ticked off again!' Emily would sigh, as they cycled home. 'I wish I could keep them as quiet as you do, Dolly.'

'They can do with livening up,' answered Dolly. 'I think they're kept a bit too meek indoors, and then they get wild as soon as they get outside. But, there you are, that's how Mr Wardle wants it, so we must do as we're told.'

'But just wait till we're headmistresses!' laughed Emily. 'We can do as we like then with the children.'

The possibility seemed so remote to the two young girls that they treated it with amusement. They might teach for a few years, they supposed, and enjoy it very much, but marriage, they felt sure, would one day claim them – marriage to someone as yet unknown, for all the known young men were far too familiar and dull to consider – and then another way of life would begin for them.

And so, happy in the present, and with vague and happy dreams of the future, Emily and Dolly passed the years of their pupil teaching in the long golden afternoon of Edward's reign, with never a thought of the shadows of war which crept slowly but inexorably nearer to their small bright world.

One June evening, about this time, Dolly came out alone from the evening institute in Caxley High Street. Emily was at home with a feverish cold. As she mounted her bicycle she caught sight of Ada in the distance, strolling some way ahead, on the arm of a thickset young man.

Dolly had heard Ada say that morning that she would be late home all the week as they were getting stock sorted ready for the summer sales. Had she finished, Dolly wondered, or had the task been fictitious?

The couple progressed slowly. They were deeply engrossed, and Dolly pedalled equally slowly to keep behind them. There was a look on Ada's face which she had never seen there before. It was a dumb, adoring look, quite unlike the bold flirtatious glances with which Dolly was familiar. The young man's arm crept round Ada's waist and they turned down a side lane towards the river.

Dolly trundled home much perturbed. She had recognised the young man, as he turned, as the son of a local publican. Though the father was respected, it was general knowledge that he had hopelessly spoilt his only child who was allowed too much money and too much licence. Harry Roper, thought the youthful Dolly, must be quite old – twenty-five at least – and Ada knew, as well as she did, that there were dozens of pretty girls, in Caxley alone, who had been as besotted as Ada now was, and who later had regretted their infatuation.

Cycling along the warm lane, with her eyes half-shut against the clouds of gnats, Dolly pondered. It was unlike Ada to lie to her mother. Then again, it was unlike Ada to be so secretive about her escorts. This affair was obviously more serious than the others, and Dolly did not like it.

She decided to say nothing to her parents, nor to Ada. But she was uncomfortably guilty that evening in her parents' presence, and glad to escape early to bed. There she lay, anxious for Ada's safe return, but it was past eleven o'clock before the girl crept upstairs, and by that time Dolly was sound asleep.

This escapade had its sequel, for the next day Francis met a friend who had been in Caxley the night before.

'Saw your girl last night,' he said brightly, his face alight with the pleasure of tale-telling.

'Oh yes,' answered Francis, observing the note of happy anticipation. 'She'd been to evening class.'

'Not this one hadn't!' asserted the friend inelegantly. 'Behind the bar of "The Crown" she was, and served me with a pint, too.'

Francis was completely taken aback, but with a countryman's caution did his best not to show it.

'I must be getting along,' he said, collecting his thatching shears and making towards the ladder.

''Bye,' said the other, setting off in the other direction, well pleased with the encounter.

Francis watched him go, and leant back against the ladder to consider this unsavoury piece of news. He was shocked by more than one aspect of it. In the first place, it looked as though Ada had deliberately lied about staying late for the sale. It also seemed that she was mixed up in company of which he had no knowledge. But worse still was the thought that she had appeared openly in a public bar. This hurt Francis deeply. She had disgraced them all.

Francis liked his pint now and again, and enjoyed his local pub, but at a time when drunkenness was rife and the wretched results were everywhere around, the idea of women, and particularly his own young daughters, being seen in a public house, was horrifying. His parents had been strict teetotallers, and he had been brought up to consider public houses as dens of depravity. If word of Ada's escapade ever reached her grandparents, it would be the end of them!

And what was the publican thinking of, to let a young girl serve in his bar? Francis grew belligerent at the thought, and found himself snapping the shears viciously.

'Best get on with my work,' he said aloud to a prowling cat. 'But I'll have a word with that young lady tonight. Maybe I'm too soft with her.'

He mounted the ladder and attacked the straw with unusual savagery.

Ada did not trouble to deny anything. She was in a hard, bold mood, offhand and insolent, calculated to send her parents into a frenzy. Dolly, cleaning her shoes in the kitchen, trembled for her sister. Mary was torn between tears and an overpowering desire to box the girl's ears, but Francis handled the affair competently.

'What's wrong with bringing the young man here?' asked Francis. 'If you like him well enough, let's see him. He'll come if he thinks anything of you.'

'Everyone's against him,' protested Ada, 'and you're the same. You haven't even seen him but you tell me I oughtn't to go out with him. And I don't see why I can't go to his home. He can't help living in a pub.'

'He don't live in the public bar,' said Francis shortly, 'and that's where you were – and serving too. His father could get into serious trouble for that, and he knows it.'

Ada's face flamed scarlet.

'I hates this place! Full of a lot of tittle-tattlers with nothing better to do than make trouble! But they shan't stop me seeing him – and neither will you!'

Francis kept his temper with difficulty.

'See here, Ada. I'm your father and I must do the right thing by my own daughter. You're young yet—'

'I'm nearly nineteen,' Ada burst in, 'and he's twenty-five, and we're going to be married as soon as we can.'

There was silence for a moment in the little room, then Francis spoke gently.

'I'd like to have heard about that from him first. The sooner I see this young man the better, I reckons, and his dad, too.'

'You don't understand—' began Ada, with a wail.

'Your mother and me has both been in love, you know,' commented Francis dryly. 'We don't want it explained to us. All we're saying is: don't do nothing in a hurry. If you've got any sense at all you'll keep away from him for a bit until I've seen him.'

'Oh, you *old* people!' expostulated Ada, flinging out of the room. Dolly heard the thud of her feet on the stairs and the creak of the bed as she flung herself upon it.

Francis and Mary exchanged hopeless looks.

'Well,' said Francis heavily, 'I'll go and thin my carrots. Need a bit of fresh air after that. Let her simmer a bit, my dear, and then you see what you can do with her. Proper headstrong hussy she's getting!'

'She always was,' said Mary candidly, to her husband's departing back.

The next day Francis made his way to 'The Crown' to see the publican. He did not relish the interview, but it had to be faced, and a steady anger helped his determination. He found his anger evaporating, as the meeting lengthened.

Mr Roper knew nothing, he said, of Ada, although he had seen his son with a girl in the parlour. His wife was about at the time, and he himself was busy with a party of travellers. He had been obliged to go into the yard to arrange stabling for their horses and had knocked on the parlour window and told Harry to attend to the bar. He was as upset as Francis to hear the news, he said; and Francis believed him.

They talked straightforwardly of the affair, and agreed to speak to their children again. If marriage was what they wanted, then Harry would call upon Francis at once.

'But if he's lukewarm,' said Francis honestly, 'you can warn him off. I'm in no mind to lose our Ada anyway, and she'll have plenty of choice.'

They parted civilly, and Francis returned to Beech Green with a more contented mind.

But for Dolly, this family row had particular significance. On the fateful night when the storm had broken Dolly crept to bed, praying that Ada would be asleep or content to lie silent. She herself was in such a turmoil of doubts and fears that she craved nothing but the unconsciousness of sleep.

But Ada was awake and in an ugly mood. She lay in bed watching Dolly undress by the light of a candle.

'I suppose you're glad I've been found out?' she said, speaking low so that their parents would hear nothing through the thin wall which divided the two rooms.

'Ada!' cried Dolly, cut to the quick.

'Ada!' mimicked her sister in a spiteful squeak. 'You know you were watching us – sneaking along on your bike! I saw you!'

'I couldn't help it—' began poor Dolly.

'And I bet you told mum as soon as you got home, that I wasn't sorting stock. Wanting to make me out a liar.'

'And are you?' asked Dolly, with a flash of spirit.

'Yes, I am then,' said Ada defiantly. 'You're driven to it in this mean rotten place. And I don't care! When you're in love you'll do anything!'

Dolly was shocked into silence. With trembling hands she hung the last of her clothes on the back of the chair, blew out the candle, and slid into her cold bed. The dreadful words beat in her brain – words all the more sinister from their sibilant whispering. 'When you're in love you'll do anything!' Lie to your parents? Shout abuse at them? Attack your sister with false accusations? Was this what love did to you?

She remembered Mr Waterman reading poems about love to his callous young pupils. Surely he had told them that love was ennobling and fired people with all that was good and beautiful? Love had not done that to Ada, it seemed.

She summoned all the courage and calm she could, amidst the tumult and the darkness, and spoke pleadingly.

'Ada, you don't really mean that. You're just upset. Try to go to sleep.'

Ada gave a hard, harsh laugh. It sounded like the cackle of a jay in the dark room, and it sent shivers down Dolly's spine.

'Don't you soft-soap me! You're a sneak, and I know it. And I mean every word I say. What do you know about being in love, anyway? You only got me into trouble because you're jealous – and that's the honest truth, Dolly Clare!'

The vicious whispering ceased as Ada thumped over towards the wall. Exhausted with emotion she fell asleep almost immediately, but Dolly lay, appalled and icily awake, until the dawn came.

During that long terrible night she came to realise that the rift which had been widening so steadily between Ada and herself was now too wide for any successful bridge. Gone were the days when Ada was always right, when Ada led and she followed, and when Ada – the bright, the beautiful, the brave – could count on her adoration and obedience.

Nothing would ever be quite the same again. The words had been said, the cruel blows given. Dolly felt that even if she could come at last to forgive, she could certainly never forget.

She fell into sleep as the cocks began to crow, and woke, two hours later, leaden-eyed, to a world which had lost some of its brightness for ever.

CHAPTER 14

LOOKING back across the years, as she lay half-dozing in the sunny garden, old Miss Clare marvelled that she should remember that wretched night so clearly. Was it true, she wondered, that she had been jealous of Ada's popularity with the young men? She had not realised it at the time. She had been furious and severely shaken by Ada's spite. But was there an element of truth there which the youthful Dolly unconsciously recognised?

Certainly her interest in boys was remarkably small at that time, Miss Clare remembered, and smiled to think of her first 'walking out', which occurred a little before Ada's escapade.

It was, not surprisingly, with Emily's brother Albert. He was now a corporal and a very fine figure in uniform.

When he came home on leave the family made much of him. Mrs Davis, all passion spent, was now proud to show off Albert in his khaki, and basked in the congratulations of her neighbours when he accompanied her about the village or took her shopping in Caxley.

He was a quiet, happy boy, pleased to be back in the overcrowded cottage but secretly a little lonely when the rest of the family were out upon their various ploys during the day. He wandered round Beech Green, leaning on a gate here and there to chat with men gardening or women hanging clothes. He stopped to talk to old school-mates, as they cut back hedges or turned the plough at the end of a long furrow, and felt mingled pride and guilt at the envy which he saw in their eyes.

'It ain't all beer and skittles,' he assured his questioners, almost apologetically. 'Sometimes I reckons you chaps has the best of it.' But he knew he was not believed. To the stay-at-homes, he had the glamour which a uniform and travel give.

To have some purpose for his meanderings, Albert frequently strolled towards Fairacre to meet his sister and Dolly on their way home from school. He was fond of them both, and a little sorry for Dolly, whom he considered overshadowed by Ada. If he had been bolder he might have approached Ada himself, but he knew that she was besieged by young men, and was afraid that he might be rebuffed. He felt safe with Dolly, and asked her one day if she would like to go to Caxley with him on the next Saturday. Somewhat surprised, Dolly agreed.

It was all very innocent and pleasant. They cycled together to the town, Albert on Emily's bicycle. It was a blue and white March day of strong sun and wind. Dolly bought some crochet cotton and a new hook, a pound of sprats which her mother wanted, and two ounces of cabbage seed for her father. Albert accompanied her into the shops, watching gravely over her purchases, and buying some cold wet cockles in the fishmonger's as a present for the Davis family's supper.

The fish was put into a small flat rush bag which was secured with a skewer. As the afternoon wore on it grew dark with dampness and decidedly smelly, but the two were in great spirits and felt very daring as they took their burden into a tea shop in Caxley High Street and Albert ordered ices.

'What would you like to do?' asked Albert, as they tinkled their spoons in the glass dishes.

'I don't really know,' said Dolly truthfully. 'I mustn't be too late because my bicycle lamp isn't right, and anyway I want to wash my hair when I get back.'

Albert looked a little relieved. He had been wondering if he could afford to take Dolly to the show in the Corn Exchange put on by the local Nigger Minstrels. It might have been good fun, but they would have been late back, and Albert was not sure if his parents and Dolly's would have approved. Perhaps another time, he told himself vaguely.

'We'll have a walk in the park,' he said firmly, and called for the bill.

The daffodils were in bud, and they sat on a bench with the fish bag oozing gently beside them. Albert rested his arm along the back against Dolly's thin shoulder blades, and finding that she made no demur, shifted a little closer.

Dolly's silence stemmed from surprise rather than shyness. She did not have the heart to tell the young man that she was very uncomfortable. Albert's arm gave her a crick in the small of the back, and he was sitting heavily on the side of her skirt. Dolly doubted if the gathers would hold at the waist, as the material was rather worn. She leant a little towards him in order to minimise the strain and found Albert, much encouraged, tipping her head to rest on his shoulder.

Her discomfort now was considerable. His epaulette was stiff and dug into her cheek, and her neck was strained unbearably. A cold hairpin, sliding from her rumpled bun, lodged inside her collar and added to her troubles. Albert took her hand and held it very tightly and painfully in his own.

They sat there in silence with a chilly wind blowing round them. A bed of early wallflowers competed unsuccessfully with the damp fish bag for their attention. Dolly, squinting sideways at the daffodils, found her view impeded by Albert's neck and was interested to observe how much larger his pores were than her own. It was a decidedly clean neck, she noticed with approval, and the lobe of the only ear she could see had a healthy glow.

At last cramp began to invade her left foot, and feeling that she could bear no more, Dolly struggled into an upright position. There was a cracking sound, but whether of gathers or stiff joints Dolly could not be sure, and then the two smiled upon each other, Dolly with relief and Albert with affection.

'It's getting very cold,' said Dolly gently.

'Best be cycling home,' agreed Albert, collecting the fish bag.

They pedalled home companionably in the twilight, talking of this and that, but making no comment on their prim embrace on the park bench. Only when they stopped at Dolly's gate were future plans mentioned.

'Will you write to me sometimes when I'm away?' asked Albert, looking very young as he screwed and unscrewed Emily's bicycle bell.

'Of course I will,' said Dolly warmly.

'And come out again perhaps?' continued Albert.

'Thank you,' said Dolly, a little less warmly.

'Good,' said Albert, and looked as though he might lean across Emily's bicycle and peck her cheek. At that moment Francis Clare opened the door of the cottage.

'Got my cabbage seed, Doll?' he called cheerfully.

'Goodbye,' said Dolly hastily, 'and thank you for that lovely ice cream.'

Pushing open the gate, she trundled her bicycle towards the

house. The lamp made a pool of light round her father's familiar figure in the doorway. It was good to be home.

This incident, touching and absurd, had no real sequel, for Albert's leave ended very soon after. But Dolly kept her word and wrote occasionally telling Albert about the doings of Beech Green and Fairacre. Her letters were beautifully penned; no blots, crossings or spelling mistakes marred their exquisite pages, and their subject matter was as blameless, for Dolly had no stronger feeling than friendship for the young man and was too honest to pretend that anything more was felt. After some months the letters between them grew less and less frequent, and Dolly heard of his engagement to a girl in Colchester, some time later, with genuine pleasure and some relief.

Meanwhile, Ada's love affair gave Dolly food for thought. After his interview with the publican, Francis tried patiently to get some sense from his defiant daughter.

'I've told you and told you,' said Ada obstinately. 'We're going to get married whatever anyone says.'

'But what if he doesn't want to?' queried Francis. 'Takes two to make a marriage, and he ain't bothered to come and speak to me about it yet, has 'e?'

'Looks to me,' commented Mary, in support, 'as if you're throwing yourself at him. That's no way to go into marriage, Ada.'

'Why should he come here to be picked over and found wanting?' demanded Ada belligerently. ''Twon't do no good to either of us, as far as I can see.'

They could get no further with her in this mood. Francis was perplexed. He disliked the idea of pursuing this young man, but if he refused to come and see him then he supposed he must make some effort to find out the fellow's intentions if Ada's happiness was involved.

'Dammit, Mary!' he sighed to his wife. 'Girls is a darn sight more trouble than boys when it comes to wedding 'em.'

He waited a fortnight, but nothing happened. Ada continued to see the young man, and short of locking her in her room, Francis felt he could do nothing about it. At length he went again to Caxley and had an uncomfortable session with the publican, his wife and their son.

The young man was ill at ease, but assured Francis that he wished to marry Ada. Harry Roper did not impress Francis. He was thickset, with a surly expression, and had the heavy, dark, good looks which would soon coarsen with corpulence. Francis was amazed that Ada was attracted to him.

There was no doubt, however, that she would be well provided for. Jack Roper, the publican, also had an interest in a flourishing market garden, and he proposed to set up the young couple in a small greengrocery business in the town as a wedding present. So far, he knew, Harry had failed to remain in any job for longer than a year. Marriage, and a business of his own, he hoped, would settle his son permanently. At twenty-five he should have sown all his wild oats, and it was time he turned his attention to domesticity and the raising of a family. The Ropers, for their part, liked the lively girl who seemed so determined to marry their son, and felt sure she had the power and energy to direct both her husband and the business.

The Ropers were invited to the Clares' cottage. The two families exchanged civilities, the engagement was announced, and the marriage arranged for the autumn. Mary seemed pleased with matters, but Francis had a heavy heart. It was not what he wanted for his best-loved child.

There was a triumphant excitement about Ada, throughout the weeks before the wedding, which Francis found distasteful.

'She feels she's got the better of us all,' he confided to Mary.

'But what does that matter if she's not truly happy herself? And do that young Harry really want her?'

It was Mary's turn to calm fears this time.

'Our Ada's always known what she's about, and she's chose a solid fellow as'll see she's always comfortable. He loves her all right, never you fret,' she added casually.

Francis was not completely convinced, but this matter-of-fact attitude of Mary's gave him a little comfort. Presumably women knew best in these affairs.

But when he stood beside his glowing Ada before the altar, his misgivings returned. She looked so radiant, so young and so trusting in her white lace frock, standing beside that dark stranger whom he disliked. Behind her stood Dolly, pale and demure in blue, the only bridesmaid.

Francis gave Ada away, feeling as though part of his heart had gone too, and all through the wedding breakfast, which was held in 'The Crown', he felt cold and wretched. With the rest of the party he waved goodbye to the young couple as they drove off in a carriage to the railway station, and was ashamed to find that tears blurred his final view of them.

It was Mary who remained dry-eyed.

Dolly and Emily had just finished their four years' pupil-teaching at this time. Little Miss Taylor at Fairacre School now retired, and Mr Wardle suggested that Dolly might like to carry on. She was appointed as infants' teacher that September, and continued to cycle from Beech Green daily. Emily heard of a post, some miles away at a village on the south side of Caxley, which appealed to her. An aunt lived in the village and would put her up, and she would be teaching children from twelve to fourteen, which was what she had always wanted.

The two friends, who had seen each other daily for most of their young lives, missed each other sorely. They promised to write once a week, and they met occasionally in Caxley or whenever Emily managed to get home for a week-end. Without Emily and Ada, Dolly felt quite forlorn for several weeks that autumn.

But the interests at Fairacre and its school grew more absorbing as the months passed. Mr Wardle and his wife left the village, a year after Dolly began her teaching, and a new headmaster, called Mr Hope, came to live at the school house. He was a shyer, cleverer man than his predecessor, one who loved animals and flowers, and who wrote poetry with some skill and feeling.

Dolly liked him, and his vague young wife. They had one daughter, Harriet, a child of outstanding beauty and intelligence. All three, Dolly thought, had charm and uncommon sympathy, but she missed the Wardles' splendid invigorating presence, the hearty good humour and the drive which was essential to stimulate the native laziness of the Fairacre children. She hoped that Mr Waterman's methods would not be repeated.

At first, all went well. Despite his delicate appearance and gentle ways, Mr Hope had the ability to catch the imagination of the children. He was more aware of the progress of the world than Mr Wardle had been. For Mr Wardle, Fairacre and its immediate environs offered all that was needed in interest and amusement. Mr Hope soon made his older children conscious of the exciting changes about them.

He told them about aeroplanes and the pioneers who flew them. He conjured up visions of air travel in the future for his open-mouthed, and slightly disbelieving, pupils. With a poet's flair for words he described the great icy wastes at the farthest Poles of the earth, whose mystery and beauty were just becoming known and explored by brave men. He told them of Peary and Shackleton and of Scott, and he made his country children realise that adventure was still to be found.

In advance of his time, the schoolmaster recognised the power of topical news, and photographs from the papers were pinned on the walls to encourage an interest in matters of the day. He was adroit enough, too, to relate these national events to their own small world, whenever possible, and Dolly listened to him one April morning as he pointed out the splendours of a mighty new liner.

'And Mr and Mrs Evans at Beech Green are going to sail in her,' he told them. 'When they come back I shall ask them to come and tell us all about it.'

Dolly had heard that the Evanses were going abroad from Mr Davis, who was their gardener.

'Taking poor Miss Lilian,' he said, 'to see some famous doctor over there. They say he may be able to cure her. Cuts a bit out of your brain, he does, and many a poor soul's found his wits again that way.'

Dolly thought it was brave of the Evanses, to go so far, and hoped that the proposed operation would be successful, for Miss Lilian grew more pathetic yearly, and it was common knowledge that her ageing parents feared for her future when they had gone.

A few days later Mary Clare was delighted to find a picture postcard on the mat. The postman rarely called at the little cottage, and a picture was far more exciting than a plain envelope.

She held it up for Dolly to see at the breakfast table.

'I call that real nice of Mrs Evans. Written just before they sail, she says, and she's never seen anything so lovely before. Hopes we are well, and Miss Lilian sends her regards.'

Mary put the card face upward beside the bread board and peered closely at it.

'You can see the name quite clear,' she said excitedly. '*Titanic*!'

* * *

Three days later the village heard the news. The names of the Evans family were not on the list of survivors. It was a stunning blow.

Mr Hope took down the picture of the ill-fated ship, but could say nothing to the children at that time. He was as stricken as they were at the horror which had come so close to them.

The house stood with its blinds drawn for three weeks. The eldest son, known to the neighbourhood as 'Mr Bertie', then moved in with his wife and young family. With him came two or three servants who had been in his employ in London.

Mr Davis gave the Clare family the news.

'There's a new chap coming to be head gardener,' he told them. 'Seems a nice enough young fellow, if you like 'em with red hair, which I don't.'

'And what's happening to you then?' enquired Francis.

'Three times a week,' said Mr Davis, 'and it suits me. Getting a bit long in the tooth these days, and the family brings us in a bit. We'll manage.'

He made his way to the door and then turned to Dolly.

'Keep your eye out for that young chap,' he said, with mock solemnity. 'You can't miss that hair. Just like a sunset it is.'

He opened the door and was gone.

CHAPTER 15

It was strange, thought old Miss Clare, that the *Titanic* disaster in the spring of 1912 had brought such unexpected happiness in its wake.

Although, at this time, she was almost twenty-four years of

age, she had remained remarkably untouched by love. There were several reasons for this. By nature she was reserved, and in company she was an observer rather than a participator. Ada's tempestuous marriage had made her cautious, and circumstances did not throw many young men across Dolly's path. At home she found that her parents grew more dependent upon her for company, and she herself, tired after a day's teaching and the long cycle ride, was very content to stay at home during the evenings.

She had not been conscious of any gap in her life. Her work, gardening, reading, helping her mother with household affairs and writing to Emily, kept her occupied and happy at the cottage. She took part in the life of both villages, helping with socials and jumble sales, fêtes and church bazaars, and considered her life completely satisfying. She was all the more surprised, therefore, to find how overwhelmingly easy it was to slide into the state of love within a few weeks of Arnold Fletcher's arrival at Beech Green.

They first met when the young man called at the cottage with a message for Francis. Dolly was weeding, squatting down with her back to the gate, and did not hear him approach. She was startled by his voice, and struggled to her feet, much hampered by an old sack which she had pinned round her for an apron.

'You should kneel to weed,' said the young man, smiling upon her. 'It saves your back.'

There was no doubt about who he was. The bright auburn hair, which flamed above his pale bony face, identified him as the Evanses' new gardener. His eyes were of that true dark brown which is so rare in English faces, and they looked very kindly on Dolly's discomfiture.

After that he came often. He had an easy friendliness which disarmed Dolly immediately, and she felt happy in his company from the first. They found that they had much in common. His knowledge of plants and trees was deep, and unlike many gardeners, he was equally interested in wild growing things. He was an avid reader and a cricketer. Beech Green found him a reliable slow bowler and a swift-running fieldsman, and by the end of May he was playing regularly for the team.

Both he and Dolly enjoyed music and Arnold took great pride in a new phonograph which he sometimes brought over to the Clares' cottage. After much adjustment a hollow nasal voice echoed through the little room: 'This is an Edison Bell record,' and after a short rushing noise, the music would begin. It all seemed miraculous to the listeners, and Dolly first became acquainted with Handel and Bach, whose music she was to love throughout her life, by way of Arnold's phonograph.

It was soon common knowledge in the neighbourhood that Dolly and Arnold were 'going steady', as the villagers said. There was general approval.

'About time that girl got settled,' said Mr Davis to his wife. 'Won't have time for much of a family if she leaves it much longer.'

'Nonsense!' snorted Mrs Davis. 'Who wants to begin a family at eighteen like I did? Dolly's got plenty of sense – and plenty of time too. I shouldn't want to see her with a long string like ours.'

'But I thought you liked 'em!' answered Mr Davis, somewhat affronted by this sidelong attack.

'Case of have to!' commented his wife shortly, pushing him to one side as she bustled by with a steaming saucepan. Mr Davis wisely held his tongue. No point in adding fuel to the fire, he told himself.

Francis and Mary both seemed pleased, but Dolly sensed that her mother's approval was not whole-hearted. Latterly,

Mary's manner had been strange. She was at an age when women are the prey of moods, and Dolly had tried to be understanding. She guessed that, unconsciously, Mary clung to her last remaining child, and it was this that caused her mother to be cool at times with the young man. Nothing was ever said, and the matter was small enough to be ignored. In any case, Dolly was so deeply happy that troubles could scarcely affect her.

They became engaged later that year. Arnold took Dolly to Caxley where he bought a delicate little ring which she had seen in the jeweller's window and adored at first sight.

'But it's a *regard* ring, Dolly,' protested Arnold. 'I feel more than *regard* for you!'

But that was the ring which she wanted, and as she turned it upon her slim finger admiring the ruby, emerald, garnet, amethyst, ruby and diamond which spelt out its message, she felt that no one could be so happy.

Soon afterwards, in the Christmas holidays, Dolly paid her first visit to London, on the way to meet Arnold's parents who lived in Norwich. She had been by train from Caxley to the county town on a few occasions, but to ride to Paddington was a real adventure, and to see the capital itself an even greater thrill. Very few of the older generation in Beech Green, and not many of Dolly's, had seen London, although they lived within seventy miles of it, for fares were expensive and there were very few holidays.

She and Arnold went by horse bus from Paddington to Liverpool Street. Dolly was appalled by the number of vehicles, most of them horsedrawn, but some motor driven. The speed and dexterity with which the bicycles moved in and out of the traffic made Dolly shudder, and she found the noise worse than Caxley on a market day. The streets too seemed very dirty, and she was interested to see how necessary crossing sweepers were as they brushed a clear way across the road for the ladies to use.

Dolly had never seen anything so enthralling as the ladies' fashions in Oxford Street. She admired the wide hats tied on with veiling, the net necklets held up with whalebone which gave their wearers a haughty appearance, and the long sweeping skirts, held gracefully to keep them from the dirt, above neat buttoned boots. The journey to Liverpool Street passed all too quickly.

She was glad of Arnold's protection in that cavernous place of reeking smoke, hooting engines and hustling people, but once the sad poverty of the slums was passed she settled back to enjoy the different scenery of East Anglia. She never forgot her first sight of those wide wind-swept heaths and the magnificent avenues of the Norfolk countryside, with great clouds bowling in from the North Sea, moving like pillars of snow across the vast blue sky.

Arnold's parents were welcoming. They lived in a small crooked road in the shadow of the ancient cathedral. Dolly liked them at once, and was taken on a tour of relatives who lived in the city, and who proved equally friendly. She and Arnold spent three happy days in Norwich, and she grew to love the place more with every hour that passed.

When the time came to return to Beech Green, and the farewells were over, she stood at the train window and watched with regret the last of that lovely and lively city slide behind her.

Arnold, amused at her pensive face, put his arm round her comfortingly.

'We'll come again,' he promised. 'Lots of times.'

But Dolly never saw Norwich again.

Long engagements were common in those days, and Dolly felt no hardship in waiting for her wedding. It was an idyllic time, she thought. She saved as much as she could from her small salary, and bought and made many things for her future home. Friends presented her with linen and china, and Dolly found much satisfaction in her well-filled bottom drawer.

Emily, who was also engaged, to the son of a local farmer, was as busy and as happy as her friend. The two girls had plenty to talk about now when they met, and despite the major distraction of their future husbands, the weekly letters still passed between them. There were things, Dolly discovered, that one could only tell to Emily, no matter how dear Arnold might be, and their shared school experiences made a constant bond.

Fairacre School had its problems at this time which perturbed Dolly. In the January following her visit to Norwich, a tragedy had occurred in the headmaster's house.

Harriet Hope, the only child, had died from the same disease which had taken little Frank Clare. She had been a child of such unusual vivacity and beauty that the blow was all the more cruel. Mr Hope and his wife could not face the village for a week after the funeral, and Dolly coped alone with both classes, glad of the extra work and responsibility which kept her from dwelling on the loss of the attractive child.

When at last Mr Hope returned, he was a changed man. His vigour had gone, never to return, and his duties were undertaken mechanically. Worse still, he began drinking heavily, and frequently arrived in the schoolroom smelling strongly of liquor. It was not long before he began to make an excuse to leave the school soon after ten each morning, and could be seen making his way to 'The Beetle and Wedge'. He returned within half an hour just in time to mark the arithmetic he had set before his departure. But his marking pencil often wavered, and the smell of beer was most noticeable. It was small wonder that the older boys and girls winked and giggled at each other behind his back, and that the parents at Fairacre, torn between pity and indignation, wondered if they should report their schoolmaster to those in authority.

While Mr Hope was out, the door in the partition between the two classrooms was left open so that Dolly could keep an eye on both classes. She took to setting her babies some quiet work in their little desks, for during the headmaster's absence she knew she would have to make several visits to his room. Through the open door she caught glimpses of mischievous dumb show. One wag would pretend to swig from a bottle, another would clutch his stomach and roll his eyes in mock drunkenness, and these capers aroused titters from the rest of the children. It was a difficult time for Dolly, and she found it better to forestall this insolence rather than deal with its effects. Her presence in the room guaranteed good behaviour, for most of the children had been in her hands only a year or two before, and young though she was, Dolly's tall dignity commanded respect.

The babies suspected nothing, and were content to set out their counters and attempt the simple adding up and taking away sums displayed on the blackboard in Miss Clare's clear hand. Sometimes, during those quiet periods when she walked the length of Fairacre School with all its young scholars in her care, Dolly grieved for the tragedy which was being enacted around her.

Standing at the narrow Gothic window, she gazed at the dazzle of fruit blossom in the school garden, and the grandeur of the elms against the sky. She could see the roofs of the village, the blue smoke spiralling against the background of the distant downs, as blue as the smoke itself. It was appalling to think that a man could throw away such beauty and the security of a home and congenial work for the sake of drink.

That sorrow had driven him to it, Dolly knew well. That same sorrow had broken his wife's health and this added to his own misery. But Dolly could not understand why he gave way. He had so much to lose, and to her mind, there was so much around him to offer comfort and sanity. The countryside alone offered untold blessings of sight, sound and scent. He had the affection and, till recently, the respect of the children and their parents, and a fine gift of teaching. His conduct was incomprehensible to young Dolly.

What Dolly failed to recognise, because of her inexperience, was that she judged Mr Hope by her own standards. She had a calm wisdom beyond her years, and the ability to stand aside from a problem and assess it rationally. No matter how troubled her heart might be, as it was at the unaccountable attack on her by 'the marsh' boy so many years before, or by the death of Frank or by Ada's sudden vituperation, yet her head took command and dictated the course to take through stormy waters. That a man might be engulfed by the storms, and finally ship-wrecked, simply through lack of judgement, was a state of affairs which Dolly could not imagine.

Nor could she realise the state of despair to which a man might be driven so that he was impervious to the world around him. Dolly's quick eye and ear supplied her constantly with a succession of small delights – a field of buttercups, a child playing with an animal, the bubbling of a clear spring in the hedge, the flaming of Arnold's hair in the sunshine. That a man might be stricken deaf and blind with grief, and so be cut off from the mercies of nature's healing, was beyond the girl's understanding, at this time.

After some unhappy months, matters improved a little, for the morning absences ceased and Mr Hope remained on duty. It was common knowledge that the vicar, who was chairman of the managers of the school, called upon the headmaster one evening and remained in his house for nearly three hours. After this warning, 'The Beetle and Wedge' saw Mr Hope no more, but he did not stop drinking. He and his wife went out less and less in the evenings. Failing health, and shame at her husband's condition, kept Mrs Hope house-bound, while despair drove Mr Hope to the bottle, which led only to further despair.

So the sad state of affairs drifted on, and it was lucky that Dolly had so much happiness in her love for Arnold and in the bright world around her that she was able to work by the side of the pathetic headmaster of Fairacre School with constant cheerfulness.

An added joy, in the early summer of 1914, was the birth of Ada's first child. Despite her robust good health, Ada and her husband had waited six years for a son, and three miscarriages made them wonder if they were doomed to have no family.

Dolly and Arnold went to Caxley one evening to see the new baby. Harry Roper let them in the door by the side of his shop. The greengrocery business was doing well and, as his father had hoped, Harry had settled down well with his young wife. It was quite apparent, though, that in spite of her youth Ada ruled her husband. It was she who urged him to buy a smart horse and cart and to employ a good-looking young man to drive it on a round. Harry would have been content to let customers come to him. Ada saw that 'H. Roper – Caxley's Finest Greengrocer' went further afield.

Dolly suspected that it was not a very happy marriage. Prosperity had thickened their figures and lined their brows. Harry's native indolence needed to be scourged by Ada's nagging tongue. Material success meant the vindication of her early rebellion to Ada, and she intended to show the world that the Ropers had succeeded. It was an attitude which jarred on the unworldly Dolly, but on this May evening she rejoiced that her sister and brother-in-law should have a new and unifying interest.

Ada lay in a vast brass bedstead, her son in a beribboned cradle at her side. Dolly had never seen her look so pretty.

'Well, there's your nephew,' said Ada, nodding to the swaddled infant. 'And your godson, too, if you like the idea.'

Dolly was much moved. She picked up the warm bundle and looked at the tiny crumpled face among the shawls. It was more than she had ever hoped for, and it meant a new and happier relationship with Ada which she welcomed gladly.

'There's nothing I'd like more, Ada,' she said softly. The two sisters looked at each other with a sympathy and affection which had been lacking for years. It was as though they were children again, sharing the joy of a precious new present.

'We're going to call him "John" after Harry's dad,' said Ada, at last. 'And "Francis" after our dad. We'll have him christened at Beech Green when I'm up and about.'

It sounded perfect, Dolly told her. She returned the sleeping baby to its cradle, kissed Ada with warmth, and made her farewells.

Arnold, cycling home beside her, noted his Dolly's glowing looks and attributed her happiness to the new nephew. It was good to be looking forward to their own marriage later this year, he thought, for Dolly was now twenty-six and it was time they began a family of their own.

But Dolly's thoughts were of the past rather than the future. In those few minutes with Ada it seemed that some of the comradeship of their childhood had been regained. In the long look which had passed between them, Dolly recognised the old Ada she had always loved, and believed that that brief vision was a happy augury for the future.

CHAPTER 16

THE marriages of Dolly Clare and Emily Davis were planned for the autumn. There were practical country reasons for this, for Edgar, Emily's young man, would have helped his father to get in the harvest by that time, and could be spared for a few days for the less important job of marrying and taking a short honeymoon.

Arnold, too, would be particularly busy in the Evanses' garden in September, and the cottage promised them by Mr

Bertie would not be vacated until Michaelmas Day. He had promised to get the decoration and repairs done immediately, and the young couple expected to be able to live in their first home towards the end of October.

Dolly was so engrossed with household plans and the making of her trousseau that she took little notice of the newspapers and the talk of troubles abroad. She was vaguely aware that a foreign Archduke, with the same name as her father's, had been shot, in a country whose name meant nothing to her. She heard her father talking to a friend about it in the garden one hot June evening, but she was bent double, with her hands thrust among the thorns and fruit of the gooseberry bushes, and her attention was otherwise engaged. This would be the last time, she told herself, that she would pick the crop to bottle for her mother. Next year she would be picking in the Evanses' garden and the fruit jars would stand upon her own white shelves.

All through July, as Dolly spent her last few weeks at Fairacre School, trouble brewed far away. She heard Mr Hope talking to the boys and girls about Germany and her military power. At home Arnold and her father shook their heads, and the names of Sir Ernest Grey and the Czar of Russia and the Kaiser and Crown Prince flew back and forth across the room. Dolly was too happy to worry about such far-off affairs, and it was not until the first day of August that Dolly realised that her own small world might well be shattered by a great explosion outside. It seemed, suddenly, that everyone spoke of Belgium – Belgium's neutrality, Belgium being overrun by the Germans, Belgium who must be helped.

'We wouldn't go to *war*, would we?' asked Dolly, much shocked, one Sunday morning. Arnold had cycled to Caxley for a paper, and it was spread out upon the table with all four grouped around it. The headlines said 'Germany declares war on Russia', and on the same page were the words 'Bank rate rises to 10 per cent.' It all seemed incomprehensible to Dolly, but from the gravity of the men's expressions she realised that calamity was threatening.

'It'll be France next,' said Arnold quietly. 'And we'll have to go in.'

'That be damned,' answered Francis robustly. For him still the French were the enemy. Hadn't his mother told him Bony would get him when he was a boy, even though the Frenchman had been dead for years? Tradition dies slowly in the country, and the idea of spilling his blood for a parcel of Frenchies did not suit Francis Clare.

'And what about Belgium then?' asked Arnold.

'Oh well,' said Francis roundly, 'that's a different kettle o' fish. If the Kaiser steps in there, he's for it.'

'Comes to the same thing,' said Arnold laconically.

In two days' time Arnold's words were proved true, and Dolly, with mounting horror, watched the enthusiasm which greeted Britain's entry into the war. Just as, faced with Mr Hope's tragedy, she deplored his rejection of reason, so now in this world-wide dilemma she was appalled to think that no settlement could be reached between nations except by the idiocy of war. She tried to talk about it to her mother, but Mary shrugged her shoulders, and dismissed the subject with:

'It's the men, dear! They govern the country, and they knows what's best.'

When Dolly retorted that it was a pity they did govern then, if that was what they thought best, she was teased by her father and Arnold.

'Our Dolly's turning Suffragette! Votes for women!' they cried. And Dolly smiled and remained silent, for she knew it was useless to try to explain the fire, kindled by injustice and deep feeling, which burnt within her.

The summer holidays had begun and Dolly had time to

think of things. She had planned to return and teach for a few weeks in the autumn term before getting married. On marriage she was obliged to give up her post, for no married women teachers were employed in that area. She was looking forward to earning a little more money before her enforced resignation, to put towards the many expenses of their new home.

Now these long-settled plans were thrown into confusion. Within a week of the declaration of war, Mr Bertie, who was in the Army Reserve, left to join his regiment, and his wife announced that the house would be turned into a hospital. She explained to Arnold that his cottage would be available if he should need it in October, but it was quite clear that she imagined that he too would be in the Army by that time. In this she was right.

Dolly and Arnold discussed their future long and earnestly. Lord Kitchener's appeal for half a million men had gone out, and Arnold was determined to become one of Kitchener's Army without delay. Dolly, though sad at heart, could not help admiring his single-mindedness. He looked upon the war as a great adventure, and something more – a crusade against the evils of subjection. She did all in her power to make his going easier. It would have been wrong, and also impossible, to deflect him from his purpose.

At first, immediate marriage seemed the right thing, but after some cooler thoughts they decided against it.

'It's best if you carry on with your teaching,' said Arnold, 'while I'm away. Something to stop you from fretting. We'll get married a bit later, say, after Christmas. It'll all be over by then, they say, and we can settle down without parting.'

It seemed sensible, and Dolly agreed. After all, it was only a few months, and maybe Arnold would worry less about her if she were still under her parents' care. Sadly and bravely, the young couple rearranged their lives, and neither spoke of the possibility of mutilation or death, for it barely entered their thoughts.

The next day Arnold and a dozen other young men drove into Caxley to the recruiting centre. Dolly never forgot that summer morning. Harold Miller, son to the man who had let Francis have the cottage so long ago, held the reins at the front of one of his own farm waggons. He was a lusty red-faced man in his thirties, grinning broadly on this unforgettable morning, and thoroughly enjoying the thought of excitement ahead.

The waggon was freshly painted bright blue, with red wheels. Two massive black carthorses pulled it, their coats shining like coal and the brasswork of their harness jingling and gleaming in the sunlight. Two small Union Jacks fluttered from the front of the waggon, and Harold Miller had decorated his whip with red, white and blue ribbons that fluttered in the breeze. It was a brave, gay turn-out, which matched the spirits of the young men riding aloft, and the villagers waved enthusiastically when it descended the long slope of the downs and stopped at Beech Green to collect the recruits.

They were all dressed in their Sunday suits. White collars, or clean white mufflers, showed up the sunburnt country faces, and Dolly thought that they looked as fine a body of men as any in England. They glowed with good health and eagerness. Normally as quiet and docile as the powerful horses in front of them, the thrill of war had woken them to life. Ahead lay adventure, the unknown, hazards to face and battles to win. Now they would see, as such lucky chaps as Albert Davis had seen, foreign parts and foreign ways. They would exchange the confines of home for a limitless new world, and at the heart of each of them lay the encouraging certainty that they were fighting for a right and proper cause.

Dolly, with a pang, thought that Arnold had never looked so happy as at that moment. His red hair glowed above his sun-tanned face. He had one arm round his neighbour's shoulders, as the great waggon rumbled away from the waving crowd, and looked as though he were one of a band of brothers, each as exulting and purposeful as he was himself. She remembered old Mr Davis's words so long ago. No woman could ever know completely the whole of a man's heart.

All through August, Dolly and her mother went several times a week to Caxley Station to help to distribute cups of tea and sandwiches to the troops, who passed through in their thousands to Southampton. Thanks to the British Fleet, the Expeditionary Force was ferried safely across to France in the ten days between August 7th and 17th. Dolly was told that this meant that a hundred and sixty thousand men were carried during that time, and sometimes, it seemed to her, the majority must have come through Caxley Station.

Hot and tired, she cut bread and butter, sliced meat, mixed mustard, tended urns and milk jugs, and carried trays up and down the length of the packed trains in the broiling heat. But she forgot her minor discomforts in the warmth of the welcome she was given by the men. Most of them had been travelling for many hours, but their spirits were as unquenchable as their thirst. To Dolly they looked unbelievably young in their khaki uniform, and had the same air of gaiety that Arnold wore. She waved to each departing train, a long, long monster fluttering with a thousand hands, until it disappeared round the line which curved southward to the sea. Then she hurried back to the trestle tables to prepare for the next train load which would follow so soon after.

Emily helped too, and sometimes Ada left her baby, and spent an afternoon at the station. Harry had also volunteered for service and was now busy putting the shop into order, before he was called up, so that Ada could run it easily in his absence. Arnold, and the others who had jolted to Caxley in the waggon, awaited their call-up impatiently, carrying on with their jobs in a fever of suspense. Suppose it should all be over before they arrived?

They did not have long to wait. As news of the retreat from Mons came through at the end of August, Arnold and his friends were sent to a training camp in Dorset.

'It won't be for long,' Arnold promised her as they said good bye. 'You look out for a nice little house for us to go to after Christmas. We'll have the Kaiser squashed by then.'

He echoed the general feeling of optimism. Despite the ugly sound of the retreat from Mons, it was only a set-back, people told each other, and a chance to prepare for a resounding blow at the enemy. Britain was the greatest country in the world, supported by the mightiest Empire ever known – it was unthinkable that such power could be beaten. Francis and Mary, and many like them, remembering the display of might at Queen Victoria's jubilee, could see no possibility of defeat at the hands of mere foreigners. Dolly had private doubts, but was glad of the robust spirit around her.

At the end of November Arnold had a short leave before going to the Western Front. He was thinner than before, but his face glowed with health and high spirits. He was more gentle and loving than Dolly had ever known him, refused to let her show any hint of sadness, and forbade her to accompany him to Caxley Station on the evening of his return.

She walked slowly with him, in the early twilight, along the road to Caxley, and they stopped beneath a sycamore tree to make their farewells. The bare branches seemed to stretch kindly arms above them, as if in blessing, and at their feet the winged seeds lay on the wet road, a sign of hope and life ahead.

He put a little packet into her hand before taking her in his arms. It was only then, and for a brief moment, that Dolly

caught a glimpse of something more than resolute gaiety in his mien. For that one telling second, darkness came into his eyes, a weary hopelessness shadowed his face, as though he knew that he was powerless in the grip of the fates.

Their faces were cold as they kissed, and Dolly's throat ached with the effort of controlling her tears. But when they finally parted Arnold's smile was as warm as ever. He took his cap from his head at the bend of the lane and waved it cheerfully. His fiery head shone with the same bronze glow as the winter sun's slipping below the shoulder of the downs behind him.

When he disappeared from view, Dolly sank on to the damp bank among the writhing roots of the old tree, and let the hot tears fall. She made no sound, but sat hunched silently, tasting the salt drops as they ran over her mouth.

When at last it was dark, she rose to her feet, patting the comforting rough bark of the tree which had witnessed her grief. She never passed it again without remembering that evening.

In the quietness of her bedroom she undid the packet. It contained an oval locket made of gold threaded on a long gold chain. Inside was a photograph of Arnold, and facing it, a lock of his blazing hair.

She slipped the chain over her throbbing head, and by the wavering light of the candle, surveyed her blotched swollen face and the beauty of the locket which lay cold upon her breast. She was to wear it every day of her long life.

One February day of biting cold, Dolly returned home from school to find an incoherent letter from Arnold's parents, written on a flimsy half sheet of paper, with the ink blurred by tears. He had been killed by a hand grenade lobbed into his water-logged trench near the Ypres Canal. Three other men had been killed instantly with him.

Dolly's first reaction was of stubborn disbelief. A flame as vital as Arnold's could not be snuffed out so easily. It was all a dreadful mistake. Why, she had had a letter from him only yesterday! She pushed the paper, almost impatiently, towards her mother.

It was Mary's anguished face which really convinced Dolly that the news was true, and later still the rare embrace of her sympathetic father. But for many days she was too numbed to cry. It was as though this tragedy had happened to someone else. She went, pale and dazed, about her daily life. She set work for the children, read them stories, bound up their broken knees and listened to their tales. Francis and Mary, Mr Hope, and all who knew her in Beech Green and Fairacre feared for her reason. There was an icy remoteness about her which frightened them into silence when she approached.

Even Emily had no power to thaw her. During those dark weeks she came daily to the Clares' cottage to do her best to comfort her friend.

'There's nothing you can do for me,' Dolly told her gently. 'Don't be sorry for me. I don't feel anything at all.' She was touched by Emily's staunch devotion and felt almost guilty that she should be so calm.

'Sometimes I think,' she told Emily one day, 'that my heart was killed at the same time as Arnold. Only my poor dull head works now.'

It was a small incident a week or two later that snapped Dolly's chains and released her grief. Every morning she fed the birds which came to the doorstep of the cottage. Among them was a robin, bolder than the rest, who came so frequently that the Clares' cat ignored it. But on this particular morning the cat, who had been watching the proceedings from a window-sill, leapt suddenly upon the robin, killing it at a blow, and returned immediately to the window-sill where it yawned indolently.

Dolly was shaken with fury at this wanton attack. This robin had been hatched in the damson tree in the garden. She had watched its parents, day after day, feeding their young. Their efforts had brought up the little family, all of whom had gone, except for this one. The Clares had thrown him crumbs daily, and Francis looked for his company when he dug in the garden. His clear piping and bright eye had cheered the wretched winter.

That such abundant vitality should turn to half an ounce of dead feathers, with the stroke of a paw, was horrifying to Dolly. Tears of pity and rage shook her as she lifted the victim. Its breast was the same colour as the hair within her locket, and it was this that made her tears fall faster. Now the full realisation of her loss gripped her. A blow as cruel and as senseless as the cat's had robbed Arnold of life and her of joy. The paroxysms of grief continued unabated all that day, to be succeeded by a week of such black and hopeless despair that Dolly longed to die.

Only then did she understand the pitiful state of those who could find no comfort. She could understand now the depths of Mr Hope's despair, his rejection of a world which could offer him no solace. Never again, in her young arrogance, would she despise those who failed to interest themselves in the bright world about them. There was no bright world for those in the pit.

It was a long time before Dolly herself could clamber slowly from it and seek the light again.

CHAPTER 17

THE war ground on mercilessly. Now there was a grimmer spirit everywhere, for it was obvious that victory would not be easily won. Fighting was going on in all quarters of the globe, but it was the losses on the western front that meant most to the people of Fairacre and Beech Green, for it was there that almost all their men were fighting.

In April 1915, while Dolly still groped her way to normality, the new weapon of gas was used at Ypres, where Arnold's broken body shared a grave with ten others.

Dolly never forgot the horror with which she heard this news. It was followed almost immediately by a message from Emily's Edgar, who was out there.

Dolly was with her when his postcard arrived. It said starkly: 'For God's sake send me a gas mask.' Bewildered and shocked, the two girls looked dumbly at each other. What was a gas mask? Where could you buy one? How could you make one?

With no time to lose they fashioned a thick pad of cotton wool which they bound with tape, adding more tapes to tie it round the head. They tried it on each other, and in normal times would have laughed at the ludicrous sight. But it was too gruesome an affair this time for laughter.

They packed it up, with a hasty loving note from Emily, and Dolly and she cycled to Caxley to catch the last post. The lanes and fields were brushed with tender green, and the downs, ineffably peaceful, brooded over all. It seemed unbelievable to Dolly that, within hours, the parcel they carried so carefully would be in another world where there were no trees left, no birds to sing, but only grey mud, guns, and suffering men.

It was gas which ended Edgar's war service. At the end of May he returned to England, a gasping, coughing shadow, and was sent to a hospital on the south coast. For months Emily made the long anxious journey each week while the young man struggled back to life. It was now Dolly's turn to be of comfort, and she marvelled at the endurance of Emily's slight frame and the light of courage that shone in her clear grey eyes. Although she taught all the week at Springbourne, where she was now headmistress, and worked increasingly hard at home, she still undertook the week-end journeys with unfailing hope.

Dolly, at Fairacre school, thought how little the war had changed it. Unlike Springbourne, its headmaster had not gone to war. Mr Hope's repeated attempts to join up met with failure through ill-health. He could best serve his country by staying at his post, he was told. He grew shakier and more morose as time went on, and the morning visits to 'The

Beetle and Wedge' were resumed. Dolly could not help hearing the gossip that flew about the village, though she herself preserved silence, steadfastly refusing to be drawn into discussions about her headmaster.

Two evenings a week she stayed late at the school with a party of local Red Cross workers. They sewed, knitted and packed parcels under the lamps swinging from the lofty roof, while the news of husbands and brothers and sons far away was exchanged. The women were extra kind to Dolly at this time. Her tragedy touched them, and they felt great admiration for her increasing care of the children.

'Carries that school along alone these days,' commented one. 'She's the one that should be head there.'

'They don't learn much after they've left Miss Clare,' agreed another.

Certainly Dolly had enough to do. The school was growing. A family of Belgian refugees contributed five more children, and there were several Londoners who had been sent to stay with local relatives to escape the bombing attacks on the capital. Dolly enjoyed their fresh outlook, and, remembering her own apprehension as a newcomer to Fairacre school, tried to make them particularly welcome.

Now that so many men were away, far more women went out to work. A munitions factory on the outskirts of Caxley employed a number of Fairacre mothers, and Dolly passed them each morning as they cycled into work. To her mind, they looked happier and healthier cycling along together in all weathers, than they had when they were cooped up in their cottages. Many of them were tasting independence, and the pleasure of earning, for the first time in their lives. This emancipation would not be lightly thrown away when the war was over.

The food shortage, which so seriously affected the towns,

was not apparent at Beech Green and Fairacre. Dolly was made aware of their good fortune one day when she was throwing maize to the chickens in Mr Hope's garden. A boy from London watched in amazement.

'We 'ad that for dinner up London,' he told her disapprovingly. 'My mum'd give you what for if she saw you doin' that.'

Dolly realised that the rebuke was a just one. Certainly they were short of such things as sugar and sweets, but corn, vegetables, fruit, and even butter, were plentiful in the quiet little world of Fairacre. They had much to be thankful for, thought Dolly, beginning once more to find comfort in the work she loved, and the ever changing natural beauty about her.

Life could never be quite as sweet again. A vital part of her had died, it seemed, with Arnold's going; a part which beauty, work or the love of friends could not replace. But from these sources came a measure of comfort for which she was humbly grateful. She learnt, at this time, the invaluable lesson of finding happiness in little things, and by picking up small crumbs of comfort as she went about her daily work nursed her damaged spirit back to health.

In the summer of 1916 Dolly was looking forward to Emily's wedding. Edgar was still an invalid, at a convalescent home not far from his first hospital. Emily made her week-end journeys regularly, and the plans for the long-awaited marriage were all ready. One of the farm cottages was waiting for them, and Edgar was expected to return to light duties on the farm at Michaelmas time.

The two young women spent many evenings together making curtains and covers for the new house. Dolly's pleasure in the preparations was occasionally clouded by her own sense of loss, but she was careful never to let Emily know her feelings.

She was sincerely glad for her friend, she was fond of Edgar, and looked forward to being a frequent visitor to the little home when they had settled in.

One sunny evening she had arranged to meet Emily at the empty cottage to help her measure the floors for lino and rugs. Edgar's farm lay beyond Springbourne, in a wide valley, hidden by the swell of the downs from the villages of Beech Green and Fairacre, and hard by the larger farm of Harold Miller. As Dolly Clare pushed her bicycle up the steep chalky path from Beech Green she thought of the varying fates which war had brought to the men of that district. While Arnold lay dead, and Edgar broken, Harold Miller went from strength to strength, and had just been commissioned on the field, she heard, at Thiepval. He would be a gallant fighter, she felt sure, remembering his tough smiling face as she had seen it last as he drove his comrades to Caxley in the brightly painted farm waggon. How many more would come back with just such honours, she wondered? And how many would share Edgar's and Arnold's fate? Accompanied by such pensive thoughts, she rode down the other side of the downs and made her way to the cottage.

The door was open, but there was no welcoming cry from Emily. Dolly stepped in and saw her sitting, dazed, upon a wide window-sill. In silence Emily handed her a letter. Dolly read it slowly in a shaft of evening sunshine which fell through the little window. The only sounds were the fluttering of a butterfly against the pane and the distant bleat of sheep on Edgar's farm. It said:

Dear Em,

I don't know how to tell you. I don't expect you to forgive me. But I can't marry you. There is a nurse here who looked after me all the time. I love her very much and we are getting married as soon as we can. I have tried to tell you before, but never managed it.

Em, I am sorry, but you will meet someone much better than me. I don't deserve you anyway.

Your loving,

Edgar.

Stunned, Dolly slid on to the window-sill beside her friend and put her arms round her. She held Emily's head against her shoulder. They sat in dreadful silence, while Emily's slight frame shook with sobs, and her tears made a warm wet patch on Dolly's print blouse.

After a time, Emily straightened up and looked dazedly about the room. She folded the letter carefully, tucked it into her wide belt, and stood up. She dried her eyes, smoothed her hair, and went from the empty room through the front door.

Dolly followed her, torn with grief and fearful for her welfare. The evening sun had turned everything to gold, and glinted on the key in Emily's hand.

Dolly watched her close the door of the house which was to have been her home. She turned the key resolutely in the lock and thrust it, with the letter, into her belt. Then she looked steadily at her friend. Her clear grey eyes were swollen with crying, but were as brave as ever. They lit with sympathy as they observed Dolly's stricken state, and she came to her friend and kissed her soundly.

'It's her house now,' she said firmly. 'Edgar's made his choice. I'll abide by it.'

Without a backward glance she mounted her bicycle and the two friends rode slowly, and with heavy hearts, back to Beech Green.

Dolly often thought, later, that Emily's lot was far harder than her own. She was fated to live for the rest of her life within a mile or two of Edgar and his wife, cloaking her feelings before all who knew the sad story. Public knowledge of one's affairs is a factor of village life which can cause annoyance. Sometimes it can cause tragedy, but sometimes it can be a source of strength. The sympathy which flowed to Emily, as a result of Edgar's marriage to another, did not show itself in words, but she was conscious of much kindness and was grateful for it.

Dolly never forgot Emily's reaction to this blow, and the turning of the key upon her hopes with such swift resolution. She had come to terms with the situation as decisively as she had so many years ago, when she had heard of Queen Victoria's death and saw in it a comfort to little Frank Clare, in a world unknown. It was her acceptance of fate, which Dolly admired. She seemed to bear no rancour towards Edgar, and refused to discuss his future wife.

'What use would it be,' she said one day to Dolly, 'to try and hold Edgar against his will? I don't want a marriage like that.'

But not many women, Dolly thought, would have felt that way. Some people wondered if Emily Davis were heartless, and if her love for Edgar had waned during the long months of waiting. But Dolly knew it was otherwise.

In the years that followed, Emily never passed the house that might have been her own, if she could help it. She would walk a mile further, along a winding lane, rather than take the steep path beside the cottage, and when, by chance, she and Dolly came across Edgar one day, resting beneath the sycamore tree where she had said good-bye to Arnold, Emily's sudden pallor told more than words, and the look in her eyes reminded Dolly of the stricken gaze of some dying animal. As she knew only too well, time would bring merciful relief from pain, but it would never cure the cause.

* * *

The visits of Ada and her children did much to cheer them all at this time. John Francis, Dolly's godchild, was a rampageous two-year-old when his sister was born, and Mary and Francis were the most indulgent grandparents.

Ada drove over in a smart governess cart from Caxley whenever she could spare time from the business. Harry seemed to be enjoying the war. He was fighting in Italy, and wrote cheerful letters home about the lovely country, promising to bring Ada there for a holiday when the war was over. His opinion of his Austrian enemies was low, and of his Italian comrades in arms not much higher, but he gave Ada to understand that Harry Roper was equal to coping with all difficulties. In truth, Harry quite liked his freedom again. His naturally buoyant spirits had been kept in check by Ada who had seen that any excess energy was harnessed to the business. Now he had a free rein, and Harry was to look upon his years with the army as one of the happiest times of his life.

Ada was now a very prosperous matron. Dolly marvelled at her extensive wardrobe, the children's expensive toys and the lavish amount of food which she generously brought to her parents' cottage.

Francis gloried in his Ada's success. Mary seemed less enthusiastic. It was the children that roused her spirits. It seemed as if she became young again when they tumbled about the cottage floor or called from the garden.

For all Ada's ostentation and finery, which jarred upon Dolly, yet she was warmly welcome. Despite the differences in temperament, the two sisters were fond of each other, and the children were a strong uniting bond. Harry's absence meant that the family saw more of one another. It was a comfort to Dolly to share the responsibility of her parents' care, and she hoped that Harry's homecoming would not sever the ties which had grown stronger during the war years.

At the beginning of November 1918, a jubilant letter came from Harry Roper describing the taking of an island called Grave di Papadopoli in the middle of the river Piave. He had helped to build bridges over which the Italians poured to victory, splitting the Austrian army in two.

'Now the way's wide open,' wrote Harry exultantly. 'With Austria down in the mud, we make straight for Berlin!'

The war news from all quarters was as cheering as Harry's. Mutiny had broken out in the German Fleet at Kiel, the Americans had cut the German eastern and western forces by taking Sedan, and the Allies were pursuing the enemy on the Meuse. The news that Foch was meeting German delegates, to arrange an armistice, sent the hopes of everyone soaring. On November 11, Harry Miller of Beech Green, with five other local men, entered Mons with the victorious British army, while the bells of that shattered town played 'Tipperary.' Early on the same morning the Armistice was signed, and fighting ended at 11 a.m.

In Caxley the rumours flew round that Monday morning. Someone said that the news had been telephoned to the Post Office. Flags began to appear on buildings and the bell ringers hurried to the parish church. But no official confirmation was forthcoming, and it was decided to wait a little longer. The market place and High Street began to fill with excited crowds.

At half past twelve official confirmation of the Armistice was posted in Caxley Post Office and the town's suspense was over. The bells pealed out, the Union Jack was hoisted on the Town Hall and flags of all nations sprouted from roofs and windows. Monday's meagre war-time ration of cold meat was ignored while Caxley rejoiced.

At Fairacre Dolly heard the news from Mr Hope, during the afternoon. One of the children had brought a collection of

French and Belgian postcards to show her. His father had sent them regularly – beautiful objects of silk with fine embroidery showing flowers and crossed flags of the Allies. Dolly was holding them in her hand when Mr Hope burst into the room.

'It's over!' he cried, his face alight. 'The war's over!'

The babies looked at him in amazement. They remembered no other kind of life. War had always been their background. His excitement was incomprehensible to them.

He called the school to attention, told them the news and then gave a prayer of thanksgiving. School ended early that day, and Dolly rode home through the grey November afternoon with much to think about. Rejoicing, for her, was tempered by Arnold's loss, but she felt overwhelming relief at the ending of suffering and slaughter.

Now the sons and lovers, the husbands and fathers, would come home again, and the village would have young men to work in the fields and to laugh in the lanes. Now the girls and wives and mothers would find happiness, glad to have someone to share the joyful responsibilities of home life.

But not all. How many cottage homes, Dolly wondered, mourned today when all the world was gay with flags and bells?

Over forty years later, old Miss Clare felt her eyelids pricking at the memory of that distant day. She knew now the price that the parish of Beech Green had paid.

Twenty-six names were carved at the foot of the stone war memorial, now weathered to a gentle grey. In the neighbouring parish of Fairacre seventeen young men had died, so that over forty men had been taken from the thousand people who made up the population of the two parishes. Miss Clare had known them all, and could never be reconciled to their loss. She honoured the high ideals of sacrifice and patriotism which had illumined the path of these young men, but the tragic pity of it all overcame her other feelings.

In the years that followed, poetry became a source of joy and comfort to Miss Clare, but the loveliest songs sung by the young war poets who were her contemporaries, moved her so swiftly to weeping that she could not bring herself to read them often. 'The heartbreak at the heart of things', as one of them wrote, was too poignant for Miss Clare's generation ever to forget.

In the heat of the June sunshine Miss Clare's old fingers strayed to the locket. She bent her white head to look at it. It was thin and smooth with years of wear, and its glitter had mellowed to a soft golden sheen. But inside, the dear face of Arnold Fletcher was still clear and unlined, and his bright hair had no touch of grey. For Arnold and his comrades would never grow old.

CHAPTER 18

OUTWARDLY, Beech Green and Fairacre seemed to change little in the years after the war. Two bungalows were built on the road between the two villages, but no other new houses for some time. Most of the men returned to the villages, but some, unsettled by the last few years, took this chance of leaving the country and moving townwards.

Harold Miller was now in charge of the farm at Springbourne, as his old father had died during the war. He found himself so short of men that he decided to sell several of his outlying cottages, including the Clares'. Francis was given the first chance to buy it for the sum of two hundred pounds. The family spent several evenings in earnest discussion, and finally decided to purchase it with the savings of a lifetime.

'Well, I never thought to live in a house of my own,' declared Mary proudly. 'Now we don't need to fret about paying the rent every week.'

'It's to be yours when we're gone,' said Francis to Dolly. 'Ada's well provided for, and this place don't mean much to her, and never did.'

He looked through the leaded panes at the trim garden, and Dolly saw the pride of possession light up his face.

'And if you was hard pressed,' he continued, 'you could always sell it. Or say you got married,' he added, somewhat doubtfully.

'We don't need to think about that for a good few years,' replied Dolly. 'You'll enjoy it for another twenty or thirty.'

Ada and Harry bought a house about the same time. Living over the shop, Ada said, was downright common, and if they didn't have a place on the hill on the south side of Caxley, like all the other people who had done well, their two children would never be able to hold up their heads. Harry, delighted to be back and to find a flourishing business and money in the bank, agreed readily. Within a year they were installed in a brand new house with HARADA in curly chrome letters on the oak-type front door.

Emily too had moved. She had been acting head teacher during the headmaster's absence on war service, and was appointed head when he moved to a larger school. A little house went with the post, and as her father had died, Emily persuaded her mother to leave the cottage where she had reared her thriving family and live at Springbourne with her. Mary Clare missed her good neighbour sadly, but sometimes made the long walk over the hill to spend an hour or two with her.

Fairacre school had its changes, too. Private warnings to Mr Hope had been of no avail. The man was now a physical wreck and the work of the school suffered badly.

One spring morning he came into Dolly's room looking vaguely bewildered.

'I'm leaving Fairacre,' he said abruptly. 'I had my notice this morning.'

Dolly was not surprised, but she was sorry that he was going. There were many things about the man that she liked, and change was always distasteful to her.

'The managers suggest that I have a holiday for a month or two,' went on the headmaster, 'and there will probably be a vacancy for me in Leicestershire.'

Dolly guessed that this opening must have been suggested by Miss Parr, one of the managers of Fairacre school, who had relatives in Leicester. Privately, Dolly thought Mr Hope was lucky to get anything. She suspected that he would have an assistant's post in the new school, and in this she was right.

He left at the end of May, and Dolly wondered who would be the next occupant of the school house. Fairacre school was very much bigger than Springbourne so that a man would be appointed. For the last few weeks of term Dolly and a woman supply teacher from Caxley coped with the school between them, and in September Mr Benson arrived.

The first thing that Fairacre noticed about the new headmaster was that he had a car and a wireless set. The car was a Ford T model with a beautiful brass radiator and brass headlamps, and the wireless set was the latest type with a superior gadget to hold the cat's whisker above the crystal.

'Go ahead sort of fellow,' commented Mr Willet to Dolly Clare. Young Mr Willet had been badly wounded during the war, and was making a modest living as caretaker to the school and by growing vegetables and plants for sale in his own flourishing garden. He was clearly impressed by the new man, and so were all the other males from six to sixty, Dolly observed, for such is the power of things mechanical.

He had other interests besides the car and the wireless set. He had served with distinction in the RNAS and had travelled widely. In the few years he was at Fairacre he reminded Dolly of Mr Hope in his younger days, for he had the power to fire his listeners with his own enthusiasm. He was a great supporter of the League of Nations, and tried to explain its world-wide task to the children who only knew the small world of Fairacre.

'There will never be another war,' he promised them, many and many a time. 'This war was the war to end all wars. Now we shall use reason to settle arguments between nations.'

He bought many magazines and papers for the children from his own meagre salary. He found that they read these far more easily than books. Arthur Mee's monthly *My Magazine* was a great favourite, and Dolly remembered the frontispiece to one of the issues very clearly. It showed a little girl, barefoot and in a pink tunic, opening the golden gates to a new world where all was peace. It was typical of the ardent hope of a war-shattered world. 'Never again!' was the cry, uttered in all sincerity.

The new world certainly seemed a happy place in the years that followed. Fairacre did not boast any bright young things of its own, but its inhabitants were pleasurably shocked to read about those who painted the big cities red. *The Caxley Chronicle* reported the dancing of the Charleston at the Civic Ball in the Corn Exchange, and some of the older generation felt that the age of decadence had arrived.

There was certainly an air of gaiety about which reached even to such leafy retreats as Beech Green and Fairacre. It was a daily wonder to wake to a world at peace, to know that one's menfolk were home again, that the guns thundered no more, and that life could be relished for the good thing it was.

An enterprising firm in Caxley started a bus service during the twenties and this made a world of difference to those living in remote villages. Twice a week, on Thursday and Saturday, it was possible to ride from Fairacre through Beech Green to Caxley by bus, and there to shop or meet one's friends, or even catch another bus to the giddy pleasures of the county town fifteen miles away. The older people, whose cycling and walking days were over, were enraptured by this new wonder, and Mary Clare became a regular passenger on Thursday mornings.

'Proper old gad-about you're getting these days!' teased Francis, but he was glad to see Mary with this new interest. Now she could go to see Ada and the children much more often, and though she sometimes wondered if she were a nuisance to her daughter, the rapturous welcome she received from her two grandchildren consoled her. It was true that Ada looked with mixed feelings upon the small shabby figure, in her old-fashioned button boots and jet-trimmed bonnet, which ambled up the gravel path, always, it seemed, when she had a party of genteel Caxley friends whom she was trying to impress.

Emily and Dolly found the Saturday morning buses very useful too. They frequently met in Caxley to shop and exchange news over coffee. Edgar was never mentioned, but Dolly knew that the marriage was successful and that he had two small children. How Emily felt about it she could only guess. They were both in their thirties now, and often spoke good-humouredly of 'being on the shelf'. Chances of marriage were very small, they knew, for their generation, and Dolly counted herself lucky in having Ada's children in the family and all the young fry of Fairacre to work among. Nevertheless, her sense of loss was great, for other people's children are a very poor substitute for one's own, and there were occasions when, at that sad time of day between sunset and twilight, Dolly could not bear to think of the long lonely years ahead.

It was during Mr Benson's period of headship that Mrs Pringle was engaged as school cleaner. This dour individual, who was 'never so happy as when she was miserable', as the villagers said, had lived in Fairacre since her marriage and worked for Mrs Hope at the school house. The shortcomings of Mr Hope and the decline of his wife had furnished Mrs Pringle with ghoulish interest. She had wanted to take over the school cleaning for several years, for the two great black tortoise stoves which warmed the building exercised a strong fascination over her, and she longed to apply blacklead and elbow grease to their neglected surfaces.

'Fair makes my blood boil to see the state that Alice got 'em in,' she grumbled to Dolly on her first day in office. Alice was the poor toothless old crone who had been taken from an orphanage at ten, set to work as kitchen maid for fifty years, first here, then there, until she drifted to a hovel in Fairacre and earned a few shillings by scrubbing the school floors and lighting the stoves. In all the years that Dolly had known her she had only heard her speak about a dozen times. She bobbed and nodded when addressed, a skinny hand fluttering to her mouth.

She had been found dead in her little broken cottage, rolled up in a thin grey blanket before an empty grate, a week or two earlier, and the neighbour who had lifted her said that she was lighter than his own two-year-old.

Mrs Pringle would have made six of her. A squat, square figure clad in a thick skirt and jumper covered with a vivid flowered overall, she stumped morosely about the premises grumbling at the mess made by the children and the amount of coke consumed by the stoves. She was to be part and parcel of the Fairacre scene for many years and Dolly Clare found it best to turn a deaf ear to most of the lady's complaints.

As time passed Dolly sometimes thought that she knew every stick and stone of Fairacre school. The grain of her desk lid, the knots in the wooden partition, the clang of the door-scraper and the sound of the school bell above her were as familiar to her as her own face and voice. Only the children changed, and now she taught many whose parents had once sat in the same desks. Miss Clare was becoming an institution. Would she ever leave, she asked herself?

Mr Benson left after five years, his successor left after seven, but Miss Clare remained at her post.

'She won't never go,' the parents said to each other. 'And a good thing too. Taught us all right, she did, and teaches our kids good manners, as well as sums and reading.'

She was looked upon with affection and with much respect. The years added dignity and authority to Dolly's upright figure. Her fair hair was beginning to grey a little, but her blue eyes were as bright and kindly as ever.

'Pity she never married,' she overheard her headmaster say. 'A bit late now, I suppose,' he added and Dolly echoed the sentiment.

It was not only age, but circumstances that kept Dolly at Fairacre. In the early thirties Francis collapsed one day, while he was digging in the garden. Doctor Martin surveyed him gravely. Mary and Dolly watched the doctor closely from the other side of the bed. He was an old friend, but they rarely needed to call him in professionally. This was an alarming moment.

'I'll call again in the morning,' he said at last, leaving Francis in a heavy sleep.

The next morning he was moved to Caxley hospital, and

Mary was inconsolable. Dolly was obliged to have the week away from school to comfort her mother. They went daily to visit Francis, who lay very quiet and still, but smiled at them and occasionally spoke. He seemed very weak, and from Doctor Martin's manner Dolly guessed that this was her father's last illness.

One May evening she went alone, cycling along the scented lane. It had changed little since the first time she had driven along it behind Bella's massive bulk, but sometimes a car passed her now, where there was none before, and the main street of Caxley had more cars and lorries than horse-drawn vehicles these days. Her dislike of Caxley had changed over the years to affection. So much had happened to her there that it now seemed as much a background to her life as Beech Green and Fairacre.

Later, sitting beside her father's bed, holding his hand in hers peacefully, the feeling that she was part of Caxley stole upon her. How many other people had sat as she did now, or lay as her father did, gazing upon the trees outside that sheltered the nearby almshouses? Caxley was the mother town to which all the surrounding villages turned. Here they came to work, or sent their children to school. Here they gathered when war broke out, or a queen died, or peace was celebrated. Here were the offices which dealt with rents and rates and other irksome matters which concerned them. And here was the hospital which took them into its shelter and restored them to health, or eased their going when life ebbed.

When she left her father that evening she made her way down a quiet by-road leading from the back of the hospital to the centre of the town. She felt curiously at peace, still sustained by the feeling of being at home in the town. A motor hearse overtook her and waited to slip into the main road ahead, leading to the market place. Four men, in sober clothes, sat beside the coffin on its way to the town undertakers. There was a decent restraint about their quiet bearing which Dolly admired. A right and proper way, she thought, to make one's last journey through familiar streets, flanked by companions, slipping along unobtrusively with schoolboys on bicycles and vegetable vans, as unremarked as any other part of the moving stream. If that was what fate had in store for Francis then she felt she could face it all the more bravely from having seen the passing of that unknown one who had walked the ways of Caxley as her father had done.

He died that same night and was buried three days later beneath a giant yew tree in Beech Green churchyard not far from little Frank. Mary was braver than Dolly had dared to hope. She went to stay for a few days with Ada, and the children's chatter and affection seemed to comfort her.

When she returned she seemed her old self. She sighed with relief at being back again, lonely though it was without the dear presence of Francis.

'Ada's is lovely,' she said to Dolly. 'Full of fine things, and hot water straight from the tap and that – but it don't seem homely to me. I'm happier here.'

Later that evening she looked across the table at Dolly, who sat sewing a shirt for John Francis.

'When you was born,' she said slowly, 'the old dame that was helping said you'd be a lucky child. She said: "That child be blessed and the day will come when you'll remember what I told you." Those were her very words, Dolly, and they've come true. You've been a real blessing to me – all my days.'

Dolly was deeply moved. Her mother rarely showed emotion, and when, soon after, she kissed her goodnight, she felt that they had never before been quite so close.

Francis left very little. Almost all his money had gone to the buying of the cottage, but his thatching tools and those of his father were carefully stored in the garden shed. It was Emily who discovered a young man in Springbourne who wanted to take up a thatcher's craft, and to him Dolly and Mary gave the tools. He was a handsome lad, with a look of Frank about him, and it gave both women much happiness to think of Francis's tools being used again, on the same familiar roofs, by one of the next generation.

CHAPTER 19

LOOKING back upon those twenty years between the wars Miss Clare realised how great a change had taken place in the lives of her neighbours.

Very few of her mother's generation had been to London, or had seen the sea, although both were within seventy miles of the village. She herself had not seen either until she was in her twenties. But with more and more cars pouring into the roads, and with buses and charabancs increasing their services weekly, there were very few children in Miss Clare's class of babies who had not seen both before they were five or six years of age.

It made life much more wonderful and exciting. When you have been bounded by the limits of your legs, or bicycle wheels, there is something deeply thrilling about boarding a coach which will take you a hundred miles away. Dolly Clare never completely lost her sense of wonder at the miracle of modern speed. Holidays away from home were not possible on her small salary, but occasionally she took her mother on a day's outing to the coast, during the school vacations, and this was a rare joy for them both.

The children's annual outing was equally exciting. When Dolly was at Fairacre school as a pupil, and in her early teaching years, a brake pulled by four horses had taken them all to Sir Edmund Hurley's park just beyond Springbourne, and there, five miles from home, they had felt that they were in a foreign land.

Another new joy was the occasional visit to the theatre at the county town. To be sure, the scenery was sometimes a little shabby and some of the acting mediocre, but to Dolly and her unsophisticated friends it was always an evening of enchantment.

Even more miraculous was the wireless. In its early days, soon after Mr Benson's coming to Fairacre, the children besieged Dolly's desk each morning to tell her what the invisible uncles and aunts in Children's Hour had told them the day before. And when, one unforgettable day, they heard 'Hello, twins!' boomed forth in unison, for a pair who lived at Beech Green, their excitement knew no bounds. Sometimes, Dolly thought wryly, they seemed to learn far more from the wireless than they did from her. Would lessons ever be broadcast to the schools, she wondered?

In the little cottage in the evenings Dolly listened to concerts and satisfied that love of music which had first been fired by Arnold's wheezy phonograph. Mary's pleasure in it increased as the years went by, for her eyes soon tired of reading and sewing, and she found this new invention fascinating. There was no doubt about it, she told Dolly, life was richer by far than when she was a girl at the farm, creeping to her attic bedroom, lamp in hand, soon after darkness fell.

But despite the new wireless sets in cottage homes, and the new excitement of modern travel, things were still difficult for those employed in agriculture. Many of the children who clamoured round Dolly's desk, eagerly trying to tell her of last night's wireless programme, were thin from lack of proper food. The lot of the farmer, and, worse still, of the farm labourer, was as hard as it had ever been, and Dolly often wondered how long the land could support a fast-growing population. It was not enough to expect industry to pay for the foreign food that packed the little village shop at Beech Green and the rest of the shops in England. The farmer must be given hope and help to be able to contribute his share. It grieved Dolly to see the heritage of the countryside, held in trust for generations to come, being so sadly neglected.

For women a new interest sprang up during these years. The Women's Institute had a thriving membership at Beech Green and at Fairacre. Mary Clare was a keen supporter and acquired many new skills. Dolly was amused to see her proficiency at upholstery, and acted as unskilled assistant when her mother boldly re-stuffed and covered the ancient sofa and matching armchair. It was Dolly's job to pull the tough strings which drew the buttons into their allotted dimples, and very hard work she found it. But Mary seemed inspired by her new ability and from upholstery she progressed to making loose covers, going from strength to strength.

The years passed tranquilly. The spring term, bedecked with primroses and violets and loud with cuckoo song outside the school, and the remains of winter coughs inside, gave way to the pinks and roses of the summer term, arrayed in 'Virol' jars along the window-sills. Hips and haws and trailing bryony welcomed the autumn in, and new babies faced Miss Clare for the first time in their young lives. And always the highlights of the year remained the same – Christmas, Easter, Harvest Festival and the school outing and the church fête, held, as always, in the grounds of the vicarage.

To some women this familiar cycle would have proved stultifying. Dolly Clare saw nothing monotonous in it. She liked order, she liked knowing the pattern ahead. Within the framework of seasons' and terms' events she found variety and excitement enough. For one thing, no child was like its neighbour. More fascinating still to the elderly teacher, no child was exactly like its parents. There was something infinitely satisfying in comparing the generations of the families she knew so well. There were hereditary tendencies in looks or behaviour which were interesting to study. She knew too the background of the homes from which they came, which child went to bed too late, and which was frightened of its father and for what reason. She knew which child was jealous of a newly born brother, which one pined for one, which one resented being the youngest. There was nothing hidden from Miss Clare, as both children and parents knew, and better still, she could be trusted to keep confidences to herself. In a village a silent tongue is rare, and much respected. Dolly Clare heard many secrets, gave advice when it was asked of her, and found the study of character endlessly absorbing. Life in Fairacre, she discovered, grew richer every year, and the slow measure that she trod there pleased her more than the giddy whirling of the world outside.

The news from abroad, during the mid-thirties, was disturbing to say the least of it. The domination of Austria by the Germans, and Ethiopia by the Italians were ugly reminders to Dolly Clare of the happenings of twenty years before. Surely such appalling things could not happen again in a lifetime? She pondered on the spirit of hope which had transfigured the world at the end of the first war. Surely the League of Nations could not fail? – it had the support of all right-thinking men and women. It seemed stupid to worry over the childish posturings of Hitler and Mussolini when one considered the forces ranged against them.

So Dolly tried to comfort herself, but she was not completely successful. There was something terrifyingly insane about the

statements made by the two dictators and Dolly trembled to think what might happen if they were allowed the time to gain further military strength. Arrogance unchecked becomes megalomania, and it is impossible to reason with a madman. Would the dearly-bought peace be shattered yet again?

That harbinger of doom, Mrs Pringle, prophesied war for many months before Munich, and at the time of that event spoke scathingly of the hopes of peace makers.

Dolly came across her before school one morning early in the autumn term of 1938. She was spreading newspaper round the newly whitened stone at the base of the stove in the infants' room. Crouched on all fours, in an unlovely toad-like position, she stabbed vehemently with a podgy forefinger at a photograph of Mr Chamberlain waving a piece of paper.

''Opeless!' announced Mrs Pringle. 'Just 'opeless, trying to deal with that Hitler fellow. My mother, God rest her, would have called this a sop to Cerebos. Mark my words, Miss Clare, we'll 'ave to pay for this all right!'

All through that uneasy year, when a nation's conscience grew more and more troubled as one German coup followed another, Mrs Pringle's dire prognostications were cast like black pearls before the surfeited swine. The headmaster at that time, Mr Fortescue, goaded beyond endurance one hot day in the summer of 1939, sharply told her to hold her tongue.

Dolly, washing a child's sticky hands in the lobby, heard the swift intake of Mrs Pringle's outraged breath. Then the floor-boards resounded to the limping gait of Mrs Pringle's substantial frame. It was obvious that her leg, always combustible in times of affront, had 'flared-up' with unusual ferocity. She stumped through the lobby, looking neither to right nor left, mouth compressed and nostrils flaring.

Dolly put her head round the classroom door. Mr Fortescue was alone, scribbling a fierce note to a dilatory publisher who had failed to send some promised inspection copies.

'We shan't see Mrs Pringle again this term, I suspect,' she said.

'That'll suit me,' replied the headmaster grimly. 'It's only another fortnight anyway. At last we shall have some peace.'

Dolly was right. Mrs Pringle sent a stilted note which said that her leg was too inflamed to use, and she did not know when she would be back.

'That means,' said Dolly, construing the letter to her colleague, who had not the same experience of Mrs Pringle's warfare, 'that we must woo her back if we want the school scrubbed out during the holidays.'

'Oh, dammit!' expostulated Mr Fortescue. 'What an old vixen she is!' He looked doubtfully at Dolly.

'Yes, I'll go,' she offered, reading his thoughts, and on the last day of term she made a treaty with the enemy.

'It's only because his lordship's going away,' announced Mrs Pringle. 'Wild horses wouldn't drag me back inside that school if he was going to be prying about. You can tell him from me, Miss Clare, I'm coming to oblige you and because I knows my duty to the children!'

Dolly promised to deliver the message, wondering privately why Mrs Pringle's strong sense of duty to the children had remained quiescent for the past fortnight.

And so this petty storm, just one of many made by Mrs Pringle, passed over, while the storm that was to darken the whole world swept closer and closer.

At the end of August, a few days before Fairacre school, freshly scrubbed and polished, was due to reopen, the evacuation of children from London began, and Caxley and the villages around it awaited the newcomers.

Dolly and Emily went to Caxley station to help. As the long trains drew in to the platform, with heads and arms sprouting from the windows, Dolly remembered that other war, so tragically near, it seemed, when she had watched her own generation on its way to annihilation. Now these younger casualties of a new war, emerged into the shimmering heat, pale faced and heavy-eyed, clutching one another's hands and weighed down with gas masks and cases.

All through the long hot day Emily and Dolly helped to sort out the children, and returned to their own cottages with two apiece. Dolly had chosen two small sisters, June and Dawn Milligan, both tearful and bewildered. Emily, as bold as ever, had returned to Springbourne with a pair of black-haired twin boys of twelve who looked as tough and unmannerly as any among the hundreds who arrived. Dolly had no doubt that Emily would win any future battles. Her own family background and many years of teaching had given Emily a rare resilience.

On the next Sunday the Prime Minister was to speak to the nation. War looked inevitable, and Dolly and her mother sat down with heavy hearts to listen to the broadcast. The cottage door was propped open. Outside, the two little girls dressed and undressed the dolls they had brought with them, and the ghostly Emily that Dolly had unearthed from the trunk in the loft. She was sadly shabby and her stuffing had shifted so that her figure was badly deformed, but the Milligan children took her to their hearts, and Dolly was glad to see poor Emily beloved once more.

The sunshine bathed the children playing by the door, and warmed the brick floor by Mary Clare's feet. The scent of tobacco plant stole into the room as they listened to Mr Chamberlain's voice. At last it came to an end. Mary and Dolly looked silently at each other, both fearful of breaking down before the unheeding children.

At that moment, the distant wailing of Caxley's air-raid sirens began to be heard, and close at hand the banshee clamour of Beech Green's began too. The two children looked up at the cloudless sky with such pathetic terror in their faces, as they clutched their dolls to them, that Dolly's own fears were transformed to fury. It was insupportable that innocent children should have to suffer in this way – torn from their homes, set down among strangers and then forced to live in constant fear! Brave with the wrath that burned within her, she brought the two little girls indoors and calmed them, and when at last they were busy in the kitchen and the all-clear had sounded, Dolly's anger cooled.

In the last war, she thought, she had seen many men go into battle. This time the battle came to them – to all of them, women and children too. Everyone would be taking part in this war, Dolly suddenly realised, and with this thought fear was inconsequently replaced by infinite relief. Somehow, it was comforting to be in it with the men this time.

Dolly had never known anything like the term that began so soon after. A London school shared the building, and overflowed into the modest village hall nearby, a building which had been put up in memory of the Fairacre men who had died in the 1914–18 war.

Fairacre school had never been so tightly jammed. Half a dozen long desks, which had not been in use since Dolly was a child there in Edwardian days, were pulled from their resting place in the playground, scrubbed and polished, and put back into use. Kitchen chairs were set by collapsible card tables, the nature table was stripped and furnished accommodation for six more children, and every inch of space, it seemed, was occupied by the children. At first, the teachers had wondered if it would be better to let the London children and their teachers take over the building in the mornings, and the Fairacre children in the afternoon, but this presented many difficulties. Thus for the first few weeks of the war, Dolly Clare shared her room with two teachers from London, twenty of their pupils, and her own normal class.

It did not last long. The weeks slid by with no expected air raids, and the children gradually drifted back to town, followed eventually by their thankful teachers. Fairacre was left with a mere sprinkling of visitors, the Milligan children among them much to Dolly's delight, and the year slipped away with very little incident.

It was a good thing that there had been this rehearsal, for when, in September 1940, the onslaught began in earnest, the children came flocking back, and this time they stayed. No bombs fell in Fairacre throughout the war, but two were dropped at Beech Green one clear night in 1942, and Mrs Pringle knew why.

'It's the solemn truth,' said that lady, folding her arms majestically across her cardigan. 'As sure as you're standing there, Miss Clare, it was Ted Prince's bakehouse as led them Germans to Beech Green.'

Dolly began to protest, but was overborne. Mrs Pringle, in spate, swept everything before her with awful might.

'He says 'isself as 'e opened up the oven to see if it was all right for the loaves. Twenty to five that was. *Twenty to five*!' repeated Mrs Pringle thrusting her face belligerently towards Dolly. 'And what 'appens?'

'I don't know,' admitted Dolly weakly.

'I'll tell you. Up goes the glare from Ted's oven! Down comes the bombs at *exactly nineteen minutes to five*! That's the answer. And lucky Ted Prince might think 'isself to have no innocent deaths laid at 'is door!'

She stumped away before her argument could be taken up, and the children who had been listening enthralled to this exposition stored up the pleasurable story of Ted Prince's villainy for future telling.

Mary Clare had been in bad health for the whole of that winter, and early in 1943 Dolly sent for Doctor Martin, despite her mother's protests. Mary was in bed with a severe cough and a temperature, and Doctor Martin closed the door of the box staircase carefully when he returned from visiting the patient.

'Sit down, Dolly,' he said. They faced each other across the table, Dolly more frightened than she cared to admit.

'Can you stay at home, do you think? Or get someone in?' he asked. 'What about Ada?'

Dolly thought quickly. She hated the idea of leaving her teaching, but her mother would never tolerate Ada about her if she were ill. There was no one that she could ask. Everyone in war time was busy.

'I think I could manage it,' she answered as calmly as she could.

'Good girl,' said the doctor, patting her hand kindly. 'If you keep her warm and on a light diet, she should be up and about again in a month or so.'

'A month?' cried Dolly. 'Is she as ill as that?'

'She'll probably see us both out,' answered Doctor Martin heartily, 'but she wants cosseting through the winter. Now, don't worry yourself too much. See if the school can run without you, and settle here with your mother and have a rest yourself.'

And so Dolly made her plans and nursed her mother for a month. Mary was an unusually good patient, delighted to see friends and fonder of her wireless set than ever. But to Dolly's anxious eyes she did not look robust, and her appetite grew smaller and smaller.

''Tis sticking in this old bed,' said Mary cheerfully one spring evening. 'Now it's getting warmer I'll sit outside in the garden and the fresh air will soon put me right.'

Dolly lifted the untouched supper tray and went towards the door.

'Bring your sewing up here tonight,' said Mary. 'I reckon that old dame knew a thing or two when she said you'd be a blessing to me. How would I have got on without you this winter?'

'Ada would have had you,' answered Dolly reasonably.

'She ain't worth the half of you,' said the old lady dispassionately, 'and never was – for all Francis thought of her!'

Dolly laughed, but could not help a warm glow at the sincerity of her mother's remark. She returned with her sewing, and they talked for an hour or so, until Mary yawned and settled down for the night.

In the morning Dolly carried up a cup of tea, to find her mother in exactly the same position, with her hands clasped lightly upon the white bedspread and a look of utter contentment upon her face. But the room was uncannily still, and when Dolly touched her mother's enlaced hands, they were cold in death.

CHAPTER 20

DOLLY was glad to return to her crowded classroom a week after her mother's death. The cottage seemed bleak without her warm presence, and Dolly was grateful for the return of the Milligan children. A neighbour had offered to put them up on the day of Mary's death, and they stayed there until after the funeral. Dolly had found her week of solitude profoundly depressing. Worn out with nursing, deprived now of both parents whom she had loved dearly, and low in health through meagre war-time diet, Dolly wondered if she were really fit to take charge of children again. All her instincts were to return to the cheering bustle of the schoolroom, but such weariness possessed her that she doubted if she could ever teach again.

She need not have feared. The comfort of the children's presence at school and the Milligans' at home did much to restore her spirits, though she often longed to have another grown-up with her in the evenings when the little girls had been put to bed.

Emily came over sometimes, but was tied with her own two evacuees and her ageing mother.

'One day we'll share a house,' Emily promised. 'And I'll give you your breakfast in bed one day and you shall do it for me the next!'

'Then it shall be in this house,' Dolly said, 'and you can choose your own bedroom – the one with the sparrows or the one with the house-martins outside.'

And so, half in jest, they made their plans for the future, though each wondered secretly if circumstances would ever allow them the pleasure of sharing a home. It seemed as if the war would never end. The drone of bombers in the night sky, as they set off from an airfield to the west of Caxley, was the noise to which the inhabitants of that area fell asleep. There was a dour, business-like approach to this war, Dolly thought, quite different from the tragically idealistic outlook of the earlier one. It was a job to be done, as efficiently and as ruthlessly as possible, and though the young men possessed the same courage and endurance as their fathers, no poets sang them into battle. Dolly's generation had lived through a war to end war, followed by a period of hopes and dreams. There could be no glamour about this conflict which shattered the illusions of a quarter of a century.

Ada's son, John Francis, was a bomber pilot, and Dolly shared his parents' anxiety for him. He was stationed in Yorkshire, and occasionally Ada made the tedious journey northward to see him, staying at the local inn with other wives and mothers. Dolly marvelled at her bravery throughout the war years. Her robust good health and spirits seemed to thrive in adversity, and she never showed her fears before her friends. She had volunteered for driving with the R.A.F. at the beginning of the war, and spent a large part of her time on the road.

The terms dragged by. After D-Day, in June 1944, some of the London children returned to town, as the war seemed to be nearing its end, but the Milligan children remained at Beech Green. Dolly wondered how she would feel when they too returned. She hoped they would stay for a long time.

At last, in May 1945, the long-awaited European peace came. Dolly's thoughts turned back to that earlier war as she listened to the joyous pealing of bells across the spring meadows around her. This time she mourned no lover. Her nephew, John Francis, remained unscathed, though many of his friends had gone, and Dolly was thankful for this mercy.

In the months that followed, while the world waited for fighting to end in the Pacific and the Far East, Dolly wondered what the future held. This war was not ending with the same firm conviction of an ever-lasting peace, as when the first world war came to an end. On the contrary, it seemed almost as if the thought of future wars was present in people's minds. Mr Willett voiced many people's feelings when he spoke to Dolly one morning.

'Got them Germans beat for a second time,' he announced cheerfully, 'and now I s'pose it's them Russians next.'

'But, Mr Willett,' protested Dolly, 'they're our allies!'

'Hmph!' snorted the caretaker disbelievingly, 'how long for, I'd like to know? Best by far polish 'em off while we're at it!'

It was not long after this conversation that the horror of Hiroshima's bombing burst upon the world. The frightening possibilities of warfare in the future clouded the rejoicing which accompanied the final stage of the war. Now, it seemed, not what kind of a world would we live in, but would there be a world at all, as mankind had always known it? Sitting before her innocent babes that summer, Dolly Clare wondered what hopes she could put before them. It had been much simpler at the end of the first world war. Then she and Mr Hope had honestly believed that the world would be built anew upon the ashes of the old, and that the sacrifice of thousands of young lives had not been in vain. They had been able to speak with conviction and hope to the children before them. But now those same children had experienced a war themselves, and many had made the same sacrifice. What could she say to their children now?

She could only pass on to them the philosophy which sustained her throughout her life. She could teach them to face whatever came with calmness and courage, to love their families and their friends with unswerving loyalty, and to relish the lovely face of the countryside in which they lived. It might seem a humdrum, day-to-day set of values, but Dolly

Clare knew from long experience that they could carry a man bravely through a lifetime's vicissitudes.

In 1944 an Act of Parliament was passed which had an important effect upon the lives of Dolly Clare and those like her. This Education Act meant that almost all the older children in the villages around Caxley would leave the small schools after eleven years of age and be taught together in one of three types of secondary school, grammar, technical, or modern. Furthermore, the school leaving age was raised to fifteen, and this meant an extra year at school.

It was impossible to put this revolutionary idea into practice immediately. Beech Green school was to have a large extension to take the over-elevens from the small schools nearby, including those from Fairacre and Springbourne, and was to be called 'Beech Green Secondary Modern School'. Children who were assessed as intelligent enough to profit by a grammar school education would go to the ancient Caxley Grammar School, as had been the custom for generations. Those who seemed best fitted for a technical school were destined to share the secondary modern schools' amenities, for no technical school was to materialise for many years.

The effect of this step was far-reaching. The children themselves much resented the extra year, Dolly found. Country children have traditionally been early wage earners, and those who were looking forward to leaving Mr Fortescue's care and launching out on their own in a year or two's time felt thwarted when they found that they must mark time for another twelvemonth. For, despite the high-flown theories about the advantages of a further year's schooling, the truth of the matter was that there were very few schools equipped, either in apparatus or staff, to make the extra time of any real value to the last-year pupils. In time this would be altered, but immediately after the war, labour and materials were short, money was needed desperately for other aspects of national recovery, and the schools struggled to put into practice a project which was almost unworkable in the circumstances. Nevertheless, Dolly and her fellow teachers realised that it was indeed a step forward which should, in time, prove a wise move.

Another result of the Act was the transfer of some church schools to the County Education Committee, for the managers had to undertake to bear half the cost of improvements and maintenance. Springbourne was one of these schools. Fairacre's managers decided to continue as a church school, and undertook to find the money for its upkeep.

During the next year or two Dolly found teaching a difficult task. Mr Fortescue was due to retire in 1949. He was certainly ready for it. To Dolly's eyes, he looked twenty years older than he had at the outbreak of war, and the addition of a dozen or so resentful fourteen-year-olds to his normal class taxed him sorely. He did his best to contrive useful work of a more advanced nature for them, but without equipment he could not undertake carpentry, metalwork or the electrical work which they would have enjoyed and profited from learning. He organised an occasional trip to Caxley to watch a council meeting or to visit factories there, but the children sensed that it was all a makeshift passing-of-time, and longed to be in a job where they could be earning money, as their older brothers and sisters had done at the same age.

Dolly was now approaching sixty, and though she was as upright as ever, her hair was snow white and she suffered from occasional twinges of rheumatism. She still cycled daily the three miles from Beech Green to Fairacre, and still looked out with fresh joy for the coming of each year's violets and wild roses along that well-loved route. During the war school dinners had come, to stay for ever it appeared, and this extra duty taxed Dolly's strength more than she realised.

Twice, during the last few years of Mr Fortescue's rule, Dolly suffered a momentary black-out, all the more alarming because she had no warning of the sudden attack. On both occasions she was in her own classroom, the children appeared to notice nothing, and she did not mention either occurrence to her headmaster, dismissing the incidents as the result of being rather over-tired, as indeed she was.

Life alone at the cottage was very quiet without June and Dawn. Dolly had grown accustomed to their chatter and the pounding of their young feet overhead in the little bedroom. She had always prepared an evening meal while they were there, but now that she was alone she could not be bothered to cook, after a day's teaching, and took a glass of milk and a biscuit to an early bed. She hated to think of the empty room next door where first she and Amy and then the two Milligan children had slept. She herself now slept in the room which had been her parents', and very lonely she found it as autumn gave way to the cold of winter.

One windy January evening Emily came to see her. They sat by the fire and Emily told Dolly some surprising news. Springbourne school was to be closed as its numbers had fallen steadily and it now boasted only sixteen pupils.

'And what about you?' asked Dolly.

'I'm to be transferred to a school in Caxley. That dreadful old place by the gasworks that's now called "Hillside Secondary Modern School". Not much modern about that ancient monument,' said Emily, poking the fire vigorously.

'But where will you live?' persisted Dolly. The thought of Emily leaving the nearby village was shocking.

'With Joe,' said Emily. 'It all works out very well. His housekeeper gave up at Christmas and he's glad to put me up in exchange for looking after things. I shall enjoy it.'

Dolly said nothing, but she wondered if Emily really would enjoy it. Her mother had died a few months earlier so that she was free to go to Joe, but the two had never got on very well. He was the youngest of the Davis brood, and a bachelor of about fifty years of age. By trade he was a plumber, and, by the Davis's standards, a well-to-do man. Natural shyness had kept him from marriage, though it was well-known in the family that a personable widow in the same Caxley road pursued him relentlessly. So far he had resisted her enticements.

'You must come into Caxley and see me often,' continued Emily, busy with the poker. 'Joe was always fond of you.'

It would not be quite the same, Dolly felt, to visit Emily in someone else's home, but she promised to go frequently, and begged Emily to spend as much time as she could at Beech Green. She looked at her friend in the firelight. Her hair was sprinkled with silver threads but was still, in the main, the crisp dark crop she had known since they were children. Emily had altered little over the years, and still had the power to give that same comfort to Dolly as the first unforgettable Emily had done in her infant years. This was a sad moment for them both. Life in a Caxley street, no matter how comfortable Joe's home was, could not be as happy for Emily as her own rural independence.

'When must you go?' asked Dolly, at last.

'I start there next term,' said Emily. 'I shall move in the Easter holidays.'

She looked at the clock upon the mantelshelf and uttered a cry of horror.

'So late! Never mind, I've only myself to think of,' she said, putting on her coat. 'When I'm a housekeeper I shall have to take more care!'

Dolly walked to the gate with her through the windy night. The light of Emily's bicycle wavered along the brick path, and the moon emerged from scudding clouds for a brief moment. By its gleam Dolly caught sight of Emily's face. It was sad, but had the dogged look about it with which she had always faced misfortune.

She watched her old friend mount her bicycle, called farewell, and watched the brave little light until a bend of the road extinguished it. Dolly went to bed that night with a heavy heart.

It was a relief to everybody when Beech Green's new buildings were ready and the long-awaited transfer of the older children took place. Fairacre's parents had been vociferous about the scandal of moving their offspring at first. Later, they said it was 'a crying shame they never learnt nothing in their last year' at Fairacre, and it was high time they went on to Beech Green's superior instruction at eleven.

Mr Fortescue had just retired, and as Fairacre was now a primary school only, a woman head was appointed. Dolly Clare liked Miss Read from the first, and the two worked well together. It was much more peaceful with the bigger children absent. Playground duty was far less arduous, and fewer numbers in the classroom meant that it was easier to give the children individual help in a quiet atmosphere.

Dolly was grateful for a less busy working day. She had been obliged to go to Doctor Martin's surgery one day and confess that she had had 'a turn'. The old doctor listened gravely to her heart and shook his head.

'Feel like retiring?' he asked.

'No,' said Miss Clare composedly.

'I thought not,' replied the doctor. He surveyed his old friend with a gleam of amusement. 'Well, take one of these tablets once a day, and try to rest more. I suppose I might just as well talk to that table there, but that's my advice, Dolly.'

It was soon after this encounter that fate struck again. One autumn afternoon, the children were engrossed in making bunches of corn to decorate St Patrick's church next door for Harvest Festival. It was a time that Dolly always loved. She loved the clean floury smell of the grain, and the sight of the busy children preparing to garland the sombre old church. She sat at her desk watching their solemn faces as they arranged the heads of corn evenly together.

It was warm and close, and suddenly the room began to tilt alarmingly. Her heart began to beat so loudly that she felt the children must hear it. She struggled to rise from her chair to open a window, but the last thing she was conscious of was the stream of water which flowed across the desk top from an overturned vase of pink dahlias.

Later she found herself in the school house with Doctor Martin gazing steadily at her.

'I'm sorry,' she whispered.

'Nothing to be sorry about,' he replied cheerfully. 'You can't control your heart's antics, you know.'

Dolly heard his voice as he made his farewells to the head mistress. She knew suddenly, with devastating clarity, that this was the end of the life she loved at Fairacre. She was no more use to the children if these attacks were to become frequent. She must have frightened them to death by this afternoon's collapse. It was not right to stay in her condition.

The room swam before her tear-filled eyes, but her voice was steady when her headmistress came in to see her.

'I shall go at Christmas,' she said, and felt as though her heart would break.

Retirement was something which Dolly had dreaded. To be idle, to be useless, to be laid aside, seemed appalling to her. But when it actually happened, and she had made the sad farewells to the school she had known all her life, and had put a generous cheque from the managers in the bank and a presentation clock upon her bedside table, she found that there were compensations in this time of enforced leisure.

At first she looked at her new clock and thought of what they would be doing in the classroom at that time. Now they would be out in the playground, now they would be at arithmetic, now washing their hands ready for school dinner. But gradually other activities engaged her attention, and she found it wholly delightful to potter in the garden when she would have been marking a register or collecting savings money.

Emily retired very soon after, for she was a little older than Dolly, but still she kept house for Joe and the two seemed to get along very well together. Once or twice she suggested to him that he might find another housekeeper, and that Dolly could do with her company, but he seemed so distressed by the idea that she did not pursue the subject. The friendly widow called as often as ever, and played cards on two evenings a week. On these occasions Emily and Dolly usually met.

To augment a tiny pension, Dolly Clare occasionally took in a lodger. Her first was a redoubtable young woman called Hilary Jackson, who taught her own infants' class at Fairacre school. It began as a happy relationship, for Dolly looked forward to the girl's return at the end of each day, and to hearing the school news. But she soon found that Hilary Jackson's love affairs were too tempestuous to endure, and when at last the girl decided to leave the district Dolly Clare was relieved to see her go.

One or two temporary lodgers followed, but Doctor Martin decided that his patient was doing too much, and finally forbade her to take more.

'Better to have less money than too much worry,' he told her. 'See how it goes, my girl. You'll manage, I expect. Pity you and Ada don't get on better. You could share a house with her.'

'Never!' said Dolly forthrightly, thinking of HARADA in all its ostentatious glory. It now had a billiard room, two tennis courts and a swimming pool, and Ada was in the throes of choosing the third car for the establishment. Dolly felt that she could never fit into such grandeur.

Doctor Martin had been right, she discovered. She went gently on her way with only a beloved cat for company in the house. She was not lonely now, for in a village there are always people to call and be called upon, and everyone was fond of old Miss Clare. Her garden was one of the loveliest in Beech Green, and the little thatched house always as gracious and serene as its owner. The furniture might be old, but it shone like silk; the rugs might be threadbare, but they were spotless, and everywhere there were flowers from the garden to add colour and fragrance to the cottage rooms.

And always, more precious with every passing year, was the friendship of Emily.

CHAPTER 21

OLD Miss Clare stirred in the hot sunshine. While she had dozed among her memories, the June sun had slid round the sky and now fell fully upon her head. It was too much even for Miss Clare's thin blood, and she rose and made her way towards the house.

Heat shimmered across the silvery thatch, and the great pink poppies had fallen wide open in the heat. A bumble bee fumbled up and down the blue spire of a lupin, and the cat lay stretched at full length in the shade of the hedge.

Stepping down into the cool twilight of the living-room was like entering a shady wood from some bright open meadow. The clock said four and Miss Clare spread the table with a white cloth for which Mary had made the lace edging long ago.

Humming happily to herself she went gently to and fro between the kitchen and living-room as she had done ever since she was a little girl of six. Soon Emily would arrive by bus, for this was market day in Caxley and an extra bus drove the villagers back in good time for their husbands' homecoming.

She set out her best china, a dish of plum jam, a plate of wafer-thin bread and butter, and a freshly-made sponge cake. The kettle was beginning to sing as she heard the bus stop obligingly at her gate.

'Must be Bill Prince driving,' said Miss Clare aloud. He had once been a pupil of Emily's at Springbourne and would look after his old teacher well, she knew.

The two friends met in the path and kissed affectionately.

'Come inside, where it's cooler,' said Miss Clare. 'I'll make tea at once, if you like to put your bag upstairs.'

Emily paused at the foot of the box staircase, her grey eyes sparkling.

'Doll, I've got the most wonderful news for you!'

At that moment the shrill whistle of the kettle shattered the peace of the room, and Dolly Clare hastened to the kitchen.

'Tell me when you come down!' she called.

A few minutes later, with the tea cups steaming and the bread and butter on their plates, Miss Clare looked across at her friend. Emily was obviously bubbling with excitement. Her clear grey eyes were as mischievous as a kitten's.

'Joe's given in at last,' she announced. 'On Tuesday he said he'd marry Caroline.'

Miss Clare put down her cup with a crash, and stared dumfounded.

'I can't believe it!' she cried at last. 'After all these years!'

The full significance of the disclosure suddenly dawned upon her. She put a thin hand upon her friend's.

'And you're free? You can come here?' she asked, with a quiver in her voice.

Emily nodded, smiling.

'If you still want me,' she said.

'As soon as you like,' said Miss Clare thankfully. The little room seemed lit with more than sunshine. A great happiness suffused her. At last the little house would be a shared home again. The empty bedroom would be occupied, and her companion for the last years of her long life would be the dearest and most constant friend of all. There were no words to express her joy at this sudden blessing.

Later, in the evening, they sat in the quiet garden and discussed plans. The wedding was to be as soon as possible. Caroline obviously had the sense to act swiftly after years of waiting, and she and Joe proposed to live in his house as soon as they were married.

'I ought to be able to come next month,' said Emily. 'In nice time to help with the bottling and jamming.'

'And to think,' sighed Dolly happily, 'that you'll be here to enjoy it next winter! I still can't believe it's happened!'

They sat there until the white owl from the elms nearby swooped out on his nightly affairs, and the moths began to flutter in the twilight. Then the two old friends walked slowly indoors and prepared for bed.

'This has always seemed like home to me,' said Emily, when Miss Clare came to say goodnight. 'It's lovely to be in Beech Green again. I started my life here, and I hope I'll end it here, Dolly. It's funny when you think of it – the furthest I've been is Dorset, and the furthest you've been is Norfolk. I suppose some people would think our lives have been narrow, and would feel sorry for us. But I think we've been two of the luckiest women alive – to have lived all our lives in this dear small place and to have watched the children grow up and have children of their own, and always to have had our friends about us.'

'I thank God daily,' answered Dolly simply, 'for the same things.'

Half an hour later, Miss Clare, in her nightdress, leant from her window to take a final look at the sleeping garden. The scent of the tobacco plant floated from below, a bat rustled on its erratic way, and in the distance the white owl hooted over Hundred Acre field.

There was still a lightness in the sky and the splendid whale-back of the eternal downs was visible. Dolly Clare looked up to them with affection. How many thousands of men and women, she wondered, through countless centuries had lifted up their eyes to those great hills and there found help as she had done throughout her long life?

Beside her, a few feet along the roof her father had thatched so well, Emily's dormer window glowed companionably. It was good to know that through summer sunshine and winter storm they would share the same roof and the same view for the rest of their time on this earth. It might not be for long, but, no matter how long or how brief their allotted time, it would be a blessing shared.

Dolly Clare took one last look at the night's beauty and then, with a thankful heart, crept softly to bed.

EMILY DAVIS

And some there be, which have no memorial; who are perished, as though they had never been . . .

But these were merciful men, whose righteousness hath not been forgotten . . .

The people will tell of their wisdom, and the congregation will show forth their praise.

Ecclesiasticus, Chapter 44

1 Two Old Friends

ONE golden September evening, Dolly Clare and her friend Emily Davis set out on a walk at the edge of Hundred Acre Field, which lay behind the hawthorn hedge of their cottage home.

It was a leisurely progress; more of a potter than a true walk. There were frequent stops to admire the scarlet rose-hips in the hedge, or to pick a spray of late honeysuckle, or simply to stand, eyes shaded against the declining sun's dazzle, to gaze across the great field to the hazy blue of the downs beyond.

But then both ladies were in their eighties, slight and silver-haired, and the track was rough going even for the young and sure-footed.

Besides, why hurry? Their time, after years of teaching in the village schools near Caxley, was their own, and had been ever since retirement some twenty years earlier. Their days were as serene and cloudless as the evening air which they were now enjoying. The clock, once their stern task-master, had no power over them now.

The two had met at Beech Green village school when Emily Davis was seven, and Dolly Clare, then a timid newcomer, was six years old.

'You can sit by Emily,' the teacher had said to the bewildered Dolly. 'Emily Davis will look after you.'

The dark little girl had shifted along the desk seat obligingly,

and given Dolly a wide smile, made more endearing by the gap left by the loss of her two front teeth.

From that moment they had been friends, and Dolly grew to love Emily even more deeply than she did her own older sister Ada.

The little house which Emily shared with her six brothers and sisters became a second home to young Dolly. Somehow, there was always room for one more child to tumble about in the crowded living room at the Davis' cottage.

The two little girls had shared their schooling at Beech Green School and later had travelled almost three miles together each morning to attend Fairacre School in the next village.

They knew every foot of the road intimately. They knew where a robin had his nest, where white violets were hidden, where there were blackberries to quench a child's thirst and the first primroses to carry proudly home. Their love of nature's treasures was doubly deep because it was shared. It was to be a never-failing source of happiness to them throughout their lives.

They both became pupil teachers, attending evening classes at Caxley, the local market town, and trying out their skills with the younger children at Fairacre.

Their ways later divided, but were never far apart, and weekly letters held the bond between the two friends. The Great War of 1914–1918 brought tragedy to them both. Dolly Clare's fiancé, Arnold Fletcher, was killed at Ypres, and Emily had, perhaps, an even harder blow to bear. Edgar, whom she loved dearly, lay ill in a war-time hospital for many months. Week after week, Emily made the difficult journey to see him, sustained by the hope of his progress to health and their future happiness.

It was a bitter day for Emily when she received a letter from him confessing that he had fallen in love with his nurse, and all was over.

Later, he brought his wife to live near Fairacre, and it was Emily's painful lot to witness the progress of the marriage.

She was careful to keep out of the way of Edgar and his family, but she heard from many neighbours that the marriage was an unhappy one. The nurse had proved a nagger, and Edgar, once so gay, had become sullen with the years. The knowledge distressed Emily, but she said nothing.

The two friends never married. There were very few eligible men left in their generation, and they filled their days busily with work for other people's children. When the time came to retire, Dolly Clare left Fairacre School, and continued to live in the same little cottage, thatched by her father Francis Clare, at the foot of the downs.

A few years later, Emily came to join her, and a period of perfect companionship began for the old friends. Their ways fell together as sweetly as the two halves of an apple, and every day held simple joys.

This evening walk was one of them. They had walked this track watching the corn sprout, grow, turn from green to gold, and had listened to the clamour of the combine harvester as it gathered the grain. The baler had been at work during the past few days, and neatly-stacked piles, seven bales to each, stood among the glistening stubble awaiting collection.

Overhead the rooks flapped slowly homeward uttering their raucous cries, and, in the distance, pin-points of flame on the hill side showed where a farmer was burning his stubble, with thoughts of ploughing to come already in his mind.

The pair walked to the oak tree which stood in the hedge. Soon the acorns would be ripe enough to fall.

'We shall soon see the pheasants gathering round here,' observed Dolly.

'I've always loved the autumn,' said Emily. They stood in the oak tree's shade, gazing up into its gnarled branches.

Emily shivered, and Dolly noticed it.

'It's chilly here,' she said. 'Let's go home. There begins to get a nip in the air when the sun goes down.'

They turned to face the silvered thatch above the hawthorn hedge and, like the rooks above them, made their way home.

The evening was spent sitting one each side of the fireplace. Dolly had put a match to the paper and sticks which always stood ready in the hearth, and a small fire of logs now crackled cheerfully.

'It seems extravagant,' said Emily, lowering her knitting and gazing at the flames. 'And only September! But what a joy a fire is, Dolly, isn't it? Thank goodness, we've still the strength to bring in a bit of firing.'

They listened to a little music on their ancient radio set, knitting the while, and basking in the warmth from the fire.

At eight o'clock Dolly fetched supper on a tray for them both. Thin brown bread and butter, a little cottage cheese, and two bowls of blackberries, dappled with the cream from the top of the milk, made their meal, with a glass of warm milk apiece to wash it down.

'We're like the good rabbits, Flopsy, Mopsy and Cotton-tail,' commented Emily, laughing, 'with our "bread and milk and blackberries for supper".'

'I wonder how many hundreds of times we've read that,' said Dolly.

'Recited it,' corrected Emily. 'We certainly never needed to look at the pages.'

They fell to reminiscing, as they did so often, while the meal was in progress. Their memories were prodigious, and their enjoyment of the follies and foibles of their neighbours, past and present, was as keen as ever.

The meal over, they washed up together in the little kitchen. Emily gave a great yawn.

'I can't think why I'm so sleepy tonight. I feel just as I did after a ten-mile walk as a girl. A lovely feeling really – but just dog-tired.'

'Go up to bed early,' urged Dolly. 'Shall I help you up-stairs?'

'No, no!' cried Emily robustly. 'There's nothing wrong with me. But I think I will go up, as you say.'

She took her book and made her way up the short staircase. Dolly, below, heard the creaking of the old floorboards as she made ready for bed, and the gentle squeak of the springs as Emily settled herself.

Dolly knitted for a little longer. The logs were almost burned through, black and zebra-striped with silvery ash. The cat had taken advantage of Emily's absence to establish itself in her chair. There, curled up luxuriously, it would stay until morning, unless the mysterious noises of the night tempted it through the window left ajar for its convenience.

The sky was clear when Miss Clare made her way to bed at ten o'clock. A great full moon silvered the sleeping world. From her bedroom window Dolly noted the luminous beauty of the field of stubble, beside which she had walked with Emily a few hours earlier. She was reminded of Samuel Palmer's pictures of the countryside. He had caught exactly that eerie moonlight transfiguring an everyday world.

In the distance a sheep coughed, rasping and rhythmic, like an asthmatic old man.

It was very still. The perfume of night-scented stock came from the garden bed beneath the window. Emily, who loved the scent, had planted the seeds that spring.

Reminded of her by the fragrance of the flowers, Dolly went softly across the landing.

Emily had put out her light, but lay awake, gazing at the bands of moonlight across the rafters.

'All right, my dear?' asked Dolly gently.

'Perfectly,' answered Emily. 'What a heavenly night!'

'Can I bring you anything?'

'Nothing, dear, thank you. I've all I want.'

'Then sleep well,' said Dolly.

She kissed her friend's forehead briefly, and closing the door behind her made her way to her own room.

She was asleep within twenty minutes, but Emily, next door, was not. Tired though she was, sleep seemed to evade her.

She plumped up her pillows and sat up in bed. Now she could see the tops of the trees in the garden, the cornfield and the distant downs. Somewhere at hand a night bird rustled among leaves, and in the thatch above her there was a tiny scratching noise. No doubt a mouse was out upon its foragings.

The peace of the countryside enveloped her. Had it ever been so beautiful? Lit by the full moon, scented with stocks, the familiar view was enhanced by the mystery of night.

Emily sat there entranced for almost an hour. She had known that scene for eighty years, and still it had power to move and delight her, to present a different aspect with every changing season, and with every changing hour.

At last, with a sigh of pleasure, she sank back upon her pillows and closed her eyes.

2 Dolly Clare Alone

MISS Clare woke early. The hands of the china clock pointed to six o'clock, as she sat up in bed to survey the day.

The sun was slowly dispersing the light mist which veiled the distant downs. The beech hedge was draped with filmy cobwebs, and the grass was grey with a heavy autumn dew.

'There should be mushrooms about,' said Miss Clare aloud.

The shadow of the cottage, elongated absurdly, stretched across the cornfield. The chimneys were just like rabbits' ears, thought Dolly Clare, with amusement.

The croaking cry of a pheasant came from the distance. No doubt he was searching for a few early acorns from the oak tree. There had been another picking of ripe blackberries close to the tree, Dolly remembered. She would take her basket there later in the morning when the sun had dried the long grass a little. Emily enjoyed a dish of blackberry and apple meringue, and there were plenty of apples and eggs in the larder.

She wondered if Emily were awake, but decided not to disturb her so early. Countrywomen both, they were usually astir by seven o'clock, but Emily had seemed so tired, it would be a good thing if she slept on, thought Dolly.

She rose, and dressed as quietly as possible, but no matter how lightly she trod, the ancient floor boards creaked and squeaked, and the staircase was equally noisy as she crept downstairs.

She opened the windows and doors, letting in the fresh morning air scented still with stocks and damp grass. It was Dolly's favourite time of day, when the world was cool and quiet, and the day was full of hope.

She fed the purring cat which rubbed about her legs, and then set the breakfast table. Next she filled the kettle and switched it on. To have an electric kettle which boiled within five minutes, was still a wonder to Dolly Clare, who well remembered the lengthy process of lighting the kitchen fire and waiting for the black iron kettle to boil above it.

She thought she heard a sound above. Emily might be stirring. She made the tea, and found an unusually pretty porcelain cup, given long ago to her mother, for Emily's tea.

The tea was just as Emily liked it, not too strong and with only a little milk. The steaming fragrance whetted Dolly's own appetite as she bore it upstairs.

She tapped upon the door, but there was no answering call. The cat, which had followed her upstairs, hoping for a comfortable bed, mewed by the closed door.

'I've brought some tea, dear,' called Dolly, opening the door.

Emily was turned away from her, her face towards the window, and the bed-clothes drawn round her motionless figure.

Dolly put the cup carefully upon the bedside table, and walked round the foot of the bed to survey her sleeping friend.

She knew, before her trembling hand touched Emily's cold forehead, that she had been dead for some hours.

* * *

Slowly, Dolly descended the staircase and fumbled her way to a chair. Suddenly, the full weight of her eighty-odd years seemed to crush her. Her heart fluttered in her breast like an imprisoned bird. Her head throbbed dully, and she rested it upon the table before her.

She lay there, felled by the blow, for ten minutes or more. Gradually, her heart quietened and she raised her head. Tears, of which she had not been conscious, had made a damp patch upon the polished surface of the table, and when she raised a hand to her cheek she found it wet with tears which still were running.

She let them flow unchecked, while her strength slowly returned. There was much to be done, but the day was still so young that few people would be astir. For this Dolly was thankful. Her private grief would be unseen, and the last services, which she intended to render her friend, could be undertaken alone.

Dolly Clare had seen death many times in her long life and had prepared her parents for their last journey. She did not flinch from the practical duties which must now be done.

Still trembling, but with quiet courage, she filled a bowl with warm water, collected snowy linen cloths, and returned to the bedroom.

An hour or so later, she locked the house, and walked along the lane to the school house where her friends Mr and Mrs Annett lived.

The leaves were beginning to fall, bright as new pennies on the surface of the road. The mist had gone, and the warmth in the sun was welcomed by Dolly's thin blood.

There was no telephone at the cottage. It was too expensive

an item for the two old friends to install. A public call box was nearer than the Annetts', but Dolly disliked the idea of transmitting her news whilst someone might be waiting outside, an interested witness to her grief.

The school house was peaceful, for the headmaster had just gone across to his duties and was at that moment taking morning prayers, and the two children of the house were also at school.

Mrs Annett took one look at the tall figure, the tear-stained face, and the ineffable air of grief which surrounded the old lady.

'Emily?' she asked swiftly.

Dolly Clare nodded, her lips quivering.

'Sit down, and I'll fetch coffee,' said practical Mrs Annett. But Dolly preferred to follow her hostess into the kitchen. Now that the first shock was wearing away, she felt the need for company.

'I wondered if I might use your telephone,' she said diffidently. 'I should ring Doctor Martin, and then I must make the funeral arrangements.'

'We'll do all that,' said Mrs Annett swiftly. 'Now drink your coffee, and I'll send a message over to the school.'

'You mustn't disturb the time-table,' replied Miss Clare, years of school discipline coming to her aid. But she was overborne.

'It was all very peaceful,' said Dolly. 'I'm sure it was just as Emily had hoped to go. We'd had a perfect last day together, and she went to bed rather tired, but very tranquil and happy.'

'I'm thankful to hear it,' said Mrs Annett, watching the old lady's frail hands twist and turn in her lap, far more poignant than any spoken expression of grief.

'I'm thankful for *everything*,' replied Dolly soberly. 'Our lives have been bound together for so long that we both dreaded prolonged pain and disability for each other. Emily was spared that.'

She rose to go.

'Do stay, please.'

'If you don't mind, I'd sooner be alone. I shall feel better at the cottage, and if you will be so very kind and make all the arrangements I shall be so grateful, my dear. Tell Doctor Martin I shall be waiting for him. No doubt he'll be along after surgery.'

Mrs Annett insisted on walking back with her. She saw her safely installed in her armchair, promised to call again during the day, and returned to make the telephone calls from the school house.

'I wonder,' she thought, as she rustled through the dead leaves at the roadside, 'how long she will survive poor Emily?'

The day passed for Dolly as if in a dream. Doctor Martin, that wise old friend, called in the latter part of the morning. He made his examination, noted the tidy body, the brushed hair and the clean linen enfolding Emily's thin frame. This, he knew, was Dolly's handiwork, and his respect for the old lady's courage grew deeper still.

He surveyed Dolly now as he put his certificate upon the mantel-shelf. Her face showed the ravages of grief, but she was as calm and dignified as ever.

'Any good advising you to stay with your sister for a bit?' he queried.

'No good at all,' answered Dolly, with a small smile. 'This is my home. I need it more than ever now.'

'Very well,' said the doctor. 'Go to bed early, and take two of these pills to make sure that you'll sleep.'

She gave him a quizzical look, but did not take the pills from him.

He put them beside the paper on the mantel-shelf.

'Stubborn girl!' he said. 'Well, there they are, anyway. I promise you, they wouldn't hurt a two-year-old.'

'I'll take them if I can't sleep,' said Dolly. 'You're very kind to me.'

'You wouldn't like me to run you along to the Annetts?'

'No, indeed. I must stay here until Emily is taken into Caxley.'

She put her hand upon his arm, and smiled at him.

'My dear, I'm not in the least frightened. Only sad – and then only selfishly, because I shall miss her so. For her, I don't grieve. She always hoped to go first, and I'm glad things fell out so rightly for her. But I must stay with her until she goes. You understand?'

The doctor nodded, patting the frail hand upon his coat sleeve, then went his way. She might be old, she might be frail, but she had a strength of spirit which out-matched his own, and this the doctor recognised.

In the afternoon, the great black car arrived from the Caxley undertaker's, and four dark-clad men carried Emily down the little staircase and out into the mellow September sunshine. Mute, dry-eyed, Dolly watched them go.

Neighbours called, unhappy and diffident, seeking to help and to offer sympathy. Dolly met them all with sweetness and dignity, but refused to be led from her cottage. Compassion she appreciated: companionship, as yet, she must refuse.

At last, as the sun sank behind the downs, she found herself truly alone. Who would have thought that so much could have happened in the course of twenty-four hours?

This time yesterday, she and Emily had walked back from the oak tree to the shelter of their shared home. She thought of that evening – aeons ago, it seemed – when they had knitted and talked, and shared the company of the crackling fire and the purring cat.

It was another world – but Death had shattered it. She took a deep breath, and walked to the window.

The rooks were flying home. The downs were deep blue against the gold of the sunset. Emily's stocks were already beginning to scent the evening air, and in the distance Dolly could hear the coughing of the one afflicted sheep.

Life went on. No matter what happened, life went on, inexorably, callously, it might seem, to those in grief. But somehow, in this continuity, there were the seeds of comfort.

Dolly returned to the table, took out writing paper and began to draft an entry for *The Caxley Chronicle.*

DAVIS: *On September 20th, at Beech Green, Emily, aged* 84. *Funeral* 2.30 *p.m. Beech Green, Saturday, September 25th.*

She looked at it carefully, checking the notice for any mistakes as meticulously as she had corrected her pupils' work for so many years.

She put it into an envelope, stamped it, and put it on the window sill for the postman to take in the morning.

The house was deathly quiet. She looked about her automatically before mounting the stairs. Doctor Martin's two pills remained untouched, and she ignored them now. She had no heart to warm milk for herself, as she usually did at this hour, and could not trouble to put on a light.

In the darkness she ascended the stairs, comfortless and friendless. She undressed, shivering, and crept into her cold bed.

She had never felt so alone and forlorn, and the night stretched before her, black, bleak and hopeless.

Could she go on, she asked herself? Without Emily?

3 Manny Back's Marrow

WITHOUT Emily!

The words still beat in Dolly Clare's mind as the dawn broke, and she rose thankfully, glad to leave behind the wretchedness of a sleepless night.

She went about her early morning tasks automatically. She felt unusually weak and, grief apart, realised that lack of nourishment was partly the reason. She had been unable to eat the day before. Now she boiled an egg for herself, and cut a thin slice of brown bread and butter for her breakfast. She must look after herself.

There was no trace of self-pity in this observation. Sensible, as always, Dolly now faced the fact that she was quite alone, and if she wished to maintain her independence, which was so dear to her, then she must take care of herself, both in body and mind.

Emily was in her thoughts constantly during the day. Memories of Emily came flooding back. Small incidents, long forgotten, swam into her consciousness, as if to compensate her for the loss of Emily's physical presence.

The name itself had been dear to her for as long as she could remember, for the first Emily in Dolly's life had been a heavy, cumbersome, rag doll, stuffed hard with horse-hair, and much battered about its painted face.

It had been Dolly's companion from babyhood. The doll

Emily was lugged about the little house in Caxley where Dolly was born, bumped upstairs, thrown down them, taken in Dolly's high wicker-work pram on the shopping expeditions in Caxley High Street, and accompanied her young owner to bed each night.

When Dolly was six, the family moved to Beech Green, to the cottage in which she was to live for the rest of her life. Of course, Emily was put into the waggonette which carried their furniture. But a dreadful misfortune occurred on the way.

Emily, who had been propped up in an armchair, the better to see the passing landscape on this great adventure, was jogged by the rough road, fell out, and lay for many days hidden by bushes.

Young Dolly was heart-broken. Even her joy in the new home was dimmed by this catastrophe.

Francis Clare, her father, who was the local thatcher, discovered Emily at last and, full of relief, handed her back to his tearful daughter.

But, somehow, Emily had changed. Rough weather had faded her beauty. Her paint was washed away here and there, and the battered face had become more battered still, so that there was a sinister wryness about Emily's looks which chilled Dolly's ardour.

It was true that Emily was still looked after. She was dressed carefully, and put to bed at night time, but now she slept in a doll's bed and not in her mistress's. Emily had changed, and Dolly mourned for the old Emily she had loved and lost.

Doubly heartening was it then to encounter the second Emily – the small dark girl with eyes as bright as a squirrel's, who took timid Dolly under her wing and made sure that no school bully approached her charge. From that first meeting the friendship had flourished, growing in strength as the years passed.

Dolly was always the quieter of the two. There was a tomboy element about Emily, encouraged no doubt by her lively brothers who dared her to face exploits which she would not have essayed on her own. It was a high-spirited family, dominated by their mother, a busy little Jenny-wren of a woman.

Dolly found the boys' society overwhelming at first. At home, there was only Ada, her senior by two years, as playmate. She was a sturdy headstrong child, with a healthy beauty which Dolly envied. Ada was soon elected as queen of the school playground. For her, the boys were creatures who must pay homage.

Dolly looked upon them differently. It was not long before she came to appreciate the humour and honesty, first of the Davis boys, and later of most of her male school fellows. Later still, when she began to teach, she found she had to guard against this secret sympathy with the boys' point of view. She liked their directness of response. If she had occasion to reprimand a boy, there was usually a posy brought the next day as a peace-offering, and then the whole affair was over.

When a girl needed correction Miss Clare often found that the results were far more complex. There might be no sign given of resentment or guilt. Very often there was a show of bravado instead. But sometimes a mother would appear, with tales of nights spent weeping, or a daughter reluctant to attend school. Certainly, Dolly Clare soon learnt that boys and girls often react differently to the same treatment, and the Davis' household was a sound training ground for her future experience.

All the Davises had a strong sense of justice and fair play. In Emily this quality was allied to an impish sense of humour which led her into many an escapade.

The case of Manny Back was one of them. Although it had occurred more than seventy years ago, Dolly Clare recalled it clearly, and with amusement.

Manny Back had been christened Mansfield Back by his loving parents because Mansfield was the town where their courtship had taken place. Manny was the only pledge of their union, and hopelessly spoilt.

He was a big child. When Dolly Clare first met him at Beech Green School, he sat in one of the senior pupils' desks which had been moved to the junior section of the big schoolroom to accommodate his bulk.

He was not bad-looking in a florid, massive fashion, and his clothes were superior to those of his raggle-taggle neighbours. In the latter years of good Queen Victoria's reign, large families were normal, and clothes were passed down from big brother to the next in line, or cut down from father's, for money was short and, in any case, thrift and ingenuity were looked upon as virtues. A neat patch here and there, or an exquisite darn, were signs of industry as well as poverty. There were plenty of both in Beech Green.

But Manny, as an only child, fared better than most. His father was a boot-maker, and although he did not actually supply all the beautiful riding boots worn by the horse-riding gentlemen of the district, he was generally entrusted with their repair which he did very satisfactorily.

His wife had been laundry maid in good service. Together they saw to it that their only sprig was well-shod and his clothes immaculate.

As much care was lavished on the boy's diet, which was unfortunate for Manny. Whereas the village children carried a homegrown apple, a plum or two, or even a couple of young carrots or some radishes as the seasons supplied them, for their morning 'stay-bit', young Manny would produce a bar of chocolate or a slice of plum-cake for his.

Like most of his fellow-pupils, he ran home for his midday meal and there received much larger and much richer helpings than they could afford. The results were predictable.

Grossly over-weight, Manny soon became the butt of his school-fellows' teasing. A strong streak of savagery runs through every child. Beech Green children, at the end of the last century, could be particularly cruel when roused. After all, it was only the toughest that survived in those days. Weaklings died in infancy, or soon fell prey to consumption, diphtheria and other diseases as yet unconquered by medical science. Those who remained were further toughened by a constant fight against poor food, poor housing, and the stark necessity of competing for work.

Jealousy, no doubt, added to the children's dislike of Manny Back. It is hard to watch a luscious slice of cake vanishing into an already over-sized face when one has only the heel of a stale loaf to satisfy the gnawing pains of youthful hunger. It is hard to see one's fellow-pupil sitting at ease in warm well-fitting boots whilst the damp chill of worn-out soles enflame one's own chilblains.

Manny took his teasing fairly well in the playground, but it was asking too much of human nature for the insults to be ignored completely. Consequently, he vented his outraged feelings on younger children on the way home.

It was unfortunate for Dolly that Manny's house lay beyond her own and that she soon became one of his favourite victims. Fearful of violence, and bewildered by this surprising animosity, poor Dolly began to dread the passage homeward. She watched the great clock on the schoolroom wall with increasing agitation as the hands crept round to four o'clock.

When they stood to sing their grace before leaving, Dolly's folded hands trembled.

'Lord, keep us safe this night,
Secure from all our fears,
May angels guard us while we sleep,
Till morning light appears.
Amen.'

She sang desperately, longing for the angels to be on guard on the homeward way. After all, she reasoned, her parents and Ada could guard her while she slept. Far better to have some assistance, heavenly or otherwise, to withstand Manny's attentions.

If the older Davis boys accompanied her, then Manny did not dare to approach, but more often than not they joined forces with others of their age and vanished on their own ploys in the woods and fields. Emily's presence was a comfort, but no real safeguard from attack. She put up a good fight, using fists, feet and even teeth if necessary, but Manny's bulk could easily overpower her.

Not that Manny took to fighting very often. His methods were more subtle. He was cunning enough to realise that parents would dismiss tale-telling about teasing on the way home. Actual physical harm – a bruise or scratch – might bring a furious parent to his door.

His ways were sly. He would tweak off a hair-ribbon, and hold it too high to be reached by a tearful little girl dreading a mother's wrath. He would threaten the two with stinging nettles. Once, on a hot summer's afternoon, he stirred a wasps' nest, deep in the bank, sending an enraged swarm to follow the girls whilst he escaped over the fields to his house.

He had managed to collect a number of filthy and blasphemous epithets which would have made his devoted parents' hair rise, had they heard him using them. Dolly and Emily found them shocking, and said so. Manny, needless to say, was only encouraged by his success, and used them all the more.

All in all, Manny Back was a menace to Dolly's happiness and, short of telling tales, which she had no intention of doing, there seemed to be no way in which she could take action.

But Emily did.

A day or two after the incident of the wasps, and while her arm still smarted with the stings, Emily vowed vengeance.

'It's not fair!' she said indignantly to Dolly. 'Not fair!'

'But what can we do?'

'I've thought of something to pay him back.'

'Oh Emily,' quavered Dolly, 'it will only make him worse.'

Emily's face took on a look of grim determination, but her eyes sparkled.

'I'll teach him,' said Emily.

'What will you do?' asked Dolly fearfully.

Emily surveyed her timorous friend.

'I shan't tell you,' she announced, 'because you'd be upset, and maybe tell your mum.'

'I *wouldn't*!' shouted Dolly, much hurt by this slur on her integrity.

'Well, all the same, I'm keeping it to myself,' said Emily, a trifle smugly. 'You'll know in good time.'

She began to laugh, and danced dizzily about the playground, her dark plaits bouncing. Dolly, recognising defeat, watched her friend rejoicing in her secret, and trembled for her future downfall.

It was the custom at that time at Beech Green School, for the boys to cultivate a large kitchen garden.

It was worked communally, under Mr Finch's keen eye, and the vegetables were bought very cheaply by the boys. By the side of the communal patch lay a narrower strip, divided into a dozen or so small plots, for any boy who wanted to till a little garden of his own, providing his own seeds or plants.

Manny owned one of these, and had devoted the entire plot to the growing of marrows. Perhaps it was the affinity between the bulbous marrows and his own stoutness which made Manny's marrows grow so remarkably well. They certainly throve, and Manny plied them with manure and rainwater and watched them swell into sleek striped maturity.

The pick of the crops from the school garden went to the Beech Green flower show in September. The school had a special display, and it was considered a great honour to have something on show for parents and friends to admire. Manny was determined to put in his largest marrow.

There was one in particular which was his pride. It was dark and glossy, with a sheen on it like satin, and it was destined to be a perfect beauty. Beside its splendour, its striped brothers looked positively peaky although, in truth, they were very fine specimens as marrows go.

Early in its life, Manny had taken a stout darning needle and scratched his name neatly along its side.

MANSFIELD BACK it said, in tidy capitals, and as the weeks passed the letters grew larger and plainer as the marrow increased in girth. Manny had no doubt that it would be chosen for display, and the thought of his signature emblazoned there for all Beech Green to see and admire gave him the keenest satisfaction.

After the show, the school's produce was carried to the church for Harvest Festival which always took place on the Sunday following the show day. With any luck, thought Manny, his marrow would be placed in the porch, or perhaps below the pulpit, there to dazzle the eyes of the devout.

Later still, the produce would be taken to Caxley hospital, there to be devoured by properly-grateful patients. The thought of his marrow being assailed by a sharp knife, plunged into boiling water, and finally eaten, gave Manny acute pain. He turned his mind from the marrow's ultimate fate and concentrated instead on the glory which was to be his.

One evening, just as dusk was falling, a small figure might have been seen, entering the school garden through a hedge at the rear. It advanced stealthily through the gathering gloom and knelt down among Manny's marrows.

A small hand, bearing a penknife, lifted the vine-shaped leaves beneath which the prize beauty lay hidden. For three or four breathless minutes, dreadful work went on in the silent garden.

Then, back through the hedge crept Emily, revenged and unrepentant.

A week of heavy rain followed, and Manny had no need to pay much attention to his marrow bed. It was some ten days later that he went to water the beauties and, as he was in some hurry, on that occasion, he did not disturb the leaves which covered the prize exhibit. The dark glossy end protruded like the polished barrel of a cannon. At this rate of growth, it should be the largest marrow in the whole show, let alone on the school stall. Manny's spirits were jubilant.

Four days later, whilst he was digging with his fellows on the communal patch, two breathless children rushed up to him.

'Seen yer marrer, Man?'

Manny looked at them with distaste. There was a gloating excitement about them which made him apprehensive.

'What's up with it?'

'Someone's bin and written on it.'

'I know that,' said Manny huffily. 'I scratched my name on it weeks ago.'

'It ain't just yer name,' retorted one of the boys. He waved his arm expansively, beckoning the group to come and see for themselves.

Mr Finch had gone into school for a few minutes leaving the boys to get on alone. Carrying forks and hoes, the boys now drifted across the private plots.

The more vociferous of the two discoverers knelt down by Manny's marrow and lifted the leaves aside.

There, plain for all to see, were the words:

MANSFIELD BACK

and below, in smaller capitals the one word:

BULLY

Grins split the faces of the watching boys as they observed Manny's face. It changed from pink to scarlet, then faded to a greyish pallor. And then, to everyone's horror, Manny burst into tears.

'And what,' said Mr Finch, returning, 'is the meaning of this? Get back to your work.'

'Please, sir,' said the vociferous one, 'somethinks happened to Manny's marrer.'

Mr Finch's sharp eye fell upon the tearful owner.

'Let me see, boy.'

Snuffling, shaken with sobs, Manny parted the leaves and displayed the outrage. Mr Finch looked stern. He then bent down to finger the added word BULLY.

'Done recently,' he said. 'Within the last week or two.'

He straightened up and surveyed the little crowd around him.

'Well, come along, boys,' he said peremptorily. 'Own up now. You are the only people to come in this garden. Who's to blame?'

There was an unhappy silence and much foot-shuffling. Manny's sniffs grew more frequent.

'Blow your nose, child,' snapped Mr Finch. Manny unfolded a beautifully clean handkerchief and did as he was bid.

'At once, boys. Who's done this mean thing to Manny?'

'I never,' said one quaking red-head, known as Copperknob.

'Not me,' whispered several more.

Mr Finch's experienced eye travelled over them all. There seemed to be very few guilty looks among them.

'Who's away today?'

'Only Jim Potts, sir. He never done it.'

'And how do you know what Jimmy Potts done? Did?' Mr Finch snapped, correcting himself briskly.

Silence fell again. Mr Finch's moustache was bristling, a sure sign of danger.

'File into school as soon as you have cleaned your tools and put them back,' ordered the headmaster. 'We'll get to the bottom of this.'

Twenty minutes later, after ruthless interrogation, Mr Finch had to admit to himself that the mystery was unsolved. He could only be certain of one thing. These boys, for once in their lives, were innocent.

Most of the schoolchildren had gone home by the time Mr Finch's class were dismissed.

'We'll see about this after prayers first thing tomorrow,' announced the headmaster. 'You may dismiss. But I want you to stay behind, Manny.'

The schoolroom was very quiet as Mr Finch asked a few searching questions. He had heard rumours about Manny's behaviour, but had had no definite evidence of bullying. What he learned from Manny's faltering replies gave him some sympathy with the unknown malefactor. But justice must be done, and would be done in the morning.

Manny, still tearful, made his solitary way homeward, leaving Mr Finch to think about the incident.

What a simple way of getting one's own back, thought the headmaster, as he locked up the cupboards! Manny would be powerless to hide the incriminating word. Any attempt to disguise it would ruin the marrow's beauty. Oh, yes, this was indeed a subtle blow!

Nonetheless, thought Mr Finch, the culprit must be punished. To deface Manny's marrow, on which so much loving care had been lavished, was a cruel trick.

The next morning the whole school remained standing after prayers and heard the sorry tale. There were a few titters which Mr Finch quelled instantly. It was pretty plain that Manny had few supporters.

'Will the boy who did this despicable thing come forward,' said Mr Finch, his eye raking the back rows where the tallest and oldest pupils stood.

'At once!' thundered Mr Finch. 'Or the whole school stays in this afternoon until we get to the bottom of this!'

From the front row, where the smallest children stood, the neat figure of Emily Davis emerged. Her dark head was on a level with the headmaster's watch chain. Her clear grey eyes looked up into his astonished face.

'I cut the word,' said Emily. Her voice was steady.

There was a stir of amusement in the ranks behind her.

'Silence!' roared Mr Finch, and there was.

'Go to your classes,' he ordered. 'And you, Emily Davis, will come with me.'

He led the way into the lobby where the children hung their clothes. Dolly Clare watched Emily's small figure following the headmaster's portly one, looking like a diminutive tug following a liner. What would happen to her in the privacy of the lobby? Dolly trembled for her friend.

She need not have suffered so. Mr Finch was a just man and, after hearing Emily's side of the story, he realized that there had been provocation.

Emily's punishment was to have no play for a week. Whilst the others rushed about the playground, she was to stand by the headmaster's desk contemplating the fearful ends of those who took the law into their own hands. Alas, it was a lesson which Emily Davis never completely learned in life, and injustice was always quick to prick her into action.

As for Manny Back's marrow, it was never displayed. A lesser giant from his marrow bed gained third prize, and with this he had to be content. Dolly Clare and Emily Davis were not molested again by the biggest boy in the school, on their homeward journeys. Mr Finch saw to that.

Years later, looking back on the incident, Dolly Clare wondered if they had not under-estimated Mr Finch's sense of humour which was so successfully hidden under his stern manner.

For could it have been coincidence alone that caused the headmaster to read the story of David and Goliath at assembly next morning?

4 Wartime Memories

IT was not only Emily's keen sense of justice that Dolly Clare remembered, as she moved slowly about the cottage, trying to accustom herself to the numbing sense of loss. Emily had always had courage in abundance.

It had needed courage to step forward and confess to the crime of defacing Manny's marrow. It had needed courage to stand by the headmaster's desk, dry-eyed, whilst the rest of the school played outside in the sunshine. But, to Dolly's mind, Emily's courage was supreme when she faced the darkest hour of her life as a girl in her twenties.

Dolly and Emily, as they grew up, made very few friends. The furthest they went from home was Caxley, where they went to evening classes as part of their teacher-training, or sometimes to shop for things which were unobtainable at the village stores.

Most of the young men had been known to them all their lives, had shared desks with them at the village school, and stirred them no more than a brother would. No one could accuse either Emily or Dolly of being flirtatious: many, in fact, thought them too prosaic and unromantic. Certainly, the flamboyant novelettes, so beloved by some of their contemporaries, did not interest them, and older women, gossiping by the village pump, looked sourly at the two friends when they passed.

'Heads too full o' book-learnin' to find them a husband,' said one, when the girls were out of earshot.

'They'll find themselves on the shelf, them two,' agreed another.

'Too hoity-toity to go out with my Billy as asked 'em to the fair,' added a third. 'Gettin' above themselves with all this teaching nonsense.'

Jealousy was at the root of such remarks. Most of their daughters were in service at twelve years old, or soon after, and to see Dolly and Emily aiming at higher things aroused maternal resentment.

It was not that the two girls were blind to male attractions. They discussed the pros and cons of the young men around as keenly as the other girls of their own age, and probably more wisely. But, whereas most of the girls talked of nothing else but their conquests and their intention of marrying, Emily and Dolly had many other equally absorbing interests. The children they taught, the books they read, the lovely natural things around them which gave them constant joy, engrossed them quite as much as the thought of marriage. Luckily for them, their work was fascinating, not something to escape from, as it was for so many of their over-worked young friends, at the mercy, very often, of dictatorial employers. If Emily and Dolly married, as they calmly assumed that they would do some day, then it would be for a positive cause, not as an escape from tedious or intolerable conditions.

It so happened that the two friends became engaged within a few weeks of each other. Dolly Clare was attracted, at first sight, by the tall young man with red hair who came to be under-gardener at the big house at Beech Green. His name was Arnold Fletcher, and his home was in Norfolk.

There was something exciting about this young man from far away. He was quicker and gayer than the friends of Dolly's youth, and the mere fact that he found his new surroundings stimulating made Dolly look at the old familiar places with a fresh eye. He shared Dolly's love of books and music, and he brought with him a breath of the salty wind which blew so refreshingly about his native Norfolk. Their engagement was considered an excellent thing, even by the most curmudgeonly of the village folk.

Emily's choice was a local farmer's son. His name was Edgar Bennett and his father and grandfather had been tenant farmers at Springbourne, a neighbouring village, for many years.

Edgar was as tall as Dolly's Arnold, but his colouring was pale. He had ashen-fair hair, and the clear grey eyes which so often go with it. He was a quiet, gentle fellow, and the general feeling was that Emily's drive and vivacity would 'put some life' into him.

He was the eldest son and it seemed likely that he would carry on the farm when his father gave up. Two younger sons were in business in Caxley, and it looked as though Emily would live eventually in the sturdy four-square Georgian farm house set in a hollow on the flanks of the downs.

But to begin with, the young couple were to make their home in a cottage near the boundary of the Bennetts' farm and that of Harold Miller who owned the Hundred Acre field hard by the Clares' cottage.

Dolly and Emily planned to have their weddings in the autumn of 1914. By that time, Edgar would have helped to bring in the harvest and there would be a break before winter ploughing began.

But these plans were made in the spring, a few months before the outbreak of war with Germany shattered their hopes.

'Better postpone it,' said Arnold to Dolly sadly.

'We'll all be back by Christmas,' said Edgar to Emily, consoling her.

The two young men went to Caxley to enlist, one bright August day, waving from a farm wagon, crowded with fresh-faced country boys going on the same errand.

Dolly and Emily were heavy-hearted, but saw the sense of a postponement of their plans. Far better to continue steadily with their teaching while their men were away. Everyone said it would be over before long. Perhaps a spring wedding would be better still?

They were false hopes indeed. Far from being over by Christmas, as the confident had boasted, it was quite apparent, by that time, that the war could drag on indefinitely.

In February, when the year was at its coldest and most cheerless, Dolly came home from school one day to find a tear-stained letter from Arnold's parents, telling her that they had heard of his death in action. Dolly's first reaction was complete disbelief.

Someone as loving and alive as Arnold could not possibly be snuffed out like a candle flame! This was some cruel mistake. It could not be right.

It was the stricken look on her parents' faces which finally brought home to her the awful truth. Even then she could not cry, but went about her affairs, numbed with grief, in a dreadful strange calm which frightened those about her.

It was at this time of her life that Dolly felt the full strength of Emily's support. Her sympathy took a practical turn. She brought her a bunch of violets to smell, or a bottle of home-made wine to tempt her listless appetite. She persuaded Dolly to accompany her on quiet walks where the gentle sounds of trees and birds could act as a balm to her friend's torn spirits.

Emily said little about Arnold's death, unlike so many neighbours, meaning well, who poured sympathy into Dolly's ears but only succeeded in torturing the girl and distressing themselves. The fear that Edgar too might die, was constantly with Emily, but she gave no sign of it to Dolly. Outwardly, she remained cheerful and loving, and Dolly, looking back later, realised just how bravely and generously Emily gave all her strength to comfort her. There was an unselfishness and nobility about Emily, at this time, far beyond her years.

A more cruel blow was in store for Emily. One spring day, when the high clouds scudded across the blue sky above the downs, and the lambs skipped foolishly below, an urgent message came from Edgar who was fighting in France. It said simply: 'For God's sake send me a gas mask.'

The two bewildered girls had done their best with cotton wool and tape to design some poor defence against this unknown method of warfare. Together they had taken the precious parcel to Caxley, cycling through the balmy evening air filled with the music of the blackbirds' song, so that it should go by the quickest possible post from the main office in Caxley High Street.

They heard that Edgar received it, but the gas attacks continued relentlessly. Some weeks later, Edgar returned from France, a victim of gas, and was sent to a hospital, not far from Bournemouth, for long months of recovery.

Emily took the blow well. She was now headmistress of the tiny school at Springbourne, for the headmaster had enlisted as soon as war broke out. Despite the hard work which this involved, Emily made the long journey to see Edgar every week-end, staying overnight in cheap lodgings near the hospital gates.

Edgar was a wraith of his former self. His eyes looked huge in his pale wasted face, and the terrible coughing attacks, which tore his damaged lungs, tore just as cruelly at Emily's heart-strings.

But Edgar's welcome and his joy in her presence were worth every minute of the long journey. She stayed with him until the last train each Sunday, and it was often past midnight when she reached home to fall exhausted into bed.

Throughout the dismal winter Emily continued to make her journeys, and now it was Dolly's turn to be comforter. Once or twice she accompanied Emily, but she could not afford to make the trip very often. Emily herself had foregone a new winter coat and boots to pay the fare each weekend, and Dolly had insisted on giving her money as a Christmas present, so that she could visit Edgar as often as possible.

Gradually, Edgar improved. They made their marriage plans anew. Now they would have a summer wedding.

Edgar was moved to a convalescent home not far from the hospital. It was an easier journey for Emily, with one less change by railway.

She was as blithe as a summer bird as the days grew longer. She and Dolly set about preparing the cottage which had been waiting empty for so long.

The two girls spent the long light evenings distempering the walls and scrubbing out cupboards and floors. There were wide serene views from the cottage windows, looking down over the sloping downs dotted with the sheep of Edgar's farm. They would perch on the wooden window seat or on upturned buckets in the porch, and revel in the last rays of the sun as they rested from their labours. Sometimes, they took a simple meal of cheese and biscuits and would sit outside, their hair lifted by the soft breeze, gazing at the view which would soon be Emily's daily one.

These busy, but tranquil, hours did much to restore Dolly's spirits, and her own sense of loss was lessened by Emily's bubbling happiness. It was plain that Edgar would never be fit for active service again. As soon as he was released from the convalescent home he would return to the farm to work as best he could. His future, it seemed, held no more war-like excursions, and Dolly rejoiced for her friend.

Doubly bitter was it then when the blow fell. One evening of golden sunlight, only a few weeks before the appointed wedding day, Dolly arrived at the cottage to find Emily sitting with a letter on her lap, and tears rolling down her cheeks.

She handed the letter to Dolly without a word. It was a short note from Edgar stating baldly that he had fallen in love with one of the nurses and that they planned to marry as soon as possible.

'I don't deserve you anyway' the letter ended. How true that was! thought Dolly, putting her arms round Emily's shaking frame.

They sat thus for hours it seemed, while the sun grew lower and the sheep's distant cries came to them through the open windows.

At last, Emily rose and left the house, followed by Dolly. She locked the front door and put the key and the letter together into her belt.

'Emily?' questioned Dolly, searching her friend's resolute face for an answer.

'He's made his choice,' said Emily, taking a deep breath. 'I'll abide by it.'

'But won't you try and see him?' asked Dolly.

'Never!' said Emily. 'It's her house now. I can't bear to look at it ever again.'

From that day Emily Davis had done her best never to look upon the little cottage where she had dreamed of happiness. It was Dolly and Mrs Davis who had removed Emily's curtains and the few pieces of furniture which were already put into the downstairs rooms.

It was they who disposed of them, for Emily would have nothing to do with this bitter clearing-up. The wounds were too fresh and raw to bear this added salt rubbed into them. For a time, she spoke to no one about the tragedy, but gradually she brought herself to say a little to Dolly, and as the months and years passed, Emily faced life without Edgar with a courage which was typical.

Only Dolly guessed how deeply Emily was wounded by this affair. Edgar married his nurse one July day of thunderstorms and torrential rain. Maybe it was augury, thought Dolly, for the years that followed were stormy ones indeed for Edgar. He had married a virago, it turned out, and despite three bonny children there was little happiness in the cottage on the downs, and later in the farmhouse which they took over at his father's death.

There was no doubt in Dolly's mind that Emily's tragedy was far more difficult to bear than her own. Edgar lived in the same small community, his marriage under constant scrutiny by his neighbours. Emily was forced, throughout her long life, to keep a still tongue and a calm face when informed of Edgar's doings.

Her love for him never wavered. It was the kind of love, Dolly often thought, which one read of in old ballads, where the woman was called upon to endure all manner of humiliations and tests before her lord would acknowledge her. But in ballads, this faithful love was rewarded. Emily's was not.

The fact that Edgar's marriage was a miserable one added to her unhappiness. Her spirit was too fine to find consolation in the 'I-told-you-so' attitude of many of her neighbours. It was no comfort to Emily to know that Edgar had chosen wrongly, but only an added tragedy.

She did her best to avoid meeting him, sometimes going some distance afield to miss him at work on the farm. Never, if she could help it, would she pass the cottage. But, one day, some eight or nine years after his marriage, she met him face to face unexpectedly, and they spoke a few words. She told Dolly about this encounter many years later.

She was walking up a rough cart track which led to the top of the downs. Spindleberries grew at the edge of a little copse on the chalky lower slopes, and she was on her way to collect some for a nature study lesson next day. Suddenly, there was a crackling of twigs from the copse, and Edgar emerged, holding a gun. He drew in his breath sharply.

'I'm sorry, Emily. Hope I didn't scare you. I'm after jays.'

Emily, speechless, shook her head.

He leant his gun against the green-rimed trunk of an elder tree and came towards her. She looked steadily into his face, and what she saw there made her start to run.

He caught her arm, and looked sadly and longingly into her eyes.

'Oh, Emily,' he said, 'what a mess I've made of it!'

'Edgar, please,' protested Emily. 'This will do no good.' She struggled to get away but he held her arm firmly.

'Hear me for one minute.'

Emily stood still. She was more stirred than she could believe. That steadfast love, which had never wavered, was now mingled with pity for the unhappy man before her.

'I made the mistake of my life when I chose Eileen. Life's hell. I'm not complaining – I brought it on myself. But when the gossips tell you tit-bits about our cat-and-dog life, Em, you can multiply it by a hundred.'

'So bad?' whispered Emily, shaken.

'So bad,' repeated Edgar. He released her arm and turned away.

'I'm sorry – *truly* sorry,' said Emily. 'You deserve happiness after all you went through in the war. But, Edgar, try not to speak to me again.'

Her lips quivered, and the elder tree, and the gun, and the man were blurred by the tears which filled her eyes.

He turned towards her, and Emily saw that tears too were on his cheek.

'*Please,*' cried Emily, 'because – can't you see? I just can't bear it!'

And, weeping, she stumbled back the way which she had come, leaving him there, forlorn.

Poor Emily, thought Dolly Clare. And poor Edgar, now an old, old man. How would he face the news of Emily's death? Did he still remember the girl whom he had once loved, so many years ago?

5 Edgar Hears the News

EDGAR Bennett sat in the September sunlight and surveyed his gnarled old hands ruefully. The dratted joints were more swollen than ever! Fat lot of good that doctor's muck had done him!

He had once been proud of those hands, now mottled with the brown stains of old age. They had held a plough steady all day long, wielded a scythe, harnessed scores of horses, and used a cricket bat, with such skill, that at least one century from Edgar Bennett, each season, was celebrated at Beech Green in the old days.

Now they were fit for nothing but pulling on his clothes each morning, and then with pain, or peeling the confounded potatoes that Eileen put before him every day.

'No need to sit idle,' she said sharply to him. 'Just because you can't get about as you used to, it don't follow that you're helpless.'

He looked at them now, swimming about in a bowl of muddy water on the bench beside him. He sat in an old wooden armchair which had been his father's, close by the back door of the farm house.

It was a sheltered spot, and whenever the weather was fine, Edgar struggled out there with the aid of his stick and looked across the fields which he had sown and tended until ill-health had forced him to retire, two or three years ago.

His son John ran the farm now, and lived in the main part of the farm house. Edgar and Eileen had the old kitchen and two other rooms downstairs for their quarters, and the old dairy had been turned into a bathroom.

One way and another, thought Edgar, listening to the distant combine churring round the farm's largest field, they were pretty lucky. No stairs to worry about, for one thing, but no one knew how much he missed the glorious view of the downs from the window of the main bedroom. It had never failed to hearten him – in good weather or bad.

The fruit trees in the garden obscured the vista, and now Edgar's horizon was bounded by the hawthorn hedge which enclosed the farm garden. It was all pretty enough, he supposed, looking with lack-lustre eye at the dahlias and early Michaelmas daisies which John's wife Annie tended so zealously; but it was not a patch on the rolling downs, undulating as far as the eye could see, filling a man with wonder and awe.

He sighed, and fished in the bowl of water for the first potato. His right hand held an ancient steel knife with a horn handle. It had been new when he and Eileen married at the end of the First World War. Now, the blade was broken short, and it had come down to kitchen work. Edgar found it comfortable to manage with his twisted fingers.

He peeled carefully, getting the parings as thin as possible. Eileen was a stickler for wasting nothing. Even the eyes must be gouged out with the least possible waste. It was a ticklish job, thought Edgar, bending over his task in the sunlight.

And one which Eileen had always hated, he remembered. When she had given up her nursing to marry him she made it clear that cooking was a penance to her. Housework she enjoyed. Her training as a nurse made her standards of cleanliness uncommonly high – too dratted uncomfortably high, Edgar said – and the farm house gleamed from every surface capable of being polished. The place reeked of cleaning materials. If it wasn't bees-wax on the furniture, it was methylated spirits from the rag which cleaned the windows, or the breath-catching pungency of the bleaching liquid which Eileen liked to use for the sink and drains.

Now that the house was mainly in Annie's hands, it smelt less like an institution and more like a home, thought Edgar. The smell of baking pervaded the house. Vases of roses or narcissi, or wallflowers – or whatever fragrant blooms were in season in the garden – gave out their own sweetness. It did not please Eileen.

'Everlasting petals all over the place,' she grumbled to Edgar. 'Messy things, flowers. Spoil the polish.'

'I like 'em,' said Edgar mildly. 'And in any case, Annie's entitled to do what she likes in her own home. Some young women would have turned us out. In-laws don't make the best house-mates, you know.'

Eileen snorted. There was small chance of getting Edgar to take her side, as well she knew. From the very first days of marriage she had discovered that, despite his gentle ways and apparent submissiveness, there was an obstinate streak in Edgar's character. She, who loved to rule, found that there were some occasions when her husband stood fast. Her temper was fiery, her voice shrill. Neither improved with age, but Edgar had grown used to these outbursts, treating them with a stubborn silence which drove Eileen to even greater fury.

Luckily, the three children had inherited their father's nature. In some ways, it made matters even worse for Eileen, for there was no one to answer her with equal fire. Her sharp tongue met little verbal resistance. John, the eldest, went so far as to laugh at his mother's tantrums as he grew to manhood, and his easy attitude did much to help his wife Annie to be philosophical about the old people's presence in the house.

'I'd put up with anything for the old man,' John said. 'He bears the brunt of it, poor old chap. Don't hurt us to have 'em here, if we act sensible, and I'm not seeing my mum and dad turned out of their home at their age.'

The two younger boys, equally mild-mannered, worked in Caxley and were both married. Sometimes they came out on a Sunday afternoon to see the old people, but they did not visit very often, and as neither enjoyed letter-writing, Eileen and Edgar heard little of them, despite their presence within five miles of the farm.

'All the same, children,' Eileen said tartly. 'Ungrateful lot. You brings 'em up and gets no thanks for it.'

'Didn't ask to come, did 'em?' replied Edgar. 'You be thankful they ain't turned out jail-birds or worse. We've got three fine boys, all doing well. What more d'you want?'

Looking back, turning the wet potato in his swollen fingers, Edgar wondered how many days of his marriage had passed without some outburst from Eileen. God, she was a nagger, if ever there was one! What madness had made him take her on in the first place?

A shadow fell across his armchair, and he looked up to see Tom More, the postman. He held out a letter.

'Shouldn't bother to open it,' he remarked. 'Looks like a bill.'

'You been through 'em all?' asked Edgar jocularly. 'Any good news?'

'No,' said Tom, settling on the bench near the bowl of potatoes. 'Got a bit of bad, though.'

'Oh? What's up?'

'Poor old Emily Davis.'

Edgar drew in his breath sharply. Tom More was too young to know what Emily meant to him, but he bent over the knife in his hand so that his face was hidden.

'She's gone,' continued Tom. 'Saw Dolly Clare half an hour back. She said they took their evening toddle up the field, had some supper and Emily was as right as rain at bed-time.

'Next morning she found her dead in bed.'

'I'm sorry,' said Edgar huskily. 'Very sorry. She was at school with me.'

There was a pause. From a distance the hum of the combine continued. Close at hand, one of the farm cats came round the corner of the house, mewing plaintively.

'How's Dolly Clare taken it? She got anyone there with her?'

'Seems all right. Looks a bit pale-like. I heard she was asked to go up Annetts' place, but she said "No".'

'Home's best at times like that,' agreed Edgar. His voice was shaky, and Tom More noticed that his hands shook too. These old people never liked to hear of their generation dying. Brought it too near home, no doubt. Maybe he shouldn't have told the old boy.

He shifted uneasily, and gave a gusty sigh.

'Ah well, must be getting along. You're looking very fit, Edgar. See us all out, you will. 'Morning, now.'

He ambled off towards the gate, hoping that he had made amends with his last remarks. Must be rotten, getting old, thought Tom, turning for a final wave at the gate.

Edgar was still bent over his task. But the shaky hands were not working, and Edgar's gaze was not upon the potato he now held, but upon a vision of Emily Davis, a life-time ago, as he remembered her.

The first time that Emily had come to Edgar's notice was on the occasion of her confession at school assembly. Edgar had been standing in the back row, among the oldest boys at Beech Green school, due to leave in a few months for the waiting world of hard work.

The affair of Manny's marrow had amused them. Mr Finch's threat of keeping in the whole school did not. He was a man who kept his word, and Edgar and his school-mates had too many activities to attend to after school to welcome any restriction of their liberty.

It was with relief then, as well as amusement, that the bigger boys saw little Emily Davis step out to take her punishment.

'Got some spunk that little 'un,' one boy had commented, as they filed out.

'All them Davises have,' said another. It was something which Edgar was to find out for himself years later.

Emily Davis did not cross his path again for some time. He saw her occasionally about the village, usually in the company of Dolly Clare, but she meant nothing to him. He was busy on the farm, and his only relaxation was the cricket which he played on summer Saturday afternoons whenever the work on the farm allowed.

But one autumn evening, when the beech trees were ablaze on the road to Caxley, and the blue smoke of autumn bonfires drifted through the village, Edgar encountered Emily.

It had been a good harvest that year, and Edgar had taken

a wagon laden with sacks of wheat to Caxley Station. When the wagon was empty, he had reloaded it with sacks of coal, ready for the winter, and set off on the return journey. He was pleasantly tired after the heavy work, and looking forward to an evening meal and early bed.

Perched high on the plank seat at the front of the wagon, he had a fine view of the surrounding countryside.

The fruit trees in the cottage gardens were weighed down with apples and plums. In one garden, a cottager was bent over his rows of bronze onions, turning the tops for final ripening. In another, a woman was tending a bonfire of dead pea-sticks and dried weeds. Everywhere there were the signs of the dying year, and the nutty fragrance of autumn hung in the air.

'Soon be Harvest Festival,' said Edgar aloud to the massive haunches of Daisy, the old cart-horse, moving stolidly along between the shafts. She snorted in reply, and shook her shaggy head. She was a companionable animal, and liked the sound of a human voice.

The thought of Manny's marrow, destined never to be the centre-piece of a Harvest Festival, flashed back to Edgar. It was the first time he had remembered it for years, and he savoured the memory now, as Daisy descended the steep hill leading to distant Beech Green.

At the bottom, there was a sharp bend, and as Daisy rounded it, she pulled suddenly to one side.

'Whoa there!' said Edgar, startled. 'All right, old girl!'

On the verge, at the side of the road, knelt Emily Davis beside a bicycle. Her small hands were black, her hair dishevelled, and her hat hung from a spray of yellowing hawthorn in the hedge.

'What's up then?' asked Edgar, leaping down.

'The chain's come off,' said Emily.

'Here, you hold it upright,' ordered Edgar, 'and I'll have a go.'

Emily struggled to her feet, and did as she was told; Daisy wandered towards the grass and browsed happily, tearing great mouthfuls and munching noisily.

'Funny thing,' said Edgar. 'I was thinking about you.'

'Honest?' said Emily surprised. 'What about me?'

'Manny's marrow.'

Emily flushed and looked disconcerted.

'Oh that!' she said discomfited. 'I try and forget that. It was a mean trick really, but that boy got my dander up.'

'You did all right,' said Edgar robustly. He lifted the back wheel from the gritty road and spun it swiftly.

'This chain's pretty slack,' he observed. 'Tell you what. You climb up with me and we'll put the old grid on the back. Can't do much to that chain without some tools, and if you ride it like it is, then ten to one it'll be off again in a hundred yards.'

'Thanks,' said Emily. He watched her climb up to the front of the wagon, as nimbly as a monkey despite her long skirt. He heaved up the bicycle, lodging it securely between two sacks of coal, and clambered aloft beside her.

'Come up, Daisy!' he commanded, and the old horse left her meal reluctantly and clip-clopped steadily towards home.

'Where've you been then?' asked Edgar, making conversation.

'Caxley. At evening class. You have to, you know, while you're a pupil teacher.

'D'you like it?'

'Teaching? Yes, I do – better now than when I started. Are you still with your father?'

'Yes. And I'll stay that way, I reckon. I'll take over the farm gradually, I expect, when he gets past it. Not that there's any sign of that yet. He's a tough old party, thank God.'

They jogged along peaceably. The air was growing chilly as the sun slipped down behind the downs.

'Do you go to Caxley much?' asked Emily, pulling her jacket round her.

'Next trip'll be to the Michaelmas Fair,' said Edgar. He looked at her suddenly. She'd grown into a nice-looking girl, small and neat, with dark hair piled untidily on top of her head. True, she had a black grease mark from the bicycle chain on one cheek, but it didn't detract from her charms, to Edgar's appraising eye.

'What about coming with me?' urged Edgar. Emily turned wide grey eyes upon him.

'Well, I *was* going with Dolly and my brother Albert,' she began uncertainly.

'Tell you what,' said Edgar. 'Dad'll let me have the little cart, and I'll pick you three up. How's that?'

'That would be lovely!' said Emily, glowing with pleasure. 'You say what time and we'll be ready waiting.'

'Good,' replied Edgar. 'Let's say half past six. I'll be there.'

They drew up at the end of the lane where the Davises lived. Their thatched roof was visible a few yards down the road.

Edgar jumped down and released the bicycle from its lodging place.

'I'll wheel it down for you,' he offered. 'Old Daisy'll wait for me.'

'No, don't you bother,' said Emily hastily. 'It's no distance.

Albert'll be home now, and I'll get him to make the chain safe. And thank you *very* much, Edgar, for the lift, and for helping me.'

'No trouble,' said Edgar. 'I'll look out for you on Saturday week then.'

'It will be lovely,' said Emily, giving him a dazzling smile. My word, thought Edgar, she's getting quite a beauty, is little Emily!

She waved goodbye, and set off down the lane. Edgar watched her until a bend in the road hid her from sight.

'That's a real nice little maid,' observed Edgar to Daisy.

Daisy snorted in agreement and quickened her pace, advancing towards her stable and a good feed. There had been enough dallying—that was her opinion.

6 Edgar and Emily

OLD Edgar put a peeled potato carefully in the saucepan and straightened his legs in the sunshine. He had been to many Michaelmas Fairs since that one with Emily over half a century ago, but it was that particular occasion which stayed so clearly in his memory.

How slowly the days had passed after that first encounter with Emily on the road from Caxley! He had been surprised by the strength of his desire to see her again, and looked forward eagerly to the Saturday evening.

It had gone well, right from the start, he remembered.

His father had given permission willingly for the little cart to be used on the Saturday evening, and had come upon his son, during that afternoon, polishing the brass work on cart and harness with unusual industry. The long black cushions, buttoned and horse-hair stuffed, which ran along each side of the cart were dusted, and the bottom of the cart swept clean.

'Who's the girl?' asked Edgar's father, with a smile.

'I'm picking up Albert Davis and Dolly Clare,' said Edgar, trying to sound casual, and failing utterly.

'And who's to be your lady for the evening?'

'Well,' said Edgar, studying a brass stud closely, 'Emily Davis is coming too.'

'Look after her then,' replied the old man. 'I like the Davises. You treat that girl right, mind.'

'Of course, dad,' said Edgar shortly. The old man continued on his way.

The three were waiting for him at the end of the lane where he had dropped Emily after the bicycle incident. She was dressed in a bright scarlet coat, which showed up her dark hair to advantage. What Dolly wore, Edgar had no idea. His eyes were only for Emily.

The roundabouts and swingboats were close by the statue of Queen Victoria in the market square at Caxley. She looked faintly disapproving, standing there among the cheerful vulgarity of the fair.

Naphtha lights flared, music blared away, children screamed as they careered round and round on the galloping horses, and the stall-holders shouted their attractions with lungs of brass.

The din was unbelievable. After sampling all the side-shows, and having taken two trips on the roundabout and switchback, Emily begged to be allowed to stand still for a few minutes to calm her whirling senses. Dolly and Albert were high in a swing-boat above them.

'Come down to the river for a minute,' said Edgar, leading the way, and Emily was glad to obey.

After the tumult of the market square, the riverside was cool and quiet. A little breeze rustled the autumn leaves, and Emily welcomed the refreshing air on her hot face. They leant companionably, side by side, on the bridge, and watched the placid Cax slipping gently along below them, gleaming dully like pewter in the night light. Somewhere nearby, a splash told of a moorhen or water-rat going about its business. The distant racket of the fair was muted and the native sounds of water and trees in harmony made the age-old music of the night.

Emily sighed happily.

'Enjoying yourself?' asked Edgar, putting one hand on hers as it rested on the wooden rail.

Emily nodded, and did not remove her hand.

Emboldened, Edgar put his disengaged arm round the red coat.

'Emily – ' he began urgently, but Emily wriggled away.

'Oh, Edgar, don't spoil it!'

'What d'you mean – spoil it? I was only going to say, won't you come out with me again soon?'

Emily came to rest again, and looked down upon the Cax for a time before answering.

'I'd like to, Edgar, I really would. Only—'

'Only what?'

Emily turned to face him.

'Only this. I don't know if you take out lots of girls – but – well, I don't want to be one of a lot. That's all!'

Edgar laughed, and put his arm round her again. This time she did not wriggle away.

'Oh, Emily! You're a plain speaker, and no mistake. I can tell you truly – if you're willing to be my girl, then you won't have no others to worry about. You're the only one for me.'

'But, Edgar, don't say that! How d'you know how you'll feel in a month or so? We hardly know each other.'

'I know how I feel well enough,' said Edgar soberly.

'Well, I don't.'

'You'll get to know,' said Edgar comfortably. 'What about coming to the dance next week?'

'Thank you,' said Emily, in a small voice.

Edgar bent to kiss her cheek, but Emily, shying away, caused him to land a rather wet one on her brow.

They laughed together, and Emily moved away.

'Let's go back,' she said. 'We haven't tried the swing-boats yet.'

Together, hand in hand, they returned, like happy children, to the bustle of the market square.

Theirs had been an easy courtship, thought Edgar, looking back. There were no lovers' quarrels, no misunderstandings and no parental obstacles to overcome.

That auspicious Michaelmas Fair was in 1913, and throughout that winter and the following spring the young lovers were happy making plans for a wedding the following year.

'Better be October,' said Edgar practically. 'Have the harvest in nicely by then.'

'So I take second place after harvest!' quipped Emily, teasing him.

'As a farmer's wife, you always will,' replied Edgar. 'You know that without being told.'

Emily spent her evenings crocheting yards and yards of lace to edge tablecloths and towels. She still taught at Springbourne school during the day, and most of her earnings now went on linen for her bottom drawer.

Dolly Clare and Arnold Fletcher were also engaged, and the four friends had many outings together. Edgar grew less shy as their social circle widened, but there were one or two people whom he disliked and with them he had great difficulty in making conversation.

Dolly Clare's sister Ada was one of them. She and her husband Harry Roper ran a thriving greengrocery business in Caxley, and she invited the four to supper on several occasions.

There was a boldness about Ada which Edgar found highly distasteful. He hated boastfulness and pretence, and in the Ropers' establishment he found both in abundance. What Harry Roper called 'ambition' or 'getting on in the world', Edgar, with his solid country background, called 'doing down your neighbour', or 'cutting a dash'. Edgar felt fairly sure that Harry was not above using some doubtful methods of making a quick profit – all in the name of good business – and he did his best to avoid mixing with Ada and Harry.

Luckily, Emily was as distrustful of the two as Edgar himself.

'She was always top dog at home,' Emily told him, 'though Dolly's worth ten of her. She did some pretty mean things at school that I could tell you about, but won't. I never took to her.'

In the early summer of 1914, Ada's first baby was born, and Dolly was delighted to be godmother to John Francis.

It so happened that Emily and Edgar encountered Ada in Caxley one Saturday afternoon, pushing the baby in a very fashionable pram. Of course, they stopped to admire him.

The child was plump and pink, his dark head resting on a pale blue satin pillow decorated with lace and ribbons. He was asleep, and in his mouth was a dummy.

'Shall I take it out now he's asleep?' asked Emily, bending over the child. Ada gave her a cold glance.

'No, thank you. I can look after my own baby, I hope.'

'I'm sorry,' said Emily, discomfited. 'I know lots of babies use comforters, but our doctor told me that they can cause adenoids when the child's older. Lots of my children at school breathe through their mouths instead of their noses – and he says comforters may be the cause.'

'Maybe he's a busybody,' said Ada pointedly. 'I must be getting along.'

She swept away up Caxley High Street, and Edgar pulled a face at Emily.

'You copped it then,' he remarked. 'And you know, you did ask for it.'

'I don't care,' said Emily stubbornly. 'That baby didn't need it when he was asleep, and I don't mind betting he'll get adenoids, and probably protruding top teeth as well, if Ada lets him go on with it!'

It so happened that the years were to prove that Emily Davis was correct. Needless to say, it did not endear her to Ada Roper.

'The cheek of it,' she had said to Harry later that day. 'A

spinster like her – telling a mother what to do with her own child! I fairly froze her, I can tell you. Adenoids indeed! She and that doctor of hers want their heads seen to!'

Edgar and Emily were never invited to the Ropers' house again. They were not surprised – only mightily relieved.

They had been happy days old Edgar mused, leaning back in his wooden armchair and closing his eyes against the dazzle of the warm sunshine.

No one, least of all young lovers, bothered about the political happenings across the Channel. The course of the seasons rolled steadily onward. Ploughing, harrowing, drilling, planting – the long days in the fields and farmyard passed swiftly away, and their wedding day was only two or three months ahead. The two were as blithe as nesting birds, when the blow fell.

War with Germany was declared on August 4, 1914, and within a month Edgar was training in Dorset with other young men from the Caxley area. He and Arnold Fletcher had leave at the same time in November, and both came to Beech Green to see their girls. For Arnold, it was the last time, for he was killed by a hand-grenade thrown into his trench near the Ypres Canal, one cold and cruel February day in 1915.

The months which Edgar spent fighting in France were like a nightmare to him. Remembering them now, in the September sunlight, so many years later, they still seemed unbelievable.

The constant noise, the habitual grip of fear, the stench of rotting corpses, the rats, the sea of grey mud broken only by the stark splinters of shattered trees, were so alien to the young Edgar's home background of quiet green beauty that he was in a constant state of horror and shock.

Some men managed to keep up a stout heart, even addressing their dead comrades with cheerful badinage as they passed up and down the trenches. This ghastly bonhomie Edgar found callous and macabre. His gentle nature was crushed and appalled by the sights and sounds around him.

When the gas attacks finally caused his collapse, and he was invalided out of the army, he returned to England with a thankful heart.

A thankful heart, indeed, remembered old Edgar, stirring uncomfortably in his armchair, but a changed one too.

What went wrong with his love for Emily in those dreadful months that followed? To say that his war experience had unsettled him was to make the whole affair seem too slight and uncomplicated. But, nevertheless, that was the root of the matter.

Lying in his white bed at the Bournemouth hospital, he had gazed at the green trim lawns and the leafy trees, remembering his comrades in that grey, shattered landscape overseas.

On some days the English soil trembled with the thunder from the distant guns in France. Edgar rolled his aching head from side to side in sympathetic anguish.

It was as though his mind were split in two. One half was here, with his suffering body, in this quiet room with birds and flowers outside. The other half, writhing and tortured, still inhabited that nightmare world of dying men and hopelessness. Perhaps there was an element of guilt in poor Edgar's mind at this time. Other men were in danger. He was safe. But should it be so? He tortured himself with thoughts of Arnold Fletcher, and other young men who had been his friends at Beech Green, sharing his background, his work and his play – men who had ploughed, sown and threshed with him, batted and bowled on Beech Green's cricket pitch, shared his laughter and his hopes. Where were they now? And could he ever return, to face those who had loved them, seeing the sadness – and perhaps the resentment – in their eyes?

When Emily came on her weekly visits, the first flood of joy at her approach gradually ebbed away in the face of these secret fears. Outwardly, Edgar seemed calm, but Emily sensed that all was not well with him. There was a barrier now across the easy passage of their affection. She put it down to general physical weakness, and to the horrors which a sensitive spirit like Edgar's would find hard to overcome. She never doubted that all would be well in time.

Remembering that steadfast trust, old Edgar groaned aloud, and buried his face in his hands. He should have waited! He should have waited! All would have come right for them both if he had been patient – as patient as poor Emily was!

He rocked himself to and fro. To think that something which happened nigh on sixty years ago could still give such pain!

He remembered his terrible tears when Emily had gone each week to catch the last possible train back to Beech Green. It was not her going which upset him so dreadfully, but the knowledge that he would never be able to face life with her. For in his present state he never wanted to see Beech Green again, or those who lived there.

He wanted to run away from all that had happened, to start afresh, where no one knew him, where he could make a new beginning, leaving the pain and heartbreak behind.

The Irish nurse, Eileen, had comforted him during these outbursts. She was kind and motherly, it seemed to Edgar, ready to hold his hot head against the starched bib of her apron.

Later, he realised, she never spoke of Emily or his return to her.

In his weakness, he clung to her for support and advice. She gave both freely, never displaying the quick temper and sharp tongue which made her so heartily disliked by the other nurses.

In truth, Eileen Kennedy was looking for a husband, and in Edgar she thought she had found one who would suit her very well. She liked the idea of being a farmer's wife. She knew that Edgar would follow his father one day, and she enjoyed country life. Also, she was tired of nursing. She was twenty five and was determined to marry. The fact that Edgar was already engaged weighed with her not at all. Emily she considered a poor thing. Victory should be easy.

She conducted her side of the campaign with ruthless subtlety. Circumstances were on her side. She was with him constantly, and he was dependent on her for all his comforts. She was careful to keep out of Emily's way, when she paid her visits, so that her rival's suspicions were not aroused.

Edgar, weak in body and torn in spirit, gave way with little resistance. Eileen, as a young woman, had physical charms which faded after a few years of marriage, but in her nursing days she was trim and comely, with fair hair neatly waving under her flighty starched cap.

By the time Edgar's convalescence came, and he was moved a few miles away, there was a firm understanding between them. Now there was a dream-like quality, for Edgar, when Emily visited him. It was if she were a ghost from the past – that past he wanted so desperately to forget.

He was too weak to tell her about his plans. This cowardice was to colour his whole life. It haunted him whenever he was unable to sleep, in the long years which lay ahead. He never forgave himself.

Eileen encouraged him to keep silence.

'You aren't up to a scene,' she persuaded him. 'Write her a letter. You can put it all so much better in a letter.'

The little she had seen of Emily made her realise that she would accept the situation more readily with a letter before her. She recognised Emily's pride, and suspected rightly that she cared enough for Edgar to abide by his decision, no matter how cruel it might seem.

The scheme worked. Edgar was freed from his engagement, and he turned to a triumphant Eileen. Emily continued as best she could. No other man came into her life. For Emily, Edgar was her only love, both then and forever.

It was a week or two after his engagement to the nurse, that Edgar first had an inkling of her true nature.

He broached the subject of where they should live when he had quite recovered.

'Why, Beech Green, surely? You say there's a house there for you,' said Eileen briskly.

Edgar gazed at her in dismay.

'But you know how I feel about going back. I want to start somewhere quite new.'

'Who'd have you, except your father?' asked Eileen flatly.

'I expect I could get a job with another farmer,' began Edgar, much shaken.

'Another farmer would want a full day's work from you,' said Eileen. 'Your dad will let you go your own pace for a bit. And there's the house. It sounds just right for us.'

Edgar roused himself.

'But surely, you wouldn't want to go back there, where everyone knows about me and Emily. You'd feel uncomfortable.'

Eileen gave a hard laugh.

'It'd take more than Emily Davis and a parcel of gossipers to make me uncomfortable. She had her chance, and lost it. It's our life now, and we'd be fools to throw away a house and a job ready-made for you.'

'But, Eileen – ' protested Edgar, tears of weakness filling his eyes.

'No buts about it,' said Eileen ruthlessly. 'It's Beech Green for us, so get used to the idea.'

She whisked out of the room, leaving Edgar to his melancholy thoughts. For the first time, he began to realise that he had made a mistake, and one which was to cost him dear.

Old Edgar sighed, and reached for the last potato.

Humiliation, self-reproach, gnawing remorse and a lifetime of bitterness had been the result of a few vital months of

sheer cowardice. God knows he had paid heavily for his mistake! Worse still, he had made innocent, loving Emily suffer too. The encounter by the wood had told him clearly all that he had suspected – that Emily's love remained constant, and that his did too. It had been his lot to see the finest woman he had ever known tortured, year after year, on his account.

And now she had gone.

He bent his grizzled head over the last of his task, and a tear rolled down his cheek.

'What's up?' snapped his wife, appearing suddenly, throwing a shadow between him and the sunshine.

'Sun in my eyes,' lied Edgar.

But he knew that, for him, the sun would never be as dazzling again.

7 Ada Makes Plans

THE news of Emily's death spread rapidly when *The Caxley Chronicle* made its weekly appearance. Most readers turned fairly quickly, after reading the headlines, to the column headed 'Births, Marriages and Deaths', choosing the one of the three divisions most appealing to them, according to the age of the reader.

Ada Roper, widow of the prosperous greengrocer Harry, and sister of Dolly Clare, naturally looked first at the 'Deaths'. When one is in one's eighties there is a certain macabre pleasure in reading about those whom one has outlived.

She sat in her sunny drawing room on this shimmering September morning, a cup of coffee beside her, and a magnifying glass in her hand the better to read the small print.

The house, 'Harada', which Harry had built in the 'twenties, weathered the years well, and though her son John had once tried to persuade her to move to something smaller, Ada was resolute in her refusal.

'Why should I?'

'Because it's so expensive, for one thing. Fuel, rates, furnishings – and so much housework. I could easily find you a nice little flat – '

'I don't want a nice little flat. And anyway, I shan't need to buy any more furniture, and if I did move into a poky little place somewhere, what should I do with all these nice pieces your Dad and I collected over the years?'

'You could sell them,' suggested John.

'Never!' cried his mother. 'No, John. This is my home and I'm stopping here. I've quite enough money to see me out, thanks to the business, and with Alice to help me the work is very light.'

Alice was the companion who had come to live with Ada soon after Harry's death. She was a gentle soul, herself a widow, but a penniless one, and glad to have a comfortable home and pocket money in return for an amount of work which would have daunted many a younger woman.

John, seeing the position pretty clearly, was sensible enough to insist on plenty of reliable daily help. Alice, he knew, was worth her weight in gold as a companion. She was genuinely devoted to his mother and took her somewhat over-bearing ways with cheerful docility.

If she left, it would be impossible to find another person so amenable. John had no desire to have his mother living at his own house. His wife and children were positively opposed to the idea when he had once broached the subject tentatively.

'No fear!' said his wife flatly.

'Grandma? Live here? Oh no!' cried his children. And though he had upbraided them with their selfishness, secretly he was very relieved. If his mother was happy to squander her money on that great house, then he would see that things were arranged to keep her there in contentment. But, now and again, a little secret resentment clouded John's thoughts. What would there be left, when the old lady died, if she continued to live in this way?

John's good business head always ruled his heart, which is

why his parents' shop continued to thrive under his management.

At the time of Emily Davis's death he was a man in his late fifties with the dark florid good looks of his father.

A fine moustache and an expensive dental plate improved his looks as he grew older. As a young man, the slightly protruding top teeth had given him a rabbity look. Whether the comforter, abhorred by Emily, and the subsequent thumb-sucking had anything to do with it, one could not be sure. His mother, rather naturally, thought not. But Emily's words rankled for many years, nevertheless.

John took infinite pains with his clothes, going to London for his suits, which did not endear him to the local tailors. He presided over the shop in well-cut tweeds or worsteds, his dark hair carefully brushed, his expensive shoes as glossy as horse chestnuts.

His wife looked across the breakfast table, on this September morning, and thought how remarkably young he looked as he read *The Caxley Chronicle*.

'I see Aunt Dolly's Emily has gone,' he said, eyes fixed upon the paper.

'Poor old thing,' said his wife perfunctorily. 'But she must have been terribly old.'

'About the same age as mother, I should guess. They were at school together, I know.'

'What will happen to Aunt Dolly?'

John lowered the paper thoughtfully.

'I don't know. I really don't know.'

He rose, tugging at his jacket and smoothing his hair.

'She really shouldn't be alone there,' said his wife solicitously. 'Anything might happen.'

'I might drive over and see her,' said John, kissing her swiftly. 'It's rotten getting old. This'll cut up Aunt Dolly badly.'

During the day he turned over in his mind the possibilities for Dolly Clare.

Could she be persuaded, he wondered, to leave the Beech Green cottage and make her home at 'Harada'? There were points in favour of such a move.

For one thing, it would be further company for his mother, and if anything happened to Alice then Dolly, presumably, would still be there. It was another hedge against the possibility of his mother having to live in his own house some day.

Again, Dolly's little cottage, humble though it was, was exceedingly pretty, and just the sort of place which was being snapped up by Londoners looking for a weekend cottage. A similar one at Fairacre, John remembered with a glow of pleasure, fetched five thousand pounds last month. The money could be invested and add to Aunt Dolly's tiny pension, thought John solicitously.

Besides, it would be keeping the money in the family.

He spent much of the day working out little sums – the possible interest that Dolly Clare would get on her problematical gains, if invested wisely – and it was almost time to leave the shop before he faced the cold fact that Dolly might not wish to sell, and that his mother might prefer to have 'Harada' to herself.

He determined to go and see his mother that evening and to make a few delicate enquiries.

Meanwhile, Ada too had been thinking. This death of Emily created some problems. She was honest enough to admit to herself that she did not feel any grief on Emily's behalf. There had never been any love lost between the two.

Even now, Ada felt resentment at the way Emily had usurped her own place in young Dolly's affections. As little children in Caxley, Dolly had always followed Ada's lead. She adored her elder sister, and had been content to do her bidding without question.

But things had changed under the influence of the Davis family, and particularly with the growth of the friendship between Emily and Dolly. Now Ada was not always right. Dolly began to question some of her decisions, and to ask Emily's opinion before her sister's. Ada considered Emily a subversive influence, and, as she grew older, she found no reason to change her views.

Then there was the affair of Manny's marrow which had made young Emily a minor heroine. The boys' attention had been diverted from Ada, the queen of the playground at Beech Green School, and although it was only a temporary defection, it gave Ada further cause to dislike Emily.

Later still, when Ada was a young mother, and not long after the little contretemps of the baby's dummy, Emily played a more important part in Ada's life. It was an episode which she remembered with shame for the rest of her life, and Emily's attitude at the time did little to assuage Ada's guilt.

Even now, over half a century later, she shied away from the remembrance, although she knew from experience that it would return before long to haunt her. Did Emily ever tell? Did Dolly ever know?

The anxiety pricked her as keenly now as it had so many years ago. And she would never know the answers! Sometimes the old Jewish God of Retribution seemed very real to Ada.

The thought of Dolly brought more practical problems to her mind. She would be left alone in the little house at Beech Green, and would be worse off without Emily's financial help in the partnership they had so much enjoyed.

It was all very tiresome, thought Ada with exasperation. She supposed she ought to invite her to 'Harada'. It would be expected of her, by her local friends, she had no doubt, and when one was so well respected in the church, and particularly in the Mothers' Union, it behoved one to act correctly.

But why should she alter her comfortable way of life to accommodate a sister who really meant very little to her? They had gone their own ways for so long, that, despite a proper sisterly warmth when they met, they had little in common.

Would Dolly mix comfortably with the prosperous widows who still came occasionally to play bridge in Ada's drawing room? She was far more likely, thought Ada, to sit in a corner, like a death's head at a feast, while the chatter went on, making everyone self-conscious.

And how would Alice like it? After all, she must consider Alice's feelings. She might very well feel hurt at another person coming to live at the house, on intimate terms. And, of course, it would make more work. There would be another bed to cope with, more laundry, more heating in the bedroom, more vegetables to peel, more meat to buy. Really, the more one thought of it, the greater the problem became.

She was restless and irritable throughout the day, wondering what to do. She wanted to appear generous in the sight of the little world of Caxley, but she very much resented the discomfort and expense it might put her to.

So like Emily, she thought distractedly, to go first, and leave such a muddle for others to tidy up!

Perhaps John might be of help. She determined to telephone him, as soon as he returned from the shop. After all, Dolly was his godmother, as well as his aunt. He should give her some attention at this difficult time. It was all too much for Ada alone.

Really, she felt quite faint with worry about it. She went to the drawing room door and called Alice.

'Could we have tea early, dear? My poor head's throbbing. Jam and cream with the scones, Alice dear.'

But there was no need to make a telephone call, for John appeared very soon after the meal had been dispatched, and broached the painful subject with masculine frankness.

'Bad news about Emily Davis. You saw it, I expect, in the paper?'

'I don't know what's bad about dying in your eighties,' said Ada tartly. 'Surely it's only to be expected. I know I feel very near my end often enough.'

John sensed from this reply that his mother was in one of her difficult moods. The dash of self-pity in her last sentence was always a danger sign.

He patted her hand kindly.

'You're a wonderful old lady,' he assured her. 'Lots of happy years ahead for you.'

She allowed herself to be slightly mollified.

'Yes, well – I suppose I do keep pretty bright, considering. But it's always a shock when one of your own generation goes.'

'Aunt Dolly will miss her,' said John, approaching the subject of his schemes warily.

'Bound to,' agreed Ada. She brushed a scone crumb from

her lap and considered how best to put her difficulties to John.

'She shouldn't be alone,' said John. 'Not at her age.'

'No,' said Ada. 'Not at her age. And she's never been really robust. She was always the weakling of the two of us.'

'It's a problem.'

'It certainly is.'

'I take it she'll be pretty hard up?'

'No doubt about it. They shared expenses, of course, which helped them both.'

John stood up and balanced himself first on his toes and then on his heels. It was a habit he had had since childhood, and indicative of mental unrest. Ada found it irritating.

'Don't keep rocking, John.'

'Sorry, mother,' he said, standing stock still. 'It's just that I'm a bit worried about poor Aunt Dolly. She is my godmother, you know.'

'I know well enough,' snapped his mother, resenting the reproachful note in John's voice. 'And you're not the only one to be worried. I've been almost distracted, wondering what to do for the best, all day today.'

John felt that some progress was being made.

'What had you in mind?'

'Well, naturally, as she's my only sister, my first thought was to invite her here.'

'That's very generous of you, mother. But do you think you are up to it?'

Ada sighed heavily.

'We all have to make sacrifices at times like this. And no doubt Dolly would appreciate it.'

'I'm sure she would be most grateful.'

'But then – I don't know. It would be such a complete

change in her way of life, wouldn't it? And we're so far here from the shops and things. Have you considered having her at your house? She is your godmother, you know.'

John, though taken aback at this surprise attack, rallied well.

'Out of the question,' he replied swiftly. 'No spare room, for one thing, and then I think Aunt Dolly would find the children too much for her.'

'Humph!' snorted Ada, thwarted. A short silence ensued.

'If she *did* leave Beech Green, I think she would get a very good price for the cottage,' said John at last. His mother's love of money was as strong as his own. He could have found no surer way of diverting her attention.

'Would she now?' said his mother speculatively. 'How much should you think?'

'Somewhere in the region of five thousand.'

Ada nodded slowly.

'She'd need some of that to see her fixed comfortably for the rest of her life, of course – ' Her voice trailed away.

'Naturally, naturally,' agreed John hastily. 'Properly invested it should bring in a nice little sum for the next few years.'

He cleared his throat fussily.

'How old is dear Aunt Dolly now?' he asked in a would-be casual tone.

'Eighty-four,' said Ada shortly.

'She's made a will, I hope?'

'I believe so. I know if she went first, the house was to be Emily's.'

'Really?' John sounded startled. 'And now what happens?'

'I'm not sure, but I've an idea it might go to a niece of Emily's.'

It was John's turn to sigh.

'Ah well, she must do as she likes with her own property, of course, but I do hope she isn't making a mistake. Well, mother, how do you feel about inviting her here? Would you be happy about it?'

'I must think it over. I'm sure poor Dolly would enjoy the greater comfort she'd get here, and she'd have company, of course, but it would mean a lot of extra work. Not that I'd mind that – I've worked all my life – but I shouldn't like to place a burden on Alice.'

'Of course not,' agreed John. 'You think it over, my dear, and give me a ring, before you write to Aunt Dolly.'

He kissed her cheek and departed, leaving her to her thoughts.

* * *

Five thousand, thought Ada. It was worth keeping in the family. She reviewed the situation anew. There were arguments for and against inviting Dolly to 'Harada'. She pondered on the problem in the gathering dusk.

At last she came to a decision. She would write to Dolly expressing sympathy, and telling her that she could make her home in Caxley should she wish to do so. Then, in all truth, she could tell her friends that she had invited Dolly to live with her, and any money would be wisely invested for her maintenance. John would see to that.

She went to her writing desk and wrote swiftly in her large, bold hand.

Dear Dolly,

I was most distressed to hear about poor Emily and hasten to send my deepest sympathy.

You can guess how worried I am to know you are quite alone now. Should you care to come and stay here with me, you know you would be most welcome. For a short visit, if you prefer it, to see how you like it here, but with a view to living here permanently, I mean.

The back bedroom is very comfortable, although it is facing north, and the little box room next door could be turned into a snug little sitting room, if you like the idea.

I know you wouldn't want to be idle, and Alice and I would welcome your help in running the house.

Do think it over. I know John would be very happy to give you any help in disposing of your furniture and so on, if the need arises.

With love from,
Ada.

She glanced at the clock. If Alice hurried, she could catch the last outgoing post at the main office in the High Street.

She stuck on a stamp with an energetic banging, and called imperiously for Alice.

When she was safely dispatched on her hurried errand, Ada rang John to tell him what she had done.

He was a trifle annoyed that she had written without consulting him again, but he was resigned to his mother's high-handed and impetuous methods.

'Well, we'll have to wait and see now, won't we?' was all he found to say.

But as he put the receiver down, he had a strong feeling that Aunt Dolly's cottage would never be his.

He was right.

Two mornings later, he called to see his mother, who handed him Dolly's reply in silence.

My dear Ada,

Your kind sympathy is very much appreciated. I miss dear Emily more than I can say, as you may imagine, and because of that I am doubly grateful for your kind suggestion of sharing your home with me.

It is a very generous gesture, Ada dear, and I have thought about the matter seriously. However, I am determined to stay here, where I am so happy, and I am lucky enough to have good neighbours who will always help me, I know.

Perhaps John would bring you out to tea one day when things are more settled, and I can thank you both properly for all your concern for my welfare.

Your loving sister,
Dolly.

'That's that then,' said John, returning the letter. They both sighed. John for the loss of a dream; his mother with secret relief.

8 Did Emily Tell?

ADA'S relief was genuine. There would have been many drawbacks to Dolly's presence in the house. Perhaps the most irksome would have been the constant nagging query in her own mind: 'Did Dolly know?'

What was this guilty memory which worried Ada so unduly after so many years? And what part did Emily Davis play in it?

It was the age-old story of a boy and a girl, and it all began when Ada went, as a young girl, to live with her grandparents in Caxley.

She had a job in a flourishing draper's shop in the High Street, and her bright good looks and flirtatious ways brought many a young man into her department.

She had many admirers, and among them was the younger son of Septimus Howard, whose baker's shop stood in the market square.

Leslie Howard was dark, gay and a lady-killer. He worked hard with his father and brother Jim, and drove a smart baker's cart on the rounds outside Caxley. Leslie Howard was known well in the neighbourhood. He was a great favourite with the young of both sexes; a charmer who had inherited the dark looks of his gipsy mother.

The older generation, particularly those sober chapel-goers who respected his father Sep Howard, shook their heads over

Leslie's goings-on, and warned their daughters about trusting such a flighty-minded young man. If anything, this increased Leslie's fascination in their eyes.

It was not long before bold Ada caught Leslie's eye, and he took to meeting her as soon as the shop closed. Ada was careful to say nothing about the meetings to her aged grandparents, but, of course, in a town of Caxley's size, the word soon went round.

In the meantime, however, the two young people enjoyed each other's company. Sometimes, Leslie made an excuse to take the baker's cart out in the evening, on the pretext of a forgotten delivery. He would pick up Ada, waiting in a quiet lane, and they would spend a blissful few hours before returning.

They attended several local dances held in the Corn Exchange. They were both fine dancers, and grew accustomed to much open admiration on the floor.

It was on one of these occasions that Ada's quick temper betrayed her. Another market square family, the young Norths, were present at the dance. Bertie North had brought his younger sister Winifred, whose pale blue frock and silver ribbons were more splendid than any other gown to be seen at the dance.

Leslie turned his attentions to his old friend Winnie, and danced with her far more frequently than Ada thought suitable. It was true that kind-hearted Bertie had taken pity on her, but Ada, becoming crosser as the evening wore on, decided that Bertie was simply patronising her.

Her anger grew. The Norths were a prosperous family. The father, Bender North, had a thriving ironmongery business in the square, and Hilda North, his wife, could afford to dress well and to see her children beautifully clothed.

Ada considered the family 'stuck up.' In those days of class consciousness, she felt that the Norths were above her. The Howards were poorer, and with Leslie she felt comfortable. Bertie's good clothes and gentle manners made Ada feel rebellious and discomfited.

It was the beginning of the end of the affair between Leslie and Ada, but although they rarely met after the dance, there was a strong personal bond between them. They both possessed outstanding vitality, and the attraction they felt for each other did not grow less by being pushed underground.

Ada heard of his subsequent marriage to Winnie North with secret envy, although by that time she too was married to Harry Roper, and was the mother of a baby son.

Leslie came into Ada's life again during the 1914-1918 war. She met him, quite by chance, one bright October evening as she walked along the tow path by the gently flowing Cax.

Baby John was safely in bed, looked after by a little maid-of-all-work who lived over the shop with Ada. Harry was serving in Italy, and from his boisterous letters seemed to be happy in the army.

Ada was bored and lonely. She worked hard in the shop all day, but when she had locked its door, and she had shared a meal with the little maid and kissed young John 'Goodnight', she took a brisk walk before darkness fell. Partly she felt the need for exercise and fresh air, but even more strongly she needed to pass away the long hours of evening time.

In war-time in Caxley, there were very few social occasions. With the young men gone, there were no dances or socials – nothing to give Ada the stimulus she loved.

She had a wardrobe packed with pretty clothes, for Harry was a generous husband, but no occasion to wear them. There were long ankle-length gowns trimmed with lace insertion and rows of diminutive buttons. There were smart fitted coats with fur at the hem and frogging across the front. There were several muffs to match the coats; and in a separate cupboard stood a dozen or more beautiful hats, some trimmed with feathers, or laden with silken flowers, or edged with fur or swansdown. Perched above Ada's bright gold hair, well-skewered with hat pins for safety, they crowned Ada's beauty with added glory. She mourned the fact that in war-time there were so few times when she could dazzle Caxley with such finery.

She met Leslie face to face as she took her walk along the tow-path, and her heart leapt at the sight of him. He looked even more dashing than usual in uniform.

He held out both hands, and she put hers into them. They stood looking at each other, without speaking for a full minute.

Beside them the Cax gurgled. A few leaves fluttered down upon its silky surface and were borne away. The dry reeds whispered as the slow current moved them, and nearby a moorhen piped to its mate.

'Ada,' said Leslie, at last, very low, 'I've been longing to see you again.'

'I've missed you,' replied Ada simply.

She turned to walk beside him. It was as though no rift had ever occurred between them. In that one short minute, they were once again in complete accord.

'I've ten days leave,' said Leslie, matching his step to hers. 'Can I see you again?'

'I usually come here for a walk about this time,' said Ada.

Neither said a word about wife or husband. There were no

enquiries about their respective families, no polite small talk about the town or general matters.

Both knew instinctively that the feeling between them was too strong to be denied, and time was short. To be in the presence of the other was all that mattered.

For the next few days, Ada lived in a state of feverish excitement which she found difficult to conceal. She met Leslie each evening, sometimes by the Cax, sometimes in a quiet lane where prying eyes would not see them.

Leslie's leave ended at the weekend, and he persuaded Ada, with very little difficulty, to go away with him on the Saturday before he reported to his unit on the Sunday night.

'But Winnie?' said Ada, speaking at last of his young wife.

'She thinks I have to be back on Saturday. We can go to Bournemouth. No one knows us there. I know a decent hotel.'

Ada's heart leapt. Here was excitement, a change from stuffy Caxley and the dreary round of keeping the shop going. The thought of the neglected gowns in the wardrobe, now to see the light of day again, made her eyes sparkle.

Leslie kissed her swiftly.

'We can go on the morning train, travelling separately until we change at the junction, in case there are any old codgers who might tell tales.'

They laughed together. They were like two children, plotting mischief. To neither of them occurred the possibility of wrong-doing or disloyalty to their partners. They were perfectly matched in selfishness and animal vitality.

The plan worked smoothly. Ada left little John with his doting grandparents, on the pretext that an ageing aunt of Harry's wanted to see her in Sussex, and she felt that she must make the journey for Harry's sake.

As arranged, Ada made her way to the head of the platform, assiduously avoiding looking at the further end where a soldierly figure waited, his eyes, apparently, gazing down the line.

Leslie had made his farewells to Winnie at home, begging her not to upset herself by saying farewell in public. Winnie, touched by his thoughtfulness, had agreed to his plan.

The train arrived in a flurry of steam and smoke. Doors banged, porters shouted, the guard blew his whistle shrilly and waved his flag.

At that moment, a small figure hurtled from the booking office, wrenched open the nearest third-class door, and leapt inside.

Emily Davis had caught the train by the skin of her teeth yet again.

She was on her weekly pilgrimage to see Edgar in hospital at Bournemouth. At this time, she was acting headmistress at the little school at Springbourne, for her headmaster was in the army, and as it happened, was fated never to go back to Springbourne. On his safe return at the war's end, he moved to a larger school, and Emily continued as headmistress in her own right.

Running the school while he was away in the army was a heavy task for Emily, but one which she tackled with her customary energy. The hardest part was the journey back and forth each weekend to see poor Edgar.

His progress was so pathetically slow. The gas attacks had affected his lungs, and a painful cough persisted. He seemed to live for the week-ends, and Emily travelled on Saturday morning and returned on the last train on Sunday.

This meant that all her domestic work had to be fitted in during the evenings or very early on Saturday morning. The school house at Springbourne was small, but inconvenient. Water had to be wound up from a well in the garden. The bath was a zinc one which hung at the side of the garden shed, and had to be carried into the kitchen, there to be filled from hot saucepans and kettles bubbling on the kitchen range.

Emptying the bath was almost as great a labour as filling it.

Emily overcame all these difficulties effortlessly. After all, this was the way in which she had been brought up as one of a large and cheerful family. But she wished, sometimes, that Edgar were nearer, for the journey was tedious and involved precious money as well as precious time.

On this particular morning, she changed as usual at the junction, and whilst she was collecting her hand luggage together, she saw Ada, exquisitely wrapped in a fur-trimmed coat, with a hat and muff to match, moving swiftly towards a waiting figure. They linked arms and, heads together, made their way to the waiting train.

Emily recognised Leslie Howard. It was plain from their behaviour that they were completely engrossed in each other.

Emily hung back out of sight, and quickly climbed into an empty carriage at some distance from the couple. She did not want to embarrass them, and she also needed to mark some tests of the children's which she had brought with her in her bag.

But as she put the ticks and crosses automatically against the answers, Emily's bewildered brain tried to take in the full import of this meeting.

At Bournemouth she waited until the couple had gone

through the barrier, and then gave in her ticket and made her way straight to the hospital.

Edgar's eyes lit up when he saw her walking down the ward. She kissed him gently and let him tell her all his hospital news – what the doctor said that morning, what meals they had been given, the excitement of a visiting soprano who had made their heads ache with patriotic songs.

Emily gave him the Springbourne news and the little presents of farm butter, brown eggs and late roses from his family. But she said nothing of Ada and Leslie.

She stayed nearby in a shabby house which supplied bed and breakfast for a small sum. The woman was kind, but too busy to take much interest in her lodgers. There was nowhere to sit, and Emily was accustomed to walking along the promenade or looking at the windows of the shut shops on Sunday morning, until it was time to visit Edgar again.

This Sunday morning was clear and sunny. The sea air was heady, the sea-gulls cut white zig-zags across the blue sky, screaming the while. Emily gulped down the salty air, revelling in the fresh breeze on her face. A bright October day had a flavour all its own. Here, by the sparkling sea, everything was extra sharp and beautiful.

She went at a brisk pace, but presently slowed up. In front of her strolled Ada and Leslie. His arm was round her waist. Her head was almost upon his shoulder. They might have been a honeymoon couple. Passers-by looked at them fondly and with some sympathy. So many young men in uniform came here for their leave, and many of them never returned to England again. Let them enjoy life, said their indulgent smiles, while they can!

Emily was about to turn round and escape when, to her

horror, they turned too. She was conscious of Ada's eyes upon her – eyes which widened in surprise. Emily bolted toward the rail of the promenade and, leaning over, gazed out to sea. She did not dare to move for a full five minutes.

When at last she turned, she saw the pair far away in the distance. They were as lovingly entwined as ever.

Emily made her way thoughtfully to see Edgar.

Ada was perturbed by the encounter.

'That was Emily Davis,' she told Leslie when they were out of earshot.

'And who's she?'

'Dolly's friend. Teaches at Springbourne.'

'I don't believe it,' said Leslie stoutly. 'You're getting fanciful.'

'I'd know that ghastly old hat of hers anywhere,' replied Ada, tossing her own furry beauty proudly.

'What does it matter anyway?'

'Supposing she tells somebody?'

'She won't. Why should she? It's none of her business what we do.'

'She doesn't like me. She might feel like making mischief.'

'Rubbish!' cried Leslie. He stopped by the end of a shelter, where they were hidden from sight, and took Ada in his arms. His kisses were not returned as ardently as before.

'Ada! Don't let this silly business upset you.'

'I bet she tells Dolly anyway,' said Ada spitefully. 'They never keep anything from each other.'

'Forget it,' said Leslie, drawing her close. She struggled free.

'It's all right for you. You're going away. I've got to go back and face them all. Suppose Harry gets to hear of it?'

'And suppose he doesn't!'

'Or Winnie?'

'They won't! Come back to the hotel and calm down.'

He guided his love back to the privacy of the hotel, and there they stayed, very happily, until it was time for Ada to catch the train home.

Emily, of course, had to catch the same train. She was careful to get into it early, and to busy herself with her books.

There was no sign of the couple and she began to think that they must be staying in Bournemouth when, at the last moment, they hurried on to the platform.

Ada climbed into a carriage only two from Emily's. There was little time for farewells for the train was about to move off, but Ada leant from the window and clung passionately to Leslie's neck for a brief moment, crying his name.

The train chuffed off, leaving Leslie, hand upraised, on the platform. Emily heard the window pulled up with a bang, and before she had time to wonder if she could slip down the corridor to a carriage further away, Ada herself appeared in the corridor.

She stopped dead, her chest heaving beneath its smart frogging, and tears still wet on her cheeks. She cast a look of venom upon poor Emily, who gazed back transfixed, as an innocent rabbit might when hypnotised by a stoat.

Ada turned and re-entered her compartment. Emily, sorely troubled, did her best to read a paper by the meagre light afforded by war-time illuminations.

At Caxley Station they reached the ticket-collector side by side.

Ada thrust her ticket into his hand and spoke in a vicious whisper to Emily.

'You keep your mouth shut,' she hissed.

She never forgot the look which Emily gave her from those clear grey eyes.

Emily said no word, but the look expressed loathing and contempt. In that moment, Ada was forced to face the truth that little Emily Davis, poor, shabbily dressed, a humble inky-fingered school-teacher was her peer in all that really mattered. There was no disguising the fact that Emily had every right to despise her.

When, in later times Ada looked back upon that mad weekend, which was never repeated, she realised that it was that look of Emily's which brought home to her the wickedness and cruelty of her behaviour.

It was the first step towards Ada's heart-searching, and her first true encounter with the feeling of guilt.

And now Emily Davis was dead, thought Ada, the old woman. She had kept silence. She had carried Ada's secret to the grave with her. Of that, Ada had no doubt. She would have heard soon enough, in Caxley, if Emily had ever breathed a word.

There had been many moments of panic for Ada in the years that followed. Harry was a loving and generous husband, but he would never have forgiven infidelity, Ada knew well. She trembled when she thought how completely she was at the mercy of Emily Davis. It made her dislike of Emily stronger than ever, for now it was allied to guilty fear.

Yet, in her heart, she felt sure that her secret was safe. That look which Emily had given her at Caxley Station expressed not only contempt, but also her own shining goodness. Emily Davis would not stoop to anything as shabby as tale-telling.

The old lady sighed, and picking up the poker, stirred the fire.

'Well, at least she made me take a look at myself,' she said aloud.

'Who, dear?' asked Alice from the other side of the hearth. She lowered her knitting and looked in bewilderment at her employer.

'Emily Davis. She made me look at myself. What's more, she made me see plenty to dislike when I looked.'

Alice studied the wrinkled face with some concern. For the first time, she saw humility written there.

9 Jane Draper at Springbourne

AMONG those who read the brief notice of Emily's death in *The Caxley Chronicle* was Jane Bentley, who had started her teaching career, many years before, under Emily's guidance at Springbourne School.

She was now a woman in her late fifties and lived in a village to the south of Caxley, some fifteen miles from Springbourne. She had not kept in touch with her old headmistress, but occasionally they had met by chance in Caxley, and were always glad to see each other.

As a child, Jane Bentley, then Jane Draper, was delicate, the type of child who spends a large part of the winter in bed, the prey of every epidemic in season.

Luckily, she was intelligent and fond of books. The youngest of four, she became an aunt in her teens and had plenty of experience with children. She decided to become an infants' teacher.

The Draper family lived in a respectable London suburb. Money was short, but with wisdom and thrift the family managed adequately. It was a sacrifice to let Jane go to the training college of her choice, for although she received a grant, and a loan which had to be repaid in the first three years of teaching, in the normal way she would have been earning at the age of eighteen, and able to augment the family income.

She was a conscientious girl doing well at college and, honouring her pledge to return to the authority which had financed her, she started her teaching career, in the bleak early thirties when posts were so scarce, at a large infants' school in her native borough.

She found the work tough going. Nervous and apprehensive, she discovered that she was expected to teach a class of fifty six-year-olds to read, to write, and to imbibe the rudiments of arithmetic. These three Rs in some form or other, and with a break for physical training, made up the morning's time-table. The afternoons were given over to such infant delights designated as Art, Music, Handwork, Free Expression, and the like.

Her headmistress was a forceful woman, over endowed with thyroid and the relentless energy which goes with it. She did her best to be patient with the succession of young teachers who passed through her hands, but it was plain that their slowness and lack of class discipline, allied to some vague and high-faluting clouds of Child Psychology which they trailed behind them from college lectures, drove the poor woman to distraction.

Miss Jolly – for that was her unlikely name – came into Jane's classroom one day to see what all the hubbub was about. She found Jane sitting at her table with half a dozen children round her, holding reading books. One of the books was upside down.

The rest of the class seemed to be wandering restlessly about the room, some children holding pieces of equipment, some gazing through the window at another class in the playground and others enjoying themselves by sweeping their fellow pupils' work from the tables with happy cries.

'What are they doing?' asked Miss Jolly in a voice of thunder.

'They're Working At Their Own Pace,' replied Jane, rising to look over the heads clustered about her.

'Half of them aren't working at all,' rejoined Miss Jolly truthfully. 'Get them to their desks.'

Poor Jane did her best by clapping her hands ineffectually and crying, in a voice faint with nervousness, for order. A few, who had noticed Miss Jolly's presence, had the good sense to obey, and sat, smiling smugly, at the chaos around them.

For almost two minutes, agonisingly long to Jane Draper, she did her best to make herself heard. At last Miss Jolly came to her aid.

'SIT DOWN!' commanded that lady, in tones which set the windows vibrating. Children scurried to their chairs.

'HANDS IN LAPS!' ordered Miss Jolly. They obeyed to a man. Even Jane's particular problem child, Jimmy Lobb, who had frequent fits – some of them quite genuine – subsided into his chair and sat mute and wide-eyed. They knew the voice of authority well enough, and most of them unconsciously welcomed it.

'You are making far too much noise,' Miss Jolly told them sternly. 'How can Miss Draper hear this group read?'

Rightly, the subdued class assumed that this was a rhetorical question and remained suitably mute.

'Has everyone got work to do?' asked Miss Jolly.

'Yes, Miss,' came the meek reply.

'Very well. You get on with it, and you STAY IN YOUR DESKS until the clock says half-past.'

She pointed to the enormous electric time-piece on the wall which jerked the minutes along in staccato fashion.

'When that big hand gets to 6,' she continued, improving

the shining hour, 'you may CREEP from your desks to change your apparatus. NOT BEFORE! You understand?'

'Yes, Miss,' came the dulcet whispers.

'Those who were reading come quietly to Miss Draper's table,' ordered Miss Jolly. 'And I want to see every book the right way up.'

A demure half-dozen tip-toed politely to their former positions. Jane found the whole exercise unnerving, and hoped that Miss Jolly would soon leave her to her usual muddle.

But for a full five minutes, Miss Jolly prowled about the room, whilst work went on in an unnatural hush. Jane found herself trembling with anxiety.

At last, Miss Jolly departed, requesting Jane to meet her in her room as soon as school dinner was over.

By the time the meeting took place, Jane was in a state of panic. She entered the well-polished room, blind to the Della Robbia plaques, the cut-glass vase of roses, the silver desk-calendar (a parting gift from another school) and the hand-tufted rug on the floor.

Miss Jolly was kind but firm. She began by praising Jane's conscientious approach to teaching, her punctuality, her neat Record Book of Work to be done weekly, and did her best to put the dithering girl at ease.

She did not succeed, for in Jane's bewildered brain the phrase 'Damning with faint praise' beat about inside her head like an imprisoned bird, as she tried to listen to Miss Jolly's controlled commendations.

'You see,' said Miss Jolly at last, approaching the heart of the matter. 'We set ourselves certain aims in this infant school – aims of *attainment*, I mean. Ideally, each child should go forward to the junior school able to read – the most important thing – to write, and with a working knowledge of the four rules, at least in tens and units, preferably with hundreds too. Then, of course, they should have some idea of common measurements, be able to tell the time – '

'But there are *so many* of them!' wailed poor Jane.

'Unfortunate, I know, but there it is. What you have to learn, my dear, is to get them to do as they are told WHEN they are told. You saw what happened this morning.'

'But they really *were* working,' protested Jane. 'They must move about to fetch the next piece of apparatus. It shows they are keen to get on when they get one card done quickly and hurry out for the next.'

'It could show that they are bored with the piece of work in front of them,' said Miss Jolly. 'As far as I could see, quite a number of them couldn't be bothered to finish one job before trying their luck with the next. It's no good letting them get slack. You must check their progress. The bright ones will get on whatever happens. It's the idle ones who need prodding.'

'But if they're *interested*,' began Jane, 'they'll *want* to work. At college – '

Miss Jolly, with one eye on the clock, and patience sorely tried, let herself be told about Self-Determination, A Child's Natural Thirst for Discovery, and Working At One's Own Pace.

'Yes, well – ,' she said, when Jane had come to a faltering halt. 'Don't forget that a very small percentage are paragons. The rest, like most of humanity, are bone idle.'

Jane, horrified by such heresy, was about to argue, but Miss Jolly raised the capable right hand which had slapped so many infant legs.

'Keep the aims in mind, my dear. We want to send these children along to the junior school well equipped. If you can get the results by the methods shown you at college, well and good. But they won't work unless you have control of the class. Without that, nothing will work.'

She rose, and Jane made her way to the door.

'You're doing very well,' said Miss Jolly kindly. 'I think I shall be able to give you a good report at the end of this probationary year.'

'Thank you,' said Jane huskily. 'If only there weren't so many in a class, I think I'd manage better.'

'Wouldn't we all?' said Miss Jolly, with feeling. She gazed speculatively at Jane for a moment, and spoke again.

'I could offer you *forty backward* children next year, if you like the idea. Think it over, dear. Think it over!'

Jane did think it over. She thought a great deal in that first gruelling year, and many a time she despaired of continuing in the career she had adopted.

Would she ever become a fully-certificated teacher at the end of this probationary year? Did she want to be one for the rest of her life? And what could she do, if she wanted to change her job?

There were plenty of long queues outside the Labour Exchanges. Some of her college contemporaries were on the dole. It was a dispiriting situation.

She was not sure that Miss Jolly was right in her attitude to the children. She seemed to be far more concerned with the school's record of achievement than with the children themselves. Jane felt that she demanded too much of them, and of her staff. Not all of them were possessed of the self-assurance and drive which had swept Miss Jolly into a headship at a relatively early age.

On the other hand, she had the sense to realise that Miss Jolly did not ask anything of her teachers which she could not do herself. She might not conduct a class as Jane's college lecturers had recommended, but she certainly got results, and the children seemed to thrive. It was all very confusing.

At the end of the year, she was relieved to know that her work had been considered satisfactory. She was asked again if she would take the 'small' class of forty backward children, and agreed.

And so it came about that one September morning she faced her new class. Most of the six-year-olds were backward because of absence from school through illness. Some were mentally unsound and a few of these children would become certifiable at the right age. Some were incorrigibly lazy and would always lag behind, and a few were rebels by nature against any sort of discipline and authority, and likely to remain so for the rest of their lives.

Jane grew very fond of them. For one thing, they were grateful for any effort made for them. They were wildly delighted with such simple creations as a paper windmill or a lop-sided blotter, and carried these treasures home with far more care than their more brightly endowed fellows. They were affectionate and anxious to please. Jane found their goodwill exceedingly touching.

She also found them exceedingly exhausting, and returned home each evening tired to death. She had no heart for any sort of social life. Early bed was the thing she craved most, and her mother grew alarmed.

The family doctor prescribed iron tablets and sea-air. The

iron tablets were taken regularly and seemed to do some good. Sea-air was more difficult to come by. The family had no car, and money was still short.

When, in February, Jane was forced to take to her bed with influenza and was unable to leave it for three weeks, the doctor spoke his mind to Mrs Draper.

'That girl of yours upstairs,' he told her frankly, 'is wearing herself out. She's no reserves of strength at all. See she gets a holiday by the sea, after this, and then a teaching post that's easier than this one. Don't you know any school that has small classes?'

The Drapers did not. But during the summer term, when Jane was back at school and still struggling feebly with her forty backward children, a post was advertised in *The Teachers' World* for an assistant mistress to take charge of eighteen infants at Springbourne School.

'Number on roll,' said the advertisement, 'forty-eight.'

A whole school, with only forty-eight, thought Jane longingly!

She looked up the village in the ordnance survey map. It was, she saw, a few miles from Caxley where one of her college friends lived.

She wrote to her, and asked for her advice and for any information.

'Come and see it for yourself,' was the answer, and with a glow of hope Jane went to spend the weekend with the Bentleys.

They were a happy-go-lucky family living on the northern outskirts of Caxley, some three miles from Springbourne. To reach the village the two girls cycled along a quiet valley beside a little river full of water-cress beds. It ambled along sedately beneath its overhanging willows on its way to join the Cax.

It was a Saturday morning, warm and sunny. The school, of course, was uninhabited and so was the school house, for Emily had gone on the weekly bus to do some shopping in Caxley.

Emboldened, the two girls pressed their noses to the class-room windows and gazed at the interior. To Jane it seemed like a dolls' school after the enormous building in which she taught. She caught a glimpse of a large photograph of Queen Mary as a young woman, wasp-waisted in flowing white lace, with pearls in her hair.

The desks were long and old-fashioned, housing five or six children in a row. But there was nothing old-fashioned about the stack of new readers on the piano – Jane was using the same series herself – and she noted, with approval, the children's large paintings, the mustard and cress growing in a shallow dish, and the goldfish disporting themselves in a roomy glass tank, properly equipped with aquatic plants.

The playground was large, and shaded by several fine old trees. Elder bushes, turning their creamy flowers to the sun, screened the little outhouses which were the lavatories.

It all seemed cheerful and decent, a kindly spot where one could be happy, and could work without heart-break.

When Jane returned, she applied for the post and was accepted. Later that summer she met her headmistress-to-be for the first time.

She was in the playground carrying a tear-stained five-year-old in her arms. She kissed it swiftly before putting it down,

and advanced to meet Jane. It gave Jane quite a shock. Would Miss Jolly do that?

'I'm so glad you can come and help us next term,' said Emily Davis, holding out her hand.

And, as Jane held the small warm brown one in her own, she felt that, at last, she had come home.

10 The Flight of Billy Dove

THERE began then for Jane a period of great happiness and refreshment which was to colour her whole life.

To begin with, she stayed with the hospitable Bentleys, for the first few weeks of the autumn term, until she could find suitable lodgings nearer the school. After so much ill-health and strain, it was wonderful to be taken into the heart of such a cheerful family, and Jane thrived.

The bicycle ride to school and back brought colour to her cheeks, and an increased appetite. In those first few weeks of mellow autumn sunshine, Jane began to realise the loveliness of the countryside.

Harvest was in full swing, and the berries in the hedges were beginning to glow with colour. The cottage gardens were bright with Michaelmas daisies and dahlias, and the children brought sprays of blackberries and early nuts for the classroom nature table. Sometimes Jane received fresh-picked field mushrooms which the children had found on the way to school, or a perfect late rose from someone's garden.

She revelled in the bracing air of the downs and, encouraged by her headmistress, took the infants' class for nature walks round and about the village.

She found the children amenable and friendly. They might lack the sharp precocity of her former town pupils, but their slower pace suited Jane perfectly. Facing a class of eighteen, after forty or fifty, was wonderful to the girl. There was so little noise that there was no need to raise her voice. She could hear each child read daily – a basic aim she had never been able to achieve before – and found the children's progress marvellously heartening.

Of course there were snags. The chief one was the range of ages. The youngest was not yet five; the oldest – and most backward – nearly eight. But Jane was used to working with groups, and found that discipline was no bother with so few children who were mostly of a docile nature. Relaxed and absorbed, Jane's confidence in her own abilities grew steadily, and she became a very sound teacher indeed.

Emily Davis played her part in this process. Jane found her as quick and energetic as Miss Jolly had been, but with a warmth of heart and gentleness, both lacking in her former headmistress.

Emily was like a little bird, Jane thought, with her bright eyes and brisk bustling movements. The children loved her, but knew better than to provoke her. They knew, too, that a cane reposed at the back of the map cupboard. No one could remember it being used, but the bigger boys, who occasionally assumed some bravado, were aware that Miss Davis was quite capable of exerting her powers, if need be, and kept their behaviour within limits.

Emily's high spirits were the stimulus which these children needed. Mostly the sons and daughters of farm labourers, they were unbookish and inclined to be apathetic.

'Don't forget,' said Emily to Jane one playtime, as they sipped their tea, 'that most of them are short of food, and quite a number go cold in the winter. Times are hard for farmers and their men.'

'But they look well enough,' observed Jane.

'Their cheeks are pink,' answered Emily. 'If you live on the downs you soon get weather-beaten. And by the end of the summer they are nicely tanned. But look at their bodies when they strip for physical training! You'll see plenty of rib cages in evidence. There's just as much poverty in the country as in towns. The only thing is it's not quite so dramatic, and fewer people see its results.'

There were such families at Springbourne, Jane soon discovered. She saw too how Emily coped practically with the situation, supplying mugs of milky cocoa during the winter to those who needed it most. Those who did not run home for their midday meal brought sandwiches, for this was before the coming of school dinners. One family, in particular, was particularly under-nourished. When the greasy papers were unwrapped, they were usually found to contain only bread with a scraping of margarine.

Many a time Jane saw Emily adding a piece of cheese to this unpalatable fare, and apples from her store shed. It was all done briskly, without sentiment, and in a way which would not make a child uncomfortable.

It was small wonder, Jane thought, that Emily Davis got on well with the parents. There were exceptions, of course, and one incident Jane remembered for years.

It happened just before Christmas one year. Emily had arranged a school outing to a Christmas pantomime, put on by amateurs, in Caxley. A bus was hired, and the fare and the entrance fee together would cost five shillings. Parents could join the party, and there was a good response, despite the fact that five shillings seemed a great deal of money to find just before Christmas.

The fact that several Thrift Clubs would be paying out about that time may have accounted for the enthusiasm with which Emily's venture was received. The money came in briskly until only young Willie Amey's contribution, and his mother's, were outstanding.

The day before the outing, Mrs Amey appeared, in tears. Asking Jane to keep an eye on both classes, Emily took the weeping woman over to the school house and heard the sad tale.

'That beast of a husband,' Emily told Jane later, 'took the ten shillings from the jug on the top shelf of the dresser, where she'd hidden it – or *thought* she had, poor soul – and drank the lot at the pub last night.'

'What will happen?'

'I shall put in the money for them,' said Emily shortly, 'and I'll see Dick Amey myself. He'll pay up, never fear!'

Jane gazed at Emily in trepidation. Dick Amey, she knew, was a big, burly, beery fifteen-stoner. Jane was afraid of him under normal circumstances. Provoked, he could be dangerous, she felt sure.

'But he's such a great *bully* of a man,' said Jane tremulously.

'And like most bullies,' said Emily forthrightly, 'he's a great coward too. I shall square up to him tonight.'

She went about her duties as blithely as ever that afternoon, but Jane was the prey of anxiety. She said goodbye to her diminutive headmistress that afternoon, wondering if she would see her unscathed next morning.

She need not have worried. Evidently Emily had put on her coat and hat as soon as she thought Dick was home, and had climbed the stile, crossed a field to his distant cottage, and tapped briskly at his door.

His frightened wife stood well back while the proceedings took place.

Emily had come straight to the point. Direct attack was always Emily's motto, and she got under Dick Amey's guard immediately.

'About as mean a trick as I've ever heard of,' said Emily heartily. 'But the money's in for both of them and they're going to enjoy the show. That's ten shillings you owe me. I'll take it now.'

Dick Amey, flabbergasted, demurred.

'I ain't got above two shillun on me,' protested Dick.

Emily held out her hand in silence. His wife watched in amazement as he rooted, muttering the while, in his trouser pocket and slammed a florin into the waiting palm.

'When do I get the rest?' said Emily.

'You tell me,' growled Dick.

Emily did.

'A shilling a week at least, till it's done,' said Emily. 'You keep off the beer for the next few weeks and you'll soon be out of my debt.'

Jane heard of this memorable encounter from Mrs Amey herself, long after the event. It must have looked like a wren challenging an eagle, thought Jane. But, no doubt about it, the wren was the victor that time.

* * *

Jane found permanent accommodation in a tiny cottage on Jesse Miller's farm at Springbourne.

It had been empty for some time, but was in good repair, for the Millers were always careful of their property.

It consisted of a living room and kitchen, with two small

bedrooms above. The place was partly furnished and Jane had the pleasure of buying one or two extra pieces to increase her comfort. The rent was five shillings weekly, and the understanding was that if Jesse Miller needed it for a farm worker sometime, then there would be a month's notice to quit.

She was now a near neighbour of Emily's, and frequently spent an evening with her headmistress and old Mrs Davis who now lived with her. Emily's father had died some years before and it had taken much persuasion to get her mother to leave the family cottage at Beech Green where she had reared her large family. But at last she consented, and had settled very well with Emily.

The two had much in common. They were both small, energetic and merry. Jane found them gay company, and often looked back, in later years, upon those cheerful evenings when the lamp was lit and stood dead centre on the red serge tablecloth, bobble-edged, which Mrs Davis had brought from her old home.

They knitted, or worked at a tufted wool rug, and chattered nineteen to the dozen. The schoolhouse living room had an old-fashioned kitchen range with a barred fire and two generous hobs on which a saucepan of soup, or a steaming kettle, kept hot. It was all very snug, and Jane was always reluctant to leave the circle of lamp light to make her way home along the dark lane, following the wavering pool of dim light from her torch.

Often, she went to Caxley to see the Bentleys, for Richard Bentley, an older brother of her college friend, became increasingly attentive. He owned a little car and worked in a Caxley bank.

As the months passed, he came to fetch Jane from the cottage more and more frequently. When they became engaged, Emily Davis was the first to hear the news.

She was genuinely delighted, though not surprised, and kissed young Jane soundly.

'And don't have a long engagement,' urged Emily.

'But we must save some money,' protested Jane, laughing at her vehemence.

'Don't wait too long. I did, and I lost him.'

Her face clouded momentarily and, for the first time, Jane realised that this cheerful little middle-aged woman must once have been young and in love, and then terribly wounded.

It was the first she had heard of the affair, although she learnt more later.

'I'm sorry,' she said, taking the older woman's hand impulsively. 'I had no idea.'

'Well, it's over and done with,' said Emily, with a sigh. 'But take my advice. Marry soon.'

The two planned to marry in the spring of the next year, and at Easter 1939, Jane was married from her parents' house in London.

After the honeymoon, they settled at the Springbourne cottage, intending to move nearer Caxley when something suitable came on the market. Jane had resigned her teaching post, but still saw a great deal of Emily and her pupils.

When war broke out in September of that year, young Richard Bentley, who was in the Territorial Army, went off to fight.

Jane resumed her job as infant teacher at Springbourne School, and went to Caxley Station, with her headmistress, to collect forty or so evacuee schoolchildren who were to share Springbourne school for the duration of hostilities.

The war years had a dream-like quality for Jane Bentley. At times, it was more of a nightmare than a dream, but always there was this pervading feeling of unreality.

Had there ever been such a golden September, she wondered, as that first month of the war?

Day after day dawned cloudless and warm. Thistledown floated in the soft breezes. Butterflies, drunk with nectar, clung bemused to the buddleia flowers, or opened and shut their wings in tranced indolence upon the early Michaelmas daisies.

It was impossible to realise that just across the English Channel terror and violence held sway. At Springbourne one might have been swathed in a golden cocoon as the harvest was gathered and the downs shimmered in the heat haze.

Of course, at Springbourne School there was unusual activity as the newcomers settled down, amicably enough, with their native hosts.

Two teachers had accompanied the evacuees, one young, one middle-aged.

The middle-aged headmistress was a tough stringy individual with a voice as rough as a nutmeg scraper. She had run a Girl Guides troop for years, played hockey for her county and had the unsubtle team-spirit approach to life of a hearty adolescent.

She was billeted with Emily in the school house, and the two got on pretty well, both appreciating the other's honesty and concern for their charges. Miss Farrer, Emily discovered, was a whirlwind of a teacher, and a strict disciplinarian.

The younger woman, Miss Knight, was a different kettle of

fish altogether, and poor Jane, whose spare bedroom she occupied, suffered grievously.

Molly Knight was one who thrived on emotion. She travelled from one dramatic crisis to another as a traveller in a desert moves from oasis to oasis. If the war could not supply enough material for sensation – and at that stage it was remarkably dull – Molly Knight created excitement from the little world about her. She was a mischief-maker, mainly because of this desire for sensation, and Jane found her particularly exhausting.

'What can I do?' she asked Emily one day, in despair. 'I try to look upon it as my contribution to the war effort, but I really can't face Molly breaking into my room at midnight to tell me how atrociously the Germans are treating their prisoners, and giving me a blow-by-blow account of her reactions to some stupid piece of propaganda.'

'I've been thinking about it,' replied Emily. 'If Miss Farrer's willing, I suggest they have your cottage, and you come here. How do you think that would work?'

Jane, despite a certain reluctance to leave the cottage, fell in with this plan, and for some time the two establishments were thus constituted. It made things easier in every way.

As the phoney war, as it came to be called, continued, a number of the children and their parents returned to London. One who did not, much to Emily's and Jane's pleasure, was a particularly attractive eight-year-old called Billy Dove.

He was a red-haired freckled boy, quick and intelligent. There was no doubt in Emily's mind that he would go on to a grammar school in time.

He was the only child of a quiet little mouse of a woman, and the two were billeted in a cottage not far from the school.

The father was in the Navy, patrolling off the coast of Ireland, it was believed.

Mother and son were devoted. Mrs Dove was a great knitter, and young Billy's superb collection of jerseys was much admired. She did not mix much with the other women, although Billy was popular with the other children, frequently organising their games.

One day in late November the tragedy occurred. By now the weather had broken, and all day the wind had howled round Springbourne School and rain had lashed the windows. Playtime was passed indoors, in a flurry of well-worn comics on the desks among the milk bottles.

By afternoon, a fierce gale was blowing, ferocious enough to satisfy even Molly Knight's passion for excitement.

'Just look at the postman!' she exclaimed to Jane, as they watched the weather through the rain-spattered window. 'He can hardly walk against it!'

They watched him struggle up the path to Billy Dove's door, letter in hand. Water streamed from his black oilskin cape, and every step sent drops flying from his wellington boots.

The children were sent home at the right time, through the murky fury of the storm, with strict orders 'not to loiter'. Emily and Jane returned to the school house for tea, looking forward to a peaceful evening by the fire.

But at eight o'clock, an agitated neighbour arrived to say that Mrs Dove was in a dead faint across her table, with her wrists dripping blood, and that young Billy was nowhere to be found.

'You go and ring the doctor,' said Emily to Jane, 'while I run along to Mrs Dove.' They flung on their coats and hurried away on their errands.

The scene at Mrs Dove's, though frightening enough, was not quite as horrifying as the neighbour's breathless description had led Emily to believe.

There was blood upon the tablecloth, on the floor, and upon Mrs Dove's hand-knitted jumper, but the slashed wrists dripped no longer for, luckily, the poor woman's attempt at suicide had been unsuccessful. Emily had snatched up her mother's smelling salts on her way out, and now waved the pungent bottle before the pale face.

The neighbour found some rum in the cupboard, and when, at last, Mrs Dove came to, she and Emily made her sip a little rum and hot water.

'What ever made you do it?' asked the neighbour, bewildered.

Emily shook her head. This was no time to torture Mrs Dove with whys and wherefores. They must bide their time.

Although conscious, the woman said nothing, but sat, head sunk upon the bloodied jumper, in silence.

But when the doctor arrived, she stirred and pointed to a letter which had fallen to the floor. He read it, and passed it to Emily, without speaking.

It was a brief communication – that which Jane and Molly had seen the postman delivering that afternoon. It said that James Alan Dove was missing presumed killed.

'I'd like to have her in hospital overnight,' said the doctor. 'She's lost a good deal of blood, and is in a severe state of shock.'

'I understand,' said Emily. 'The boy is missing. I'll ring the police and start searching myself. He can stay the night at the school house when we find him.'

'By far the best thing,' agreed the doctor. If only more

women were like Emily Davis, he thought, turning to his patient!

The memory of that night stayed with Jane Bentley for the rest of her life. The two of them set out through the storm with only the faintest glimmer from torches, dimmed by tissue paper over the glass in accordance with black-out regulations, to guide them.

'We'll stick together,' said Emily. 'And keep shouting his name. Not that we stand much chance of being heard in this wind.'

'Which way?' asked Jane, at Mrs Dove's gate.

'Towards Caxley. He may have had some muddled idea of catching a train. Anyway, he wouldn't make for the downs in this weather. There's not a shred of shelter there.'

They splashed along the valley lane, past the school. The water gurgled on each side of the road, sometimes fanning across the full width where the surface tilted. Above their heads the wind roared in the branches, clashing them together and scattering twigs and leaves below. The elephantine grey trunks of the beech trees were streaked with rivulets of rain-water.

Jane's shoes squelched at every step. She could feel the water between her toes, and wished she had had Emily's foresight and had thrust her feet into wellington boots.

The little headmistress kept up a brisk pace. Every now and again she stopped, and the two would cry:

'Billy! Billy Dove! Billy!'

But their voices were drowned in the turmoil about them, and Jane began to wonder if the whole venture would have to be abandoned.

She followed in Emily's wake envying the older woman's unflagging energy.

'Are you aiming at anywhere particular?' she shouted above the din. Emily nodded.

'Bennett's barn and the chicken houses,' she responded. Jane knew that these buildings were Edgar Bennett's – that same Edgar, so she had recently learnt – who had jilted the indomitable little woman before her, so many years ago.

They splashed onward. Now the lane ran close by the little river. The watercress was now large and coarse, and swept this way and that by the torrent of water rushing through it. Who would have thought that the pretty summer trickle of brook, overhung with willows and long grasses, could become such a snarling leaping force, carrying all before it!

Emily turned left, and struck uphill along a rough track now streaming with chalky water from the downs. Some hundred yards up the hill, she left the track and beat her way, head down against the onslaught of rain, towards two large hen houses standing side by side in the field. Jane followed doggedly.

'Stand round here. There's more shelter,' said Emily. 'I'll only open the door a crack, otherwise the hens will be out. They're kittle-cattle.'

It was the first time Jane had heard this phrase. She savoured it now, watching Emily's small hand fumbling with the wooden catch of the door.

'Billy! Billy Dove!' she called through the chink. A pencil of light from the dimmed torch searched every cranny of the house.

There were a few squawks of alarm from the hens, and a

preliminary rumbling from the rooster before taking suitable action against those who disturbed his rest. But there was no human voice to be heard.

'No luck,' said Emily, shutting the door, and squelching across the grass to the next.

They were just as unlucky here.

'We'll try the barn,' said Emily, tucking wet strands of hair under her sodden head scarf. 'Back to the road, Jane.'

Jane found herself stumbling along, almost in a state of collapse. She was not as strong in constitution as Emily, and this evening's tragedy had taken its toll. She longed for bed, for warmth, for shelter from the cruel buffeting of the weather, and for the relief of finding the missing child.

She did not have to wait long. At the barn door, Emily motioned her forward. Together they moved inside, out of the wind and rain. It was quiet in here, and fragrant with the summer smell of hay.

Emily pushed aside the wet tissue paper from the torch, and a stronger light came to rest on a dark bundle curled up in an outsize nest in one corner of the barn.

Emily knelt down beside the sleeping child. His eyes were tightly shut, his red hair dark with moisture and clinging to his forehead. The cheeks were blotched and his eyelids swollen with crying. But he was unharmed.

'Billy,' whispered Emily. The child woke, and sat up abruptly. There was no preliminary stretching or yawning. Billy Dove was awake in an instant, and remembered all that had brought him to this place in blind panic. Emily knew how it would be.

'Mummy?' he asked, turning anxious eyes upon Emily. She took one of his grimy hands in hers.

'She's well again,' she told him. 'The doctor is looking after her.'

'And Daddy?'

'No one knows yet.' She gripped his hand more tightly. Obviously, the child had read the letter and understood his mother's action when he had found her slumped across the table.

'But what do *you* think?' said Billy, his bottom lip quivering piteously.

Jane, the silent spectator, never forgot Emily's reply, or the expression on her wet face as she made it.

'I think it would be wrong and wicked to stop hoping,' said Emily straightly.

The child sighed and struggled to his feet. Emily brushed the wisps of hay from his raincoat.

'You're coming to sleep in my house now,' Emily told him.

He managed a watery smile.

'Thank you, Miss Davis,' he said politely, holding open the door for her.

Jane Bentley put down *The Caxley Chronicle* slowly. Over thirty years had passed and yet she could remember that dimly-lit scene in every detail.

And now Emily Davis was dead!

Or was she, wondered Jane? What was that saying about those who lived in the hearts of others? Something to the effect that they never really died. If that were the case, then Emily Davis would certainly live on.

She herself owed much to Emily. She had gone to Springbourne a nervous, delicate girl with little to look forward to in the career which she had chosen.

Emily had given her strength and encouragement. She had sent her out into the healthy downland to regain her youthful spirits. She had taken in this apprehensive stranger and turned her into a happy confident member of the Springbourne family.

Whilst she was with Emily she had found health, happiness and a husband.

And more than that, she had found, by Emily's example, a way of living and a strength of character, both of which were to remain as guide-lines for the rest of her life.

Little Emily Davis's influence must have spread far, thought Jane, gazing into the September sunshine. Just as a small pebble, dropped into a still pool, spreads ever-widening ripples, so must Emily's impact have travelled through all the friends and pupils she had encountered.

What became of Billy Dove, she wondered? He certainly fulfilled the promise Emily foretold, and went on to Caxley Grammar School, then to a university, and was doing something quite important connected with mining, Jane believed.

There had been a happy ending to Billy Dove's war-time experience, Jane remembered, for his father had been picked up from the sea by a German ship and he spent the rest of the war, tediously but safely, as a prisoner. Billy's eyes had been like stars when he told Miss Davis the news, months after that never-to-be-forgotten night of storm and horror.

Dear Billy Dove, thought Jane, bestirring herself! He ought to know the news, but it wasn't likely that he took *The Caxley Chronicle* these days. He probably read *The Financial Times*, now that he was a prosperous man of nearly forty. No doubt he had done well for himself, but no doubt he often thought of Springbourne School and how much he owed to the guiding spirit who ruled it so wisely when he was young.

And in that, thought Jane Bentley, he would not be alone.

11 Billy Dove Goes Further

JANE BENTLEY was wrong.

Billy Dove read *The Caxley Chronicle* as well as *The Financial Times.* It arrived regularly each week, in a wrapper neatly addressed by his mother, wherever he might be in the wide world. The issue carrying the notice of Emily's death came to him in Scotland.

When his father, Petty Officer Dove, returned from prison camp at the end of the war, he found that his old London employer had died and the firm was no more. In a way, he was relieved.

He had had plenty of time for thinking in camp, and more and more his thoughts turned to the English countryside where he had been brought up. Now he longed to return.

After leaving the village school, he had been bound apprentice, at the age of fourteen, to a family firm of cabinet-makers in London. He lodged with an obliging aunt in Mitcham, worked hard, and gained steady promotion with the firm as the years passed.

In one of the terraced houses opposite his aunt's home, he found his future wife, a pretty little auburn-haired girl, who caught the same train into the City as he did to work as a copy-typist in an insurance firm.

They married when he was twenty-five and she was twenty-three, and made their home in a tiny flat two streets away from their former abodes.

Jim Dove often thought of those early married days, as he went about his tasks in the German prisoner-of-war camp. They had been happy enough, for they were young and very much in love. Young Billy arrived within the year, and was an added joy – a good-tempered, healthy baby, with his mother's red hair and his father's cheerful disposition.

It was now that the Doves began to long for more room. Their flat was on the first floor. Their landlady lived below, a hard-bitten widow who resented the necessity of letting part of her home.

Billy's pram was left in her tiny hall with her grudging consent. Billy's napkins and other family washing were allowed to blow on a two-yard line near the garden rubbish heap, screened from sight by a large golden privet bush. Except for the purpose of hanging out the washing, the Dove family was not allowed in the garden.

Peggy Dove bore the restrictions patiently. Times were hard, and she knew that it would be several years before they could hope to move to a house of their own. Meanwhile, she took Billy to the nearby park for his daily outing, and did her best to keep on good terms with the landlady.

Jim Dove fretted far more. When war came, and settled their future for them willy-nilly, he was relieved to know that his wife and son would be settled safely at Springbourne. He knew the Caxley area fairly well, for he and his father had been great cyclists, and had camped many a time on the banks of the Cax, and had pushed their bicycles up the steep flanks of the downs nearby. At sea, and later in the prison camp, he had found comfort in the thought of Peggy and Billy enjoying the countryside he knew so well.

He was determined that he would not return to London to live. It was no place for a boy to be brought up. Who knows? There might be more children, and a flat in London was little better than the prison he now inhabited, he told himself. He was tired of being cramped and confined. When he got back he would find a job in the country.

But would he? That was the problem. Would any other firm employ him? Peggy, cautious as a mouse, would tremble at the thought of any risk. She would try to persuade him to return to the old life, he felt sure.

Ah well! No use fretting about it whilst in German hands. He'd face that problem when the time came, Jim decided.

As so often happens, the problems resolved themselves by the time he was reunited with Peggy and Billy. The old firm had gone. Billy was now doing well at Caxley Grammar School, and Peggy had found a little cottage to rent on the edge of commonland within walking distance of Caxley. She wouldn't go back to London for a thousand pounds!

Jim found a post with a local firm of furniture makers, and the Doves settled down to make their life afresh. Jim and Peggy were destined to spend the rest of their long lives in Caxley, and to find contentment there.

Billy remained an only child, and a highly satisfactory one. He was almost thirteen when his father returned, and working well at the grammar school. He had found the transition from the little school at Springbourne to the large boys' school somewhat unnerving, but by the time his father came back he had settled down and was enjoying the work.

Eventually, he gained a place at Cambridge, obtained a good

class Honours degree, and became a mining engineer. His work took him all over the world, but at the time of Emily Davis's death he was in Scotland with his wife and two children. His assignment there was for approximately two years, and the Doves had rented a house for that time. It stood among pine forests, on the edge of a sizeable village where the children attended the local school.

The job was an interesting one. On the site of a long disused coal mine, other mineral deposits had been discovered, but at a depth and angle which made them difficult to work. It was Billy Dove's job to overcome the problem.

He had been chosen expressly for it by his firm because he had done so well on a similar project for the Italian government. On the slopes of Mount Etna in Sicily, certain minerals had been discovered in the volcanic rock which were of great interest to the chemical industry. The deposits were at a considerable depth, in one particular stratum formed by lava ejected some hundreds of years earlier. Billy found the work arduous but fascinating.

He was at work there for six weeks, and there was a possibility of returning for a further month when the drilling had reached the second stage. It was a prospect which he viewed with mixed feelings. For, to his mingled delight and guilt, sensible, steady Billy Dove, devoted husband and father, regular church-goer and wise counsellor to those asking his advice, had fallen head over heels in love with a girl in Sicily.

It came about like this.

Billy's firm had booked a room for him at a modest but respectable hotel in Taormina, a few miles from the working site.

He lost his heart to the little town at once. Perched on the sunny hillside, tall cypresses towering like dark candles above the freshly-painted houses, the place had unique charm. It was at the end of April when he saw it first, and the public gardens, laid out in broad terraces, were fragrant with wallflowers, pinks and stocks. The orange trees added the warm scent of their blossom and the beauty of their golden fruit to the scene. Wistaria hung in swags from the pergolas, and, in the sheltered garden of the hotel next door, sweet peas were already in flower.

In all his wanderings, Billy Dove had never yet discovered a place which enchanted him so swiftly and so completely. He gazed at the vivid green-blue sea far below, at the craggy mountain which overhung the town, and at Etna against the blue sky forming a majestic backcloth to it all.

In his spare time he explored the town thoroughly. The ruined Greek theatre fascinated him, and the view from its heights across the Straits of Messina to the distant mainland of Italy was one which never failed to thrill him.

He enjoyed plunging down the steep steps from one level of Taormina to the next. He sampled all manner of places to eat and drink, from tiny cafés, murky with smoke and crowded with noisy Sicilians, to cosmopolitan hotels offering the accepted variety of French cooking found in every tourist centre.

It was not long before he entered the San Domenico Hotel. It had once been a monastery, and about its ancient courts and stairways still clung the gentle silence of earlier days. Here Billy Dove found hushed peace and rare beauty. He also found unexpected, and shattering, love.

* * *

The girl was small and golden. When Billy saw her first, she was clad in a brief white frock which contrasted with her glowing sun-tanned skin.

She was climbing up the steep slope from the swimming pool, carrying the bulky paraphernalia of an afternoon spent swimming and sun-bathing. Billy stood aside to let her pass, and the towel which was flung over one shoulder slid to the ground. Billy bent to retrieve it.

'Thank you,' said the girl, holding out a hand. Immediately, a Penguin book and one sandal clattered to the path.

The girl laughed as Billy bent again.

'I'm so sorry. It's like one of those circus acts, isn't it? You know, the clown drops one thing after another and then turns out to be an expert juggler.'

'And are you?'

'Does it look like it?' replied the girl. Her teeth were very white and even. Her eyes were a peculiarly light hazel which gave them a sunny look.

'Let me take some of the things,' offered Billy, genuinely concerned by the untidy collection of articles in her arms. 'Couldn't we put the small stuff in your bag?'

He squatted down and packed the book, two sandals, a spectacle case and a tube of skin-cream into the enormous beach bag. He then stood up and folded the towel neatly.

'You take that, and I'll bring the bag,' said Billy.

'No, really. I can manage perfectly now that you've tidied me up. You were going down to the pool, I expect.'

'I wasn't really going anywhere. Just savouring a perfect evening.'

More people began to descend the path, and Billy and the girl found themselves in the way.

'Well, thank you,' she said, moving on. 'I was going to have a drink before dinner. May I offer you one after all this porterage?'

'I should love it,' said Billy truthfully, following her nimble figure up the slope.

Over the drinks they introduced themselves and Billy told her about the work which brought him to Sicily.

'And you are on holiday, I expect,' he said.

'I have been. That's why I'm staying at the San Domenico. But I've come to a tremendous decision in the past fortnight. I'm hoping to settle here for good.'

'In this hotel?'

'Heavens, no! I should soon be broke. No, I've found a little house, higher up the hill. I've rented it for six months to see if life in Taormina is all I hope it will be. I've been looking for somewhere to settle ever since my father died last year.'

It appeared that her father had been a prosperous manufacturer in Yorkshire until a stroke had finished all activity for him. Mary had left her job as almoner in the local hospital to nurse him. Her mother had been dead for some years.

On her father's death she found that everything had been left to her. He was 'a warm man', as they said locally, but a large house on the windswept moors, despite two old-fashioned hard-working maids to help in running it, was not what Mary wanted.

She was over thirty now, and longed to get away. Too long, she felt, she had been mewed up in the old home. She craved for sunshine and change.

She left the house in the maids' care while she set about her restless wanderings. Almost a year was spent in this way, and now she longed for a home, and somewhere to settle, as urgently as she had yearned for flight. In Taormina she believed she had found her goal.

'If I find it to my liking,' she told Billy, twirling her glass thoughtfully, 'I shall sell the Yorkshire place and stay here permanently. I've nothing to take me back – no relatives, no ties of any sort—'

Her voice trailed away, and she looked directly at Billy.

'Are you staying for dinner?'

'I ought to go back to do some work.'

'Do stay,' she said impulsively. 'It's lovely to talk to someone again, and you've been so very kind.'

Of course he stayed. And every minute that passed made her company dearer to him. He promised to come and inspect the little house on the morrow, and to help in any way he could with the move.

Billy Dove walked home, through the moonlit scented night, tingling with the most unusual sensations.

'My God!' said Billy, addressing a stone dragon on a gatepost, 'it's love again!'

In the days that followed, Billy felt himself the battleground of conflicting emotions, and very exhausting he found it. He had been a fairly uncomplicated character for almost forty years, distrusting violent emotion, and impatient with those who seemed to have no control of their feelings. He had met many philanderers in his travels, and had a hearty dislike of them. Those who boasted of their conquests he found doubly boring. They did not impress Billy Dove.

'Time you grew up,' he would tell them, yawning, and walk away.

And here he was, behaving in exactly the same way. The guilt he felt when he thought of his disloyalty to Sarah and the boys was overwhelming, but only momentarily so. It was swept away by this new wave of fierce, youthful, exulting happiness. Before its onslaught he was powerless.

Mary's passion matched his own. It was as though, with so little time before them, their love had an added urgency. They spent every possible hour together, turning their minds away from the inexorable advance of the day of Billy's departure, like children who hide their eyes from a wounding light.

Taormina, and the golden girl, were heartrendingly beautiful when that last day came.

'You'll come back? Say you'll come back!' pleaded Mary, clinging to him.

'You know I can't promise that,' said Billy. She knew about Sarah and their two children, and he had been careful not to raise her hopes by telling her of the possibility of further work on the site. Cruel though it seemed, they must make the break.

He flew from Catania that morning and he saw the green and golden island tipping beneath him. He changed planes at Rome, and found he had to wait for three hours. He spent the time pacing restlessly up and down in the windy sunshine, his mind in turmoil.

He flew from Catania that morning and he saw the green and golden island tipping beneath him through a blur of tears. He changed planes at Rome, and found he had to wait for three hours. He spent the time pacing restlessly up and down in the windy sunshine, his mind in turmoil.

By the time he arrived at Heathrow, in pouring rain, he was calm enough to have made two decisions. This sweet mad interlude was over, and he would not see Mary again. Secondly, Sarah must never know anything about it.

12 The Return of Billy Dove

IT is easy enough to make good resolutions. Keeping them is another kettle of fish.

The decision to keep his guilty secret from Sarah was comparatively simple. He was deeply ashamed of his behaviour, although the remembrance of those few idyllic weeks would never fade, and would colour the rest of his life.

Billy was not the sort of man to unload his guilt on to another. What good would confession do to Sarah? No, he owed it to her to keep silent, and by his extra care of her, and the boys, to salve his smarting conscience.

But the decision to make a clean break with Mary was seriously undermined when a letter arrived from his firm asking him to return to the Sicilian site for the second stage of the work. Could he let them know how the Scottish project was moving? At a pinch, young Bannister could take over one or the other while he was away. He would need thorough briefing, of course, and it was to be hoped that Dove could arrange to carry on with both jobs. What did he feel?

What did he feel, echoed Billy! He put the letter to the side of his breakfast plate, and gazed out at the wooded Scottish hillside. In the garden John and Michael raced round and round pursued by a floppy-eared puppy. There were his two fine boys, full of roaring high spirits. He must do nothing to hurt them.

He looked across the table to Sarah, immersed in *The Caxley Chronicle* which had arrived with the morning letters. She looked very young and defenceless, despite her thirty-odd years, in her blue and white cotton frock. A little frown of concentration furrowed her smooth brow.

'There's an Emily Davis in the "Deaths",' she remarked. 'Could it be your old teacher?'

'I should have thought she'd died years ago,' remarked Billy absently, his mind on his problem.

'Well, she was eighty-four,' said Sarah, her eyes still fixed on the paper. 'Died at Beech Green. Might well be, don't you think?'

She looked up. Billy was standing at the window, gazing into the garden. It was apparent that he had not heard her remarks. She was accustomed to his complete withdrawal from the world around him when his mind was perplexed, and was not unduly upset.

'Heavens, it's late!' she cried. She ran to the open window and called to the boys.

Billy shook his head, as though he had just emerged from deep water. He put his arms round her swiftly and kissed her with sudden fierceness.

Sarah laughed.

'Don't dally, darling,' she said, 'or the boys will be late for school.'

Within two minutes, the three were in the Land-Rover waving goodbye to Sarah at the window.

The road was steep, and wound its way downhill between dark fir woods which Billy found beautiful on a sunny morning, but sinister and silent at other times. Nothing grew beneath their shade, and Billy often thought longingly of the oak and hazel woods of his childhood at Caxley, starred in spring with primroses and anemones, and gay with the golden tassels of catkins.

The village school stood back from the road with a wide green verge before it. As Billy drew up, the bell was clanging from the little bell-tower, and the children were already forming lines ready to lead in. The two boys gave him hasty wet kisses, scrambled down, and raced to join their fellows. The schoolmaster was a stickler for punctuality.

He waited to see them take their places in the lines. John turned towards him and gave an enormous wink of triumph, as if to say: 'Done it!', just as the lanky form of the headmaster appeared at the school door.

Amused, Billy drove off slowly. There was a lot to be said for a village school education when one was eight, robust and cheerful.

He had been eight, he remembered sharply, when he was at Beech Green Village School. But, though he may have been robust, he had been far from cheerful at that time.

What would he have done without Emily Davis just then? At the same age as John, frightened and horror-struck, he had been rescued by her efforts. He had never forgotten that night of storm and terror.

And she was dead? Is that what Sarah said this morning? Eighty-four, and at Beech Green? He mused as he wound his way towards work. That would be Emily Davis, without doubt.

He sighed deeply. She was a grand old girl! His thoughts strayed from the events of that wild night to another phase of his school life when, as a bewildered eleven-year-old, Emily Davis had come, once more, to the rescue.

* * *

The transition from the tiny world of Springbourne to the comparatively large one of Caxley upset the boy more than he would admit.

Instead of racing the few yards along the village street from his home to the school, he now had to rise much earlier and catch a bus into the town. His comfortable hand-knitted jerseys and flannel shorts, now gave way to a grey flannel suit with long trousers. Black laced shoes, polished overnight, took the place of easy well-worn sandals, and on his head he wore the familiar Caxley Grammar school cap, with much pride, but some irritation – for wasn't it just one more thing to take care of, and to remember to bring home at night?

At times, young Billy felt burdened with all these belongings. They weighed as heavily upon him as the shining new leather satchel which bumped against his hip as he walked.

He was bewildered too by the sheer size of his new school and by the hundreds of boys. When you have been one of forty or fifty children at school assembly, and one among only twenty or so in the classroom, it is unnerving to be cast among four hundred-odd boys, all larger than oneself.

To Billy, some of the prefects were men. Certainly, some of them looked quite as mature as some of the young masters. They filled the boy with awe with their tasselled caps, their gruff voices and their sheer size when they passed him in the corridors.

The standard of work, too, presented a problem. At Springbourne School he had held his own with little effort. Now he was among boys brighter than himself. There were new subjects to tackle, such as French, Latin and Algebra. At times, sitting at the cottage table, with his homework books spread out in the light of the Aladdin lamp, he came near to despair. Would his mind ever be able to hold all this mass of new knowledge?

But it was the affair of the conkers which brought all his troubles to a head. Billy had always loved the glossy beauties which tumbled from the Springbourne trees in the autumn gales. He collected them with the eye of a connoisseur, and Billy Dove was recognised by the other boys as a champion in the conker-playing field.

He owned a metal meat skewer which bored a hole beautifully. Only Billy's closest friends were allowed to borrow it. He was equally particular about the type of string he used to thread his collection. All in all, Billy Dove brought the care and use of conkers to a fine art.

He was delighted to find a stout horse-chestnut tree on the way from Caxley station to the school, and he filled his new jacket pockets with some splendid specimens. At playtime (which he tried, in vain, to remember to call 'break' now), he turned out his collection on the grass of the school field and, squatting down, began to sort them out for size. His metal skewer was in his inner pocket with his new fountain pen and propelling pencil. He produced it, ready for action.

At that moment, a shadow fell across him, and looking up he saw one of the prefects who was on duty.

'Whose are these?' said he disparagingly.

'Mine,' said Billy, blinking against the sunlight.

'Stand up when you talk to me.'

Billy obeyed briskly.

'What are these for?' continued the lofty one.

'To play with.'

'To play with,' mimicked the older boy. 'You'd better learn

pretty smartly that we don't play kids' games like conkers here. Chuck them away.'

'But why—?' began Billy rebelliously.

'Don't argue. Throw them in the dustbin. And pronto!'

'Can't I take them home?'

The prefect took hold of Billy's left ear, and twisted it neatly.

'You talk too much, young feller. Do as you're told or I'll report you. And pick up every one. Understood? If they get in the school mower old Taffy'll murder you.'

His eye lit upon the skewer.

'And I'll confiscate that. Dangerous weapon, that is. You can ask for it back at the end of term.'

There was nothing for it but to obey. Furious at heart, Billy collected the shining conkers, grieving over the satin skins so soon to wither in the dustbin.

The prefect accompanied Billy to the dustbin and watched him deposit his treasures. He tossed the skewer nonchalantly from hand to hand as the disposal of the conkers went on.

Billy made one last bid for his property.

'If I promise to leave my skewer at home, can I have it back?'

The prefect stood stock-still, his eyes narrowing menacingly.

'Don't you understand the King's English? You'll get it back – IF you ever get it back – at the end of term. Clear off, and think yourself lucky not to be reported for disobedience!'

A dangerous weapon, thought Billy murderously, watching his enemy depart. That's what he'd called his beloved skewer. At that moment, in Billy's hands, it might well have been an instrument of fierce revenge.

This happened on a Friday. He returned home, moody and pale-faced, his satchel heavier than ever with weekend homework, and his heart heavier still. His mother was wise enough to refrain from questioning, but she watched anxiously as the boy fiddled about with his exercise books at the table, obviously unable to concentrate.

He slammed them together eventually, and spent the rest of the evening slumped in a chair with a library book. There was still a good deal of work to be done, his mother knew. Usually, Billy tried to get the major part of it polished off before the weekend began, but it was plain that he was in no mood to tackle it tonight.

He was little better next morning, and his mother sent him to the village shop for some goods. It was there that he met Miss Davis, also armed with a basket. Her quick glance noted the heavy eyes and unusually sulky mouth.

'How's school?' she asked amiably.

'All right,' said Billy perfunctorily.

'Lots of prep?'

'Too much. Much too much.'

Billy sighed. Miss Davis felt a pang of pity.

'Have you got time to help me saw some logs this afternoon?'

Billy's face brightened.

'Yes. I'd like to. What time?'

'Any time after two. Ask your mother if she can spare you for a couple of hours. I'd be glad of a hand.'

She packed her basket neatly, smiled at Billy, and departed. Cheered at the prospect of some physical activity, Billy set about his shopping in better spirits.

Clad in his comfortable old jersey and shorts, Billy reported for work at a quarter past two. Emily was already hard at it, at the end of the garden, saw in hand.

'My poor old apple tree,' she told him, pointing the saw at

the fallen monster. 'It's been rocking for two or three years, and last week's gale heeled it over.'

'We'll never get through the trunk with these saws,' observed Billy.

'No need to. It's just the branches we'll have to do. A man's coping with the main part next weekend.'

They applied themselves zealously to the smaller branches. Billy found the work wonderfully exhilarating. The smell of the sawn wood was refreshing, and a light breeze kept him cool.

He enjoyed stacking the logs in Emily's tumble-down shed, and made a tidy job of it. The rough bark, grey-green with lichen, was pleasant to handle, and his spirits rose as the stack grew higher and higher.

'It will probably be enough for the whole winter,' he said,

sniffing happily. Emily straightened up and, hands on hips, looked at their handiwork with satisfaction.

'Easily, Billy.'

She gave a swift glance at the boy, now flushed and panting with his exertions.

'Have you had enough, or shall we finish the job?'

'Let's finish,' said Billy decidedly.

They worked on in companionable silence. Sawdust blew across the grass, as the saws bit rhythmically through the branches. By half past four the job was done, and only the twigs and chips remained to be collected into a box for kindling wood.

'I've got two blisters,' laughed Emily, holding out her hands.

'I haven't,' said Billy proudly, surveying his own grimy hands.

'We deserve some tea,' said his old headmistress, leading the way to the house.

It was over home-made fruit cake and steaming cups of tea that Billy told his tale. He had never felt any shyness in Emily's presence, and their shared labours that afternoon made it easier for him to speak, as Emily had intended.

There was little need for her to probe. The boy was glad to find someone to talk to, and the new problems came tumbling out. They were not new, of course, to Emily Davis. She had seen many children in the same predicament. There were very few, in fact, who went on to the large Caxley schools from Springbourne, who did not find the journey, the pace of work and the numbers surrounding them, as daunting as young Billy did.

And then came the sorry tale of the conkers. If Billy had expected sympathy, he was to be surprised. Emily took the account of his discomfiture with brisk matter-of-factness.

'If "no conkers" is a school rule – although I doubt it – you must just abide by it. Nothing to stop you enjoying a game at home, anyway. And as for that prefect, well, you'll find people like that everywhere, and he was only trying to do his duty, poor young man.'

'Poor young man', indeed, thought Billy resentfully! But he had the sense to remain silent.

Emily refilled his tea-cup and went on to talk, as though at random, of the difficulties of adjusting oneself to new situations. Billy was soon aware that he was not the only person to have suffered growing pains. It was true, as Miss Davis said, that one's world grew bigger every so often. It was an ordeal to leave home for one's first school; it was a bigger one to change to a larger school, as he had just done.

'And then you'll plunge into a deeper pool still, if you go to a university,' said Emily, 'and probably nearly drown when you dive into the world of work after that! But you'll survive, Billy, you'll see, and be able to help a great many other young people who are busy jumping from one pool to the next and floundering now and again!'

It was all said so light-heartedly that it was not until many years later that Billy realised how skilfully the lesson had been imparted. At the time, he was only conscious of comfort and the resurgence of his natural high spirits, and put both down to energetic sawing in the open air, and Emily's excellent fruit cake.

At the gate, Billy turned and surveyed the old familiar playground next door.

'I wish I were back,' he said impulsively.

Emily shook her head, smiling.

'You don't really. You're much too big a fish for that little pond now, and I think you are beginning to know it.'

She looked at Billy thoughtfully.

'What was the name of that prefect?'

Billy told her. She was silent for a minute, and then seemed to come to a decision.

'I'm going to tell you something which you must keep to yourself, but I think you can do it, and I think it will help you.'

'I can keep a secret,' promised Billy.

'That boy went from Fairacre School to Caxley. The family moved later, but this is what I want you to know. Miss Clare told me that he was so upset in his first term that his parents thought he might have to leave. From what you tell me, he seems to be keeping afloat in his bigger pond now.'

'He's unsinkable!' commented Billy ruefully.

'Well, think about it. I've only told you because I believe it might help you to understand people. But not a word to anyone, Billy.'

'Not a word,' he echoed solemnly, and ran home with half a crown as wages in his hand, and new-found hope in his heart.

Wisps of white mist were drifting in from the sea as Billy Dove drove his Land-Rover over the rutted site to his office.

The sun was almost blotted out now, faintly discernible now and again, riding moon-like through the ragged clouds. Billy hated this sea-mist, which local people called 'the haar', which swept in unpredictably and wrapped the countryside in icy veils.

He shivered as he entered the small granite house where his office was situated on the ground floor. He was the first to arrive. His colleagues would be coming within the next quarter of an hour, but now he had the little house to himself, and had time to think.

He took out the letter and read it again. Taormina! And Mary! Gazing into the swirling whiteness outside, he longed to return to the sunshine, the flowers, the cypress trees – and, above all, to the warmth and love of Mary. It would be so easy to return, and have a week or two of utter happiness in the sun. The work here could go on under young Bannister's eye without much effort. God, it was tempting!

He stood up suddenly, hands in pockets, and went to the window. Coins jingled as he turned his loose change over and over in his nervousness.

This was a situation he must face alone. No wise old Miss Davis to turn to now.

He gave an impatient snort of derision. What would Emily Davis know, anyway, of a man's feelings? Much use she would be to him with a problem like this. Her advice would come out ready-made, as automatically as a packet from a slot machine.

'Your duty, my boy, is to your wife and children! The rest is temptation. It is SIN, put before you by the devil himself.'

How simple life must have been to those old Victorians with their rigid rules of conduct! But how much they must have missed!

He faced about, turning his back upon the blank whiteness now shrouding the hill side in impenetrable clammy fog.

Nevertheless, it was the only course to take. He had made up his mind to stay in Scotland as soon as he read the letter. Temptation, the devil, Emily Davis and all the other faintly ridiculous issues which clouded his mind, at the moment, as confusingly as the mist outside, made no difference to his decision. He had made the break with Mary. He would not go back.

He had a sudden memory of Sarah that morning, laughing in her blue and white cotton frock, and of John's conspiratorial wink across the playground.

He smiled as he drew a piece of writing paper towards him. Young Bannister would see Sicily for the first time. He would remain in Scotland.

He banged on the stamp as his assistant's car drew up outside, and went outside to meet him. It was like stepping naked into a wet mackintosh. God, what a climate!

Some men, thought Billy Dove, would say he was out of his mind to turn down the opportunity of leaving it. Perhaps he was. Who knows?

Ah well, the decision was made and, bitter though it was, it was the right one. He began to smile.

'What's the joke?' said his assistant.

'I'm trying to decide if I've come to my senses – or lost them completely,' said Billy.

The assistant raised his eyebrows, and Billy laughed ruefully.

'One thing, Miss Davis would approve.'

He clapped his bewildered colleague on the shoulder.

'Come along, son. We've work to do.'

13 Mrs Pringle Disapproves

THE village of Fairacre is some two miles from Beech Green, but news – particularly bad news – travels swiftly in the country, and Emily's death was heard of within a few hours of its happening.

The people of Fairacre knew Emily well, but their first concern was for Dolly Clare who had taught them, and their children, for so many years at Fairacre School.

As children, Emily and Dolly had attended Fairacre School, and later had taught there as pupil teachers. Dolly had remained there for the rest of her teaching life, whilst Emily had gone first to Caxley and then to Springbourne. When Springbourne School closed, as a result of the 1944 act, Emily was transferred to a Caxley school, and lived with a younger brother for whom she kept house. She was glad when he married, and she was free to join Dolly Clare. In the last happy years of their shared retirement, the two old ladies had frequently visited Fairacre, and indeed they were as well known there, by young and old, as in Beech Green.

'I'd have taken a bet on Dolly Clare going first,' observed Mr Willet to Mrs Pringle. Mr Willet is a man of many parts. He is school caretaker, sexton, verger, local nurseryman and a pillar of strength to all needing practical advice on such matters as faulty plumbing, pruning roses, tiling a roof and coping generally with a householder's problems.

Mrs Pringle is as gloomy as Mr Willet is sunny. She acts as school cleaner, is the bane of her headmistress's life, and a terror and scourge to all those with dirt on their shoes. Mrs Pringle is one of this world's martyrs, but one who certainly does not suffer in silence.

On this mellow afternoon of autumn sunshine, Mrs Pringle encountered Mr Willet as she made her way homeward from washing up the school dinner plates and cutlery.

St Patrick's clock had struck two, and Mr Willet was perched on a ladder picking early black plums from a tree in his front garden. He was suitably impressed with the gravity of Mrs Pringle's news of Emily Davis's going, and dismounted the ladder to converse over the gate.

Mr Willet knew what was fitting. One could not carry on a conversation on such a serious matter when engaged on plum-picking, ten feet above ground. It would be disrespectful to the dead, and an affront to Mrs Pringle.

'Yes, I'd have taken a bet on Dolly Clare going first,' he repeated, pushing back his cap. 'She'll miss her, you know. Anyone with her?'

Flattered by his attention, Mrs Pringle launched into her narrative. It was not often that Mr Willet treated her words with such respect. She made the most of this rare occasion, and propped her black oil cloth bag against the gate, at her feet, as if she intended to be some time imparting her news.

Mr Willet, anxious though he was to hear it, watched the gesture with some foreboding. He had some hoeing to do, after the plum-picking, and some seeds to water. Mrs Pringle, launched upon the tide of her story, could take an unconscionable time getting to its end, as he knew well.

'I thought, the last time I saw Miss Davis,' began Mrs

Pringle lugubriously, 'as she was on the wane. Funny how you gets to know. There's a look about folks, as no doubt you've noticed, Mr Willet.'

'Can't say I have,' replied Mr Willet shortly, his eyes roving to the plum tree.

'Ah well!' conceded Mrs Pringle, with a certain ghoulish smugness, 'there's some of us more in tune with the Other World. You gets to recognise the Hand of Death, before it's even fallen. Miss Davis had that look – just as though she was seeing the Farther Shore.'

'Stummer-cake, more like,' said Mr Willet sturdily. He did not hold with morbid fancies, and in these realms of psychic fantasy Mrs Pringle could lose herself for a good ten minutes, if not checked. Dear knows when he'd get the seeds watered, at this rate!

Mrs Pringle ignored his coarse interjection. It was not often that she had such a valuable captive audience. She returned to her theme with all the concentration of a terrier with a rat.

'I saw the same look on my poor mother's face the night before she died. "She won't last another day," I told my husband. "She got that hollow-cheeked look".'

'You should have put her teeth in again,' observed Mr Willet.

'And next morning I found her cold,' continued Mrs Pringle undaunted. 'She looked a young woman. At Peace. We had them words put on her stone actually.'

'I might get my bike out later on and see if I can do anything for Dolly Clare,' said Mr Willet.

'With Emily Davis still in the house?' cried Mrs Pringle, scandalised. 'Where's your sense of fitness?'

'Dolly Clare might be glad of a hand. You can do with an old friend when you've taken a knock like that.'

'They say the Annetts are keeping an eye on her,' said Mrs Pringle. 'Very good thing too. She's none too strong, is Dolly Clare. A shock like this could be the death of her.'

There was a glint of pleasurable anticipation in the old terror's eye which riled Mr Willet.

'Don't start thinking of double funerals,' he said tartly. Mrs Pringle bridled. Her thoughts had indeed strayed into this delectable and dramatic field. She changed her tactics swiftly before Mr Willet escaped from her clutches and returned to his plum-picking.

'The very idea!' she protested, her double chin wobbling indignantly. 'As a matter of fact, I was recalling how good Miss Davis was to my brother-in-law – the one at Springbourne. She often found him a little job when times were hard. You knows what a family he had.'

Mr Willet began to despair of ever getting his jobs done. He was about to make a firm break, and risk Mrs Pringle's displeasure, when he saw help at hand.

A large shabby pram, squeaking to high heaven, approached from the Springbourne direction. A slatternly girl, with dishevelled red hair, pushed it, a toddler clinging to her skirts.

Mr Willet's spirits rose.

'Here's one of the family now,' he said joyfully. 'I'll get back to work.'

With remarkable speed for one so thickset, he remounted the step ladder.

It was Minnie Pringle who approached. She was still known to the neighbourhood as Minnie Pringle, although she was now a married woman. A feckless body, 'not quite all there', as people said, she had produced three children before marriage, and two since. Her husband was much older than she was, a dour widower with a number of young children of his own. The combined families occupied a dilapidated semi-detached villa on the outskirts of Springbourne and seemed to thrive under Minnie's erratic care.

The house reeked permanently of neck-of-mutton stew, which was the only dish which Minnie had mastered over the years. This, with plenty of potatoes, innumerable sliced white loaves from a Caxley supermarket, and pots of strong sweet tea, constituted the household's diet. They all seemed to thrive on it.

Their clothes were given to them by kindly neighbours or bought for a few shillings at local jumble sales. Minnie's husband reckoned that his wages as a road-sweeper paid the rent of their shabby house, provided the food and left him ten shillings a week for beer and cigarettes.

Minnie found the arrangement perfectly satisfactory. After her haphazard upbringing it all seemed a model of household efficiency.

She greeted her aunt boisterously, sniffing the while.

'We've bin in your place, but you wasn't there.'

'Not surprising, is it?' said Mrs Pringle.

Sarcasm was lost upon Minnie.

'Just going to the Post Office to get me family.'

Mrs Pringle rightly translated this as 'family allowances', and snorted. This was a sore point.

'It's people like you, Minnie, as keeps people like me *poor*! About time you stopped having babies and expecting us hard-working folk to keep 'em for you.'

'I don't ask 'em to come,' replied Minnie, tossing her unkempt head.

'You don't do much to stop 'em as far as I can see,' boomed her aunt. She looked with disfavour upon the toddler who was wiping his nose on his coat cuff.

'I'll drop in on my way back,' said Minnie cheerfully. She was not one to harbour grudges. Mrs Pringle sighed heavily, picked up her black oil cloth bag, and faced the inevitable.

'I'll go and put the kettle on,' she said resignedly. 'Don't dilly-dally now, Minnie. I've plenty to do when I get home, so don't keep me hanging about.'

Mr Willet, high among the branches, echoed this sentiment, and watched Mrs Pringle's squat figure stumping homeward into the distance.

* * *

What a family! What a disgrace to decent people! thought Mrs Pringle, setting out the cups and saucers on a tin tray. Of course, they were only relations by marriage, but even so!

Mrs Pringle shuddered at the thought of her husband's younger brother Josh. Nothing but a byword, as far as Caxley, and further. The police of three counties had been after him, for one thing or other. If it wasn't petty thieving in the market, it was breaking and entering, or being picked up dead drunk. Or else it was poaching, thought Mrs Pringle, putting out a few broken biscuits for the children.

Yes, poaching. And Miss Davis knew a bit about that too, come to think of it. It wasn't the sort of story you would tell to Mr Willet, say, but it just showed you that Emily Davis had her head screwed on, and her heart in the right place too.

The sight of that dratted girl Minnie had brought back the memory very sharply. Mrs Pringle shifted the kettle to the side of the stove, picked up her crochet work, and sat down, with a sigh, to await her niece's coming with what patience she could muster.

It had all happened when Minnie was eight or nine years of age – the scruffiest and most scatter-brained pupil in Emily Davis's class at Springbourne.

The child's work was atrociously done. Her writing always appeared to have been executed with a crossed nib dipped heavily in black honey. The pages bore the imprint of dirty fingers, despite Emily's insistence on frequent washings in the lobby.

After super-human efforts by Emily, Minnie had begun to read. Figure work seemed to be completely beyond her. Numbers to five had some reality for the child, and Emily had hopes of her comprehending those up to ten in the future. A realist, Emily faced the fact that double figures would probably always be beyond Minnie's ken. In this she was to be proved right.

Emily concentrated on Minnie's newly-acquired reading ability, substituted a pencil for the pen with the permanently crossed nib, and began to see the child making some headway.

It was not surprising that she was so backward. Her father, Josh Pringle, was the black sheep of his family, constantly in trouble, easily led by his dubious companions, and a mighty consumer of beer whenever he could afford to buy it. Occasionally he obtained work as a labourer, but his income was mainly derived from petty thieving, or from keeping a watch for the police whilst his cronies were 'doing a job'.

Minnie's mother was a brow-beaten wisp of a woman, prematurely grey, who looked twice her age, and had long since given up the struggle to keep her home and children tidy.

Meals were erratic. Sometimes she cooked a rabbit stew for the family, or a simple pie or pudding. More often, the children were told to help themselves to bread and jam from the cupboard. There was no money to buy meat, but Josh's poaching supplied them with a certain amount of nourishment in the form of snared rabbits and hares. Now and again, he took his old gun and picked off a roosting pheasant on Sir Edmund Hurley's estate. Bob Dixon, the gamekeeper, was Josh's implacable enemy.

One night, in October, Bob Dixon sat in 'The Crown' at Springbourne. He had a pint of draught bitter on the table in the corner, and his companion was the local policeman, Danny Goss, off duty.

Bob was a taciturn individual, and made few friends. He was

not particularly fond of Danny Goss, but at least they had a common enemy – poachers. And another thing, Danny Goss played a hard game of dominoes, and this Bob relished. They were in the middle of a game when old Tim Ryan came in and sidled up to them.

'Evening, Dan. Evening, Bob.'

They acknowledged his greetings with grunts, resenting interruption of the game.

Tim watched a few moves in silence, and then spoke in a low tone.

'There's some shootin' going on up Narrow Copse. Thought you should know.'

Bob stood up immediately. Danny finished his drink, put back the dominoes into their greasy box, and followed suit. Bob put a florin on the counter and nodded towards Tim.

'Give the old boy a drink,' he said to the barman.

The two men emerged into the cold night air. It was a light night, for it was full moon. Clouds covered its face, but a silvery diffused brightness made visibility easy. A shot rang out as they emerged, and without speaking they ran, one behind the other, along the grass verge which muffled the sound of their footsteps.

The small copse sloped at an angle to the road, and met it about a quarter of a mile from the pub. The two men entered the wood, and stood motionless for a minute or two.

They heard the cracking of twigs nearby and held their breath. From behind the oak tree which screened them they had a view of a small clearing. Across this, gun in hand, went the figure of a man, followed by another.

'Now,' whispered Bob.

He and the policeman ran into the clearing.

'Beat it, Arth!' shouted one of the men. They ran in opposite directions, crashing through the undergrowth, pursued by the game-keeper and policeman.

Bob Dixon caught his man within fifty yards of the clearing. But as he made a grab for his jacket, the man turned and smote Bob with such viciousness in the face that the game-keeper fell to the ground with a cry of pain.

The man ran off, as Bob was struggling to his feet. At the same time Danny Goss returned.

'He had a bike in the hedge,' he said bitterly. 'But I'd take a bet it was Arthur Coggs from Fairacre. Your chap called out "Arth", didn't he?'

Bob, staunching his bloodied nose, nodded.

'And I'm pretty sure mine was Josh Pringle. I'm going over there now.'

'I'll come with you,' said Danny grimly. 'They're a right pair, those two.'

Josh Pringle sped for home by a roundabout route, two fat cock pheasants thumping his thighs as he ran. He was in roaring high spirits. He had outwitted his enemy and he had paid off old scores with that satisfying crash on his nose.

Full of triumph, Josh did not fully realise the danger which he was in. The thought that Bob Dixon or Danny Goss might pursue him further that night did not seriously worry him. Tomorrow morning, perhaps, there might be a few awkward questions to face if they found him, but surely they'd had enough for tonight?

He was a little perplexed, though, as he ran, about the hasty disposal of the birds. He wasn't going to hide them in the woods or hedges. He'd been fleeced that way before by unscrupulous neighbours. Besides, Bob knew every hiding place as well as he did. Better by far to get them home and cooked as soon as possible. The gentry might prefer their game hung. Poachers could not afford the time.

'Get 'em under the crust,' he had told his wife often enough. 'No one can tell what's under the crust.' There would be pheasant pie tomorrow – enough for all.

He found his wife kneeling before the fire, poker in hand, when he burst in breathlessly.

'Don't rake that out, gal,' he told her roughly, tugging the birds from his poacher's pockets. 'We got to get these plucked straight away. Had a job gettin' away from Bob Dixon.'

'You ain't been seen, 'ave you, Josh?' quavered his wife, Agnes.

'He didn't 'ave no time to see anythink,' responded Josh, beginning to strip feathers expertly. He threw the second bird on to his wife's lap. 'Him and that great lump Goss come after us, but we give 'em the slip. You keep your mouth shut if they turns up tomorrow. Don't know nothin', see?'

Agnes nodded dumbly, her hands busy with the feathers. She took a sheet of newspaper from the table and spread it at her feet to catch the bronze plumage as it fell. Josh's bird lolled upon the table top, its long tail feathers brushing his jacket.

The fire whispered as they worked in silence. Josh raised his head suddenly.

'By gum, there's someone outside,' he whispered, gazing at the dirty drawn curtains. 'Nip upstairs with these while I burn the feathers. If it's Bob Dixon – '

His face was dark with fury. He thrust the two half-plucked birds into his wife's arms, and began to roll up the newspapers.

'Get on upstairs,' he told her in a fierce whisper.

'But where can I put 'em?' squeaked poor Agnes.

'Bung 'em under the bed clothes with the kids, you great fool,' hissed Josh, stuffing the bundles of paper and feathers to the back of the fire.

Agnes crept away, up the box staircase to the room above, on her errand. A strong smell of burning feathers floated about the room, and Josh cursed as he picked up a stray feather or two and added it to the blaze.

A thunderous knocking came at the door. Josh ignored it. By now the bundles on the fire were black and almost burnt through. He blew on the fire to hasten its work.

The knocking came again, and then a voice.

'Open up, Josh Pringle. Police here.'

Josh swore violently, and stirred the bundles until they disintegrated. He put on some chips of wood from a wooden box nearby, and watched them burst into flame.

He approached the door and opened it.

The sight of Bob Dixon's swollen and bloodied nose frightened him. One eye too was blackening fast. He had not realised that he had done so much damage. Too late now to worry about that, he told himself, putting on an innocent expression.

'What's all this about?' he asked truculently. 'Kicking up a fuss like this! We've got kids asleep, I'll have you know. And one's got spots – scarlet fever or summat, we reckon. Only just got off to sleep, he has.'

'We'd like to come in,' said Goss.

'I daresay,' responded Josh, with spirit. 'But I don't want you.' The longer he could keep them from the reek of burning feathers, the better.

'There's such a thing as obstructing an officer of the law in the execution of his duty,' said Goss ponderously. 'I want a word with you on one or two matters.'

'Such as?'

'Such as poaching,' broke in Bob Dixon warmly. 'And knocking me down, you ruddy swine.'

'Leave this to me,' said Goss, to his hot-headed friend. 'I've reason to believe,' he said to Josh, with a return to his official manner, 'that you have articles in this house which are not your property. I'd like to take a look round.'

'Got a search warrant?' queried Josh. 'I knows me rights.'

'There'll be one tomorrow morning,' promised Goss. There was a menacing ring in his tone. 'If you've got nothing to hide, what are you hedging for?'

Josh appeared to waver. By now the feathers should have vanished. The smell too was practically non-existent. He opened the door grudgingly.

'Come on in then, if you must. You won't find nothin' here, I'm warning you.'

Danny Goss made straight for the fire and stirred it with the poker. He saw at once that he was too late. But on the shabby mat he noticed two small brown feathers.

'Pheasant's, eh?' he said. Josh began to bluster.

'Don't make me laugh. Folks like us don't 'ave pheasants. We leaves that to chaps like Bob Dixon 'ere.'

At this point Agnes opened the door from the staircase and entered timidly.

'These 'ere feathers,' said Josh loudly, giving his witless Agnes time to sum up the situation. 'They're from that old hen your mum gave us. That's right, ain't it?'

'Yes,' whispered Agnes. Growing bolder, she added: ' 'Twas

a Rhode Island Red. Finished laying. My mum give it to me to boil for the kids' dinner.'

'That's right,' agreed Josh, nodding approval. 'I told you, they've bin poorly. One's all over spots, ain't he, Ag?'

'Spots?' cried Agnes, her hand flying to her mouth. 'Who's got – ?'

Josh broke in loudly. Lord, was she thick? He'd have to get it through to her somehow, or they'd be upstairs in two shakes.

'Our Tommy. Just bin up to see him, you should know. I was telling these chaps we wondered if it was scarlet fever. Don't want them catching nothin'.'

'That's right,' said Agnes wonderingly.

'You have a look down here,' said Josh, throwing open his arms expansively. 'Look in the washus, out the back, in the privy – we ain't got nothing to hide here.'

'Take a look, if you've a mind,' said Goss to Dixon. The gamekeeper went through the kitchen to the ramshackle outbuildings at the rear of the house. They could hear him opening doors and stumbling among the heap of logs in the corner of the wash-house.

Danny Goss raked the living room with an experienced eye. There were few places to hide a pheasant here. He'd lay a wager they were upstairs, but without a search warrant he was helpless. Nevertheless, he tried.

'I'd like a look upstairs. I won't disturb the children.'

'You can wait then! Them kids is asleep, I tell you. Can't you take a chap's word?'

'No,' said Goss briefly.

'I lets you in,' protested Josh, with a fine show of affronted innocence, 'and shows you downstairs. I'll show you more!'

With a magnificent gesture, he wrenched open the door to

the box staircase, displaying bare wooden stairs, much splintered, and the vanishing tail of a startled mouse.

'There! See anythink? Any pheasants, partridges, hares, or whatever old codswallop you reckons I've got here?'

'It's upstairs, Josh,' said Danny calmly.

'Don't talk so daft! When could I 'ave got it? I bin sittin' 'ere all evening. That's the truth. Eh, Ag?'

Agnes nodded obediently. She was wondering how soon it would be before the children awoke and discovered their gruesome bed-fellows, and how loudly they would scream the news.

As if sensing her thoughts, Josh prudently closed the door. Bob Dixon returned, his discoloured face wearing a sullen look.

'Dam' all,' he said briefly.

Danny Goss, knowing he was beaten, prepared to leave, but not without a stern warning.

'Bob saw his assailant, you know,' he said. 'He'll give evidence in court.'

'Who else saw?' asked Josh pertinently.

'You should know,' said Bob hotly.

'I bin sittin' here all evening,' repeated Josh with emphasis.

'You'll have to prove that.'

'Me brother come up with the paper about nine,' said Josh glibly. His brother would agree to anything Josh suggested. He was smaller than Josh. 'And Ag will vouch for me.'

'You'll need to do better than that,' observed Danny Goss, opening the door. 'We'll be back.'

Josh accompanied them to the rickety gate, and watched them until they were out of sight. He returned to hear the frenzied wailing of a child.

'Mum! Mum! There's chickens in our bed! Dead 'uns,

mum, but they're pricking us something awful! Mum! Mum!'

Agnes started to climb aloft.

'Chuck 'em under our bed till morning,' advised her husband. 'We'll finish 'em off before his lordship comes back. All this bloomin' fuss,' he growled. 'It's enough to make a chap go straight.'

It so happened that no charge was made by the police against Josh on this occasion. Evidence was flimsy. No firm case could really be made. It would be Bob Dixon's word against Josh's. But both the gamekeeper and the policeman vowed to keep a sharp eye on Josh Pringle, and to make sure that next time he transgressed then justice would be done.

Rumours flew about, of course, but Josh played the injured innocent and weathered this particular storm with some skill. In the privacy of his own home he boasted of his triumph, but he kept a still tongue abroad, and congratulated himself on having deceived his neighbours. He would not have been so smug if he had known that Emily Davis knew all.

Some days after the poaching incident, Emily set her class an essay to write. She knew, from bitter experience, that it was little use to expect flights of fancy from the majority of the children. They were, on the whole, unimaginative and ploddingly prosaic. As she wanted, on this occasion, as lengthy a piece of writing as they could manage, she gave them a simple, down-to-earth subject which all could tackle.

My Favourite Meal

she wrote in a fair copper-plate hand on the blackboard. There were murmurs of approval from the victims.

'And I want two or three pages,' said Emily briskly. 'Don't

worry too much about spelling and writing this afternoon. Just show me how much you can do.'

After a few preliminary enquiries, such as: 'Must we draw a line under the heading?' and 'Is jam tarts all one word?' which Emily dismissed smartly, the class settled down to literary composition with all its accompanying sighs and groans.

The children worked well, and at playtime Emily collected their books. They were left in a pile on her desk, and were carried across to the school house for marking that evening.

Halfway through the pile she came across Minnie Pringle's effort.

'Well done, Minnie,' murmured Emily, surveying the laboriously pencilled page. 'The longest essay to date. If only I can read it – '

The spelling and the writing rendered Minnie's composition well-nigh incomprehensible. Minnie had no use for punctuation, so that the whole narrative appeared as one long breathless sentence.

Translated, it read as follows:

My Favourite Meal

Best of all I likes pheasant pie what mum makes with pastry to hide whats inside as my dad tells her with gravy my dad finds them up the woods they just walks about the other night some men come and my mum put them pheasants in us kids bed to keep them warm she said they tickled us and had fleas we had two pies one Wednesday one Thursday today it was bread and sauce pheasant pie is best

Emily who had heard the rumours smiled at this artless account. But it was Minnie's best effort to date. She was very pleased with the child. Taking out her box of gold stars, Emily stuck one securely at the end of the essay. 'For good work,' she wrote beside it.

Gold stars were rarely given. They were much prized by those who earned them. Emily usually allowed the child to take home the work to show the proud parents. In this case, Emily thought, it would be wiser not to do so. She could imagine Josh's reaction to his daughter's innocent admission.

Minnie was scarlet to the roots of her red hair when she found her star.

'Can I take it home, miss? Can I?' she begged.

Emily spoke gently.

'I've put a star on a piece of paper, Minnie. You can take that home to show them. Tell them it was for a good piece of writing.'

She wondered if she should warn the child not to mention the subject matter of the essay. It would seem rather hard to Minnie if Josh's leather belt greeted her success.

'Just for good work,' repeated Emily carefully. Minnie nodded, dumb with delight.

Emily need not have worried. The gold star was given a cursory glance by Agnes and no attention at all by Josh. Not that this worried Minnie. She expected nothing more at home. Her hour of triumph had been at school. But she would have liked to take her book home, nevertheless.

It had been Minnie's aunt, Mrs Pringle herself, Fairacre School's formidable cleaner, who had warned Minnie about disclosing the theme of the essay.

The child had shown her the famous star soon after it had been won.

'What was it for?' asked Mrs Pringle, and listened, aghast,

as she was told. She had already heard the rumours about that fateful night, and suspected that they were true. This confirmed them.

'Have you told anyone else?' she asked.

'No, auntie.'

'Then don't. Your dad'll leather you if he finds out.'

'Miss Davis knows.'

'Maybe. But Miss Davis won't tell.'

The child had seemed bewildered. Mrs Pringle often wondered if she realised the reason for keeping quiet. She doubted it. Minnie was as dim as a dark night, thought her aunt, but at least she'd kept her mouth shut after that, and Josh had got away with it.

But not for long, remembered Mrs Pringle, with satisfaction. A month or two later he had been caught with a carrier-bag stuffed with stolen silver. With a string of other cases taken into consideration, this escapade earned him six months in jail. Agnes and the children missed the rabbits, but the house was wonderfully peaceful.

> 'Though mills of God grind slowly
> Yet they grind exceeding small,'

Mrs Pringle hummed to herself, recollecting Josh's imprisonment with pleasure.

The squeaking of Minnie's pram became apparent, and Mrs Pringle warmed the teapot. She must let Minnie know about poor Miss Davis. It ought to upset her nicely.

That is, if she remembered her at all, she thought, with some asperity. Knowing Minnie she wouldn't be surprised to find Miss Davis had been forgotten completely.

Sighing deeply, she reached for the tea-caddy.

14 Peeping Tom

MR WILLET filled his basket, stepped carefully down the ladder and went into the kitchen. His wife was ironing, a clothes horse beside her laden with Mr Willet's striped pyjamas and substantial underwear, and some snowy sheets and pillow cases. The comfortable smell of warm linen filled the air.

'Old Misery Pringle's just stopped by,' said Mr Willet disrespectfully. 'Got bad news as usual, and enjoying it.'

'What's that?'

'Emily Davis has gone.'

'No! Why, she was at church the Sunday before last!'

'She'll be going again, poor soul,' said Mr Willet. 'And for the last time.'

He watched his wife sprinkling some water over the handkerchiefs.

'Thought I might pop up and see if Dolly Clare wants anything.'

'Oh, I wouldn't do that just yet!' protested Mrs Willet. 'Leave it a day or two.'

Women! thought Mr Willet. All the same, maybe she was right.

He puffed out his stained moustache with a resigned sigh.

'Maybe that's best,' he agreed, and went off to his hoeing.

* * *

Emily's death had stirred memories for Mrs Pringle of her reprehensible brother-in-law. The event had stirred memories too for Bob Willet, memories which even now filled him with some shame. Both Mrs Pringle and Mr Willet kept their recollections to themselves with much prudence, but this did not render them any less painful.

It had all started when Bob Willet was at the impressionable age of seven. He lived then, with his four brothers and sisters, in a little house between Springbourne and Fairacre, and attended Fairacre School.

At that time the schoolmaster was a dreamy idealistic fellow called Hope. He was looked upon as 'a bit of a milk-sop' by the parents, but the children liked him. For one thing, he believed in reading them stories, which children always enjoy. Those who are attentive learn a great deal. Those who close their ears and daydream can get away with such behaviour with impunity. One way or another, storytime is universally popular.

Young Bob Willet was one of those who did attend. Mr Hope read them all manner of tales from the myths of Greece to passages from *Midshipman Easy*. He also read some of Andrew Lang's fairy tales, and it was these which impressed Bob particularly. He became fascinated by witches.

It so happened that a poor old crone called Lucy Kelly, then about eighty years of age, lived alone in a tumbledown cottage near the Willets' home. She was a fearsome sight, with one long eye-tooth overhanging her bottom lip, and tangled grey locks escaping from the man's black trilby hat which she usually wore.

Her clothes were deplorable, her cottage worse. Neighbours had long since given up trying to help her, for she was half-mad, muttering to herself constantly, and violent if provoked. Bob Willet had heard her called 'an old witch' by several people in the village. No doubt it was said in jest, but the boy believed it.

How could he prove it? Fearfully, he put his problem to Ted Pickett, a boy a little older than himself. Mrs Willet did not approve of the Picketts. She considered them dirty and untruthful, and wished her Bob had made friends elsewhere. But nothing could be done without giving offence, and Ted Pickett called for Bob, on his way to Fairacre School from Springbourne, and Mrs Willet could only hope that time would part them one day.

Ted Pickett was something of a hero to Bob. He was an intrepid tree climber and good at football. What more do you ask of a hero when you are a seven-year-old boy?

Bob half-hoped that Ted would give him some comfort when he told him about Lucy. It would have been a relief to have been laughed to scorn for harbouring such a wrong notion. But Ted Pickett did not laugh and Bob did not know whether to feel glad or not. According to Ted Pickett, Lucy might well be a witch. The only way to prove it was to catch her flying on a broomstick at the full moon. On that Ted Pickett was positive.

'Come with me?' asked Bob.

'No fear!' said his hero. 'I'm scared of anything like that!'

It was not very reassuring, but Bob's curiosity got the better of his fear, and one night of full moon he crept from the house and made his way to Lucy Kelly's cottage.

Everything seemed eerie in the silvery light. It was warm and still. The harvest had been gathered, and stooks of wheat stood in the stubbly fields, throwing sharp pointed shadows. The scents of the fruitful sun-warmed earth hung everywhere.

Bob approached Lucy's house stealthily, his heart in his mouth. The front of the shabby place was in full moonlight, and to Bob's horror he saw a stout besom broom lodged against the wooden lean-to at one end of the cottage.

So she had got a broomstick! For two pins, Bob would have run home, but having come so far he braced himself to investigate further.

The garden was full of waist-high docks and nettles, but by keeping close to the house he managed to make progress. Fearfully, he peeped into one grimy window. By the light of the moon he could see some ramshackle furniture. All was silent. Where was Lucy? Was she already preparing herself for a midnight flight?

He gazed spell-bound into the room, noting the battered kettle on the hob, the broken armchair with the stuffing oozing from its sagging seat, and the opened tin of condensed milk standing on the table with a spoon lodged in it.

There was something wholly fascinating in seeing a private life so plainly disclosed. Young Bob had never visited a theatre or he might have recognised the excitement which mounted in him, despite his fear. Here was a stage and although no actors could be seen upon it, a drama must take place.

Action was about to begin. The clock of distant St Patrick's began to strike twelve, each note floating clearly across the tranquil countryside. The boy grew cold with mingled terror and excitement. It was midnight – the time for witches' flights.

At that moment, a dark shape rolled from some low couch hard against the wall where Bob stood. It had been hidden from his sight as it was immediately below the window through which he was looking.

It was Lucy! Dry-mouthed, Bob watched her throw a black shawl round her shoulders and make for the door. It was enough for the terrified boy.

Lucy was off to her broomstick!

Bob Willet fled.

You may think that such an experience would scotch a boy's desire for private investigation, but funnily enough, it seemed to whet young Bob Willet's appetite for more. That glimpse into someone else's life affected the boy deeply. He always loved a story, and was to become a fine raconteur in later life, but this was something better than a story. It was experience at first hand – real people occupying a real place, an actual story unfolding while he watched.

He took to loitering past lighted cottage windows, and treasuring the glimpses of life within. Here was a baby being bathed by the fire. Here was a man setting down a foaming jug of beer on the dresser. Here was an old woman, nodding by the fire, her head on one side and mouth open, while the cat lapped milk from a jug on the table. These little vignettes fascinated the child.

He did not speak about them for some time, knowing full well that his mother would scold him for prying. But one day, he mentioned his new game to Ted Pickett.

By now it was winter-time and lamps were lit at tea-time. Children were told to be sure to be in by dark. Mrs Willet was a stickler for obedience, and one Saturday afternoon young Bob was allowed to go and play at Ted Pickett's only on the strict understanding that he was home before dusk.

The two boys spent a blissful afternoon kicking an old ball about a muddy field. Dusk began to fall and the cottage windows gleamed golden as the lamps were lit. Bob Willet, seeing them, reminded Ted Pickett of his game.

'Bet you wouldn't dare to look in Miss Davis's window,' challenged Ted. The village school stood nearby, and the school house adjoined it, surrounded on three sides by grass which Emily kept shorn with a hand mower which frequently went wrong.

Bob's heart gave a jump. Emily Davis was someone to be respected, even feared. Supposing she saw him at the window?

On the other hand, Ted had dared him. And Ted was older and bigger. If he did not take up the challenge, Ted might put an end to the friendship. There were plenty of boys at school who would be proud to take his place at Ted Pickett's side. Swiftly, the younger boy made up his mind.

'Who said I wouldn't dare?' he boasted, his heart fluttering. 'Come on then. Let's go over now.'

In the grey moth-light between day and night, the two went stealthily across the road from the field. A light burned in the little sitting room of the school house. They could see the lamp quite clearly, standing centrally on the table, for the window was a low one.

'Get round the side,' whispered Ted, 'and creep along below the window level.'

Bob led the way, Ted following. They skirted a row of lilac bushes which grew between the school playground and Emily's garden. It grew darker every minute. The two crouched down in an angle formed by two walls, waiting for an opportune moment.

A farm labourer, with his dog, clumped along the lane, only

a few yards from them. The dog raised its muzzle, sniffing the air, and for one awful moment Bob thought that they would be discovered. But the man was intent on getting home, and calling his dog to heel, he made off down the road.

Two small children then appeared, and took a long time to pass the school premises. Then one of their neighbours, who had been wooding, trundled an old pram piled high with dead branches, along the lane. Bob was terrified that she might see him. His mother would soon hear about it, if she did.

The thought of his mother made him more nervous still. It was time he was home. It was cold squatting there, and getting dangerously late. Now he had taken up Ted's challenge he must get on with it – and the sooner it was over, the better.

Now the lane was clear, and Bob nudged Ted.

'Coming?' he whispered.

Ted nodded.

Bent low, young Bob crept along the front of the school house until he was squarely below the lighted window. Ted joined him, and they sat on their haunches side by side.

Bob listened. Not a sound disturbed the twilight. Face to the wall, he raised himself, inch by inch, until his eyes were level with the lowest pane of glass. Beside him, Ted Pickett followed suit.

There was only one person in the room, and that was Emily's mother. They could see the top of her white head above the back of the armchair. An open book lay on a stool beside the chair, and a large ball of white wool. They could see the old lady's right hand moving dextrously and rhythmically as she worked at her crochet. At that very moment, just as the usual magic was beginning to work for Bob, a terrible blow smote him, and he banged heads with Ted Pickett violently. Both boys tumbled to the ground.

Through the stars born of this sudden assault, Bob looked up to see Emily Davis, who had approached noiselessly over the grass, standing over them.

'And what,' she said grimly, 'are you two doing?'

'Only looking,' quavered Bob, rubbing his ear.

'I call it *prying*,' said Emily. 'It's not only extremely rude, it could be very frightening to anyone inside the room. People's homes are private places. How dare you behave like that!'

Emily was very angry indeed. Looking back, Bob realised that she was anxious for her mother, as well as being affronted by such anti-social behaviour.

The two struggled penitently to their feet and apologised.

'Do you know what people like you are called? 'Peeping Toms', that's their name, and pretty mean they are reckoned to be. The police look out for 'Peeping Toms', so you'd better not do it again.'

The boys, thoroughly scared, promised fervently never to pry again.

'Then be off home with you. If I catch you at this again, there will be real trouble,' said Emily fiercely.

In silence, the two boys left the garden. In silence, they walked home along the muddy lane.

'See you Monday,' said Bob diffidently, when they reached the Picketts' gate. Ted grunted in reply.

Severely shaken, Bob Willet went on to his own home. It was the end, for him, of his secret game. Was it the end of his friendship, too, with Ted Pickett?

Mrs Willet was at the sink, washing up the tea things, when he entered. The table had been cleared.

'You're too late for your tea,' said his mother shortly. 'You should get home at the right time. You've been told often enough.'

She tossed him a tea-towel.

'Make yourself useful,' she said.

Dejected and hungry, wiping up the plates of those who had eaten, Bob Willet learnt his bitter lesson.

It didn't pay to be a Peeping Tom.

He never was again.

Mr Willet straightened his aching back and leant on his hoe.

Funny how fierce those little women can be when roused! Emily Davis could not have been much taller than he was, all those years ago, and yet the memory he had of her, on that distant evening, was of a vengeful giant.

Well, she'd put the fear of the Lord into him sure enough! It had been the right thing to do, no doubt, but what pleasure he'd had while the game lasted! Pity it had to end like that, but Emily was the very person to make a boy see sense. He might have scared the life out of some poor old soul one day. As it was, Bob's shameful secret was known only to Ted Pickett and Emily Davis. And they never told.

Mr Willet plucked a piece of groundsel from the earth and put it tidily with the heap of weeds.

'Good old Emily!' he said warmly, to the robin perched on the runner bean sticks, waiting for worms.

It would have made a fitting epitaph.

15 Off to America

IT was Mr Willet who passed on the news of Emily to Mr Lamb who kept the Post Office at Fairacre.

They were on their way to choir practice, prepared to tackle the usual Ancient and Modern hymns for the next Sunday, a fairly simple psalm, and a new anthem, which their choir-master Mr Annett, the Beech Green schoolmaster, called 'a refreshingly modern piece of music', and which the much-tried choir referred to privately as 'that hell-of-a-thing in E flat.'

'I'm sorry to hear it,' said Mr Lamb, entering the lych-gate. 'My brother George will be too. I'll mark the notice in *The Caxley Chronicle* when I send it on next week.'

'Does he find time to read the paper in New York?' asked Mr Willet, half-jokingly. George Lamb was known to be a prosperous restaurant owner there. His progress had been viewed with mingled admiration and envy by the Fairacre folk, but George's stock had risen considerably recently by his generous contribution to the repair of Fairacre's church roof. Those curmudgeonly souls like Mrs Pringle had been considerably sweeter in their attitude to George Lamb since that warm-hearted gesture of George's and his American friends.'

'He likes to keep in touch with things back home,' replied Mr Lamb. 'No friends like old friends, I always say. Emily

Davis was one of them, come to think of it, though we never saw a lot of her. George would be the first to say so.'

They crunched up the gravel path to the vestry door. The sound of the organ greeted their ears.

'Lord love old Ireland!' exclaimed Bob Willet, 'Annett's started already! We'll cop it.'

Like two naughty schoolboys, the two middle-aged men slunk shame-faced into the choir stalls, and Emily Davis was temporarily forgotten.

It was a cold blustery day when George Lamb opened *The Caxley Chronicle* faraway across the Atlantic.

'See P. 16' was written in his brother's handwriting on the top of the first page. He turned to page sixteen obediently, and read the brief notice of Emily Davis's death, marked by the pen of Fairacre's Post Office.

He lowered the paper to the counter, folded it carefully, and adjusted his coffee machine. His eyes strayed to the window. On the sidewalk the citizens of New York struggled against vicious wind and rain. In the shining road the traffic edged its way along, the windscreen wipers flicking impatiently.

But George saw nothing of the scene. He was back in time, back in Caxley, back in the Post Office living room at Fairacre, where his trip to the States had first begun, so long ago.

When George Lamb left Fairacre School at the age of fifteen, the Second World War had been over for almost two years.

Times were hard. Rationing of food was still in existence, and the basic necessities of life, houses, work, transport and even clothes were all in short supply.

Old Mrs Lamb still ruled at Fairacre Post Office, assisted by her older son. George, it was decided, should try for work at Septimus Howard's new restaurant in Caxley market-place. With any luck, he might be taught the bakery business too. There was a double chance there to learn two trades. One, or both, could provide George Lamb with a livelihood.

The boy cycled daily to work in all weathers, and thrived on it. At that time, Septimus Howard, respected tradesman and chapel-goer, was an old man, and within a year or two of his death. Mrs Lamb had a great regard for him, and was proud to think that George was in his care. Many a time she had listened to Sep's preaching, for she was a staunch chapel-goer herself, and Sep, as a lay-preacher often came to the tiny chapel at Fairacre to give an address.

'If you do as Mr Howard tells you, and follow his example,' she told young George, 'you won't go far wrong.'

She had been widowed whilst George was still a small boy, and sound instinct told her that a man of Sep's worth could be of untold value to the boy in his impressionable years. He certainly influenced George's thinking, and gave him an insight too, into the way of running an honest business.

It was Sep's idea that George should learn the bakery business first, and he began in the usual humble way of watching methods, weighing ingredients, checking the heat of the ovens, and so on, before proceeding to mixing and making himself. He was a conscientious lad, and Sep, always gentle with young people, took extra pains with the promising boy.

As time went on, he became skilled at decorating both iced cakes for the baker's shop and the enormous rich gateaux for which the restaurant was becoming famous.

He had his midday meal in the kitchen at the rear of the restaurant, with its view of the peaceful Cax through the window. This substantial meal was a great help to Mrs Lamb whilst food was still hard to come by. In the evening the boy ate bread and cheese, washed down with a mug of cocoa, with the rest of the family.

There were still contingents of United States troops stationed in the Caxley area. Howard's Restaurant was a favourite rendezvous for the men, and young George became friendly with several of them. One in particular, a blond young giant with a crew-cut, was a frequent visitor, and he and George struck up a friendship.

He was the son of a restaurant owner in New York. His father, so George gathered, was another Septimus Howard, hard-working, teetotal, and a stalwart of the local chapel. His son was inclined to be apologetic about his father's somewhat rigid views but it was plain to George that Wilbur was secretly very proud of the old man and of his business ability.

'You want to come and see the place for yourself sometime,' said Wilbur.

'No hope of that,' responded George. 'No money for one thing. And I've got a lot to learn here yet.'

'My old man expects me to go into the business.'

'Well, you will, won't you? Lucky to have something waiting for you.'

Wilbur looked thoughtful.

'I guess I don't take to the idea, somehow. Been brought up among pies and cookies all my life. I kind of want a change.'

'Such as?'

'Well, now you're going to laugh. I've a girl back home who works in a dress shop. I reckon the two of us could run a shop like that pretty good.'

'Have you got enough to set up a shop?'

'Nope. That's the snag. But if my old man could put up the cash, we'd make a go of it, never fear. It's just that he's looking to me to take over some of his jobs when I get home. It'll take a bit of breaking to him.'

'And you want me to take your place?' queried George jokingly.

'Well now, who knows? You keep it in mind, George. You might do a lot worse than try your luck in the States. Plenty of scope there for a chap like you.'

George did not give much thought to the conversation. His present mode of life was full enough, and besides he doubted if his mother would approve of a son going so far away.

Mrs Lamb was a strongly possessive woman, and hard times had made her calculating as well. With the wages of both John and George she managed fairly easily. She had an eye for a bargain, went shopping regularly in Caxley market on Thursday afternoons, and took advantage of every cheap line offered by the shops. The thought of losing either son's contribution to the housekeeping was a nightmare to her, although she was better off than many of her neighbours.

At that time, John was courting a local girl, and having considerable trouble with his mother on that account.

'I've nothing against her,' said Mrs Lamb, mendaciously.

'Except her being in existence at all,' thought John privately, but keeping quiet for the sake of peace.

'But can you afford to get married? Where are you going to live? She's welcome here, but I don't suppose this place is good enough for her.'

'It's not that, mother—'

'I'm quite prepared to take second place, hard though it is. I haven't had an easy time, as well you know. Bringing up two boys all alone, with mighty little money, is no joke. Not that one expects any thanks. Young people are all the same – take all, give nothing.'

This sort of talk nearly drove John Lamb mad at times. He saw quite clearly that self-martyrdom pleased his cantankerous old mother. He also saw the cunning behind it. As long as she could stave off the marriage, the better off financially she would be.

Things came to a head when his girl delivered an ultimatum. Her younger sister became engaged, and their wedding day was already fixed. This galvanised the older one into action. It was unthinkable that young Mary should steal a march on her!

'Well, do you or don't you?' demanded John's fianceé. 'If we have to live here for a bit, I don't mind putting up with your mum as long as we know we're getting a house of our own, in a few months, say. But if you can't leave your mother, then say so.'

'Don't talk like that,' pleaded poor John, seeing himself between the devil and the deep sea.

'I'm fed up with waiting. If you don't want me, there's another man who does. He's asked me often enough.'

'Who's that?' said John, turning red with fury.

'I'm not saying,' replied the girl, a trifle smugly. As it happened, John Lamb never did discover who the fellow was. Could he be mythical? John often wondered later on.

But the upshot was that John's wedding was arranged very quickly, and a double celebration took place in Caxley that autumn, much to the delight of the brides' father whose pocket benefited from 'killing two birds with one stone,' as he put it bluntly. As the poor fellow had four more daughters to see launched, one could sympathise with his jubilation.

The atmosphere in the Lamb household, between the time of the girl's ultimatum and the wedding, was unbearable. Old Mrs Lamb went about her Post Office duties with a long face, and had the greatest pleasure in confiding her doubts and fears to all her customers. Most of their sympathy went towards John and his wife-to-be.

'Miserable old devil!' was the general comment. 'I wouldn't be in that girl's shoes for a pension! If John Lamb's got any sense he'll clear out and let his old mum get on with it.'

It was at this unhappy stage that George began to think seriously of Wilbur's suggestion. He began to dread his return home, as he cycled back from Caxley each evening. Sometimes a brooding silence hung over the kitchen. Sometimes his mother was in full spate – a stream of self-pity flowing from her vigorously.

'How I shall manage I just don't know,' she complained one evening. 'It's bad enough keeping three of us going with what little comes in. When there's a fourth to feed, it'll come mighty hard.'

George's pent-up patience burst.

'Maybe there'll be only three after John gets married. I'm thinking of leaving Howard's.'

There was a shocked silence.

'Leaving Howard's?' shrieked his mother. 'What's this nonsense?'

'I'd like to go to the States. Got an opening there.'

This was not strictly true, but George was enjoying his mother's discomfiture.

'You'll do no such thing,' declared Mrs Lamb, recovering her usual matriarchal powers. 'You've got a good job with Mr Howard, and you're a fool to think of throwing it up.'

'I could do the same work in New York and get twice the money. Besides I want to see places. I don't want to stick in Fairacre all my life. If I don't go now, when I'm free, I'll never go. I'll be like old John here, married and stuck here for life.'

'And what's wrong with that?' demanded his mother. She looked at her younger son's rebellious face, and changed her tactics.

'And doesn't your poor mother mean anything to you?' she began, summoning ready tears. 'The sacrifices I've made, for you two boys, nobody knows. I've skimped and saved to feed and clothe you, and what do I get? Not a ha'p'orth of gratitude!'

She mopped her eyes.

'I only hope,' she went on, raising her eyes piously towards the ceiling, 'that you two never find *yourselves* unwanted by your family. A widow's lot is hard enough without her own flesh and blood turning against her!'

'Now, mother, please—' began soft-hearted John, who could always be moved by tears.

But George was made of tougher stuff.

'Any children of mine will have a chance to do as they want in life,' he told his mother stoutly. 'What's the sense in keeping them against their will? We all have to leave home sometime. I'm thinking about it now. That's all.'

'And what about the money?' said Mrs Lamb viciously.

George looked at her steadily.

'Let's face it, ma! That's all you're worried about.'

His mother turned away pettishly, but not before George saw that his shaft had struck home. He followed up his advantage.

'I'll get better opportunities in America. After a bit, when

I've got settled, I'll probably be able to send you a darn sight more each month than I give you now in a year.'

An avaricious gleam brightened his mother's eye. Nevertheless, she clung to her martyrdom.

'And how do we manage until you make your fortune?' she asked nastily.

'As other mothers do,' said George. 'I'm going to talk to Mr Howard. He'll understand how I feel. I shan't let him down, but I intend to go before long.'

Knowing herself beaten, Mrs Lamb rose to her feet, reeling very dramatically.

'I shall have to go and lie down. All this trouble's made my heart bad again.'

John took his mother's arm and helped her upstairs in silence.

Sitting below, at the kitchen table, George heard the bed springs creak under his mother's eleven stone.

John returned, looking anxious.

'D'you mean it?' he asked. 'Or are you playing up our mum?'

'I mean it all right,' replied George grimly.

As luck would have it, he came across Wilbur next day, and told him how things stood. Would he mind asking his father what the chances were for a young man in the trade?

Wilbur threw himself into George's plans with a whole-hearted zest which gave the boy encouragement when it was most needed. He was now quite determined to leave home. He would stay until John's marriage, but as soon as that was over he hoped to get away.

He did not intend to approach Sep Howard until he had heard from Wilbur's father. If he was discouraging he might just as well stay a little longer with Howard's, finding lodgings in Caxley. Whatever happened, he was not going to stop at home.

For one thing there would be little room for him when John married. For another thing, he foresaw that there would be trouble between the two women, and he was going to steer clear of that catastrophe.

But for all his determination, George suffered spells of doubt, particularly at night.

Lying sleepless in his narrow bed, he watched the fir tree outside the window, as he had done since he was a little boy. The stars behind it seemed to be caught in its dark branches, as it swayed gently, and reminded him of the Christmas tree, sparkling with tinsel, which he and John dressed every year. He would miss Fairacre, and his home. There would be no sparrows chirruping under the thatch, close to his bed-head, in

New York. There would be no scent of fresh earth, or the honking of the white swans as they flew to the waters of the Cax.

And was he treating his mother roughly? In the brave light of day, he knew that he was not guilty. At night, he became the prey of doubts.

There was, too, so much to consider. Suppose he hated America when he got there? Could he ever save enough for the return passage? He knew no one there – not a soul. Here he knew everyone, and they knew him, and his mother, and his forefathers.

And that, thought young George, thumping his pillow, was what was wrong! He felt stifled in this closed little world. He must get away to live, to breathe, to be – simply – George Lamb, a man on his own, not just a son, a grandson, a work-mate or a neighbour – but someone in his own right!

The letter from Wilbur's father was lengthy and full of good sense. There were plenty of openings. He gave him a rough idea of wages to be expected, and the cost of living. He pointed out certain difficulties a country-bred boy might find in a foreign town, and prejudices which might have to be overcome.

On the second page he came to his proposition. In a few months' time his assistant was leaving to take over a new restaurant which Wilbur's father was opening. If George's references were completely satisfactory (this was underlined heavily), he would consider taking him on when the vacancy occurred. If, at the end of a month, either of them wanted to end the arrangement, well – fair enough. There were plenty of caterers in New York who would give a steady young man a chance.

Until he found suitable lodgings he was very welcome to stay with Wilbur's family. Any friend of Wilbur's – and so on.

George's spirits rose as he made a note of the address. He would write as soon as he had talked with Sep.

* * *

The frail old man listened attentively to the boy's tale. He had lived in Caxley all his life, and knew something of Mrs Lamb's possessiveness. He knew, too, that young George would prosper wherever he went. Rarely had he had such a promising pupil. He was a lad brought up on hard work, ambitious and adventurous and with a strong sense of justice. It was this last, Sep surmised, which had sparked off his revolt.

He advised the boy to talk of the matter, yet again, with his family. He told him that he would be able to give him excellent references, and he suggested that his own solicitor, Mr Lovejoy of Caxley Market Place, might find out more about the proposed job and his employer, so that the affair could be put on a business-like basis.

Within a month it was almost settled. If only his mother would bow to the inevitable, thought George! He would go so much more cheerfully if she gave the venture her blessing, but she continued to play the martyr.

It was at this stage that Dolly Clare and Emily Davis entered the scene. They had called together in the late afternoon to buy stamps. Dolly Clare, who had been button-holed many times to hear about Mrs Lamb's woes, hoped that they would escape this time, but it was not to be.

Emily Davis had not heard the tale first-hand, Mrs Lamb noted with satisfaction, arranging her face into the drooping lines of suffering widowhood.

'And so, off he goes, in a few weeks' time, whatever happens, I suppose,' continued Mrs Lamb lugubriously, after ten minutes' brisk narration of George's unfilial actions.

'They're all the same, Miss Davis, aren't they? No thought for their parents. Everything taken for granted. What happens to us old folk, don't matter. They must do as *they* want, no matter who's hurt by it'.

'You don't expect him to stay here all his life, do you?' said Emily, smiling.

'John will,' replied Mrs Lamb.

'Then you are very lucky,' responded Emily. Mrs Lamb began to look even more disgruntled than usual. It was a fine thing when your own generation turned on you!

'I wouldn't mind so much,' said Mrs Lamb, changing her ground, 'if he was going to someone we knew. But to be thrust among strangers! Well, it's hard for a mother's heart to bear, I can tell you. To think of my boy, alone and friendless in that wicked city—'

'No worse than London, I expect,' said Emily mildly. Mrs Lamb ignored the interruption.

'With all its temptations – and we all know what those are for a young man! No, I wouldn't say a word against this trip,' went on Mrs Lamb, waxing to her theme, 'if I thought there was anyone there he could turn to, if he was in trouble. Just one, just one single person! It's all I'd need to set my mind at rest.'

'That's easy,' said Emily. 'I've a brother in New York. I'll give you his address.'

She put down her handbag and reached for a pen and paper. Mrs Lamb's jaw dropped. Here was a blow!

At that moment, she heard the sound of George's bicycle

being lodged against the wall. The door burst open and there stood the young man, wind-blown and boisterous.

'I'm just telling your mother,' said Emily, still writing busily, 'that I hope you'll look up my brother in New York. He's a policeman there. Been there nearly twenty years. He's married with four children. He'd love to see you. This is his address.'

George held out his hand gratefully, and studied the slip.

'This isn't far from Wilbur's father's place from the look of it,' he said. 'I'm very grateful, Miss Davis.'

'Well,' said Emily, with a hint of mischief in her voice, 'your mother said she wouldn't mind you going one bit, if there were someone there you knew. So now you are settled.'

Mrs Lamb's face was a study in suppressed wrath. Her heavy breathing boded no good to George when the ladies had left, he knew well. He could have laughed aloud at the situation. This had taken the wind out of the old girl's sails all right!

'I'll write to my brother to tell him you are on your way,' promised Emily. 'How lucky that I called in! It must have been meant, mustn't it, Mrs Lamb? Good luck, George. I'm sure you're doing the right thing!'

Eyes sparkling, Emily Davis followed Dolly Clare through the door.

'Doing the right thing,' echoed Mrs Lamb, when the couple were out of earshot. 'That Emily Davis! Always was too fond of interfering in other people's business.'

'It pays off sometimes,' said George, tucking the address in his pocket-book.

He had such a grin on his face that for two pins his mother would have reached up and boxed his ears, but she forbore.

She would keep her recriminations for that meddlesome Emily Davis next time she saw her, the hussy!

'You look pleased with yourself,' said one of George's regular customers, offering a dollar bill. 'Had good news?'

'Not really. Heard of a death actually.'

'Gee, that's sad! Sorry I spoke.'

'That's all right. She was a very old lady – over eighty.'

'Don't suppose she's many friends left to mourn her then. Not at that age.'

'You'd be surprised,' said George, handing over the change. 'You'd be surprised! Emily Davis has got a lot in common with our John Brown.'

'Our John Brown?' echoed the man, puzzled.

'Sure. The chap whose body lies a-mouldering in his grave.'

'And whose soul goes marching on?'

'That's the lad. Emily Davis is right beside him, take my word for it.'

The customer nodded and made his way to the door. These English guys had the screwiest ideas, no matter how long they'd lived in a decent God-fearing country, he told himself.

16 Heatwave in London

THE day of Emily's funeral was quiet and grey. No breeze stirred the leaves or rustled the standing corn beyond the churchyard yew trees. Only a wren, hopping up and down the stairway of the hedge, added minute movement to the scene.

The church at Beech Green was small and shadowy. It was also deathly cold, despite the warmth outside. The congregation shivered as they waited for Emily to make her last journey up the aisle.

Dolly Clare sat in the front pew with several of Emily's nephews and nieces. Doctor Martin, who had attended both friends, sat behind her with Mr and Mrs Willet beside him.

Other Fairacre friends were nearby. There were relations and friends from Caxley, and a great many from Springbourne. But very few were Emily's contemporaries, for she had outlived the majority of them.

Among those from Springbourne was Daisy Warwick, whose husband was a bank manager in Caxley. She represented Springbourne Women's Institute, on this occasion, for she was the President of that branch. But she was also there on her own behalf, for she had been very fond of Emily Davis, and grateful to her for the care and affection she had shown to her only daughter Susan.

Daisy Warwick contemplated her well-polished shoes as she

waited, and wished she had put on a thicker coat to withstand the bone-chilling damp of the church. Her fore-arms, protruding from the three-quarter length sleeves of the sober grey coat which had seemed the most suitable garb in her wardrobe, were covered with gooseflesh, and her hands grew colder and colder inside her gloves.

This would not do any of them any good, she thought practically; particularly poor old Miss Clare, and the vicar, Mr Partridge, who served the parish of Beech Green as well as Fairacre, and had recently returned from hospital. At least he was warmer waiting outside for the coffin to arrive.

At that moment, the sound of the bier's wheels on gravel was heard, and the congregation rose as the voice of Gerald Partridge fluted the unforgettable words at the west door.

'I am the resurrection and the life, saith the Lord: he that believeth in me, though he were dead, yet shall he live: and whosoever liveth and believeth in me shall never die.'

Later that evening, Daisy Warwick made a note on the telephone pad in her hall. It was the last of several such notes. The page now read:

> 1 yard black petersham
> Buttons or zip?
> Mary's baby
> Lunching at Aunt Bess's on Sunday
> Cushions?
> Miss Davis dead.

For this was the evening when she made her weekly telephone call to Susan in London, and unless she had a list before her she found that the precious minutes had slipped by, and the things which she really wanted to tell the girl had been forgotten.

The weekly list was always a source of great hilarity to her husband whenever he waited by the telephone. There was something surrealistic about the juxtaposition of such items as: 'Uncle John's asthma cure' and 'Try really ripe Stilton', or 'Theatre tickets' and 'Bed socks'. The present week, with its jumble of dress-making, births, deaths, lunches and cushions, was well up to standard, and he commented upon it to his wife.

'Well,' she said truthfully, 'life's like that.'

And her husband was obliged to agree.

Susan Warwick shared a flat in Earls Court with four other girls. The rooms were large and lofty. The windows were the sash variety, of enormous size, and as the flat was on the first floor, it was light. This was one of its few advantages.

Susan shared a bedroom with Penny Way. The other three shared the second bedroom. The sitting-room, heated by an archaic gas-fire whose meter gulped down shillings at an alarming rate, overlooked the front garden. The kitchen and bathroom, both small and dismal, were huddled together on a landing at the back of the house half a floor below. It was hardly surprising that the girls lived mainly on toast, made over the gas fire, with various spreads upon it, or bowls of soup which could be heated easily on the kitchen gas stove and carried aloft to be drunk by the fire.

The house had been built in 1890 when three resident servants had been considered the absolute minimum for keeping such an establishment running properly. It was now owned by a gentleman who lived very comfortably in

Switzerland, and whose interest in this house, and a number of others which he owned, was purely financial.

Susan's house was now divided into four parts. The ground floor and basement were occupied by two young men, one with a sable coat and a pink rinse, the other with a black velvet cloak and a blue rinse, who minced off at eleven each morning and returned long after midnight, invariably squabbling at the top of their high-pitched voices.

On the floor above lived two young couples, and a newly-born baby who cried nightly, and wrung Susan's soft heart with its misery.

Up in the attics, where once the three maids had slept in more affluent days, lived a middle-aged artist who sometimes emerged with a portfolio of drawings, but more often sat in a haze of cigarette smoke, a bottle beside him, in his eyrie, and contemplated fame – preferably without working for it.

Of all the motley inhabitants, Susan found him the most repulsive. They occasionally met on the stairs. During the year in which she had lived there, she had watched him deteriorate from a slovenly, garrulous good-for-nothing into a shaking, morose wreck of a man. He had lost a great deal of weight, his eyes watered, his head trembled uncontrollably. His clothes, always stained and spotted, were now filthy and torn. Susan suspected, from the reek of the man, that he was now drinking methylated spirit. She flattened herself against the wall, and held her breath as he passed, praying that he would not engage in facetious conversation. She need not have worried. He now scarcely noticed her as he groped his way up and down the stairs.

After a year of London life under these conditions, Susan was beginning to have doubts. During her last year at school in Caxley, the thought of living in London in a flat, away from all who knew her in Springbourne, seemed the height of sophistication. Oh, to be free!

She was happy at home, and fond of her parents and brothers. The two boys were some years older than she was, and were already out in the world. Susan envied them, and was rather sorry for herself, left behind, over-duly cosseted, in her opinion, by her father and mother.

It was too much, she felt, to be obliged to be in by ten every night. And why on earth, she asked herself privately, should she tell her parents who she was with every time? Couldn't they trust her? Heaven knows, at seventeen she was old enough to look after herself!

Or was she? In her less rebellious moments, Susan admitted that her parents were only doing their duty. There were occasions when Susan had found herself non-plussed – even frightened. There had been that drunken youth at the bus-stop. Only Susan's speed and natural agility had kept her from his unwelcome embrace. Then there was that dubious party at Roger's where everything was plunged in semi-darkness and everyone seemed remarkably gloomy until mysterious tablets were passed round. Susan had had the sense to make her way to the bathroom, throw away her tablets, and creep from the house.

Her own home seemed doubly welcome after that incident. She lay in bed and looked with pleasure at all her much-loved treasures. There were her books, ranging from babyhood's Beatrix Potters to last week's purchase – a Penguin edition of a pop-singer's autobiography.

The bedside lamp cast a cosy amber glow over the patchwork quilt her mother had made. Normally, she considered it hideous and rather sentimental. Her mother was given to fingering sections here and there, saying: 'Isn't this sweet? Part of your first smock, darling.' Or, 'Grandma gave me this. It came from a tablecloth she bought in Lisbon.'

But after Roger's horrible party, even the patchwork quilt had its charm, and her parents, looking up from their books when she returned early, had seemed so sane and wholesome that she had kissed them heartily, much to their surprise and pleasure.

After she left school, she took a secretarial course in London, living in the hostel attached to it and going home thankfully most week-ends.

She found the work gruelling, particularly shorthand. On the other hand, the rudimentary French and German which she had already taken at school, was so slowly and so badly taught that she sat through each class becoming more and more furious. She tried, in vain, to get her parents to cancel these extras.

'Oh, I'm sure it will come in useful, dear,' they replied vaguely. 'Just do your best and be patient.'

'But it's wasting your money!' Susan persisted.

'Well, that's our loss, isn't it? We want you to make the best of your time there.'

The greatest attraction of the secretarial college was Penny Way. Penny had been at school with her, but a form ahead. She was an attractive girl, dark and lively, and outstandingly good at acting. To Susan, she had always been something of a heroine. At college, Penny was still one jump ahead, for she was living in the Earls Court flat whilst Susan was incarcerated in the hostel.

Penny was kind, in an off-hand way, to her junior and Susan

was suitably grateful for her condescension. Occasionally, they travelled back from Caxley to London on the Sunday evening train, but Susan was careful not to intrude if Penny happened to be accompanied by a young man.

In the last week of the last term, Susan obtained a post in an advertising agency in Kensington. She was talking about lodgings to a bevy of friends when Penny approached.

'We need another girl,' she said. 'Barbara's off to Geneva. Like to join us?'

Susan glowed with pleasure.

'Better come and see the dump,' said Penny, 'and meet the others. Then we can tell you about rent and so on, if you're interested. Come about eight. We usually eat at seven.'

If Susan thought this was rather cavalier treatment, the unworthy thought was instantly dismissed, and she presented herself at the shabby front door with its flaking paint, at eight o'clock promptly. No-one answered the bell, and she stood at the top of the flight of dirty steps, surveying her surroundings.

They were not inspiring. The minute front garden had two jaded variegated laurel bushes as its sole adornment. On the sour black earth, which did its best to nourish this natural growth, were cigarette cartons, sweet wrappings, a saucepan lid, several grimy plastic bags and a child's plastic beach shoe.

On the steps, leading from this square yard of flotsam to the young gentlemen's basement, stood a posse of unwashed milk bottles, a small red dustbin with no lid, and an extraordinary number of screwed-up bags which had contained potato crisps. Presumably, the occupants consumed these as their main item of diet, thought Susan.

Having rung the bell a second time, with no result, she

opened the door timidly. She was in an outer hall, once whitened daily with hearth-stone no doubt, but now grey and dusty. A door, with frosted glass in its upper half, led her into the main hall.

This, and the stairs leading from it, were covered in brown linoleum. Susan mounted the stairs, hardly conscious of the grime around her, so thrilled was she at the thought of emanicipation ahead.

It was very dark on the first floor, but the sound of music thumping away behind one door must mean that someone was home. She banged loudly upon it, and Penny flung it open, looking surprised.

'Oh, hello! I forgot you were coming. Come in.'

The noise from the ancient gramophone was deafening, and the fumes from the gas fire were equally stupefying. Two girls lolled, one at each end of the vast broken-down couch, their trousered legs lodged on the back of it. They did not move as Susan was brought forward.

'Barbara,' said Penny, giving no hint of which one she was. 'And Jane. Dobby's out, and Pam's doing her face. This is Susan.'

Barbara and Jane nodded in a friendly way, but said nothing. They seemed to be attending closely to the music, in a stunned sort of way. Susan was not surprised.

'Well, this is it,' said Penny, waving a hand vaguely to indicate the amenities of the room. Susan looked about her, observing the frayed and dirty curtains, the sagging armchairs, the greasy rug in front of the fire, and the two enormous oil paintings of Highland scenes which occupied most of the wall space. But her spirits rose. She could settle here very happily – particularly if Penny were here.

'Better see the bedroom,' said Penny, leading the way across the landing. 'This is ours.'

Two single beds were lost in the vastness of what had once been the main bedroom of the house. In the enormous bay window, in front of the sagging net curtains, brown with London dirt, stood a small dressing-table *circa* 1935, with plenty of chrome fittings and a badly-spotted looking-glass. Apart from two cane-bottomed chairs and a rickety chest of drawers with grained marmalade paint, this seemed to be the only piece of furniture in the room. Here again was the ubiquitous brown linoleum, but beside each bed lay a thin strip of carpeting which had once been a stair carpet, judging by the worn stripes across it.

'The beds aren't bad,' said Penny, giving one a thump. 'But you'd better bring your own sheets and blankets. Towels too, of course – and a few tea-towels would help.'

'I could do that,' said Susan, still besotted.

Penny went before her to the kitchen. If the rest of the accommodation had been disheartening, then this was downright repellent, and even Susan's spirits quailed. An enormous black frying-pan, full of congealed fat containing pieces of burnt onion, potato and bacon rinds, dominated the gas stove. This itself was an ancient monster, furred with the black grease of many years.

The walls of the kitchen ran with small rivulets of condensation which had left lines of brown encrustations over the years. A naked electric light bulb, covered with a fine film of grease, hung over the stove. The one window was tightly shut, and papered with an oiled paper representing stained glass. It was not very convincing.

'Window won't open,' commented Penny laconically, observing Susan's glances. 'All the windows have the jim-jams, but there's such a hell of a draught from most of them I think we get all the fresh air we need.'

Susan nodded half-heartedly.

'Next door's the loo,' went on Penny, throwing open the door of a dismal room housing a vast peeling bath, encased in pitch-pine, and a regal-looking lavatory seat with tarnished brass fittings. A snarl of tangled water pipes, flaking generously, wreathed about the walls and gurgled.

'How do you heat the water?' asked Susan.

'There's a boiler down below, and an old dear is supposed to keep it going. She comes every morning – in theory, that is. Mostly the water's tepid. We chuck in a kettleful of boiling water to pep it up, and get a decent bath when we go home.'

'What about rent?'

'We pay thirty quid a week.'

'What? Each?' shrieked Susan, appalled.

'Don't be funny. Six quid apiece. Can't get anything for much under. The gas fire's extra, of course. And our grub. We usually buy our own.'

'I think that will be all right. I'll have a word with my parents next week-end and tell you then. Is that all right?' asked Susan anxiously.

'Fine,' said Penny carelessly. 'Start the first of next month, if you want to come. Barbara's off then.'

She closed the bathroom door after three resounding bangings. At the third, the brass door knob came away in her hand. She thrust it back expertly.

'Better say farewell now. I'm due to go out in ten minutes and my current young man swears like a trooper if he's kept waiting.'

Susan said goodbye, and made her way downstairs and into the street. A small Negro girl, her frizzy hair sticking out in a dozen small plaits, each ending in a flighty scarlet bow, was busy jumping up and down the steps. She looked up at Susan, bright-eyed.

'You live there?' she queried.

'I'm going to,' replied Susan, smiling.

'I wouldn't,' said the child, still jumping.

Susan went on her way, elated by this exchange. Later, she was to wonder if it had not been some sort of warning.

Her parents had been very understanding about the flat, although Susan's mother was shocked when she saw it, by the conditions under which Susan was going to live, and she said so.

'It's nothing but a slum. Will you really be happy there?'

'Of course I will. Hundreds of other girls live in far worse places than this. It only wants a good clean.'

'It needs blowing up, and rebuilding,' said Daisy Warwick. 'But if you are prepared to live here, my dear, we'll do all we can to make you comfortable.'

Sheets, blankets, towels, a chair, some saucepans and crockery were carried from Springbourne to Earls Court. A large box of useful tinned food and some jars of home-made jam and marmalade, as well as bottles of fruit from the Warwicks' garden made their way into the rickety store cupboard in the flat's kitchen. Susan prepared to enjoy life.

On the whole, she was happy for the first few months, although there were several things about sharing which annoyed her. During the first week she spent Saturday afternoon washing the paintwork and scrubbing the floor of their bedroom. She cleaned the windows as far as she could reach, and polished the battered furniture. Even if the room did not look much more attractive, at least it smelt clean.

It was as much as she could do to remain silent when she saw Penny flicking cigarette ash to the floor that evening. She realised before many days passed that Penny was hopelessly untidy, and thought nothing of borrowing anything in the flat without bothering to ask permission. Scarves, jewellery, tights, even coats were missing when Susan looked for them, and her opinion of Penny, once so high, now plummeted.

It was annoying too to see how the groceries, which she brought to the flat, were eaten readily by all and not replaced. She did not mind putting in her share, nor doing her part of the sketchy daily cleaning and shopping, but it soon became apparent that she was carrying most of the burden. Hating to quarrel, she did her best, but resentment began to grow.

The advertising job did not work out as she hoped, and she left after three months and took a post with a typing agency. This meant that she was sent out to different offices which were short-handed. The pay was good, and she thought that the varied experience would be useful.

She found that the experiences were varied all right. One of her temporary employers turned out to be a dipsomaniac, two were addicted to stroking her legs, and another – a hard-faced woman journalist – had such a vitriolic tongue that she reduced Susan to tears within half a day. But on the whole, she enjoyed the work and gloried still in her independence.

She went home less and less, and when her parents did see her they began to grow increasingly anxious. Hurried meals, late nights, stuffy offices and the slummy flat were taking their toll. Susan had lost weight, had a series of painful boils, and was so tired that she spent most of the week-end asleep.

'Why don't you come home for a time,' urged her mother. 'You can always go back if you want to, but whatever's the good of earning these large wages if they all go on rent and fares? And just look at you – all eyes, and as thin as a rail!'

'Lovejoys need a secretary,' added her father. 'They'd be decent people to work for. And I met Mallet at Rotary lunch yesterday. He is looking for an assistant. There are plenty of openings locally. Do think about it. Your mother and I would love to have you at home.'

That had been in June, and very tempting Susan had found the offer. But she still clung to her independence. It would be a retrograde step, she felt, to return to Springbourne – almost an admission of failure. She turned her back on the garden, sweet with roses and strawberries, on the haymakers in the fields and all the joyous freshness of early summer, and went back to London.

It was harder to bear than ever in hot weather, and that summer was long and fine. The journeys across London by bus or tube were a nightmare in the rush hour. After a day at work, it was almost unendurable to squash among hundreds of other tube-travellers, all hot, perspiring, and as cross as she was herself. One evening of sultry heat, she fainted on her feet, but the crush was so great that she remained upright, supported by a kindly Jamaican giant who insisted on refreshing her from his hip flask, and poured most of it down her new cotton frock.

The flat was more squalid than ever. The windows refused to open, and the smell of stale cooking hung about the place revoltingly. By late summer, Susan was heartily sick of the whole sordid set-up. It was as much as she could do to speak civilly to the other girls. She was tired of having no privacy, no quietness – for the gramophone seemed to play endlessly – and no time in which to sit and rest, to mend her clothes, to read or to write letters.

On the day of Emily Davis's funeral, while her mother was shivering in Beech Green church, Susan was pounding her typewriter in an airless top-floor office. She sat immediately below a large sky-light, which would not open, and was hotter than she had been all the summer. She had elected to work through her lunch hour, as the letters upon which she was engaged were urgent. An apple and a glass of tepid water from the cloakroom tap were all that she had eaten during the day, and by the time she arrived at Earls Court station she was almost too tired to walk to the flat.

Everywhere seemed filthy. A hot breeze raised the dust, swirling pieces of paper across the pavements. Dogs lay panting in the scanty shade of porches. Children in bathing suits lolled on the steps of houses, too hot to play. Men, stripped to the waist, sat at open windows, their arms dangling across the sills, to catch what little air there was. Querulous babies cried in stuffy prams, turning their wet heads this way and that to try to ease their wretchedness.

The traffic rumbled and roared continuously, like some snarling monster. To sit in a moving vehicle was misery on a day like this. To sit in a stationary one, in a traffic jam, was more than human flesh and blood could endure. The blaring of horns added to the din.

Susan stripped, and had a tepid bath, then lay, exhausted, upon her bed. She must have fallen asleep for the telephone bell roused her. Bemused, she struggled from her bed to the sitting-room. For once, it was mercifully empty.

Her mother's voice sounded reassuringly near.

'And how are you?'

'Terribly hot.'

'Here too, dear. Thunder, I think. Mrs Smith is getting on with the suit and says will you get a yard of black petersham for the skirt top, and do you want a zip or buttons?'

'Buttons. I'll get them.'

'Right. Now the next thing. Mary Bell is having a baby at Christmas. Isn't that nice?'

Susan forbore to say that Mary had told her this some time before, so early, in fact, that Susan had felt it was tempting fate to mention it.

'And Aunt Bessie's asked us to lunch on Sunday, so bring a frock, dear. You know how she feels about trousers.'

'If it's as hot as this, I'll probably go nude.'

'Yes, well – I thought I'd let you know. And do you still want those two cushions? If not, they can go to the Scouts' jumble sale.'

'Can I tell you at the week-end?'

'Of course. And the last thing. I've been to a funeral this afternoon at Beech Green. Now, *there's* a place to get cool! That church is like an ice-well.'

'Anyone I know?'

'Miss Davis. Your old teacher at Springbourne.'

'I'm sorry. Poor old dear – but I thought she'd died years ago. She must have been a hundred.'

'Eighty-something, I believe. She'll be missed. She was always so kind.'

'She was indeed,' agreed Susan. The pips sounded peremptorily.

'Well, we'll see you on Friday night, dear. At the station. Goodbye.'

'Goodbye,' said Susan, putting the sticky receiver back in its cradle.

She must make a note about the petersham and buttons, and get them tomorrow in her lunch break. And the cushions? She looked about her, at the depressing airless room, and the broken couch which, she thought, the cushions might make more bearable.

To hell with the cushions! Why should she bother to make the place look decent! No one else did. She'd fought a losing battle long enough. She wished she need never set eyes on the dreary place again.

She went to the window and tried for the hundredth time to open it. A sash cord broke under her onslaught, but the window remained firmly closed, sealed tightly by the paint.

Panic seized her. She could have smashed the grimy glass at that moment, in her frantic longing for air. Oh, to be on the downs at Springbourne, to feel the wind lifting one's hair, or to feel the cold rushing breeze as the swing flew up and down from the beech tree in the garden. If you swung high enough, you could see over the hedge to the village school across the way.

The village school! And Miss Davis! Susan rested her hot forehead against the grimy window pane, and stared unseeingly at the traffic pounding below.

Miles and miles away. Years and years away. And now Miss Davis was dead. A different world – a quiet, happy world of light and air and sunshine – or so it seemed, thought Susan, looking back.

17 Snowdrops at Springbourne

SUSAN had known Miss Davis and the village school for as long as she could remember. The Warwicks had moved to Springbourne when Dudley Warwick was appointed to be manager of the Caxley branch of his bank, a few years after the war.

The house was a comfortable and solid building, put up between the wars. The first owner had made a fine garden, and the Warwicks, who were keen gardeners themselves, were glad to find mature trees and hedges, settled pathways and well-tended flower beds, when they took over.

Susan was born at Springbourne, and her earliest memories were of her afternoon outings in the pram. The school was less than a quarter of a mile away, and the children were usually setting off for their homes, after school, when Mrs Warwick and Susan returned from their walks.

Miss Davis was often at the gate, seeing off the children safely, and always had a word with Mrs Warwick and the child. Emily's hair was greying by this time, but her eyes were as dark and sparkling as ever they were. They reminded Susan of the bright glassy eyes of her much-loved toy monkey. There was a humorous twinkling look about them both, which the child found irresistible.

At five years old she went to the school herself. It was the autumn term, and the beech tree in the garden was already beginning to drop leaves as bright as new pennies.

She was happy from the first day, for several of her friends were there, and she knew that home was only a short distance away.

As so often happens, the newcomer picked up measles as soon as it appeared in the village. She had it more severely than most, and Doctor Martin insisted that she stay at home for the rest of the term.

'It's not a thing to take lightly,' he told Mrs Warwick, who privately thought that the old man was making a mountain out of a molehill. 'It goes in cycles. At the present time, it's very severe. We don't want complications. She can go out, well-wrapped up as soon as she is out of quarantine, but I don't want to risk any further infection.'

Susan chafed at the delay in returning to school, but revelled in the short walks she took with her mother when she had recovered.

She loved to collect flowers and stones, or any other lovely treasure which she came across in the hedges or fields. In those few weeks was born the deep love of natural things which was to stay with her for the rest of her days.

When she returned to school after the Christmas holidays she seemed perfectly fit, but Mrs Warwick noticed that she still tired easily if she took too much exercise. Miss Davis promised to keep an eye on the child.

One morning in February, Miss Davis came into the infants' room and told them that they were going to have a treat.

Mrs Allen, the farmer's wife, who was also one of the school managers, had invited them to her garden to see the snowdrops. They grew in vast drifts in a small copse at the edge of the garden, and thicker still in a dell near the house which had once been a sawyer's pit, many years earlier. The garden was famed in the Caxley area for its profusion of snowdrops, and the children were excited at the thought of an outing to such a lovely place.

There was much bustling in the school lobby as the young children buttoned coats and wrapped scarves round their necks. The infants' teacher was left in charge of Miss Davis's class, while the headmistress shepherded her little flock through the village to the farm.

It was almost a mile distant, but the sun shone and their spirits were high. A thick frost still sparkled on the grass verges and the bare twigs, but some golden catkins told of spring at hand, and a blackbird sang from a thornbush as boisterously as if it were April.

Mothers at their dusting waved and called to them as they passed, and tradesmen gave them a friendly toot on their horns as they went by. Altogether, it was a glorious occasion, made even more splendid by the knowledge that normally they would have been closeted in the schoolroom.

Susan skipped along with the others joyfully, but was glad when the farm gates came in sight, for her legs had begun to ache. Miss Davis, noticing, offered to carry her, but Susan would have none of it. However, she held Miss Davis's warmly-gloved hand, and was secretly glad of this support.

The snowdrops were so unbelievably white and pure, so numerous and so far spread, that the children fell silent in wonderment for a moment. Susan thought how like snow they were – not only in their whiteness, but also in texture. There was something crystalline in the drooping heads, delicate and opaque in the morning sunlight. The greyish-green spears of leaves set off the purity of the flowers perfectly. It was an unforgettable sight.

They were allowed, by kind Mrs Allen, to wander about freely and to pick a small bunch each. What is lovelier than picking flowers, especially when they are the first after so many dark months of winter? The earth was moist and fragrant beneath the trees, and here and there the tiny leaves of the honeysuckle showed the first brave touches of spring.

When they had had their fill of these joys, the children walked back along the drive to the farm kitchen. On the way Mrs Allen picked ivy leaves to put with each bunch. Susan thought the dark glossy leaves, mottled like marble, were a perfect contrast to the white beauty of the snowdrops. Every year, she promised herself, she would have just such a February nosegay to remind her of this wonderful morning.

Beyond the back garden of the farm, a row of calves pressed against the low hedge. Their shaggy heads hung over it inquisitively. Their beautiful eyes, heavily fringed, gazed solemnly at the children, who gazed back just as solemnly.

The ground fell away gently into the distance, and then rose again to the swelling flanks of the downs, scarcely visible in the morning haze. To Susan, the distance seemed vast. She was suddenly conscious, for the first time, of the infinity of space about her, as she stood on the little hill in the shelter of the farmhouse.

The calves' breath floated up like steam, in the forefront of this picture, from their shiny wet noses. Far away, the farm dog must have seen the children, and began to race down the slope of the distant hill towards them.

At first he was a dim black shape moving swiftly towards his home, but as he drew nearer Susan thrilled to the sight of his splendid movement as he stretched his legs as rhythmically and as proudly as a racehourse. His ears flapped, his white teeth were bared in a grin of ecstasy, and when he finally reached them, he was so warm and panting, so full of vigorous life and spirits that Susan felt her own strength and excitement rising at the sheer joy of being alive on this tingling day of early spring.

They went into the great farm kitchen, after much shoe-wiping supervised by Miss Davis.

There on the table stood two steaming jugs of milk and an array of mugs and glasses. There was also a yellow china bowl filled with ginger biscuits.

As she sipped her milk among her chattering companions, Susan was conscious of the sudden contrast between this warm room, full of colour and conversation, and the great empty airiness outside. Both were lovely, one in its cosy domesticity, the other in its limitless mystery.

Her physical tiredness made the child more sensitive to her surroundings than usual, and she suddenly became aware that, for her, she must always have both worlds – each was necessary and complementary. One was her nest. The other was the place in which she stretched her wings, and soared, as effortlessly as the lark outside, into a different dimension.

When elevenses were over, and the mugs had been put into the sink, and the beautiful ginger biscuits had all been eaten, the children thanked Mrs Allen individually and shook hands with her, as Miss Davis had told them to do earlier. When it came to Susan's turn she felt that such formality could only express part of her feelings. She put her arms round Mrs Allen's ample waist and gave her a loving hug, when the official handshake was over.

By the time the little crocodile had reached the end of the farm drive, Susan's legs refused to carry her further, and she looked up at Miss Davis in despair.

'My legs ache,' she began, but did not need to add any more, for Miss Davis swung her up on to a high bank and sat down in front of her.

'A piggy-back for you, Susan. Up you get!'

The child gratefully put her arms round Emily's neck. Her teacher's dark wiry hair tickled Susan's face, but this was pleasurable.

She enjoyed jogging along, her cheek against Miss Davis's scarlet coat. Below her the children bobbed along, their bunches of snowdrops clasped carefully in their gloved hands. Their breath rose in silver clouds, as they clattered along in their sturdy country boots, and reminded Susan of the adorable calves standing against the background of mistily distant hills.

There was something wonderfully reassuring and comforting about Miss Davis's small strong body which bore her along so steadily. Emily had given many a piggy-back to younger brothers and sisters, as well as her own pupils, and had the knack of carrying a child in a way which gave most comfort to them both.

Susan never forgot that welcome ride. The experiences of that shining morning culminated in the new bond forged between teacher and pupil as they made their way together through the village.

Standing listlessly at the stubbornly-shut window of the flat, Susan noticed once again the small Negro girl sitting on the kerb opposite.

She was clad in a grubby elasticised white bathing suit. Her bare feet were thrust into a pair of silver evening sandals which might have been her mother's, so large were they. She rose to her feet lithely, and began to teeter along in the grotesque shoes, looking, for all the world, Susan thought, like Minnie Mouse.

Suddenly her amusement changed to pity. There she was, poor child, about the same age as she had been on that far morning of sparkling light and infinite airiness, but doomed to spend the day in a noisy prison of stone and brick. It was all wrong! No child should be forced to endure this claustrophobic squalor!

For that matter, no one – child or adult – should have to endure such conditions.

The memory of the snowdrops, the memory of Miss Davis, the memory of the calves and the emptiness beyond their endearing heads, flooded back to Susan. Why not go back?

She knew in her heart that these two worlds still existed side by side – the small and the limitless. Too long she had suffered from being penned. It was time to find her true self again, and for that she must have space and air and beauty.

It could be done. She could give in her notice tomorrow, telephone to her mother and ask if she could come for a week or two's holiday. She knew how joyously she would be welcomed. Who knows? She might find that job in Caxley after all.

But that was in the distance. All that mattered immediately was to escape – to put her affairs in order, in this swarming filthy ant-hill she had once thought so glamorous, and to find quietness and space for the survival of her body and mind.

Perhaps that had been the secret of Miss Davis's strength, she thought suddenly. She went at her own pace, and had time to relish all the lovely natural things in Springbourne and thereabouts. And when the occasion arose, that happiness, fed by inner serenity, could succour the weak and give, as Susan could so poignantly recall, strength and heart to those who needed it.

She went into the bedroom and began to pack in readiness for a longer stay at home than usual. She was not going to make up her mind one way or the other. No doubt London would pull her back before long, just as Springbourne tugged her now with an urgency her starved spirit must obey.

But she would go forward with her immediate plans. Her spirits rose as she moved about her work in the sultry heat. Soon she would be out on the windy hills above Springbourne, where the small happy ghost of Emily Davis had beckoned her.

Her mind raced ahead. She saw herself at the booking office in the deafening and dirty London terminus. Aloud, she rehearsed the words:

'Single to Caxley!'

18 Doctor Martin's Morning Surgery

A WEEK or two after Emily's funeral, Doctor Martin sat in his surgery at Beech Green, awaiting the first of the day's patients.

The morning was warm and rather close for October, and the windows looking on to his garden were wide open. A bed of mixed roses stood immediately below the windows, and in the quietness the doctor could hear a blackbird busily scrabbling the earth for worms. Now and again a delicious whiff of the roses' scent wafted into the room, giving the old man much pleasure. His love of roses grew greater as the years passed.

He glanced at the silver clock on the mantelpiece. Nine-thirty. Time he opened shop, he told himself.

He smoothed his grey hair and opened the door into the little waiting room. Not many today, thank heaven. Fine weather cut his queue by half. It was in January and February that extra chairs had to be put in the waiting room.

'Good morning! Good morning!' said Doctor Martin cheerfully.

'Good morning,' replied his sufferers, with varying degrees of joy.

Doctor Martin consulted his list.

'Mrs Petty?'

A stout young woman rose, carrying a toddler, and followed Doctor Martin into the surgery. She was, in fact, Miss Petty, but the birth of Gloria, who now accompanied her, accounted for the change to a married title.

The Pettys were a large family, originating in Caxley. They ran to fat, were short-necked and inclined to respiratory diseases. They were also good-tempered, happy-go-lucky and quite incapable of keeping to any diet prescribed by their various doctors for weight reduction.

'Well now, what's the trouble?' asked the doctor kindly.

It appeared that Gloria's 'summer cold' refused to go. She complained of a sore throat, and had a stubborn cough which grew worse at night.

'Let's have a look,' said Doctor Martin, fishing the spatula from a glass of disinfectant.

Gloria began to wail.

'Give over, do!' begged her mother. 'And open your mouth.'

Doctor Martin expertly held down the child's tongue during one of the lulls in her whimpering.

'Tastes nasty!' whined the child when the instrument was removed.

'Maybe,' said the doctor amiably. 'I should think most things taste nasty with that throat.'

He pressed her neck glands, and then took out his stethoscope. After the examination, he sat at his desk and wrote the prescriptions.

'Now, this one is for tablets which she must suck slowly. Not more than six a day, mind you. Read the label carefully. You can read, Mrs Petty?'

The question was asked casually. There were still several people among Doctor Martin's patients who were unable to read despite a century of compulsory education.

'A bit,' replied Mrs Petty

'Not more than six during the twenty-four hours. They should settle the infection.'

He held up the second slip of paper.

'This is the cough cure recipe. A teaspoonful when it is troublesome.'

She took the two papers almost reverently, and put them carefully inside a dilapidated patent leather handbag. She was about to leave when Doctor Martin motioned her to the chair again.

'This child's tonsils want attention. Bring her back in a fortnight. And her teeth have caries – are going bad. That means the second ones may be infected. She's having too many sweets, Mrs Petty. Cut them out.'

'But she likes a bit of chocolate! Her gran brings her a bar every day!'

'Ask her to bring an apple instead. Chocolate will rot her teeth and make her too fat. She's overweight now. You're storing up trouble for the future, if you don't feed her properly. We've talked about this before.'

'Well, I'll try,' said Mrs Petty grudgingly, 'but it's her gran you ought to talk to.'

'Are you still working?' asked the doctor, showing her to the door.

'Every afternoon,' said the woman, her eyes brightening. 'Down the new fish shop. It pays for me bingo, Mondays.'

'D'you take the child too?'

'No, Gran comes up. I leaves a bit of tea for 'em both.'

Doctor Martin had seen those teas once or twice. Bought pies, packets of crisps, sliced wrapped bread, glutinous shop jam and a pot of well-stewed tea. Not a ha'p'orth of nourishment in the lot! Even the milk was tinned. He had seen the opened tin standing on the table, with a large blow-fly in attendance.

'See the child gets eggs, fresh milk, some meat and plenty of fruit,' said Doctor Martin for the hundredth time. 'She needs building up.'

He opened the door, and Mrs Petty made her departure.

'Building up,' she echoed, when she gained the lane. 'He's gettin' past it. Says the kid's too fat and then, in the next breath, wants buildin' up.'

'Can I have an ice-cream?' cried the child, as the village shop came in sight. 'Can I, mum? Can I?'

'I'll see. Doctor only said: "No sweets." Yes, all right. I'll get you a lolly, love.'

She felt quite sure an ice-cream wouldn't hurt her. After all, mothers always knew best.

* * *

Doctor Martin worked his way steadily down the list of patients. There were a few unexpected visitors among them, such as Joe Melly the shepherd, who had nicked the top off a troublesome spot on his wrist, and who now had a fat shiny hand which throbbed painfully, and a dangerous red line creeping up his arm.

There was seventeen-year-old Dicky Potts, with yet another boil to be lanced. There was garrulous Mrs Twist, who enjoyed fainting fits when life became too much for her – or she was getting the worst of an argument. Jane Austen would have diagnosed the vapours. Doctor Martin could do little more. There were the two youngest children of Minnie Pringle, smothered in spots, hot, flushed and tearful, with furred tongues and high temperatures, who were despatched to bed promptly by the old doctor.

'And I'll call in on my rounds,' he told scatter-brained Minnie, who stood looking more like a bewildered hen than ever. 'They've got measles. You should have had more sense than to bring them out, Minnie.'

Might as well talk to a brick wall, he told himself, watching the trio depart up the lane.

'Who's next?' he asked of the two or three remaining patients. Mrs Barber, a comparative newcomer to Beech Green, rose with her daughter, a fair-haired schoolgirl, and the two followed Doctor Martin into his surgery.

'What's the trouble?' asked Doctor Martin of the mother. She gazed at him in silence and, to his dismay, her mouth began to tremble and her eyes fill with tears.

The doctor turned to the girl who was looking at her mother with mingled impatience and disgust.

'Are you the patient?'

'I s'pose so,' the girl shrugged.

Mrs Barber produced a handkerchief and blew her nose noisily.

'We think she's in trouble,' she said tremulously. There was only one condition which was described to Doctor Martin in these terms.

'Then I'd better ask you a few questions,' said the old man gently.

He put them simply, and the girl replied in an off-hand way. Obviously, the mother was more upset than the daughter.

'Lie on the couch,' directed Doctor Martin, 'and we'll have an examination. There's nothing to fear.'

When it was over, and the suspicions confirmed, the doctor told them that the baby would be born early in March, and gave them the address of the ante-natal clinic. He was kind and uncensorious, doing his best, by being completely matter-of-fact, to ease the tension of the unhappy situation.

'Perhaps you would wait outside a moment, while your mother has a word with me,' he said.

When the girl had departed, the mother's tears began to flow again.

'The shame of it! Only sixteen – barely seventeen when the baby comes – and no father! What will the neighbours think? We've given her everything she wants, tried to bring her up nice, and now look what's happened!'

Doctor Martin let her run on in this vein until she had had her outburst.

'Did you explain the facts of life to the child?'

'Well, no. It's so embarrassing, isn't it? You know, it never seems the right moment. Anyway, the school should teach her that these days.'

'These days,' said the doctor, 'are much the same as any other days. Parents still have duties towards their children.'

'I blame her Gran,' said Mrs Barber, sniffing. 'She was supposed to go there straight after school on the days I was working. She never bothered if Audrey was late. I bet all this happened then.'

'And how old is her grandmother?' asked Doctor Martin mildly.

'Eighty – but very healthy.'

Doctor Martin felt some sympathy with this absent and elderly scape-goat, and said so.

'It's no good casting round for someone to blame,' he

continued. 'You know the situation – it's all too common, unfortunately – and you must all make the best of it as a family.'

'That boy'll have to marry her,' said Mrs Barber fiercely.

'If he loves her, he'll want to,' agreed the doctor, 'but I can't see anyone benefiting from a shot-gun wedding, least of all your daughter and the baby.'

He patted the woman on the shoulder, and walked with her to the door.

'Say as little as you can to her until you've had time to cool down. You'll say things you'll regret all your life if you are too hasty now. Look after that girl of yours. She needs all the help she can get, silly child, and you're the one she'll turn to, if you'll let her.'

He watched the two depart, and beckoned his last patient into the surgery.

Elaine Burton was fifty-two, as Doctor Martin knew well, but she might have been sixty-two from her haggard looks. Her husband worked at a printer's in Caxley and her two children also worked there. They were unmarried and still lived at home.

Mrs Burton's main problem was her old mother, now nearly ninety, who lived with them. Brought up in a strict Victorian way, the old lady remained a martinet despite failing health. Her daughter, acting as buffer between the demands of the younger generation and the old, came off worst in the household, as Doctor Martin knew well.

'I think I need a tonic,' said his patient wearily. 'I'm tired all day, and when I get to bed I can't sleep. Mother needs seeing to at least twice in the night, and I think I've got into the habit of being on the alert all night. It's really getting me down, Doctor Martin.'

He surveyed the woman with an expert eye. She had been pretty once. He remembered her as a young woman with her first baby. She had been trim and lively, with soft dark hair, and a quick smile which revealed dimples.

Now she was running to fat, and was pale and listless. Blue smudges under her eyes bore testimony to lack of sleep. Her hair was lank, her neck decidedly grubby. Her whole bearing spoke of exhaustion and self-neglect.

'I'll put you on some iron tablets,' said the doctor, drawing his pad towards him. It was plain that the woman was anaemic and over-worked.

'How's your appetite?'

'I don't fancy much. By the time I've spooned mother's food into her, I don't want my own.'

'Do you have a cooked meal?'

'When the others get home, but I don't really want it then.'

'Milk? Eggs?'

'I could never take them, even as a child.'

The old doctor sighed. Here was yet another case of the dying sapping the living, but what could one do?

'And how is your mother?'

'To be honest, a terrible trial, doctor.'

'Can't your brother have her for a while? To give you a break?'

Mrs Burton snorted.

'He's under his Ethel's thumb, and she refuses point-blank to give any help with ma. Besides, ma hates her like poison. It would never do.'

She could have added that her own husband's attitude was much the same as Ethel's, but loyalty kept her silent.

'We might be able to get the old lady into a home, you know.'

'She'd never hear of it. And I wouldn't want to send her away, despite all the work. It's the washing and drying that gets me down. I have to wash bedding and nightgowns every day – sometimes twice a day. It's far worse than having a baby to look after. Still, it's got to be done. I wouldn't have her moved. She's my mother, after all.'

'Do the young ones help?'

Elaine Burton gave a hard laugh.

'They take the tray up now and again, and switch on the radio for her, but that's about the lot. They nag me to send her away, and she nags me to keep them quiet, and tells me I've not brought them up respectful. You know how it is.'

Doctor Martin nodded sympathetically. He knew indeed.

He felt sorry for them all – the unhappy, cross old lady, confined to her bed; the exuberant young people criticised at every turn, the husband condemned to watch his wife's health slowly seeping away and, chiefly, Elaine Burton torn this way and that, by the demands of all, and fast becoming too tired to carry the heavy burden of the combined duties of daughter, wife and mother.

'You should get away with your husband for a holiday,' he told her seriously. 'If your brother won't have your mother, I can arrange for her to go into hospital for a fortnight. Now, talk it over. I know it won't be easy, but it's no good knocking yourself up. Where will the family be, if you have to give up?'

The woman was visibly moved and gave him a shaky smile, as she held out her hand for the prescription.

'I'll think about it, but I can't see it coming off,' she said honestly.

Doctor Martin showed her to the door.

'I'll drop in and see the old lady one day soon,' he promised. 'Meanwhile, take those tablets, and some good food.'

He watched her go sadly, then returned for his bag. Off to see two of his patients in Caxley Cottage Hospital, and then he must set about his rounds, he told himself.

He locked his desk, and the drugs cupboard, and went thoughtfully to his car.

19 Doctor Martin Looks Back

CAXLEY Cottage Hospital was a small building erected in the twenties, and opened by the Mayor of the day with considerable civic pomp.

It served the area well, but now there were rumours of its closure, much to the indignation of the local people. As they pointed out to each other, by the time you had been dragged all the way to the county hospital, twenty miles distant, and waited in the queues of traffic which had to be encountered on the way, you would probably be dead on admission.

'And who wants to go all that distance to visit relatives?' they demanded. 'And who can afford the fares there, anyway? A dam' silly idea shutting the Cottage. Hope it never happens.'

Doctor Martin agreed with them. He could quite see that a more modern operating theatre was necessary, and that the place was uneconomic to run, but there was still plenty of minor surgery and certain illnesses which could be dealt with in this little place, thus relieving pressure on the larger hospitals at the neighbouring towns.

His first patient was in high spirits when he went to see her in the children's ward. Mary Wood was seven years old, and had had her tonsils removed.

'Mummy's fetching me tomorrow,' she told him triumphantly. 'And I'm going to be home for tea. And I'm going to have a puppy.'

'What? For tea?'

The child smiled indulgently at this little joke, revealing a gap where her two front milk teeth had vanished.

'I'm not a *cannibal*,' she answered, bringing out this new, half-understood word with considerable pride.

The remark amused Doctor Martin for the rest of the day.

His other hospital patient was less cheerful. Old George Smith was recovering from acute bronchitis, and was fearful of what the future might hold.

'My old woman ain't up to nursing me, sir, and we can't abear the idea of living with our Nell, good girl though she be. They've got them two strapping boys, hollering about all day, and playing that electric guitar all night fit to blow yer 'ead off. Us old folks couldn't stand it, and they don't want us anyway.'

'Would she be able to look in to your home and give a hand? The district nurse could call each morning. We'll fix up something, never fear.'

'We likes to be independent,' said the old man obstinately. 'And anyway, our Nell goes out cleaning every morning; she's got enough to do. No, let's face it, doctor, you keeps us old folks alive too long these days – and we're not wanted. Time was, this bronchitis of mine would've carried me off. Now I'm still 'ere, and a nuisance to everybody.'

Tears of self-pity rose to his eyes.

'Rubbish!' said Doctor Martin robustly, patting the wrinkled hand on the coverlet. 'You're just a little low in spirits. Wait till you're home again! You'll be as fit as ever.

'If there's one thing I 'ates,' continued the old man, 'it's the work-house. I knows things is better now, but I can recall the time when 'usbands and wives were parted at the gate, and sometimes never saw each other no more. 'Twas a terrible thing that – to be treated worse than animals.'

'Things like that don't happen now,' the doctor assured him, but the old man rambled on, unconscious of interruptions.

'Seems to me the young people ain't got no respect for their parents today. They do say that in China the old folks are looked up to because they're reckoned to be the wisest of the family. Don't see much o' that in these parts. It's time I was dead, doctor, and that's the truth of it.'

Doctor Martin did his best to speak comfortingly to the old man, but it was clear that he was sunk too deeply in his own miseries and fears to heed much that was said.

Doctor Martin returned to his car and drove carefully through Caxley High Street. It was with a sigh of relief that he turned the nose of the car northwest, and regained the leafy lanes leading to Beech Green, Springbourne and Fairacre.

'Thank God,' he said aloud, 'my practice is in the country.'

He pulled off the road, as he so often did, on the brow of a hill. Here there was a fine view of the countryside, backed by the splendid whale-back of the downs.

The doctor wound down the window and breathed in the fresh air, tugging a pipe from his pocket as he did so.

He filled it, meditating upon his morning's work, and the people with whom it had brought him in contact.

What problems people had! If one believed all one read in newspapers and magazines, or saw at the theatre or on the ubiquitous "Box", the only problem besetting people these days was sex. Good grief, thought the doctor impatiently, that was a pretty minor problem, taking all ages of men and women into account! He'd put the problems of health, family and money, as being quite as important as sex – certainly from the age of forty-odd onward, which included a goodly proportion of the nation, after all.

His mind dwelt on poor old George Smith's worries. Here was the age-old difficulty of keeping the older generation happy and cared-for. Something had gone amiss with the pattern of family life today, making this problem even greater than it had been in earlier generations.

Yes, George had a point about being kept alive too long – but a doctor's first duty was to his patient, and he must do his best to prolong life. Nevertheless, it created problems for all.

He looked back upon his own memories. His grandmother had lived in a tall town house, four storeys high, and two unmarried daughters and an unmarried son lived with her. She had borne twelve children and eight had survived. The house always seemed full of nieces and nephews, of all ages, coming and going, bearing little presents, chattering about their families, showing Grandma their new babies, or pirouetting before the old matriarch as they displayed the latest fashions. There was a lot said against those large Victorian families, but at least there was a feeling of belonging – and even if there were battles now and again, a common enemy had only to appear to weld the clan into solid unity.

And then, there was always someone with time to spare. His maiden aunts seemed to be able to drop whatever they were doing to play shops with him. When Grandma's sight began to fail, one or other read out the items of news from the daily paper with real kindliness, it seemed to the child. No one seemed cross, or in a hurry, or resented serving the old lady, although no doubt there were times when they found her as tiresome as George Smith's grandchildren and poor Elaine Burton found their ancient relatives.

Of course, the burden had always fallen hardest on the unmarried daughters, and still did, for that matter. And then, so much depended on the old people's attitude to life. If they could keep busy, and avoid self-pity, it was half the battle against depression.

His grandmother, he remembered, always made herself responsible for the midday meal. She spent the morning preparing it, and the rest of the day planning for the next day's menu. She did little else in the house, but this one important chore eased the strain for everyone and, above all, gave her the inestimable reward of knowing she was useful.

He took out a match, struck it, and drew his pipe into life. Through the blue clouds, he gazed at the view spread out below him. The spire of Beech Green church pierced the surrounding trees, and his thoughts turned to his last visit there, when Emily Davis had been buried.

Now, there was a family which had managed its life well, he mused! When he first met them all, most of Mrs Davis's family were out in the world, and Emily went out to her teaching at Springbourne each day, but returned at night.

Every Sunday there seemed to be a family reunion. Sons and daughters from Caxley brought over their children for Sunday tea, and news was exchanged. They were a lively collection, Doctor Martin recalled, and there was plenty of laughter in the tiny cottage.

Perhaps that was the secret of happy family life – or one of the secrets. Nowadays people didn't seem to have time to laugh. All too busy rushing from place to place, like scalded cats, mused the old doctor, stirring the tobacco in his pipe bowl with a match-stick.

The Davises travelled very little. Poverty had its rewards sometimes. If one had to remain in the same place, then one made one's pleasures there. Certainly the Davis family created their own delights. They gardened, and saw the results of their labours in the fine string of onions hanging in the shed, the sack of home-grown potatoes, the jams and jellies ranged upon the kitchen shelf. They knitted and they sewed. Doctor Martin remembered the beautiful dolls' clothes which Mrs Davis made each Christmas for her granddaughters' presents. He had admired tucks and feather-stitching on the minute petticoats – work which no modern parent would bother to do – but which would be prized by the owner of the lucky doll, and give pleasure too to the needlewoman.

The little cottage overflowed with the results of their handiwork. The walls were papered by one son, the paintwork done by another. Rugs, cushions, chair-covers, all were made at home, and most of their clothes, too, were hand-made. It was a way of life which had endured for centuries, but which was now fast vanishing.

Doctor Martin recalled one of his favourite characters who had lived in the eighteenth century and kept a diary. Parson James Woodforde, although a fellow of New College, Oxford, did things with his own hands just as the Davises did. He brewed his own beer, he salted pigs, he kept his house to rights, he pruned and dug in his garden, as well as visiting his parishioners and serving the church. He had a great deal in common with the country folk of Doctor Martin's earlier memories, and his sense of family duty was as keen. He was concerned about Brother Jack, the black sheep of the family, and considerate to his niece Nancy who lived with him.

The latest over-worked word 'involved' came into the old doctor's mind. Those earlier people really were involved. Emily Davis, a good daughter, cared for her mother until her death, and did it cheerfully, just as she did her duty towards the many school children who passed through her hands.

She had been a wonderful person – perhaps the finest character in that fine family. One did not meet many quite as selfless these days. That perhaps was one of the causes of Emily's strength.

She was completely devoid of self-pity, unlike poor Elaine Burton and George Smith.

She shouldered responsibility bravely, unlike Mrs Barber who thought that the school alone should tell her daughter the facts of life.

She had an unswerving sense of justice, based on her Victorian upbringing of recognising right from wrong. It may have been too rigid a code, but it produced some good steadfast people who engendered those old-fashioned virtues of respect and duty.

Doctor Martin looked at the clock on the dashboard. It was time he moved on. His pipe was almost finished, and he had day-dreamed long enough. He must blame Emily Davis for much of it!

He wished he could tell her so. She would have enjoyed the joke. She always did.

He switched on the engine and drove gently down the hill to Beech Green.

20 Two Old Friends

As Doctor Martin slowly descended the steep, winding hill, he caught a glimpse of the tall figure of Dolly Clare moving about in her garden. On impulse, he drew into the side of the lane, and made his way up the garden path.

Miss Clare was cutting a few late roses, and she held them up for the doctor to admire.

'For Emily's grave,' she told him. 'Now that all those lovely funeral flowers have gone, it is beginning to look rather bare.'

The doctor nodded. He approved of the way in which Dolly

Clare talked so lovingly, and yet so calmly, of her dead friend.

'Mr Willet is going to plant a low bush of red roses for me on the grave. There won't be a headstone. Emily always set her face against any sort of permanent memorial.'

'She left her own memorial,' commented the doctor, 'she'll never be forgotten.'

Dolly smiled at him.

'Come inside. I've something for you.'

She led the way into the little cottage. It was as fresh and shining as ever. A vase of flowers stood on the polished table. The curtains stirred gently in the breeze from the open window. There was a delicious smell of something baking in the kitchen. It was quite apparent that Dolly Clare, old and bereft though she was, was still self-reliant, and still revelling in her independence.

'Do sit down,' she said, 'while I put these in water. I shall go up to the churchyard this afternoon, after my rest.'

He did as he was told and looked about him. It was obvious that Dolly was busy sorting out Emily's effects, for a large suitcase, propped open, was filled with clothes, and on the little bureau by the window were some trinkets which the doctor recognised as Emily's.

Dolly Clare returned with the roses in a vase and put them on the window sill.

'Coffee?' she asked.

The doctor shook his head.

'Not for me, Dolly. I'm getting up an appetite for lunch. It's curried lamb today, I'm told.'

Dolly laughed, and crossed to the bureau.

'As you see, I'm sorting out Emily's things, and I've practically finished. The nieces and nephews were remembered, of course, but she asked me, several times, to give you this as a little remembrance of her.'

She brought over to him a silver pocket-watch on a silver chain.

'It was given to her brother when he retired. He left it to Emily, and she always kept it on the little table by her bed. It's an excellent time-keeper. She hoped you would find a use for it.'

The old doctor was too moved to speak for a moment, as he turned the beautiful thing in his hands.

'How generous of her,' he said at last. 'I shall always treasure it, Dolly. Always.'

He undid his jacket and patted his waistcoat.

'Help me to put it on now, Dolly. It's going to be my constant companion.'

Miss Clare helped him to thread the chain through a button-hole, and the doctor put the watch very gently into his pocket. He stood up and surveyed himself in the mirror on the wall.

'Do you know, Dolly, I've always wanted a pocket watch, and never felt that I could indulge myself. This is doubly welcome – a remembrance of dear Emily, though she would be remembered well enough without it, as you know – and something I've always longed for.'

Miss Clare smiled.

'It would have pleased Emily so much to know you like it,' she told him. She turned to the bureau and held up a gold locket for the doctor to see.

'I wish I had found this earlier,' she said seriously. 'I should have put it in the coffin with her.'

She handed it to the doctor. It contained the portrait of a young man in uniform. He studied it for some moments, then looked questioningly at Dolly.

'Edgar,' she nodded. 'The only man she ever loved. Sometimes we used to say we'd both been unlucky in love. After all, we both lost our lovers – but we were wonderfully blest with all the affection we had from the children at school and all the friends about us here. It helped a lot, you know.'

'You both deserved happiness,' exclaimed the doctor.

Miss Clare sat down in the armchair by the fire.

'I was so touched by the dozens of letters I had. Some from as far afield as India and Australia – mostly from old pupils who had read the news in *The Caxley Chronicle* or in letters from home. And then there were a great many from people I scarcely knew – Jane Bentley, for instance, who taught with Emily many years ago, and Daisy Warwick. She wrote so kindly about Emily's care of her daughter.

'And the flowers, as you know, were unbelievably lovely. I'd no idea that Emily was so widely known. Even Mrs Pringle sent a beautiful heart made of Michaelmas daisies.'

'Well, that really is a tribute to Emily,' agreed Doctor Martin, laughing.

'And so many little kindnesses to me too,' went on Dolly. 'Mr Willet brought me a marrow – which I can't look at, incidentally, without remembering Manny Back, and Emily at her most mischievous. And I've been given enough fresh eggs by kind neighbours to keep me in omelettes for weeks.'

'I'm glad to hear it,' said the doctor. 'Mind you eat them, and look after yourself.'

He rose, and looked down at his new watch-chain proudly.

'I can't tell you how much I appreciate this,' he said soberly.

'This is a typical gesture of Emily's, generous and practical. I shall wear it always.'

He turned at the door.

'I'll call again, Dolly. Don't get over-tired. What are you doing for the rest of the day?'

'Finishing my sorting. I'm thoroughly enjoying looking through the old school photographs. I've recognised several Pringles and Billy Dove, and a host of others.

'Then I shall take the roses up to Emily's grave, and also plant a clump of snowdrops which I've dug up from this garden. Emily always loved them, and I went with her several times to see them at Mrs Allen's farm. What a glorious sight! Emily used to reckon it was one of the high-lights of the winter.'

'You're going to be busy I can see,' commented Doctor Martin. 'Well, better to wear out than rust out, as my old grandmother used to say.'

He waved goodbye, and Miss Clare watched him drive along the lane into the distance.

That evening, as dusk was falling, Dolly Clare took her accustomed walk at the edge of Hundred Acre Field, behind her home.

All her little duties were done, and she felt free to enjoy the evening air before settling by the fireside.

She reached the oak tree, and stood very still, watching three fine pheasants searching for acorns at the foot of the gnarled old trunk.

Above her the rooks were flying homeward. The great field before her, gleaming with gold when last she walked there with Emily, was now freshly ploughed, the furrows dark and glistening. Within a few days the seed would be planted and she would watch, alone now, the first tender blades appear, then the ripening crop and, finally, its harvesting.

The comforting cycle of the seasons continued unchanged – the sowing, the growing and the reaping.

Dolly Clare turned, and made her way homeward with a grateful heart. Life went on, and was still sweet.

MISS READ is the pen name of Mrs. Dora Saint, who was born on April 17, 1913. A teacher by profession, she began writing for several journals after World War II and worked as a scriptwriter for the BBC. She is the author of many immensely popular books, but she is especially beloved for her novels of English rural life set in the fictional villages of Fairacre and Thrush Green. The first of these, *Village School,* was published in 1955 by Michael Joseph Ltd. in England and by Houghton Mifflin in the United States. Miss Read continued to write until her retirement in 1996. In 1998 she was made a Member of the Order of the British Empire for her services to literature. She lives in Berkshire.

The Fairacre Series

"Miss Read, a gentle soul with kindly interest in all around her, is the master of the kind of detail that shows place and character in delicate focus . . . there's no underestimating the power of rural English charm." — ***Publishers Weekly***

Village School ISBN 978-0-618-12702-3

Village Diary ISBN 978-0-618-88415-5

Storm in the Village ISBN 978-0-618-88416-2

Over the Gate ISBN 978-0-618-88417-9

The Caxley Chronicles ISBN 978-0-618-88429-2

The Fairacre Festival ISBN 978-0-618-88418-6

Miss Clare Remembers* and *Emily Davis ISBN 978-0-618-88434-6

Tyler's Row ISBN 978-0-618-88435-3

Farther Afield ISBN 978-0-618-88436-0

Village Affairs ISBN 978-0-618-96242-6

Christmas at Fairacre ISBN 978-0-618-91810-2 (hardcover)

Village Centenary ISBN 978-0-618-12703-0

Summer at Fairacre ISBN 978-0-618-12704-7

Mrs. Pringle of Fairacre ISBN 978-0-618-15588-0

Changes at Fairacre ISBN 978-0-618-15457-9

Farewell to Fairacre ISBN 978-0-618-15456-2

A Peaceful Retirement ISBN 978-0-618-88438-4

20241569R00269

Made in the USA
Middletown, DE
20 May 2015